Samson's New Day

Lynn Andrew

Samson's New Day

First published in 2024 by
Sorek Valley Books
sorekvalleybooks.com

ISBN 979-8-218-49602-9
(soft cover)

Scripture citations are paraphrases by the author based on the American Standard Version of 1901

All characters are fictional.

Composed in OpenOffice.org Writer.

Preface

Seeing as I owe Samson (who is Earl Kenneth Clark, you understand) my salvation and am still connected to him in an odd way by a bond that was never dissolved, I was given the task of writing this biography of his later life. I am called Lalomi now—Leila Lalomi—which is my name in heaven. Earl is still Samson to me, though he called himself Ichabod Samson.

What I have set down in this book is taken partly from my own experiences during the times I spent with him, partly from public information, and the rest is from what he told me near the end of his life.

Unfortunately, Earl missed the Rapture and remained a mortal resident of earth while I was taken with the church to heaven. But he was blessed to avoid the worst of new earth's birth pains by an exceptional translation in time and place. This landed him in the messianic kingdom some years after its beginning: he advanced through decades of time to get there, spending less than a heartbeat of his life in the leap. It was not like a mid-tribulation Rapture because he missed spending time in heaven.

Samson told me about the fateful day when he visited Melchior for the last time. The ancient priest surprised him with incredible news: he had been summoned to the future. His immediate question to Melchior was whether he would meet me.

"Yes, you will, but not in heaven."

"Then where?"

"You are being translated forward in time and to a place where you will find your vocation."

"I'll be whole again?"

"The distance in time is not so great as that. You will be spared the tribulation, and that is all."

"Then I will have to endure my limitations—for how long?"

"That is yet to be seen. It is your thorn, but do not let it get you down. I have every confidence in you, my son."

Earl could think of only one thing:

"I don't want her to see me in this condition. I'm afraid it would break her heart."

Many of us in heaven have duties on earth now, so we go down regularly and mix with mortals. While I, as a *novu-corpus* citizen of heaven owed nothing to entropy, Samson had to endure his aging natural body that bore the marks of injuries which he suffered the same day I left him. He had determined that he would avoid meeting me under that formidable disparity. And I was very busy and had no leave to go looking for him until later, so it was some time before we met.

I write this for you, dear reader, so do not question how it could be possible to read something from the future. Time and space are no longer the inflexible things for us as they once were. It is easy for me to go almost anywhere I desire to go, and if I were to appear as an angel with a manuscript in my hand, no one would suspect that I had come from the future. Of course, doing that would be unnecessary because it is so very easy to have anything published. I simply add to the list of books that have been attributed to Ms. Nice's *nom de plume*, Lynn Andrew, since this really is a sequel to that incredible week that she wrote about and the awful period of disarray afterward before Samson was transported into his future.

> *Of the increase of his government*
> *and of peace there will be no end—*
> *upon the throne of David*
> *and his kingdom,*
> *establishing it*
> *and upholding it,*
> *with justice*
> *and righteousness,*
> *from henceforth,*
> *even for ever.*
> *The zeal of Yahweh of hosts*
> *will perform this.*
> Isaiah 9:7

Introduction

Well buried as he was under the ruin of a building he had brought down upon himself, Samson escaped, but when he emerged he was disfigured and crippled. You will recall, if you read *The Day and the Hour* series, that he had determined to resist the tyrannical "Reorganization." Indeed, the loss of the government building that nearly killed him would have set that program back, but in retributive response to its loss the entire town was destroyed—bombed and burned—by the authorities.

The Beach House is the only building that was not destroyed, and Samson found refuge there for a short time before going to visit Melchior for the last time, when he was surprised to learn that the ancient prophet-priest had received a call for him from the future. As Melchior described the summons, it was for "Mr. Kenneth Earl Clark, sometimes known as Samson."

Samson told me he was sitting on a wooden chair in Melchior's cabin when the call was presented to him. After a short conversation with the ancient prophet, he found himself similarly seated somewhere in what he assumed was the new earth. There had been neither sensation of the passage of time nor of motion through space, but the place in which he found himself was definitely different. He had understood that his destination was on the same planet but not necessarily at the same geographical location and definitely not in the same period of history: he would skip over some decades of years. Melchior had told him he had been called to fulfill a particular assignment and that he was being sent directly and immediately in order to avoid the ravages of time that would make him unsuitable for the task for which he was being summoned if he were to live through those years in the natural way. He was told he would arrive at a point in the future some years (Melchior was vague about this) after the return of Messiah and the establishment of the theocracy. He was being given the privilege of leapfrogging over the times of tribulation in which ordinary mortals would be subjected to extraordinary plagues, solar events, and earthquakes while being coerced on pain of death or isolation into ultimately fatal Satan worship.

Others were enjoying that privilege too: members of the body of Christ had been taken out of the world, exactly as promised, in time to avoid the tribulation period. These had placed their whole confidence in Christ and had become members of the church that is called the betrothed "bride of Christ," and just as the best Bible teachers had said, Christ would not subject his bride to the wrath being poured out upon those who had rebelled against the advice of the Scriptures and had attempted rather to maintain independence from their Creator. So while the true church was enjoying her refuge from the punishing events during the tribulation, Samson had been left to suffer briefly with the unfaithful, but his visit to Melchior's cabin and his translation in time and space occurred well before (and well after) the years of great tribulation.

Although there were others who had, and would, take this exceptional route, Samson was in his own right a remarkably exceptional man. His role in life had been exceptional. He did not fit any category: he was neither saint nor skeptic, but neither was he quite an ordinary mortal. He had not arrived at some advanced state of existence by his own efforts or by some divine infusion, but like Samson of old he had been born under a promise and for a purpose, and he had fulfilled it in an extraordinary manner; he had not wavered from the course he found himself on, though he had no certain knowledge of where it would lead.

Where it led him was to the brink of death. As far as most people knew, he *had* died, crushed under the rubble of the collapsed building that he had brought down by his own hands. Some were of the opinion that he had taken up the faith at the very last and would be reunited with his friends who had gone the way of the Rapture shortly before.

Samson had escaped what should have been his grave, but no longer was he Earl Clark: he had become Ichabod Samson. That, as you know, was the new name he adopted for himself to help conceal his identity, because if the fact of his survival had come to the ears of the authorities, it would have cost him his freedom immediately.

Introduction

Under this new name he reappeared in the disguise of severe physical deformity: his left eye was blind; his left arm was almost useless; his left leg was partially lame; and there were ugly gashes on his face that had not healed well. His voice had changed too: it was raspy and rather hoarse. Though it was a fortuitous disguise, not one devised for the purpose of deceit, it served well for that.

Most of his deformity could have been avoided: those injuries could have been completely healed with better medical care, but he chose to have the myth of his demise perpetuated rather than be exposed to the doctors, which meant his recovery had to proceed without the aid of medical expertise. The best efforts of his caring neighbor with whom he sought confidential doctoring were not sufficient to save the eye or repair the arm or get the alignment of the bones in the leg perfectly correct or sew the gash on his temple and forehead with enough skill. Karen Martin had little medical training. She had been the wife of a close friend of Earl's who had deserted her in the Rapture. Her only qualification to act as an emergency medic, much less a physician, was that she found herself sheltering a wounded man who insisted she not seek outside help for him. With proper medical attention, Earl may have kept his eye, and the nasty scar on his forehead would have been erased, and the nerves in his arm perhaps could have been saved.

Karen loved Earl and would have done anything for him. The experience became doubly painful for her as she gradually came to realize that he was too much attached to another woman[1] to have his affections turned in her own direction by any amount of her loving care. The object of his devotion was not on earth; but that did not seem to matter to him.

Earl was a pitiful creature at that point. He was crushed in body and soul, but eventually there came to him a spirit of determination to serve in the place of someone who was not present. With such ghosts Karen could not compete. She was limited to being his confidant in restoring him to a degree of physical mobility and freedom. She had to be satisfied with being a caregiver.

---

1. Yes, that was me.

It was not her first experience giving care. Karen Martin had been forced into the care-giving mode earlier when her husband developed dementia. If she had one compensation for being left behind, it was being relieved of that difficult duty, but her reprieve did not last long. On the day after Kenneth Martin disappeared with the other followers of Christ, she found Earl Clark, whom she had given up for dead, hobbling out of the woods near her house.

After three months, the result of Karen's effort was the appearance of a new, mysterious figure in the community—such community as was left after the Rapture had taken some of its leading citizens. Although there still lived within Ichabod Samson the heart of Earl Clark, he had lost not only the woman of his choice but also his best friend, his home, and his several roles in the community. Initially, it seemed to him that Ichabod was destined merely to march through the next phase of his life until death delivered him to his final destination, whatever that might be. He had to assume that this experience was a necessary segment of his journey, and he was determined to make the best of it.

Ichabod had no home and no job, but he did have some money that his friend Pastor Adam Murphy had left in the care of Karen (whose absence from services had predicted she would not be among those who would accompany the church to heaven), and being a longtime friend of Earl's, she would be .... Well, it's a longer story than I have space for here. It's told in its completeness elsewhere. Suffice it to say that Karen was a good accomplice for Earl in making sure he was not without material resources.

Samson's first move as he applied himself to serving the remains of his old community in a new way was to take the lad Homer Foster into his confidence. They worked together to rekindle the fire of the Gospel as they imagined that Earl's best friend, Adam Murphy, and Homer's father, Harold Foster, would do if they were present. But the response was dismal.

In fact, the community itself—the entire town—was not destined to survive more than a few months.

Introduction

After nearly all of its citizens were packed into buses and hauled away, the town was bombed and completely destroyed by fire. Very few that were left survived, other than those who had heeded Al Cypher's warning and migrated to Herne. Five souls took refuge immediately in the Beach House, which was unaccountably spared: Enid and Ernie, Brother Ned, Larry Link, and Claudia Nice. Homer, fortunately, had rushed off to hang out with Melchior. Earl showed up at the Beach House the next day, having sheltered in a cave. Karen was found badly injured and brought to the Beach House where Earl spent two weeks caring for her while they all worried about Homer who had not returned.

Many knew the legend of Melchior, the mysterious prophet-priest living at the foot of the mountain across the lake. He had no beginning, it was said, and he had been a king over the region in prehistoric times. Homer and Earl knew exactly where Melchior lived because Harold Foster, who had visited him more than once, had drawn a map. (I think Harold happened across Melchior's cabin accidentally, but I'm not sure.) So they knew that Melchior was real, not just a legend. He was an ancient priest and prophet of the living God.

When Homer sat with Melchior on the day of the attack, he learned that his father had made arrangements for him to rejoin the church after his work on earth was completed. The priest prayed him directly to the place where he was to begin his new life —still on earth but in the future (which I explain in chapter four) —before joining his family in new heaven.

It was in pursuit of Homer that Earl made the trek to Melchior's cabin for the last time, where the news of Homer's departure was shocking enough, but beyond astonishment was that he himself had been called to an assignment in the future.

Earl assumed initially that he would be given a new body, just as those who had been resurrected and Raptured were promised new bodies free of the curse of sin. To be healed of his deformities and live during the kingship of the glorified Christ, bypassing more tribulation, was a greater gift than he could imagine.

But what excited him most was the prospect of finding the friends he had lost. In truth, he told me, it was that one friend in particular. I was the glimmering light who had been his burden for years and who had suddenly become the desire of his life just before he lost me to the Rapture. That I be in the kingdom he had no doubt because, as he understood those things, many of Christ's followers would be taking part in the royal government throughout the world. Since I had been a successful administrator, I was prepared to serve in a similar assignment on earth.

He knew that I, along with the other Raptured saints, would possess timeless, glorified bodies. (Samson told me he could scarcely imagine how glorification could enhance the beauty of certain women, for in his eyes they were already perfect.) Surely within the thousand years he would recognize me, regardless of where I was in the world, even if I had a new name.

When asked about his chance of meeting me, Melchior assured him that we would meet. But then when he asked about his physical restoration, his brief reverie got shattered: the promise was about a translation in space and time only, nothing else. Sadly, Melchior was not promising that Samson's physical infirmities would be removed. He would still be Ichabod.

Samson was afraid that the horrific scene across the lake which he viewed so clearly through Melchior's window—the heaps of bricks, the charred trees—would haunt him forever; and lest he wonder, he had a suspicion he wanted to confirm.

He asked the prophet: "Was it Al Cypher?

"Yes."

"Will I encounter him again?"

"Yes."

• • •

When Samson arrived somewhere in the future, he found he was sitting on a similar chair in a very small room, much smaller than the one he had left. Indeed, the space was far too small for a room; it appeared to be a booth or a cell. It turned out that his portal into the age of glory was a public restroom.

The Epistle of Silas

Chapter One

The story of how the planet came to be as it was when Earl leaped into his future begins with the sealing of the 144,000 men of Israel who were sent to secure Mt. Zion. I know of no better record from that time than this famous letter written by a man we know only as Silas.

To Brother Gavrel:

Inasmuch as there is still misunderstanding about the 144,000 who stood against the antichrist occupation of the Holy City; and since you requested my written testimony as a member of that company, here it is for your records.

I was at Ephesus when John's Revelation came to us. We were all intensely interested in every detail since we were grasping at anything that would reassure us and hold out hope that our beloved city, which was in ruins, would be restored according to Ezekiel's grand plan; but what we found instead was the mysterious "New Jerusalem," and we could make nothing of that. Frankly, we hardly understood any of the manuscript beyond the notes from Yeshua to the churches, and even that section seemed very odd and raised many questions.

The mention of 144,000 Israelites from twelve tribes seemed to us purely symbolic since we doubted that so many Jewish believers were still alive after the fall of Jerusalem and slaughter in Judea. Yet we hung our meager hope on them and what they might do, pretending it was literal because of that one mention of Mount Zion where it was said the 144,000 would appear. At that time if someone had told me that I would be one of the 144,000, I would have thought it a joke, and not a funny joke at all.

I did not live long after that—not on earth, I mean. The time I spent in heaven,[1] if you can call it "time," was the most refreshing experience you can imagine magnified seven times—or let us say times twelve. I have no words to describe the love that emanates from the throne of our God. There are no words to adequately convey what it meant to me, and I will not attempt to do so in writing.

---

1. This is not the "new heaven." Days and hours in new heaven correspond to time on earth.

But I can tell you that there is no fixed relationship between time in heaven and time on earth. We could observe certain things as they took place on earth (if we had a need to), but it wasn't like we could look down and watch the future unfold. There was no unfolding and there was no looking down. The past and present on earth were equally present to us as we viewed earth from heaven, but it was not for our entertainment or to satisfy curiosity.

In fact, yielding to entertainment in heaven would be like admiring a noxious weed in your garden of lilies, if you know what I mean, because curiosity has no foothold when you feel so complete.

No need or lack of any kind existed near the throne of God, only abundance and superabundance, which was overwhelming to those of us "lesser spirits" who had not grown as much in our earthly life. It's not that curiosity was discouraged as a matter of policy or anything like that; but you had to be able to detach your intellect a little and go beyond mulling over your blessings.

Yes, your time in heaven is quite apart from the sequence of events on earth. That's why John's Revelation is difficult if you have in mind an unfolding of events on earth.

In order for John to write what he did, he had to translate into words of the Greek language what there are no words for. In heaven there are no words like we use them here. We communicated and understood without words and without language. Words in heaven are used for other purposes. Unlike on earth where idle words and untruths prevail (usually with little lasting effect), spoken words in heaven cause things to happen—but don't take "happen" in a quite literal sense because the cause and effect is not like that. It's difficult to explain. The words are not the direct causation of events; they're patterns that yield events when time is applied to them.

But the written word in heaven is much the same as on earth, and there was plenty of opportunity to read. What I read reminded me of some of the Psalms in our terrestrial Scriptures, particularly those which seem unreasonable when you take them quite literally; nevertheless, they make you thankful for where you are and what you've been saved from. For example, there was one with a superscription that said it was written to restrain progress on earth and for that reason had not been included in the Psalter. I did not understand that because I couldn't imagine a lover of God being interested in the world and pursuing the world's rewards to achieve wealth in material things. What this unpublished psalm said, in effect, was that certain people are so insistent in their prayers for material prosperity that the Lord decrees they be blessed without restraint as Job was but without any interference by Satan, the reason being that it is so much easier to deal with them that way: just pour out the blessings and let them suffer the consequences on their own rather than negotiate with them as they constantly pester heaven with their insistence that they were promised certain health and/or wealth (not to mention fame).

But I digress.

John's Revelation is a marvelous work for what it achieves. It's true to heaven while being couched in the language of earth. Most of Scripture, with the exception of visions, comes ready made in earth-words as the writer writes. John, witnessing the perspective of heaven, had to describe in words what has no earthly counterpart. The difficulty comes about by the fact that heaven is spiritual and bounded by its peculiar fourth dimension while earth is physical and bound by its elementary time dimension—for the most part, though I learned there are exceptions in that too.

Spiritual heaven is to earth what a playwright's desk is to the stage on which the play gets acted out. Just as the play, when produced with all its props and costumes, is more detailed than the script, so the physical universe is more detailed than its plan as seen in heaven, but the details are results of the repetitive execution of designs that stand timeless in heaven. The whole of the physical universe, past, present, and future, is represented there as a plan like a script of a play (though that is a poor analogy unless we allow that the script has within itself many possible variants). But unlike the script of a play, the plan has no time markers and is, in fact, a system of systems of sub-plans that interconnect as needed; so it would have been impossible for John to use what he saw to predict and describe some event in time. Only the Spirit of God can trace through a script independently of time.

13

Time may execute the script, but the structure of the script as you behold it in heaven does not correspond to time at all. The plan is beautiful and you get excited about it just looking at it. It does not have the appearance of a written document; in outward appearance it is an arrangement of images—no, not simply pictures but sights and sounds of the most amazing forms, including unique creatures that embody certain subscripts. You realize that everything in the grand plan is potentially present in every moment of its revelation. It seems that everything is about to happen "soon," and yet the possibilities will never be exhausted. If that doesn't make sense, I'm sorry. It's the best I can do.

This is what John saw and was told to put down in writing; and when he did so it came out in the form of that apocalyptic narrative, which was quite appropriate. Indeed, I don't know how else it could have been written without being misleading. Those who have been misled by it have worked hard misleading themselves; the path they take is arduous, skirting the simple fact that heaven is a spiritual place and the view in the Revelation is from the perspective of the Spirit—not the creativity of a man on an island inventing riddles to mystify his enemies and inform his friends. If they really believed in John's heaven, they would not export earth's constraints into it. For example, you must understand that the time which threads John's narrative is primarily in the domain of heaven, not earth.

So when we first read this Revelation of Yeshua Messiah and tried to match it to the events that we knew of up to our time at the end of the first century, we got a poor fit. In later centuries more of it would make sense, but you know that better than I, for you were born twenty centuries later than I was. Of course it had to be that way because the plan does not fully reveal itself until the script is executed, and then the purpose and design of each element becomes understandable—as it slips into the past. A little extrapolation into the future is possible, however: you look for patterns in the past which may reveal a loop destined to be executed again. This was explained to me when I wandered away from the environs of the temple and made the acquaintance of a pair of friendly angels who traded some questions of theirs for mine.

At some point—I cannot say in earthly years how long I had been there, and it doesn't matter—I was told I had been drafted into a special-forces company of 144,000 that would be deployed to earth to hold our claim on Jerusalem against Antichrist's move to possess it for himself. In heaven there was never a question about Jerusalem being the seat of the Kingdom, though the plan seemed to be steeped in peril (Jerusalem was one bit of earth we could observe without a special need because we all had the desire for our city to come into its fruition predicted by the Prophets).

Now this detail about the 144,000, which had been one of the curiosities described by John, came to our attention. There it was, fully revealed: what I had taken to be symbolic was that, but it was also going to take place as an event in earth's history! I was elated more than usual, if that were possible, but I had a lot of questions!

First off I thought there must be some mistake because I did not know which tribe I was in, and I was not a virgin! But of course that was my old body, which had been partly digested by a lion. I quickly realized that it was about our bodies in the resurrection. It was the most awesome thing to think about: getting back to one's own familiar body yet as a pristine creation like Adam. Though we were infinitely comfortable in our spirits, divorced from material bodies, we all yearned to be back in a physical body because that's what we were made for.

Information about one's history is readily available there. Heaven knows everything in one form or another! It turned out that I'm mostly from the tribe of Dan, but I was assigned to be deployed under the banner of Judah.

The tribal divisions in this army were nominal at best. If you were primarily of one particular tribe, you would most likely be assigned to it—unless it was Dan or Ephraim. Ephraim and some of Manasseh were to be combined under the new flag of Joseph. There were enough of more-or-less pure Manassehites to make up a division on their own with some to spare, and that surplus joined with Ephraim to make up Joseph. What there were of the Danites were put in with various tribes. I would have chosen Judah, so I was fortunate. I was wishing Samson was there to carry the banner for Dan, but there was to be no banner for Dan. (Samson, of course, was waiting his turn for resurrection in the company of the old-dispensation saints.)

Also, I remembered that when we first read John's Revelation, we wondered why Judah was listed first. It became obvious to me when I understood the purpose of the 144,000, which was to defend the right of King Yeshua to renew David's throne in Jerusalem—since the nation Israel was to be overcome by her enemies and her citizens driven out of her capital. So this campaign was not about the whole of Israel, and that's why Levi had to be represented: it was not about the divisions of the Promised Land; it was about keeping our claim on Jerusalem current, which the Levites were concerned with more than anyone—especially more than Dan.

The number 12,000 from each tribe was indeed symbolic, being Israel's signature number in thousands. Eventually there were enough of us Israelite men in heaven to fill out the full 144,000, but even so it was a real privilege to be chosen. Again, when I say "eventually" don't think of time that progresses as it does on earth. It was like when John says "after these things," which is by the sequence in heaven and as such is arranged according to a system of purposes and causes, not of outcomes or effects.

Developments on earth we were told would increase at a very rapid pace as the gentile age drew to a close, and we would have to become a bit familiar with the latest things before we actually stood on the soil of Mount Zion.

We also were taught to speak an updated version of Hebrew as well as some modern languages. Of course it was the Spirit of our Lord who revealed what we had to learn, because even the angels did not know, and he instilled it in us as a new song no one else knew and we could not forget, the meaning of which would come to us to meet our needs as they arose. This was very special.

Remembering John's mention of the "marriage supper of the Lamb," we wondered if this event was to be in heaven. That was a question everyone had, and like so many other episodes mentioned in Scripture from heaven's perspective, there was a vagueness about it. We were given time's clarity on it when we were being schooled in the things we would need to know on earth. You see, we were to be the "first fruits" of Yeshua's resurrection, appearing in earth-time ahead of others. So if the marriage supper were to take place just before the King's return, it seemed that we could miss out on it—which it seemed would be a reasonable sacrifice to compensate for the privilege of being the first of the "dead" to reappear on earth.

The actual *marriage* of Messiah to his bride, his church of believers, was in heaven; and, no, we would not miss it—no member of the body of Messiah would miss it. In fact, we learned that it was a prerequisite to becoming perfectly obedient to him in the Resurrection. To be resurrected into his service without being married to him would be a ticket to a lonely limbo on earth. But, yes, the marriage supper was to be on earth. I thought about it later and saw that it could be no other way because: 1) the marriage was for the church that had not only been saved by his blood but also called out by the Holy Spirit, beginning when he first indwelt ordinary earthlings at the Pentecost following Yeshua's resurrection; 2) the supper included guests of the bridegroom, who were to be resurrected directly on earth, as was their expectation; and 3) heaven could not host a real supper with physical food.

By the way, the question I have been asked most about heaven is what the food is like or if gastronomy is even an issue there. Like so many theological conundrums, the answer follows from a statement made at the beginning of the first book of Moses:

God created man in his own image;

in the image of God he created him;

male and female he created them.

I can tell you that our image of God is stamped all over heaven, not the distortions of devils like pagan religions depict, but very human-looking faces on angels and even some beasts. Yeshua Messiah himself is in perfect likeness of a man, though a resurrected and glorified man. I can say no more about that because there are no words for it. John did the best he could, and I would not know how to improve on the way he described him. The shocking effect it has on the reader is essential. Was it heaven's sacrifice that he became the second Adam? If so, the sacrifice was made in the beginning when God created the first Adam in his own image. But there was always the glorification in view, I'm sure of that.

Mouths in heaven, however, are not necessary for taking in food and water to sustain physical life because there is no physical life there. The food is spiritual like everything else and consists of the words of God in various forms. We had thought it odd that John, like Ezekiel, was commanded to eat the little scroll. But that's the image that comes to mind, is it not? How else could John describe it in a few words?

Well, I've gone off the track again; I promised you my own testimony, not an amateur's theology of heaven. I repent.

The sensation of your spirit joining its newly created body is painless and wonderful. I knew it as my body immediately, but it was so much stronger and more responsive. I welcomed the weight of gravity and the sure footing it gave me on solid earth. I was standing upright, fully in control of my members, and I felt clean and pure—none of the nagging of the old flesh, which I could recall only vaguely. I was of the same stature and build, and seemingly the same age as when I last stood on earth two thousand years ago.

I looked around. We were not all alike. There were various lengths of beards and hair. My companions were of various ages, some much older than I (which was not surprising since we had a definite sense of being different ages in heaven, though it was not very evident in our appearances). Later I inquired about this and learned that age did not diminish one's strength. I never heard that anyone had a scar or deformity, weak eyesight, or any of the other imperfections that compromise physical bodies. Yeshua in his resurrected body manifested some of his old wounds from the cross, but that must have been a badge he wore by choice. None of my wounds were worth anything, and I'm glad to have the evidence of them gone. But his are worth more than the whole world, in my estimation.

Were we flesh and blood? It felt like it, and I'm sure of it now.

We were all uniformly dressed. In heaven our garments, and indeed our bodies, were numinous, like light, not reflectors of light. Here in our resurrection we came suitably clothed and outfitted for action. The material was not of woven fibers; it was like supple animal skin, but it also reminded me of silk. The colors were earthy, not white. (You see white robes in heaven, where they are symbolic of being clothed in the righteousness of Messiah, in certain images celebrating the achievement of defeating inevitable death.) The style of our uniform has, as you commented, the suggestion of ancient military dress.

We thought it a marvel that material objects had been created along with our new bodies, but I dare not digress and go into the theories we had about that. We also found colorful banners that had materialized along with us, ready to be unfurled for displaying our tribal identities. No one was very much surprised when we found them: you are not easily surprised after you have been in heaven—at least not when you come back as a miracle yourself. Never think lightly of the resurrection of the body! I believe it is a higher level of creation than was the creation of the first man.

Just showing up *en masse* as we did took the breath out of our enemies. We were there to replace the witness of the Jews who had not been deceived by the antichrist (the one you nicknamed Nero), most of whom had been killed in the purge or driven out, and it would not be so easy for Nero's army to get rid of us.

The marks on our foreheads were symbolic, meaning that on earth the famously hard foreheads of our race had given way to brows that were permanently in tune with our miracle-working God. But the names of Yeshua and Yahweh were literally tattooed on our foreheads, it turned out. This was a visible badge for our particular service, not a general feature in the resurrection. Those inner and outer marks combined to give us extraordinary boldness. We were not afraid of anything, confident of our calling, and I think it was evident in our manner.

It was a very dramatic moment. As if to get everyone's attention, the air suddenly became very still, and it seemed the earth itself stood still in apprehension as we materialized, dozens at a time, in Bloomfield Park on the southwest side of the Old City.

The appearance out of nowhere gave us immediate credibility, but I think what made the biggest impression was our tribal banners: the guards looking out from their garrison on the Mount of Olives were confronted with a massive delegation of the whole house of ancient Israel, looking like we had come to life from the time of David, dry bones resurrected from the valley of history and claiming their old capital. Angels could not have done it: they would not be Israel; and there was nothing about us that looked like the citizens of modern Israel. We represented ancient Israel of the Scriptures; our prophets wrote about the Kingdom, and here we were, looking like living relics to stand as witness to the imminent fulfillment of their prophecies.

What John wrote about next, after introducing the 144,000, follows heaven's source script: it is no surprise that it was not next in earth-time sequence. The "great multitude" he saw in heaven was no more a product of the latest season of persecution than our present tour of duty in Jerusalem progressed materially from an earthly sequence of events. I suspect that the multitude that John saw in heaven was there when I was there.

It was hard to tell. Something of significance was always in place around the throne, but I was never fully aware of what the proxy beings meant. There were so many angelic beings involved— angels everywhere. Heaven is like a nation of angels—so many shapes, sizes, and even kinds of angels. Did you know there were female angels before I mentioned it? Yeshua came close to letting out the secret when he said that in the resurrection we are like angels, neither marrying nor giving in marriage. I got the impression that female angels seldom visit earth because they are busy counseling newly arrived spirits and changing the decorations.

Anyway, back to the "great multitude." The "great tribulation" they had come out of was heaven's perspective: it was not a reference to a particularly difficult period of time on earth; it was a reference to the extreme sufferings they had endured while on earth.

Well, all this may or may not be interesting to you, but in any case I must get back to my story in order to finish this before I meet with some brothers about the recruitment potential here.

As we spread out on the south and west and north sides of the Old City (we were warned to stay away from Kidron Valley), there was a very strange thunderclap sounding as if an opening had been rent in heaven, and we heard familiar sounds of heaven's harpers harping, but I think only our resurrected ears could hear it. In any case, we heard the music of heaven, which had a very stimulating effect on us.

Need I emphasize that it was an alarming situation we were in? I know John wrote that the Lamb was there with us, but remember John was in the Spirit in heaven and what he saw was not the same as what we saw on earth. I have no doubt that the Lamb was there, but we couldn't see him. Heaven is not far away, you know, because distance of that kind is irrelevant in the spirit realm since it has no position in the created universe.

Our presence made the clear statement that Jerusalem belongs to Israel, but the enemy around us needed to know more than that. While the harp music was still in our ears we heard the voice of an angel—it seemed from the sky—prompting us with words to repeat, and we called out so all could hear for miles around:

"Fear the God of Israel, for the hour of his judgment has come, and he will be glorified. Worship him who made heaven and earth and the sea and the fountains of waters."

No sooner had the echoes of our twelve twelves of thousands of voices died away than we heard more words from above. We listened and repeated:

"His wrath has taken down your Great City: Babylon the Great will no longer supply the nations with the wine of her fornication."

Again we listened and repeated what we heard:

"If you worship the Beast and bear his mark, you will drink the wine of the undiluted wrath of God in the cup of his anger; you will be tormented with fire and brimstone in the presence of the holy angels, and in the presence of the Lamb."

After that, a fierce wind suddenly swept in from the east. Whether it was due to our threatening announcements or the startling wind, the opposition forces, which had been virtually paralyzed by our appearing, began reacting to their orders and noisily firing everything they had. We were perfectly calm, and no bullet or drone or missile of any sort touched us. We had the music of heaven, which they couldn't hear, on our side, and our tribal banners kept streaming.

John didn't mention the banners, for some reason, but I'm sure they had an effect on the black-uniformed enemy force. The appearance of these ancient names of our tribes acted like a spell on them; it was impossible for them not to acknowledge and respect the presence of Israel in the spot they had been trying to purge of every Jew. They deliberately aimed low and blasted the graves in the Valley.

We did not all go into the streets of the Old City, for we were advised of the coming earthquakes that would reduce it to rubble once again. If we had not firmly believed the Prophets, we would have been disheartened once again. But we knew. Yes, we knew and could doubt the Word no longer.

We did not have long to wait. A thick dark cloud came with the wind from the east and the quake struck there on the east side, directly under the Mount of Olives where the guards had their main station. The rocks crumbled around them and the earth sank beneath them, swallowing the garrison. Some of the guards got out on foot fleeing to the north and south, but most did not.

You will be reminded of Zechariah. Though we couldn't see him, King Yeshua had just arrived in the cloud. This is a good example of the difference of how heaven's perspective renders out on earth. In the plan of heaven it is all romance and glory: Yeshua rides in on a white horse followed by angels on white horses. In the reality of eternal values, that's the true image, but in the moment of time on earth it appeared as the gloom of doom to us.

We could see that some damage had been done within the walls of the Old City. Some buildings had collapsed. The new song told us that people who did not belong to the "beast" were hiding in there. The Levites went in and found them all and led them out. It was not safe for those people to stay anywhere in or near Jerusalem, so Levi led them out to the east and found the valley newly cut in the Mount of Olives passable, just as Zechariah had said.

The remaining 132,000 of us retreated to the west on foot, crowding every street. We passed through Kiryat Hamemshalah and on down into the valley. We avoided the highways, preferring the hike across country.

During that time the wind stopped suddenly. It was obviously supernatural. And the sky lit up with a blaze of light. There were roaring sounds of an enormous storm in the north, wind and lightning and hail. We knew it was the angels waging war.

We made it to Bet Shemesh before stopping, and that's when the big quake struck. Where I was, the ground shook and I had difficulty walking. Thankfully, there was only minor damage to the buildings here.

Some have reported that the earth opened up in fiery fissures, devouring Jerusalem's streets and buildings like jaws of a giant dragon. Streams of water are reported to be coming out on the west and the east.

During the march we took in marvels of the modern world, but our new song revealed that we would live without them. We will serve as guards to protect crews and work sites during the rebuilding of Jerusalem's walls. We will establish camps as needed. There are skills among us from times when food was basic and things were simply made, when architects and engineers used methods you would call primitive—valuable abilities carried over from former lives that not even heaven's school could improve on.

But initially we were to bring in labor for rebuilding, and you were the right person to get me started on that. What you suggested worked out well. You were the first glorified person I met.

Avoiding the war zone, I took a boat out of Jaffa that was sailing for Kuşadasi. Lacking the "Nero chip," I had no way of paying the fare, but the operator let me go anyway. I guess it was my unusual dress that he took to be the uniform of some official. (So far, at least, there has been no indication that this resurrected body of mine has abilities to translate instantly from one place to another or to let me pop over to heaven whenever I want to. Yeshua Messiah could do that. The servant is not greater than, or even as great as, the master.)

When I got there the few people I encountered out in the open, who did not flee when they saw the sign on my forehead, were desperate, and they responded immediately to the news that employment was available. They were all biblically ignorant and had no understanding of the times we were in. But they were eager to hear me and put me in contact with others.

So this is where I am, and this is where I will be stationed for a while. I have organized a thousand young men who are willing to walk to Israel if necessary, but I'm working on transportation.

I took a day off and got a ride to Ephesus. I was curious. It was barren, almost a desert. The ancient ruins, including the façade of the library of Celsus (which I understand was standing until this year), are down flat. Not that I would have the old pagan temples, but I was sorry to see what that region had become. Someday it will be beautiful again—not "Lord willing" because he is willing; he told me that.

I am looking forward to returning to Judea and seeing for myself the progress that has been made in laying out the new city. I know from Ezekiel's vision that the Temple will be north of its old location. If the old temple area is left undeveloped it would delight the archaeologists. That earthquake we felt and heard could have made some changes almost instantly. I'm not sure what Ezekiel meant by the temple being high and lifted up, if it meant in the political sense or the geographical sense. I have a notion of what to expect, but there are certain aspects, such as the river flowing out of the temple and down to the Dead Sea which I would almost say Ezekiel meant as metaphor, but the details that anchor it to physical things preclude that. And there are those new streams. Yet its dimensions seem miraculous because it increases its size as it flows, apparently without tributaries. I get the impression that the whole Jordan Valley will come to life like the Garden of Eden, and that the flow will bring the Dead Sea to life and from its waters the oceans of the world will be renewed. I must see this river with my own eyes! Yes, and the western branch as well.

P.S.

As you were so keen to document everything, you asked me insightful questions about my resurrected body and how it differs from a natural body. There were some things I couldn't answer at that time which I have since learned. You asked me if I had all my parts, and I knew what you meant, and I said I did. But what you really wanted to know is if everything was functional, and I didn't know that myself. But now I do. I believe everything is possible, but not everything is profitable. It is actually possible for me to be seduced by a beautiful woman, but it is no match for the love of Yeshua which lives within me since the wedding, and it is profitable for everyone when I share his love.

Baruch's Chronicle

Chapter Two

Baruch's Chronicle is a popular essay based on one man's experience during the rebuilding in Israel. He was a rabbi in Jerusalem during the days before the Rapture when he came to acknowledge Jesus of Nazareth as Israel's messiah and embraced him as his personal savior; hence he joined the body of Christ in new heaven where he learned what his role was to be in bringing about the transformation of his nation.

Other than the 144,000, not many were resurrected initially because food and shelter in Israel were limited. Baruch and other glorified saints like him had no need to feed themselves, and they never needed a place to sleep, benefiting from nights of refreshment in new heaven.

I include here Baruch's Chronicle in an abridged form.

The task before us was immense, but we had the can-do spirit of heaven in us and the certain knowledge that we would succeed as we worked to carry out the King's plan, because there could be no doubt: he had revealed the design to his prophet Ezekiel; it had reposed in Scripture for twenty-seven hundred years—disbelieved and misunderstood, of course. But we adopted it as our outline, and all the incorrect interpretations were soon forgotten.

My several colleagues and I, being leaders tasked with the rebuilding of Israel, descended first to Bet Shemesh where a single-floor office building suited to our purposes had withstood the earthquakes and been made ready for us.

Before any new building or rebuilding could take place, there was an enormous amount of cleanup to be done. Carnage disdained by the birds had been covered over when hills were shaken down in rock slides, and much of the urban ruins were swallowed like Korah's clan when fissures opened beneath them. But debris of every kind still had to be cleared from the land. For this task we needed raw manpower because few serviceable machines were left, and no functioning factories remained to make machines or parts to repair them. The angels of heaven became our mighty arm that provided the necessary workforce.

I don't mean that angels performed the labor. The laborers were "beasties"—people who were unable to buy or sell because they bore the mark of Satan's beast. Miserable souls, attracted to free rations dropping like manna, migrated to labor camps in Egypt. Once proud slaves of the devil, their former master was in chains and so were they. Their new masters were angels. Cleanup in Israel was performed by millions of these slaves of the Crown who might have worn crowns themselves had they heeded the Gospel—or at least been free if they had read the last pages of the Bible. After serving their time they will be released and have their economic freedom restored, but by then slaves of the King, wielding "rods of iron," will have been established to rule over them.

While the cleanup was going on we worked out the many details required to bring Ezekiel's plan to life. This was like no engineering project that had ever been performed on earth because the infusion of codes from heaven into the primal laws of nature gave us more options. Water flowing from springs in Israel is literally living water now. It has intelligence and is no longer incompressible: it has the ability to expand to fill dry places when necessary. As a beverage, nothing is better tasting, and such health benefits to the natural body are no longer supernatural.

The buildings located on the old temple mount had collapsed—except for the recent small temple which had to be razed because it never should have been built. The ruins of Jerusalem's modern and insignificant buildings are gone. The whole area has been cleaned up, and now it is a historical preserve. The contested mount where holy buildings stood will be mined for its history.

What is sometimes called the "new city" is a district located north of the historical preserve. Unlike the rambling old city walls, the walls of the new city form a perfect square and enclose a relatively small area, less than two miles on a side. Inside the walls is the palace of the King and prince. On east and west sides of the city walls are extensive gardens twice the size of the walled area.

Just north of the city district is a large district maintained by the priests. It extends to ancient Shiloh where the temple and sanctuary is now located. A similar allotment of land for Levites is adjacent to the priests' portion on its north side.

The sanctuary or temple complex forms a perfect square surrounded by a low wall with a tall gate in the middle of each side. Inside is an outer court and another wall enclosing an inner court and the holy house. The orientation aligns the temple with the earth's rotation, its entrance facing east.

Extending due north from the city is a broad, tree-flanked highway joining the north city gate with the temple at its southern gate.

The famous expanding stream of water originates beneath the temple stairway. It flows east in a channel across the courts then exits under the eastern wall where it turns south and runs parallel to the highway all the way to the city. Inside the city it divides into two rivers which turn east and west, one going out under the east wall, watering the garden on that side and continuing on to freshen the Dead Sea, the other flowing west to the Mediterranean.

Since this is the seat of world government, very large areas are set aside for administrative buildings—the prince's portion—extending to the Jordan Valley on the east and the Mediterranean Sea on the west.

We laid out boundaries for the tribes following Ezekiel's prescription. These are more commemorative than functional, but saints with clear tribal identity are being located accordingly. Benjamin is next to Jerusalem on the south side; then come the territories of Simenon, Issachar, Zebulun, and Gad. The lands belonging to Judah, Reuben, Ephraim, Manasseh, Naphtali, Asher, and Dan lie north of the Levite portion in that order.

As soon as an area was pronounced clean, fields were marked out for crops, and moderate rainfall commenced. Irrigation was not necessary. Also seeds fell from heaven, and now we have the plants that were in the Garden of Eden. New animals appeared as well, all of them herbivores, naturally docile with no fear of man. Farms and herds in Israel are cared for by families of resurrected Jews, their "mansions" and barns having been prepared for them by natural workers supervised by Jews from new heaven.

The construction crews were made up of naturals, including Hebrew-speaking Jews. Their bosses were Jews from new heaven. Some crews included slaves from Egypt and volunteers from other nearby nations. There were friendly Arabs among them too, but most Arabs disagreed with the plans and opposed the building of walls. The 144,000 resurrected Jewish men guarded the construction sites and protected the builders from protesters.

Stone was used for building, all of it quarried, cut, and fit in the old way. Some of the stone craftsmen and artisans from Solomon's time were resurrected, but modern Hebrew was difficult for them. Added to these were cathedral masons from centuries past and architects with later experience. All had to learn the language first.

After the temple and palace were completed, Solomon arrived along with his godly sons and slaves—and priests who had served during his time. Solomon had studied the role of the prince in Ezekiel's vision and knew what to expect. He had much to learn about the modern world, but he applied himself to studying everything that has a bearing on the matters he would be dealing with as chief administrator under his glorified Savior and son. Solomon has repented and declared that not all is vanity.

The priests went to work preparing sacrifices. This was fascinating to modern Jews such as myself who had dreamed of it prior to our being completed in Yeshua. Sacrifices are loud and clear proclamations of the hard fact that there is no pardon of sin possible apart from the shedding of blood. Whether we be resurrected or glorified and ever so obedient, we are still forgetful humans needing to remember the awful cost Christ paid for our salvation.

By this time free naturals had built up local economies. Solomon began conscripting them and had them build houses for the Crown, and as housing became available, saints began arriving.

In the order of general resurrection, first came late Christians in waves of saints having similar backgrounds. All resurrection events take place in one of the seven wedding banquet halls, each seating twelve hundred and located within the palace. During this "supper" they are seated in groups fifty and reintroduced to their millennial families. The head waiters are apostles, and the kitchens are staffed by Jewish naturals. Jews from before the Christian era are select guests eager to hear about the church age. On the last day of the week-long feast, Yeshua addresses them, telling them about the mansions prepared for them, where they are located, who their leaders are, and how they will serve in the Kingdom.

One of the problems with bringing down saints in resurrection is providing them with compatible environments. People who lived during times when travel was quick and easy and tools and labor-saving appliances were common do not want to live without electricity and indoor plumbing. After all, this is the perfect heaven they had been anticipating. It had never occurred to them that compromises might have to be made. Of course, the underlying problem is that the popular doctrine of emotional gratification in the afterlife—according to one's particular conception of bliss—was celebrated above every other practical consideration.

There is no excuse for that. We knew that Yeshua had demonstrated his resurrected body by consuming broiled fish—but that was Galilee, not heaven. However, we know that "resurrection" means a standing up of the body (hopefully in good condition), not the creation of a new kind of body. Thus it was hard to escape the conclusion that the afterlife of the saved must be on this same earth—but we thought it would be a complete remake because we demanded, or at least expected, Nirvana-like conditions.

While in new heaven, prior to the day when Yeshua asserted his right to rule the earth, we addressed these problems, but we viewed life on earth as moderns having little appreciation for the methods ancients used to achieve comfort. At first we imagined that life could be made pleasant enough to please everyone if modern technology were applied by a wise and perfectly benevolent technocracy under the direction of King Yeshua and his wise prince. But after examining that concept closely we found no proof that it would work, because modern technology had made life easy for some but had impoverished many and had enslaved everyone. Could Yeshua make it work? No, not without making fundamental changes in the laws of nature that he had written.

For some reason Yahweh had left us to ponder this. We all assumed that *he* knew the answer and would reveal it in due time, but we were not begging him to do so because we were having fun imagining that we could design a better world. Someone suggested that if everyone were given the opportunity we were enjoying—designing a perfect world—then everyone would be happy. That was good for a laugh, of course, because it had been tried.

In the end Yeshua came to our rescue by changing the subject. We had assumed a need for collective regulation by the government. He said the collective intelligence of his servants would work things out, and what we needed to be concerned about was bringing to everyone's mind the ongoing dispute with Satan.

I raised my hand. "How so, your majesty?" I objected. "What can an individual do to help you win that war?"

"You will prove to Satan, like Job did, that the human nature which I create and share my spirit with is not essentially faulty. Because Satan slipped easily into his habit of rebellion, he believes the same is inevitable for anyone who has the freedom of choice, given sufficient temptation over enough time. You, and especially your resurrected friends, will have opportunity to serve me faultlessly over the next thousand years because you are legally blameless, and with your bodies free of the corrupting influence of Adamic flesh, you have the ability to trust and obey me with your whole heart in spite of every temptation to try another way."

"I am eager to do that, your Majesty," I said.

"Are you?" he said. "I have been watching, and you sometimes step away from my Spirit. There is no essential sin in that; it is your right as a free being, but you become vulnerable to temptation. Yes, Satan is locked down for now, yet situations that invite you to explore another way still abound—but they do not interest you when you walk in my Spirit. Satan agrees that you were created to walk in my Spirit—and so was he—but he does not agree that a human creature can do it faithfully. Consequently, Satan demands that he be treated no worse than followers of mine who were likely to disobey several times in a day. New heaven will not be a peaceful place, according to him, because he demands equal treatment and will be walking to and fro and raising hell."

As the conference delved deeper into a servant's capacity for strict obedience, it was brought out that perfection is not even definable when the servant has choices to make that involve others. Perfect obedience can exist only in the eyes of the master who makes the law or gives the command. Less than perfect obedience is apparent when the servant tampers with the law or privately interprets the command. But who decides if that is justified?

The question came up about Satan's disobedience: Did Satan ever petition for pardon?

We were given that the answer to "ever" was not within the scope of our understanding. But for the purpose of judgment, the answer was, "No." Satan had come to the point where repentance was impossible for him; indeed, the line of contention had been drawn in the timeless realm.

So what evidence of obedience on the part of human servants has Satan agreed qualifies as "goodness"? If someone disobeys and later repents during the millennium of testing, will that servant still qualify as a bit of evidence for the goodness of the creation?

It would have to be argued in court, was the answer. To avoid a complicated trial, there will be such a showing of faithful servants that it will absolutely impress the angel jury. Satan will not appeal the judgment because he knows that the court's ruling is Yahweh's justice. But he also knows that the same standard must be applied to everyone. If he is banished to the outer darkness, then many whom Yeshua died for must go with him. Yahweh might decide that obtaining peace in heaven is not worth damning his beloved!

We all equated joy with being in heaven, but since we were there in the presence of our all-knowing Master we were not afraid to inquire beyond our fond expectations. We learned that "harmless" is not an attribute of a creature made in the image of God. Even with the love of God being primary in the heart of the human creature, he is not always harmless, the reason being that divine creative energy is in the image of God as well.

Joy in heaven radiates from Yeshua like light from the sun, but within each person exists a glow as well. So long as the light within resonates with the ambient light, we are happy and well guided. If we play with harmonizing hues, we may still receive light and even bless others; but dissonant chords, though private, inevitably escape us like contagions to infect others. So the enemy of joy in heaven is not simply someone's public departure from heaven's etiquette: the threat to perpetual peace resides in creative minds.

I had thought about this kind of thing with respect to peace on earth, but to realize that maintaining peace and joy in heaven will require vigilance among sanctified souls was a shocking revelation.

We had many questions, and some were answered. We learned about social structures:

The resurrected folk remain in their arrival groups for the duration of the millennium, living in many-roomed mansions with common areas—not apartments. An overseer from new heaven visits each group daily, bringing work orders from Jerusalem and returning with reports about compliance.

The natural population retains its families and community structures, including its religions, initially at least. But at the higher levels they are governed by servants from new heaven who come with charters and appoint managers over cities and towns.

Both resurrected and natural people have educational opportunities in schools chartered by the Crown with glorified teachers.

Law enforcement is staffed by naturals. They also operate the prisons. The courts are operated by resurrected magistrates with glorified judges.

The banking and the money supply is controlled from Jerusalem. Manufacturing, transportation, communication, and agriculture are all chartered and regulated by Solomon's councils in Jerusalem. The economy, including construction and renovation, is based on markets designed in Jerusalem and implemented locally by resurrected managers. The job market is for naturals.

In some places roads, railways, and bridges survived the tribulation with minimal damage. These go back into service, but very tall buildings that remain standing have demolition schedules.

Digital infrastructure was wiped out during the tribulation, which left no communication and almost no operable vehicles. Conversions to diesel-powered engines and simple electric motors were inevitably undertaken by naturals immediately, fuel needed to run them being produced in simple small-scale refineries.

Antique automobiles, locomotives, and aircraft from museums have been pressed into service, for that was their purpose.

A first priority was the establishment of points for transit between heaven and earth. Glorified bodies do not consist of earth's elements, but neither are they without mass on earth. So in order to materialize without colliding with or inconveniencing someone on earth, special places are designated for that purpose.

Chapter Three

S amson stood up and peered over the top of the stall. The place was clean and looked new. His door lacked a latch, but presently it clicked and swung wide open in the outward direction. He noticed the flooring was a mosaic of colors and shapes seemingly floating below the crystal-like surface. Or had his vision been affected by the journey?

After he stepped out, the door of the stall closed behind him of its own accord and clicked shut.

"That's odd," he muttered.

The doors of the other two stalls swung inward. The door of the one he left had swung outward, and there was no handle or any indication of how one might get in.

He limped toward the exit, passing a pair of sinks with mirrors above them. Prior to leaving the old world he thought that under this new order of life on earth his body would be less vulnerable to disease and injury, and he had harbored a hope that he would be restored to the physical wholeness he enjoyed before he got pinned under the wreckage of the FSA building. It was not a hope for his own well-being as much as it was for me: as he understood things, there was a high probability that he would encounter me during this blessed time on earth, and he dreaded my having to see him in this unsightly condition.

It was painfully obvious that his limbs were no better. He still had difficulty controlling his left leg, and and his left arm was still numb. He shifted the patch over his left eye and closed his right eye to make sure, and, yes, the left eye was still blind.

There was one more thing: might his facial deformity have been softened in some way? He guessed that the answer was "no," and he resisted the urge to turn and look in a mirror.

Maybe there are healing powers here—perhaps the lights or some magic in the floor will begin working or perhaps the water has restorative properties. That would explain why I was sent here.

He went to one of the sinks, still afraid to look at his reflection in the mirror. The water came on as he lifted his left hand into the basin. He splashed his left arm and raised a cupped palm to wet his face. The water was effervescent and refreshing yet slightly warm. Indeed it had an invigorating effect, and it soothed the scratches on his arms which he had gotten from pushing through the dense undergrowth in parts of the wooded trail on his way to Melchior's cabin. He got as much of the wonderful liquid on his hands and arms and face as he could, still resisting the urge to look at his image in the mirror, afraid that this last hope of the water making some improvement would be disappointing as well.

After two minutes of the running water, Samson shook off the excess, stood up as straight as he could, and looked at his reflection. The shock put his last hope to rest. It was never a strong, reasoned hope anyway, and its death was nothing to mourn because Melchior had warned him. But it was the last vestige of the expectation he had pinned on his assumption that the new age would not be marred by human deformity. Apparently there was to be no change at all, at least not for him.

Samson had not been in the habit of reviewing himself in mirrors, and after his injuries he avoided looking at his face as much as possible, for it was much easier to slip the eye patch on and ignore the poorly-healed scars rather than trying to get used to seeing his new look. So the shock of seeing it now was not surprising. But his image above the sink reminded him about his clothes. He had not realized that his shirt had gotten marks in the woods, and there were little tears that he had not known were there. He had been wearing it three days when he got to Melchior's cabin.

Furthermore, he had not trimmed his beard for several days and had no means of doing so now.

Maybe Melchior's powers weren't infallible. Maybe I'm somewhere else—landed in a different place or at the wrong time.

Earl turned to the hand dryer, which blasted out warm air just as any common dryer would. He was eager now to go out and get his bearings and discover where (and when) he had come to.

He checked his pockets. His wallet was still there, and it still contained the little cash it had before, but the identification card from Melchior was missing. It seemed that whatever miraculous power Melchior invoked to transport him to the future could have easily made such details as his attire and the money in his pocket conform to the new place—more evidence that Melchior failed to get him to the expected destination. He considered taking his shirt off and laundering it in a sink. It would not take more than a few minutes to dry if he held it in front of the dryer. But what difference would that make in the overall image that his broken body presented? He was still a repulsive-looking creature in his estimation, and a cleaner shirt would only create a starker contrast.

So with nothing else to do, he was ready to go and face whatever was out there and determine—assuming he had arrived at the intended destination—what he was summoned for.

Samson—I should call him Ichabod now—had been aware of voices, the sound of many voices punctuated by laughter, coming from the other side of the restroom door; and now as he opened it, the sounds were clearly from a crowded eating establishment. The short hallway led him to the side of a large dining room. Heads turned in his direction, and some of the talking stopped.

In spite of his desire to remove himself from this awkward circumstance as quickly as possible, piano music coming from the far side of the room riveted his attention and caused him to pause, for he was reminded of his own playing. Although some of the diners had become aware of his presence, none were staring at the cripple in shabby clothes with the disfigured face. The waiters were dressed in traditional Japanese attire and appeared to be members of that race, but many of the diners' faces were black and as many were white, making it unlikely that he had arrived in Japan. And they were speaking English. Evidently it was a Japanese restaurant located somewhere in southern USA.

Looking around and seeing what he guessed was the exit, Earl limped toward it, and finding it a door to the street, he stepped out onto the sidewalk. It was a warm evening.

Everything seemed to be under construction on this city street, but all the equipment was old and sat still and silent. He looked at his watch: 6:30. It had said 6:20 when he last looked at it sitting on the magical chair in Melchior's cabin.

"It took no time to get here," he muttered with a chuckle.

No vehicular traffic was on the street, and few people were on the sidewalks. The point where Earl emerged from the building was in the middle of a block. He turned right for no particular reason and walked toward the intersection where some automobile traffic was going by on the cross street. He paused at the corner, undecided about which way to go then turned to the right again. A man came out of a building and crossed the sidewalk a few yards ahead of him. He glanced at Earl—or Ichabod, rather—before going to the driver's side of a car parked at the curb, a rusting convertible with the top down. The man paused and watched limping Ichabod as he approached.

"Would you like a ride?" the driver called out.

"Sure would," Earl answered without hesitation.

The man got into the car and reached over to push open the door for Earl. The upholstery was torn and the seat had a hole in it. Ichabod felt an affinity for the car, which naturally extended to its driver, who asked him,

"Where are you headed?"

Ichabod had caught a glimmer of water beyond the end of the street several blocks away. "Down there by the water. I'm still getting used to this place."

"Where are you from?"

"Well, I'm from .... I'm just here."

"Have you been in Peter's Japanese restaurant?"

"I think so."

"So that's where you came from?"

"Yeah."

"The restroom?"

"Yeah. Is that where you came from too?"

"No. But it's well known."

36

"You mean the restaurant?"

"No. Well, yes, it's a popular spot. I meant the restrooms."

"I noticed the door seemed to be a one-way affair for letting people out but not in. This is the famous Millennium, is that right?"

"That's right."

"Why on earth would they have people arrive on a toilet?"

"I don't think there's one in there, actually. It's just a wooden chair anchored to the floor—so I've heard. Didn't you notice that?"

"No. I just assumed. Either way it's an odd arrangement."

"Compared to what?"

"Well, I don't know. Something a little more in keeping with the purpose."

"It could be that something better is in the planning. For right now we're trying to get the essentials up and running. But you realize, don't you, that the way you arrived here is exceptional. I wouldn't say there is anything illegal about it, but it's definitely not the way most people got here."

"How did they get here?"

"There were several ways. I'm one who got to spend some time with the saints in heaven."

"The Rapture?"

"That's right."

"What was it like?"

"I'm not able to even try to tell you. ... Then there are those who lived through the rough times. You will find some of them around here still."

"And the way I came .... Are there many?"

"Very few, I think."

"It seems like there should be a more formal reception, though."

"I agree; that part does seem odd. I think it's because you're off the record—rather unofficial. Almost an afterthought."

"There was a certain convenience about it, I must admit."

"Well, I'm glad for that. What is your name, by the way?"

"Ichabod."

"Mine is Louis. You're the second exceptional arrival I've picked up. I'll recognize them now for sure—that lost look. ... Things will get better. I think the answer to your question has to do with coordinates. The wizards who do the transporting need to have a definite spot they can count on that won't conflict with anything else. If you tried to materialize in a place that happened to be occupied by another person, or even another object of any size, it would not be pretty. So they made that stall with the one-way door that no one can get into from the outside. The restaurant is open 24/7, so there will always be a way out. And it's a setting that everyone is familiar with. Nobody is going to wait in there too long wondering what is going on or waiting for someone to meet them."

"I see. Who would have thought? ... Too bad I'll never have grand-kids to tell it to."

"Where would you like me to let you out?"

"Anywhere along here is fine."

"Just take it easy, Ichabod. Enjoy the park here by the river."

"Uh, Louis .... I'm just wondering—are there any others like me—crippled, I mean?"

"I'm sorry, Ichabod. No, all who have been in heaven are perfectly whole. But we're only half-citizens here. Some of those that survived without the mark were ... as you can imagine."

"Are they in a special place."

"Yes; they're being taken care of."

"Do you think anything can be done for me?"

"That depends on your particular circumstances. I really can't speak for special cases, but I'm sure you'll get an answer to that soon."

"You seem to know quite a bit. May I ask what your job is?"

"I'm the mayor of Louisville."

"Is that where I am?"

"Yes, sir. That's where you are."

"Louisville, Kentucky?"

"That's right. This is the Ohio river. Actually we're upstream of the original city which was flattened by earthquakes."

"You're not kidding me, are you?"

"No, not at all. What would make you think that? Because I drive an old rusty car?"

"And your name being Louis. It sounds like a joke."

"Well, maybe it is a joke. I thought it was funny when I got the office because I wasn't an experienced urban administrator. So maybe it was because of my name."

"I guess you're better qualified than most Louisville mayors were in the past. Weren't you elected?"

"Heavens no. Democracy is out. This is a theocracy, don't you know? And regarding the car, as long as it keeps running, I've no complaints. Probably if I did they'd get another mayor and give my car to him. It's enough just to have transportation."

The mayor's car had stopped beside a walkway overlooking the river. Ichabod hesitated. He wanted to ask more questions but did not feel he had sufficient invitation to do so.

"Do you have a plan in mind?" Louis asked him.

"Frankly, no. I'm here because of a summons, but it's mysterious so far. Can I expect clarification soon?"

"That seems reasonable. What's your full name?"

"Ichabod Samson. Can you make an inquiry?"

"I'm doing that, but nothing is turning up."

Earl turned his head so his right eye could see the driver, and he saw no evidence of an instrument of communication.

"That's incredible efficiency," said Ichabod. "How did you make your request known without me being aware of it?"

"Prayer. Yes, it's incredibly efficient. If I don't get the information you need, someone else will. Or better yet, put in your own petition. One way or another you'll get your assignment."

Since the mayor seemed ready to move on, Ichabod thanked him and pushed the car door open. It made a scraping sound as it skimmed the sidewalk. With some difficulty, for Louis had planted his wheels snug against the curb, Ichabod extracted his legs and stood up.

This was the river side of the street. He stood surveying the scene for a minute after the car pulled away. On the face of the river a fitful breeze ruffled the water and toyed with a lone sail. It was near the middle of the wide stream. He watched with admiration as the sailor handled the tiller of her tiny vessel and kept the sail drawing against the vagaries of the wind.

Included within the scope of his view on his right and downstream was a small cluster mastheads, evidence of a marina nearby.

Samson turned and walked in that direction.

On his left, twenty yards distant from the sidewalk, ran a low stone barricade furnished on its top with a polished brass railing. Evidently, a bulkhead beyond it protected the river bank from erosion by swift current at high water. By what he could see of the masts he judged that the level of the water must be thirty feet or so below the level of the sidewalk on which he walked.

Ichabod limped on, expecting to find a way of access to the marina, but the stone wall and its brass railing went on without interruption. Ornamental gardens filled most of the area between the sidewalk to the wall. He watched for an opening but encountered nothing like a path inviting him to cross the gardens and approach the wall where he might see down to the lower level and the water's edge.

After going a little farther he glimpsed parking spaces ahead beyond a row of trees. He guessed there would be a connecting ramp from there to a lower level. But already he had wandered too far from the place where he would be expected to be found— should anyone be sent to find him. He turned and headed back.

While nearing the spot where the mayor had dropped him off, Samson stopped at a bench situated on the river side of the walk and facing the water. He sat down there to wait and ponder his next move.

And I think he prayed.

The lack of information from the past and the difficulty of obtaining information about people in the present day is one of the things that differentiates my new job from the one I held in my former life as CEO of the Federal Services Administration. Here I am Leila Lalomi, CEO of the North-Central North American branch of the Anointed Services Administration, a role for which I was prepared during a period of years much later in the millennial era than when I began to serve.

Yes, I began my employment in this capacity prior to receiving my entire sanctification. In other words, I'm benefiting from experiences that took place in the future, according to the natural progression of time.

One of the silly things we sometimes said in the old life was that we would like to have an opportunity to "do it all over again." It turns out that this is almost possible. When I try to imagine having been in the future, I have to conclude that my training experience must be cyclical: perhaps a hundred years from now I will find myself being trained again and then sent backward in time to do it over again only a little better.

But that is not how it works. My training was a one-time future event that paradoxically is not in my future from here. Another strange thing is that although I benefit from that life experience, I have little specific memory of it: all of the benefit resides in my intuition.

We might imagine that it was astounding to the millennial citizens when training camps and freshly raptured saints began showing up out of nowhere. But no, we were expected, and the facilities were prepared—I say *were*, but from where I am now it really is future.

In former times it was widely assumed that if a saint would need preparation for a role in the millennial kingdom, the training would take place in heaven. Whether it was a magical sort of transformation that happened in no time or whether there was some schooling that transpired during the period when the earth was undergoing its kingdom birth-pains, the possibility of such training taking place on earth *during* the millennium was not seriously entertained by theologians.

It seemed that the principle of a miraculous transition from earth to heaven, where everything is suddenly made right, should work just fine. They agreed that it made adequate sense until mothers asked about babies growing up in heaven and wondered about giving birth in heaven if the Rapture should catch them before delivery. And whether we admitted it or not, we all wondered how heaven could reconcile and make blissful the character defects that everyone carried either to the grave below or to the clouds above—and still be who we are.

To answer the latter question (the problem of incomplete sanctification) an intermediate purgatorial stage was commonly hypothesized, which raised questions such as, "Where is purgatory?"—not only where is it in Scripture, but if it is not part of heaven, how is it connected with heaven and earth, and what sort of body and society does it entail?

As it turned out, strange as it may seem, the translation at the Rapture was not a trip to another place: we who disappeared never left the earth. The translation was primarily in time; it was neither a journey through outer space nor a trip to a separate universe or mode of being. That was to come later.

Essentially, it was a trip involving the *time* dimension of space-time. But it was not like the fabled time machine where the brave or foolish person emerges at a different point in history—past or future—but is otherwise unchanged. The Raptured bodies were entirely remade, as in the "transporter" of science fiction, at a different location.

Our Maker received us in a most intimate way: his touch remade each of our bodies. The programming and memory that constituted body and mind were used to reconstruct a new body for the same spirit and with the same essentials of mind. But unlike the *Star Trek* version of teleportation, there were changes:

physical defects were healed; bodies were free of disease and deformity, but still they were natural bodies. They were of the same order of being as before but in a pristine condition and a "new nature" like the first humans. Yet apparent age was not erased in this process, even right down to the fetus. Stature remained the same, for the new bodies continued to develop as would any natural body. But on the upper end of the age spectrum, where gray hair and wrinkles that are part of the natural aging process were potentially carried over, people looked much younger because life expectancy now was upwards of a thousand years. The centenarian, in fact, looked less than half his age.

What about the bodies that seemed to disappear at the Rapture? Vaporized. Buried in space. (Some say turned into clouds—bodies are mostly water.) Nothing is ever as romantic as it first appears to be. But no one remembers any pain. Some say the process was painless because it took place in the twinkling of an eye—quicker than the smallest unit of time. At that quantum level, what seems impossible becomes possible.

Purgatory, if I may use the term, was our destination, and it was located on this earth in the millennial age. It was carefully planned—each person having a dwelling place and a course of instruction prepared. Finally, after completing one's course, there was a graduation to heaven, not *en masse* as in the Rapture, but one by one—as it was for Enoch and Elijah. People made their exits to heaven after they had passed the final examination. Thus the Rapture ultimately did lead to heaven—after this detour.

The experience of those saints who had died in Christ and whose bodies were positionally resurrected coincident with the Rapture was different. Their abandoned bodies needed no disposition, having been assimilated into earth and air, while the elements of the Raptured bodies were scattered among the stars.

But the resurrected are the stars of the millennium because they are most like our first parents whom our Creator declared were very good—before sin entered the world. Some of them will demonstrate to Satan that perfect obedience is normal.

It is obvious that the time difference between a saint's funeral and the instant of his physical resurrection is insignificant when you consider the fact that various shifts in time were involved for everyone. In other words, if you let your imagination take you out of the linear time experience that we all depend on for normal life and consider time as being on par with spatial distance, it is not hard to see that it would be no different than two people traveling from cities on opposite shores of the continent and arriving at some midland city to attend the same meeting. Though the distance between their departure points is great, from the point of view of the meeting, the difference in travel is insignificant, because whatever mode it was, it brought them to the same place.

You may remember from Claudia's *The Day and the Hour: Saturday* that Philip Evans had a dream in which he found himself in the middle of the kingdom age in order to receive preparation for participating in the reconstruction of his town at the beginning of the same millennium. The way it came out in Philip's dream is not far from the truth. An intermediate step was omitted in his vision, and the training as he dreamed it was symbolic, but the result was on target. That is typical of prophecy, by the way.

While it was necessary that the first wave of disciples be familiar with the modern world, there was no attempt initially to preserve modern technology and maintain dependence upon it. The capital of world government at the outset was, as it is now, Jerusalem. When the general resurrection began, the new city and the new temple had been built according to Ezekiel's specifications using ancient methods, only with modern plumbing. Prior to that, when the King of kings returned he brought angelic armies with supernatural powers, not modern weaponry. In no time, he 1) cut short the antichrist campaign to erase Israel and annihilate the chosen race, 2) judged the nations, and 3) had Satan bound. The immense cleanup project that followed was organized and conducted by angels. The administration was literally the resurrected dynasty of King David, and the prince—Solomon and his associates—had no use for modern devices.

Training in Righteousness

It was not necessary that we be trained to be slavemasters, though slaves from Egypt contributed labor, food, and materials for the rebuilding and early sustenance of Jerusalem. Their masters were angels. (Few of them were Egyptians: Egypt is where the angelic armies enticed them to go in search of food, for bearing the mark of the beast they were permitted neither to buy nor sell. Many who were unfit for manual labor died in the first year.)

Indeed, the training I and other raptured saints had received was not focused on tasks we would be doing in a modern world. It was training in righteousness through obedience to the laws of the kingdom. It was a rigorous character-building and faith-solidifying experience in close spiritual proximity to the King himself. There were separate camps for men, for women, and for families with children, I am told. This "school in righteousness" was administered by sanctified Jewish priests. The camps are remote from population centers but within the borders of Israel.

After completing my course, I was translated to the temple and into the Holy of Holies, never to be seen again as a mortal. I have a clear recollection of this event. It was like I was presenting my whole self as a living sacrifice. But as I approached the veil I was overtaken by an eagerness, for I knew I would soon be like him and see him as he is. I suddenly realized that I was approaching my wedding chamber. On the other side of the veil was Jesus Christ himself waiting to personally receive me into the glories of heaven and glorify my body. My earthly nature was purged at that point, and the training in righteousness was permanently engraved in my soul, freeing my mind from even the memory of the old nature. The fruit of the training became the living Spirit of Christ magnified within me. Then I ascended to new heaven, which my body was able to do.

Insofar as the Spirit affects our ability to think clearly, we call it "sanctified" or "holy" intuition. Insofar as the way I affected other people in heaven ... the delight they exhibited in meeting me was almost as if they were meeting Jesus Christ himself. We are all like that in heaven.

I should mention the final examination that I and everyone else had to pass before being allowed to approach the veil. The purpose of the test was safety. There was a definite danger in that transition if you were not adequately prepared for it. The weight of glory cannot be supported by a soul in which the new nature does not have a solid foundation. Metaphorically, the flame of true holiness would destroy a soul not founded on solid rock.

Thus the simplified doctrine that had the Rapture sending saints to heaven without having experienced physical death was correct as far as it went. The enemies of that doctrine generally objected to it for the literal way in which it interpreted the tribulation as having much to do with the Jewish nation. What would they think about the details of the process involving sanctification by strict obedience to the Law and the necessity of entering heaven through a literal temple at Jerusalem?

The fact of separate and distinct time domains on earth and in heaven (not speaking of the millennium here) was recognized by some Bible students even before the Rapture took place and the knowledge of these things got filled in. Therefore, it was not surprising to everyone when every last one of the Raptured and pre-resurrected saints appeared in high heaven in time to participate in the formal marriage of the Lamb together as one body—before the Lord descended with his armies to set things right on earth! Linear time became irrelevant then, with the "purgatory" experience and even sanctifying resurrected life having been forgotten. It was as if there had been no intermediate steps in getting to heaven. But so evident was the beauty and genius of Christ in each person's personality that one had to wonder.

By the time all of the Raptured saints were perfected in this manner, the thousand years on earth were nearly over. The college of righteousness closed its doors just in time; the final judgment of the devil was at hand.[1]

---

1. Satan will be given the remainder of his freedom and a last chance to respect the Law that by then will be revered throughout the earth. Although it is not a necessary step in the legal case against Satan, it is within the mercy of God which he extends to all his creatures to make this final offer. The outcome facilitates the final judgment, and those unable to befriend their Maker will be delivered to their final fiery abode completely free of the bonds of righteousness.

Thus the "new" earth with its holy administration began almost immediately, not waiting for the resurrections to be completed, but depending initially on glorified saints.

A thought just occurred to me: The training camps are off limits, but if I were to go and meet myself as I was in my old natural body, it would not be a contradiction because I am not in the same body at all. My spirit is the same, yes, but the spirit is non-physical and timeless, and theoretically it is possible for a soul-mated spirit to be in two places at once.

Being administered by glorified—and increasingly by resurrected—saints, this planet is truly like a new earth: the difference is like night and day: the devil is a spectator but not a participant; the devil-marked "beasties" have now died out.

How do we know all this if our training happened on a separate track of time? It is quite simple, really. Here we find ourselves as "glorifieds" running back and forth between earth and heaven in glorified bodies. We have little memory of being in purgatory or any sort of accelerated sanctification program, yet holy we are! It had to happen somewhere, sometime. And another thing: those early Christians who, according to the conventional wisdom, would have been waiting a long time in some intermediate body for their resurrection, have no recollection of long times in that phase of existence; nor do they seem more advanced in Christlikeness than those of us who arrived by way of the Rapture.

When the time was right I appeared on the scene to take the reins at the ASA headquarters in Appleton, Wisconsin. How did I get here from heaven at just the right time? My glorified body gives me certain advantages, and there are certain places other than Jerusalem where I can transit between heaven and earth. One such place is a doorway off the lounge in my offices on the top floor—that is the second floor—of the ASA building. It is not a special door; it is a special place and the reason the building was erected on that spot. They call it the Jacob's-ladder effect.

There is a disadvantage too, because the glorified body was not designed primarily for living on earth. People like myself have to go back to new heaven periodically to get recharged. At the end of every workday, and until I reappear the next morning, I am back home in heaven, breathing the air my glorified body needs and enjoying for some length of heavenly time the warm fellowship of my companions.

Regarding specific training for my present task, it is certainly significant that I held the corresponding office in the previous dispensation. But the similarities do not go far. Nearly all of my time then was spent dealing with differences between people and accidental violations of regulations—that is, near the end of my career before the Rapture took me away. Earlier, when I was CEO of the FSA at the national headquarters in Washington DC, my primary concerns were the new regulations aimed at holding the lid on theft, dishonesty, and misappropriations within the system. There is very little of that now.

In the old regime an extensive accumulation of data on every person made it possible to be effective against the criminal will of the FSA clientele. There is no such thing now, and there is no need for the regulations. Trust comes easily here, and it makes for simplified lives. But when I do need to locate a person for some reason, one of my staff has to begin making inquiries as was done before the age of the computer. Some people are missing, and records seem to be incomplete. This is a problem I encounter every day. Where are they? Are they here on earth? Are they in heaven? Are they anywhere? We joke about someone being away in a training camp, but that cannot happen, of course.

So my job now at the ASA involves a great deal of direct contact with people, where as in the old FSA I relied on intelligence that had been gathered automatically. Now the telephone system is the tool most often used by ASA personnel, and instead of security officers I employ people who scout not for people bent on doing harm but for opportunities to serve the citizenry.

The ASA *is* the government. Each of the regional branches such as the one I oversee reports to a national headquarters, and those in turn report to the ASA headquarters in Jerusalem.

The seven departments within the ASA are,

- Lands & Resources
- Transportation
- Cities & Industries
- Employment & Commerce
- Housing
- Food & Health
- Education, Libraries & Sanctification Testing

Staffing for the organization has been my major concern to this point. I am insisting that heads of the departments not be natural people, for so I was instructed from Zion. In due time the resurrections with just the right executive skill set will appear; I am confident of that. Some have appeared already, and I have been working with them to fill the positions within their departments.

The process of hiring mortals requires more than advertising job openings and waiting for applicants. Individual people are called to the service based on research within the community. My belief is that the people I need already live in Appleton. The ones that will be recruited are presently engaged in some kind of work. They might be doing almost anything. If they have proven that they can be trusted with responsibility at a certain level and appear to be capable of more than is available in their present situation, they are made available to other employers.

Most of the citizens of Appleton are natural survivors (unmarked) of the tribulation, happy to be alive, to have been given strength to believe, against threats of torturous death, that Jesus Christ would return to release the tyrannical grip of the antichrist. Compared to what they've been through, there is no hardship here—nothing at present that registers high enough to bring about a single complaint. Nevertheless, the essentials, let alone the luxuries, of life are not readily available to anyone at any time. Supplies are limited, and there is no general consumer market for goods and services. Employment opportunities are few because most jobs are within family businesses.

Jobs are available on contractual basis but very hard to find without making a commitment that involves living arrangements. While informal bartering takes place, most trade is mediated by the ASA. To get an account you have to be an organization—we call them families—and meet certain requirements. So it's almost impossible to get by for very long without joining a family. You can hang out with friends without joining one, but sooner or later you will be expected to join or move on.

When you join a family you are really on probation. You can leave or be let go at any time as needs and circumstances change. So it's a little scary, especially if you're the type of person who finds it hard to get along with others, because when you're let go you find yourself shuttled to a restrictive arrangement. But if you like the family you're with and you're well liked, you can apply for permanent status. If you're accepted, you're basically a slave: the family owns you, but in turn the family cannot dismiss you.

The food supply has improved and will be adequate this year. Quality housing is still short of what could be used, but several winters have been endured with less, each one becoming easier. Transportation is still severely limited and mostly reserved for commercial needs because heavy manufacturing has yet to be restarted, and when new vehicles are produced, we're not sure yet about how many of various types will be made.

Recreation is whatever one can devise, and I see an example of that right now. Out on the lake someone has lashed what looks like a bed sheet to a spar and rigged it to a pole on a raft-like vessel venturing along the edge of the lake not far from shore. It reminds me of Earl Clark and his fleet of sailboats which I could observe from my office window at the top of the FSA building.

I hope Samson is safe.

Now that's a surprising thought. Never since I entered my glorification had a worry of any kind crossed my mind until now.

But is that a worry?

No, I think not. It's far from a worry because I had no anxiety about it. Whatever his whereabouts and condition, he is within the love of God, and that is enough. For that very reason I had not been thinking about him.

Yes, that explains it perfectly—there is no reason to worry or even be concerned.

The tasks I have been assigned and the people that have been placed within the scope of my activities and my relationships in heaven fill the hours of my life to overflowing. It's all joy. There is nothing lacking. Earl is not someone I have been put with; likewise, he has been provided with whatever he needs to fulfill his life. That's the beauty of the social arrangements in a sphere illuminated by the glory of Christ.

His name just never came up, so .... But why should it?

Again, this thought surprises me. It surprises me because it is irrelevant. Why should I have *any* question about Earl?

Yes, I see that to be entertaining these thoughts means that I'm on the verge of questioning the divine design. But so far I have only found myself being concerned for his safety.

He's safe in the love of God. ... I wonder where he is.

Why should that matter? Am I peering beyond the limits of the sphere of grace in which I was placed? Or is this concern for him possibly being urged upon me for a purpose?

If it were that, I would know the purpose, and I don't.

I'm still watching the clumsy little sailing raft. The wind has just gotten on the wrong side of the sail and twisted it around, pressing the boat over and capsizing it. The sailor has jumped into the water and apparently is doing something to the sail that has become too heavy to rise again.

It was a foregone conclusion that the type of feelings I had toward Earl Clark in the old life had no place in the glorified life— whatever those feelings were that were tainted by the old nature that no longer exists. So much has been made clean and new. Nothing is left of that old nature. If I ever encountered him again it would be to start over.

That was my foregone conclusion. But if that were true, if there were no carryover, why should he concern me at all?

The old life is dead and gone. There is no reason to be concerned about him.

But now that I've put that down as an axiom, I hear a voice calling for a correction.

"No reason is needed where there is love."

I'm breathing a sigh of relief, and that surprises me too! I did not realize I had become tense over the issue. But I'm smiling now. I was free to ... free to what? To be concerned? For what purpose?

Never had I doubted since my glorification that everything was proceeding exactly as it was meant to be. But now comes this thought of Earl, and it seems that I'm being called upon to be concerned for him. Was I wrong to assume that he was safe?

The sailor has untied the stays, letting the mast float free, and he's attempting to right the vessel. I can see the bottom of it and it appears to be made of many gallon water jugs somehow welded together to form pontoons.

How could he not be safe? Surely he would not have taken the mark of the beast. That's unthinkable. Earl would be the last one on earth to swear allegiance to the devil.

Well, he could be in heaven.

The Spirit tells me he is not a citizen of heaven, and the revelation strikes me as a disappointment. But now, I'm quickly realizing, if I follow my thoughts about him I am not alone.

He would be a "natural" then. ... He must be saved. How could he not believe after the Rapture?

The Spirit is suggesting that I pray for him!

I'm inclined to slip back to heaven right now and run to the city and call on Adam. But it seems I'm being called to pray now, where I am. Could that be Earl out there in the water with that makeshift boat? That thought makes me laugh.

No, Samson would find a better boat than that. Or else he would make one. ... Where are you today, Samson? Do you perhaps need help building a boat? ... Yes, you do. I pray it will work out for you.

Chapter Five

The sun was sinking low and shadows were growing long when Ichabod rose stiffly from the bench where he had spent the last hour. He made his way back toward the spot where the mayor had dropped him off, which was not a great distance, perhaps fifty yards. Either Louis had forgotten to send someone or that someone had not found him. Since nothing had been said about staying close to the spot at which he had been discharged, he had assumed that his unique appearance would mark him out if he remained in sight.

He watched a policeman crossing the street, who then turned and came toward him. Clearly the officer was interested in him, so it was no surprise when he heard his name called out.

"Ichabod Samson?"

"Yes, sir."

As the cop came closer he noticed the name on the badge: Headworthy.

How very odd. What are the chances?

Earl had disarmed and gagged a Headworthy on that dreadful night when he sought refuge with Carmen. While he dismissed the unlikely possibility that this was the same man, a doubt remained which he relegated to the safety of his disguise.

Headworthy immediately questioned him: "How long have you been in Louisville?"

"Not long at all. Two hours at most."

"Have you had anything to eat since you got here?"

"No."

The officer took a granola bar out of his shirt pocket, and then another one.

"The only difference is one has raisins and the other doesn't."

Earl looked but saw no guile in the officer's face.

I must be dreaming.

"Thank ... thank you. I appreciate this very much," he stammered. "The one without raisins will be fine."

"I'm going to take you to the homeless shelter where you can get cleaned up and spend the night. Then tomorrow morning at 7:30 I'll come by and take you the courthouse."

Earl signaled his ascent and followed the officer back to the corner. As they crossed the street, Ichabod was pressed to keep up even though the cop walked like an old man with bad knees.

"This way," Headworthy said, turning right. Then suddenly he slackened his pace and gestured for Ichabod to walk beside him. "I'm sorry; I'd forgotten you need to take it more slowly. It's not too far, though, really. About four blocks. Let me know if you need a rest or if we need to get some transportation."

"Thank you; I'll make it," said the cripple. Then sensing that his captor would not object, he asked the critical question: "Are you originally from this part of the country?"

"No. I lived on the West Coast. I was lucky enough to get out before the city was destroyed."

It could be him. ... I wonder if that's why I was sent here.

A saying of Jesus came to Samson's mind:

Agree with your adversary quickly, while you are in the way with him, lest he deliver you to the judge, and the judge deliver you to the officer, and you be cast into prison.

"Destroyed? I didn't know," Earl said hoarsely.

I'm afraid it's him. Why is he taking me to the courthouse? He must know already, and he's assuming I know why I'm in his custody. That's the only crime I committed, really. I can agree with him on that ... except for the theft of the cop car ... and pulling down the FSA building. ... But no, this is all unreasonable. He'd be taking me to jail, not the homeless shelter. ... But those granola bars are just like the ones I stole from him.

"Okay, I was told that you appeared in the exceptional manner. I take it you skipped over some years. Are you aware of the new world order?"

"No. Was there a world war?"

"Just like Isaiah and all the rest said there would be—the whole world against Messiah, or the other way around, actually."

"Does that mean ... that Christ has returned?"

"Oh, yes. Ohhh, yes. He returned all right!—along with count-less angels."

Ichabod shivered.

So that's the new world order: Justice. No tolerance. Where does that leave me? Should I confess now and ask him to forgive me? According to what Jesus said, I should. But Headworthy isn't indicating that he has anything against me personally, or even that I'm under arrest. Maybe I'll ask him about it later. This isn't the time. Probably they're only wanting to get me checked in.

"Then were you warned to get out somehow?" Samson asked.

"Jerusalem had been surrounded by Yahweh's enemies when the 144,000 showed up out of nowhere and spooked the troops. It was funny. Everyone all over the world saw the whole thing unfold, and we knew then that the Return was at hand. Ever since the Rapture, things had gradually gotten worse year by year. You might remember that. Then when the plagues hit, and it looked like the tribulation, we figured which nations would be judged, and we thought the USA was exempt for defending Jerusalem. But not all of the USA was spared. All the major cities on the West Coast were destroyed, like Babylon was, in less than an hour."

"Was there a voice that warned you to leave?"

"I took Babylon's warning as applying to every place like it—a word similar to that was going around in the underground church. I don't know who started it, but when we saw the 144,000 show up I joined some others and we came out of our Babylon."

"Did you arrive in Louisville without a job and a place to live?"

"There was nothing left of Louisville when we got there—nothing but heaps of rubble. It was awful, and I don't want to talk about it."

"What about today? Are there jobs available here now?"

"That's hard to answer by yes or no. You have to belong to a family of some kind in order to get a real job. The homeless shelter qualifies as a family."

• • •

Ichabod was assigned a small private room and allowed to select a change of clothes that were not new but better than what he was wearing.

He slept little that night. He was not comfortable with his failure to ask forgiveness. But why should he feel that way? He had spent a number of years under a false identity to avoid arrest without feeling that he owed anything to the state for opposing their repressive plan. So why should it concern him now? This new government would have nothing to do with that, anyway. The only thing relevant today was the personal matter. But it was not personal, really. He accosted the cop because he had laid a trap for him; he had nothing against the man personally—it was against the order that put him there, which ironically came from me. Poor Samson! Nothing had gone well for him since that night, and now having left the old world behind, a relatively minor part of his old trouble was keeping him awake.

His thoughts ran ahead, trying to guess what might follow if he revealed his true identity. It would put him in the public record under his real name, and someone who knew him in the past might look him up and be painfully disturbed that his glory had departed—someone like me, for example. And what if the kindly cop turned out to be not so kindly if he learned he had lost three granola bars to Samson/Clark and not just one? If this is the age of justice, would he be required to press charges? Then what? Jail? Parole? Community service? Might he have to pay the "uttermost farthing"? Was it worth the risk?

Earl was surprised at his own thoughts. Why should one be concerned about an old trespass that most likely had been forgotten if not forgiven? A profound difference in the spiritual atmosphere was the reason: the heavy air of ignorance and rebellion had been lifted, and the effect on everyone who came directly from the old world was an expansion of one's conscience. Though he did not realize it at that time, Ichabod was experiencing the absence of evil.

At breakfast he talked with a man who had lived through the tribulation and the Louisville earthquakes. Having refused the mark of the beast, he lived on fish which he caught at night in a secret trap he had made. Being alone in his hideout by the river he had escaped the plagues, but the fires nearly got him.

"What caused the fires?" Ichabod inquired.

"You know about the eruptions, right?"

"I know nothing. I've only been here since yesterday."

"Where are you from?"

"The past, mostly. Somehow I got transported through some decades of years in an instant and found myself here, and I don't know why or what I'm here for."

"Oh, you're one of those exceptionals. I never met one before, and I thought they were probably a myth. But if you say you're one, I'll take your word for it."

"How did you come to be in a homeless shelter?" Ichabod asked.

"I decided to leave my family."

"You mean you left your wife and children?"

"No, I never had a wife. I mean the working family. I'm up there in years, as you can see, and there was little for me to do, so I came here to see if there was another opportunity where I could fit in better."

"Are there many opportunities?"

"No. But when one comes up, someone has to take it. If nobody wants it particularly, someone will be assigned to it."

"It sounds like the family is a commune."

"That's what it is."

"How do folks get motivated?"

"It works out surprisingly well in this new atmosphere of brotherly kindness."

"Last night I was thinking about the difference I felt. How would you describe it? I say it's lighter somehow."

"We're in the light, brother. Compared to the old world it's like day compared to night."

. . .

Ichabod was ready and waiting when Officer Headworthy showed up at 7:30.

"I hope you don't mind another short walk," he said. "We're only two blocks from the courthouse. I gave us plenty of time because your parole officer keeps a strict schedule. She says she respects people's time and hates to keep anyone waiting. She says it's the one thing she learned in her former life that's worth anything."

"Then I hope I'll not keep her waiting either," said Ichabod.

Parole officer? Then they know about my past, and why wouldn't they? It was foolish to believe that Ichabod Samson would continue to give me cover. I should have assumed a different name. ... It's too late now.

They walked in silence for some time, while Earl turned over in his mind the few clues he had about his standing in that new world. The cop seemed to think there was nothing odd about a man being on parole without having been tried for a crime. Or maybe Headworthy's testimony was equivalent to a trial. The other possibility was that he was being confused with someone else who had been tried by the court and found guilty.

"Since no one has informed me about this, I'm wondering what it is that I'm being punished for," Ichabod said. "Or am I to assume it's for that time—"

The officer interrupted, preempting Ichabod's confession: "That I can't tell you because I don't know," he said.

Earl tried to catch the expression on his escort's face. He saw nothing except perhaps a trace of impatience, and for that he was grateful. He had to believe that Headworthy was truly unaware of the crime for which he was being paroled. But the fact that he had committed a crime against this man made it seem unlikely that it was a mistake. Nevertheless, it might be a fortuitous accident; and crossing paths with this man was his opportunity to clear his conscience. Should he blurt it out now? He imagined reversed roles: how would he feel being forced to revisit an embarrassment?

Having covered two blocks now, Ichabod's thoughts were forced back to the present when Headworthy said,

"This is the place. Get your bearings because you will have to find it on your own next time."

The courthouse was not an impressive building by modern standards, and the ground floor was arranged simply. The entrance led directly to a large room with doors in its four walls and seating clustered near each door. The atmosphere seemed very old-fashioned to Ichabod because it was quiet, which he soon attributed to the absence of a TV screen. Instead, the four faces of a large clock standing at the center of the room were easily seen from all sides. Its hands pointed to 7:58.

"We're just in time," said Headworthy. "This is the parole office on our right by the blue chairs."

He motioned for Ichabod to be seated and sat down next to him as if they were connected by an invisible chain. Immediately, the door opened and a young woman came out just as the clock struck eight. She reminded Earl of Lucy Link. He had written a piece on Lucy when she came home from college and started her internship at the dental office of Dr. Carmen Harab. But now, if it was indeed Lucy, she had a graceful, unaffected poise that some-how fit her better than the nervous demeanor of her old self.

"Ichabod Samson?" she said, and her smile was lovely.

"You're on your own now," said Headworthy. "Good luck."

"Thank you," returned Ichabod. "I appreciate you kindness more than you know."

"This way, please," Lucy sang. "Carmen is ready to see you."

Earl gulped.

No. This can't be. Is this a dream?

Yes, it is a bit overwhelming when you first get there. The say-ing used to be "it's a small world" when strangers discovered a common acquaintance. You soon come to expect it.

He was ushered to an inner office and left with the probation officer. He knew beyond a doubt that she was his old paramour, but she gave no indication that she recognized him.

This was the last person Earl wanted to see if he had any hope of escaping his past. Except for that, he was glad to see her, for like Lucy she had acquired beauty almost beyond belief, and yet she was still unquestionably herself, like the fresh bloom of a thirsting flower after a gentle rain.

"Please have a seat, Mr. Samson," she said, and her voice was surely Carmen's yet it had a new musical quality.

After he had complied and was seated, she asked him, "Do you know why you are here?"

"No. At least not definitely."

"I don't either."

I can't believe what she said. Was it a jest?

"You arrived here by an exceptional means, is that correct?"

"Yes, ma'am, that is correct."

"Then I'm not too surprised that neither of us knows what brought us together. Since there is no specific behavior that we need to correct, you can go about whatever business you are here for and check in with me once a week. I have an opening at this same time on Fridays."

Her inquisitive look that was meant to solicit his approval of the weekly appointment made him wonder if she did know who he was—or used to be. Was this meeting arranged somehow to give him an opportunity to ask her to forgive him?

"Yes, that will be easy to remember," he replied.

"How long have you been here?" asked the glorified Carmen.

"Not even a full day. I got here yesterday."

"Do you have living arrangements?"

"I stayed at the homeless shelter last night."

"How was it there?"

"Quite good, really."

"I think when you arrived you had nothing, is that correct?"

"That's correct."

"You were supplied with a toothbrush, I hope."

"Yes, there was one in the room."

"Good. I'm glad to hear it."

Ichabod opened his mouth to comment about her toothbrush reference, that it was something a dentist might say.

"The homeless shelter is for limited stays," she went on. "Do you have a plan to join another family?"

"No, not yet."

"You will have to find one. What skills do you have?"

Dare I tell her? She suspects I know her. Now if I tell her I worked for a newspaper ... that and my last name—if I ever told her about the play.... I'll have to chance it.

"I have experience in the news business."

"It might be worth inquiring at the information ministry. Someone there should know if there is a particular family they look to when they need to fill a position. The information ministry is located on the next block in the downstream direction."

"Thank you, Dr.—"

"You may call me Carmen."

"Thank you. I'm a bit overwhelmed by your kindness."

"All right, Er ... Mr. Samson. I will see you here at eight o'clock AM one week from today."

"How many of these visits can I look forward to?"

"Four—three more after this one—if all goes well."

"Is there some way I can know what 'going well' means? Are there things I need to do or avoid doing?"

"That is what you are expected to find out on your own. I cannot tell you what actions or restraints are appropriate in your case. If things are not going well, you will be telling me about it, and then I may have some advice to offer you."

"At this moment I cannot tell you that things are going well because I have yet to be told why I'm here. Can you enlighten me or suggest a means of finding out?"

"You're not alone. We all question why we're here. For now your answer is to be at peace with the question. If you have to leave the shelter before you're accepted elsewhere, come back and see me. I have a place you could stay for a little while. Remember, Sabbath starts at six o'clock. No work and no travel tomorrow.

So it happened that Ichabod was on his own for the rest of the day, with one possible lead at the information ministry, and then it would be back to the homeless shelter unless another person having advice for him had been planted in his path.

He found the information ministry building in the next block, another unimpressive two-story structure, and he wondered whether these government buildings were temporary. Seeing his reflection in the glass doorway, he hesitated before going in.

What do I have to lose? ... Nothing but my pride.

He approached the reception desk in the lobby and asked with the humble simplicity befitting his utter ignorance of the way things were done in this new world:

"I have had newspaper experience in the old world, and being new here, I'm looking for a job."

He thought the attendant was unaccountably unfazed, which led him to suspect that Carmen had sent over a warning and that his appearing was not a surprise. Nevertheless, he had reason to be surprised when she rang up someone and described his case as if it were not unusual: "A man came in off the street inquiring about employment. ... I'll send him up. Oh, hold on a moment."

"There is no elevator," she said to Ichabod. "Would you prefer that he come down and meet you in a conference room on this level?"

She led him to a nearby room and told him someone would be down to interview him shortly.

Who might this be? Another person from my past wouldn't surprise me.

When the answer walked into the room, he almost broke down and blurted out his delight at seeing his old boss.

"So. You were in the newspaper business," said Chester Matthew.

Earl was torn. He knew he could trust Chester to keep his secret, but he was not in a mood to explain his injuries and rehearse the crimes he had committed, and he assumed the newsman would want to know how the town had fared since he left.

"The news publishing business here bears little resemblance to the media machine you were familiar with in the old world," said Chester. "Every story we write imparts true meaning, has a high moral purpose, and reflects God's glory. Have you written for Christian publications?"

"No. But my boss, though he wasn't a Christian as far as I know, had high standards, and he published a religion column."

"What was the source of the religion column?"

"It was written by the same local clergyman every week."

"Was that in the Sunday edition, or was it a weekly paper?"

"It was a weekly."

"Was the contributor from a denomination?"

"No, his church was independent."

"Did you ever have a hand in editing his material?"

"On one occasion I did, but usually we had no objection beyond slight grammatical errors."

"What was that one occasion?"

"He was a little rushed; it was a busy week for him. It was his last submission before the Rapture took him away. In view of that I thought it needed a stronger appeal to make sure every reader understood the seriousness of the upcoming event."

"Yet you missed the Rapture yourself. I was told you got here by an exceptional means. Let me guess: the column's author was a good friend of yours."

"That's true."

"Just out of curiosity, on what day of the week did you publish?"

"Tuesday."

"That's relatively uncommon. Was this one of those small-town paper-and-ink weeklies?"

"Yes, it was."

"And you were a writer or a reporter?"

"Both."

"Do you have an interest in sailing?" The question caught Ichabod off guard. Chester was watching for a reaction.

"Earl Clark," Chester said in a hushed tone before Ichabod could answer. "You didn't want me to know. You wanted to spare me the pain of seeing you like this. But I'm very happy you came to see me."

Well, it was an emotional scene, I'm sure. Earl explained as well as he could why he had chosen to avoid professional medical services in the old world.

"We should get you to a medical clinic and see what can be done to make that leg work better at least," Chester said.

"I inquired about that at the homeless shelter where I stayed last night, and was told I needed documentation to prove I'm not a beastie."

"Because of that scar on your forehead?"

"Right. They said it looks like the mark has been removed."

"And I guess as an exceptional arrival you have only your old-world documentation in your wallet, if that."

"If that, is right. When I became Ichabod Samson I gave Karen most of my cash and had her shred everything else in my wallet."

"I'll see what can be done. Now you need to join a family, but until you're documented that won't work. Even if I needed a reporter or a writer, I wouldn't be able to hire you without a family to receive credit for your work. But I'll find something for you, Earl. We do have a potential assignment which requires travel. We're still getting it set up, and I think I can get you qualified for that one. If you're on an assignment where you travel away from home, your employer is essentially your family. In this job you would be sniffing out heresy and reporting it."

"I don't think you knew I was a local intelligence agent."

"If I'd known that I never would have hired you; but here you can put that skill to better use."

"I know you'll believe me when I tell you I turned soft and never reported anyone."

"Perhaps you shouldn't have told me. In this capacity you'll have to be very clear about the lines of demarcation between careless and intentional challenges to truth and authority."

Chapter Six

Every day had been so full of administrative challenges that I had not been able to begin searching for Earl. Oh ... you did not know I decided to search for him?

It started with the expectation that he would contact me, not due to any rightness or inevitability of it but simply that it was a possibility, something like a far-fetched fulfillment of an extravagant dream that hangs about the fringes of one's imagination without ever justifying itself. It was startling. I say that because, as well as I could determine, that expectation had never been substantial. And then suddenly it was ever-present.

I knew that harboring a wishful thought amounted to a prayer but that it was not in good taste, and to me that made it repulsive. Yet something might be made of my memory of Earl and the mistake I made that drove him away. Once I opened the door to consider that, the dream of him finding me without my doing anything faded like morning fog; the door itself disappeared, and there stood the matter in clear daylight: I would find Samson. I would go somewhere and find him there.

If optimism could support certainty, I would not have had the slightest doubt that he would appear even unsought for at just the right time. Joy is a component of the atmosphere in heaven, and it clung to me and followed me when I entered the terrestrial world each morning. Though joy does not befriend every hope, if the hope is approved it does; and in this case I found the hope of finding him was keeping peaceful company with my joy.

Even though the ravages of sin were still evident on earth, joy had purged the evil from the deep waters of my soul; I was therefore unaffected by every difficulty that would have dredged up a sad memory on which to form a doubt, and joy reigned supreme over everything that in my old life would have been called a setback and a disappointment. So I believed that when I met Samson again there would be no sorrow that could not be quickly resolved. How wrong I was!

Near the end of the day, when the breath of heaven had been nearly used up, and it would soon be necessary to go home and be recharged in what had become my native atmosphere,[1] I would often see where the afternoon sun shone like diamonds on the waves of Lake Winnebago. Whenever I took a few seconds to look out at the lake, I thought of Earl and his sailboats. If he were to discover that I worked here, and he wanted to live close to me, being by a large lake like this would suit him better than a desert. But that thought, I realized, was a useless vestige of the old dream. I had to make a plan and begin looking for him myself.

Two means of searching for persons were at my disposal: one was the records kept in ASA files, and the other was the records in heaven. Neither were in a form that was instantly searchable. The records that ASA kept were located in its individual offices around the world and were in handwritten form. To go beyond this office I would have to ask some busy person to spend a few minutes looking through files for a Kenneth Earl Clark born on February 29. I had already checked the records we have here; in fact, I'll admit that I've done that repeatedly.

The books in heaven are not for everyone to look at. Even if they were, they would be of little use to someone like me because of name changes. But another way to search for information is to ask others. To explain why that works better in heaven than it would on earth I will have to describe the structure of heaven.

Heaven is built on a globe, somewhat like earth in that respect, but there is little else of its geography that compares with earth. There is no sea and no weather. There are no light sources and no shadows; no day and no night because everything is luminous. The sky overhead is black, and there are stars like we see at night on earth, but they are really angels, and they see everything we do. Yes, we have government surveillance in heaven!

There is gravity, or what serves as gravity, because we walk—yes we walk like we do in our materialized bodies on earth. We don't fly in heaven, though the angels seem to.

---

1. Because while breathing the air on earth I was missing that ingredient of heaven's joy that my glorified body needed to sustain its life.

Our glorified bodies in heaven look nearly the same as the materialized version on earth, but better. The substance they are made of is the spiritual analog, or rather the spiritual prototype, of the physical body. In heaven we do not require food. We take in energy when we breathe the air, and the air we breathe is a mixture of the spirits of joy and love. Consequently, there is no opportunity for stress at all. We go down to earth for that!

Yet three things are lacking in heaven: the need to create, the need to instruct, and the need to mend a broken heart.[1] No one becomes unhappy over this, for they are not felt needs, but the chance to work and live on earth is a prize and a reward.

This is new heaven, by the way. It is not the original heaven and not the only heaven. Even though it is a spiritual dimension, its time dimension is synchronized with time on earth. In heaven we mark the passing of time by our worship and prayer schedule. For eight hours each day our social activities cease: we read and meditate on Scripture instead. This has the refreshing effect of sleep. But there is no need for sleep. In fact, sleep is impossible.

I mentioned earlier that heaven's geography is based on a sphere, and I will complete that picture for you now.

At what you may think of as the north pole stands the City— the only city—which is the Jerusalem of heaven. The city, not the sun—for there is no sun—is the source of your energy. As you go south, the atmosphere thins until at the bottom of the sphere there is no air—no love and no joy at all, I am told. But temperature is the same all over. Temperature in heaven never varies. In fact, there is no temperature like earthly hot and cold, the reason being there is no molecular structure in the spiritual world and therefore none of that kind of energy. There is the full range of sound, nonetheless. Figure that out if you can, because I can't.

A circle of dwellings surrounds the city, connected to it by twelve lanes—much like spokes connect the rim of a wheel to its hub—each lane leading directly to one of Jerusalem's twelve gates. Because the city is so large, the lanes are relatively short.

---

1. The reason is we are more perfectly in the image of God.

The circle of dwellings is really a series of concentric rings,[1] and there are many of them. The one nearest the city enjoys the richest atmosphere, while life in the last ring, the one farthest from the city, is for stolid saints who are more comfortable with lower energy. This arrangement has nothing to do with rewards for faithful service on old earth; it is about capacity—about comfort and maximizing happiness, if you get what I mean.

Your own feet are your transportation—no vehicles and no animals are there to ride. If you live near one of the lanes leading to the city, you can walk there in half an hour. But once you enter a gate you find Jerusalem is wider than you can cross in a day.

Since there are only twelve lanes to the city serving the entire circle of dwellings, the distance on the first ring from one lane to the next is a six-hour walk. So your travel time to the city and back takes seven hours if you live in the innermost ring midway between lanes and walk steadily without stopping. But it takes much longer because you never go far without meeting someone you know, and then you must exchange greetings and news. Or if you meet someone you would *like* to know, you have as much right to engage them as you would an old friend.

Dwellings are of different sizes and arrangements and most are multi-leveled. There is no space between them except for cross streets at intervals. With streets between the rings plus the radial cross streets, the appearance is like residential blocks in some old European city. But you never have the feeling of being independent of the city because the Jerusalem walls are very high and visible from every cross street and from the higher floors in most houses.

The globe of heaven is smooth, so the horizon is like looking out on an ocean. Beyond the horizon where the light is dim there are ghostly buildings, I am told, built by unsaved spirits who carry on much as they did in their fleshly lives on old earth. It is possible, and often happens, that someone goes out seeking a relative or friend, but rarely does the spirit consent to come into the light.

---

1. The great plan in heaven is reflected in the square layout of terrestrial Jerusalem's perimeter. Here in new heaven the implementation is circular with the full compliment of gates.

Over a number of evenings, six days a week, I discussed my desire to locate Earl with everyone I met, describing the place we lived—which few knew about, of course. All were willing to pass the request on, and I did get one return via that grapevine: some-one who had gotten news from a natural person on earth. That was when I learned that my FSA building had collapsed and that Earl was inside it when it happened.

After that I took a week off and went to see Adam Murphy (I mentioned him before; I will call him by his old name) because he would know where Earl had gone if anyone knew.

Without getting into much detail, I will tell you that the saints who live closest to God live within the walls of Jerusalem full time, whether it be Jerusalem in heaven or Jerusalem on earth. In heaven, those who live in the rings (and that includes me) are not really in the service of our Master as intensely as are those who live within the city gates. Out in the rings we have more freedom to spend time according to our own desires while many of the city dwellers are literally slaves. By that I mean they are fully engaged with the Master's business and their lives are ordered entirely around him and the work he assigns them to.

Adam Murphy lives in the city. Before I could meet with him, I needed to submit my request and wait for an answer. And in order to do that I had to visit the city myself and wait there, which could take more than a day. You see why I allowed a week. Just inside the gates are waiting rooms for this purpose.

I had been there two days when Adam appeared. I was sur-prised that he knew what I had been doing. He was informed about many people we both knew. But he had lost track of Earl.

I reproduce here the conversation we had—after greetings and words of gratitude for having been given this time to be together.

"Do you have the means to find out where he is?" I asked.

"Potentially, yes. But I don't initiate things like that. You have more ability to make inquiries because your time is not so strictly dedicated to our Father's daily business as mine is."

"If he died for Christ, might he be considered a martyr?"

"That depends on how it happened, of course. But I know he's not among the martyrs because all martyrs live here in temple residences, and my primary duty is seeing to their comfort. The first thing I did when I got here was check the roster for Earl. (It's organized geographically.) Our town had no martyrs."

"I think you know I'm not unhappy about that."

"Yes, my child, how could you not hope to find him in a place where you will be able to commune with him?"

"Could you point me to some resources?" I asked. "Is there a way I could find out if he's in a training camp?"

"No, because that's future even from here. They're all back now, as you are. If Earl were among them, his current address would be in your neighborhood."

"I've been looking for him in Wisconsin long enough that I had to come and ask you for help."

"If he's a natural on earth, you may encounter him yet. We both know he wouldn't have taken the mark, so he might have lived through the tribulation and still be in the flesh."

"So ..."

"Do we have records on them? Yes, we do, but I have no authority to search the books. However, for you I will ask. Can you wait here another day?"

"Yes, I can and I will."

I wanted to ask Adam why it takes so many to administer heaven. I understood what had to be done on earth to govern a mixed populace, but why heaven needed an army of servants was a mystery to me. I had mentioned it to several acquaintances, but none of them were much interested. Either they did not know that heaven had an administration or they assumed that everyone serving near the throne was there as an honorary assignment without any real duty or responsibility. So before he left I asked Adam about the army of servants I had been observing.

"It *is* an army," he answered. "There's war going on in heaven, you know."

"Well, I didn't know."

He explained:

"The war is what brought about the creation of earth—indeed the whole material universe. You and I wouldn't exist if it were not for the war. We're expecting the end of it now, and preparing for the final battle is what this army of servants is about. We need a massive force to face the enemy, and that entails compiling records on regenerated people like you who have come out of your training with perfect scores. If you resist every temptation to exercise your own judgment when it opposes a clear instruction from our Master, then your record will give you an opportunity to serve in the front line. The final battle will be held here in the courtyard of this city. If we have overwhelming strength, we'll answer Satan's accusation beyond any doubt, which will satisfy the justice of his banishment to the lake of fire deep below the surface of this globe. But he'll be given a final temptation even after losing the court battle, and for that some rebel hearts must continue on the earth for a long time yet. I know that's not good news for one in your position. Think of it as job security!"

"Am I to understand that Satan, in spite of all his lies, is claiming he doesn't qualify for punishment?"

"Not exactly that he's undeserving of punishment under the law. He's insisting that obedience to the law is unattainable because rebellion against authority is in the nature of every created free-willed being. Therefore, the law is unrealistic and should not be enforced."

"But our past—"

"Yes, I know. You see, we're new creatures now; the old things have passed away. That's our immunity."

"Will Satan agree with that?"

"He has to agree with it. You may remember some old things, but God does not remember what is covered by the blood of his Son. Satan cannot accuse us of what doesn't exist in God's eyes."

"What a price he paid!"

"Yes, he was willing to pay the price to rid heaven of evil. He will lose quite a number of angels too, but hey! we're here!"

Adam came back the next day with the news that Earl had not died when the building came crashing down and buried him.

"But his appearance was severely marred from injuries he sustained," he told me. "You will be surprised, as I was, to learn that he attempted to continue the work I had been doing, though his message had to be different, of course. He urged people to repent and be baptized, telling them that the kingdom of God was at hand. But he had no success, partly because no one knew him. To avoid being arrested for his crimes—that's another story—he had taken advantage of his altered appearance and assumed the name Ichabod Samson, which he still goes by. I'm sorry to say that we have no evidence that he has come under the blood of our Savior."

Adam paused and looked at me sadly before continuing. He knew how I felt because he felt the same way. Never think you escape the full range of emotions just because you are in heaven!

"But his career as kingdom advocate was cut short. For some mysterious reason, he was called out of the old world and transported across years in virtually no time. He is not a regular natural because he did not pass through the tribulation. Yet he is a natural because his body never died. He has none of the benefits that we enjoy in our resurrection and glorification. He's classed as an exceptional for having arrived in that very unusual manner."

"Where is he now?" I asked eagerly.

"Such information is rarely if ever given out. But I was given the impression that you will find him on the North American continent and not far from a body of water."

"You speak as though there is more than chance in this."

"Oh, yes. Absolute chance never existed in the old world, you know; chance was the appearance of things going wrong. But on the new earth Murphy's law has been rescinded. You will find out if you haven't already that all things work together for good here and now. I must tell you, Leila, that I came away with a definite feeling that if I had been inquiring about Earl on behalf of anyone else, none of this information would have been available to me. This exception was granted for your sake."

Do you understand what that meant to me? I had justified my desire to find Earl, you remember—to myself. While I had not dis-obeyed any command, neither was searching for Earl an obliga-tion that had come with my assignment. I knew that in my old nature it could easily become an obsession, and on that basis I would have done well to deny myself and keep my entire focus on the work I had been given. This special favor now being granted to me was like I had not only been given permission without ask-ing for it but also my Master had encouraged me in the search. Thus my will cannot now be easily distinguished from his.

As I thought about this I wondered how much of our right-eousness is achieved by our loving Father making adjustments in his expectations so as to undermine and nullify a devil's accusa-tion.

"I will have to keep my eyes open, then," I said, "because if he .... I hope his injuries were healed."

"I hope so too, but nothing was said about that."

"Do you know how long he's been there?"

"No, but I know what you mean. At least he would be a few years younger than his contemporary naturals who lived through the tribulation period—and some of them are still around. He could be decades younger if he has arrived here recently."

"What happens to him when he dies?" I asked. I knew the answer, but I was desperate to hear some exception in that too.

"All the vacant streets are reserved for resurrectees, so at best he comes here with an address on Outermost Ring Street. But if he continues to be as stubborn as when I knew him and fails to believe he has a higher calling—heaven forbid—he'll be among the shades below awaiting sentencing."

"I hate to think of it, but might he make an appeal at the time of his sentencing? He thinks he can get out of any sort of trouble."

"Not the kind of appeal that might have the outcome of bring-ing him back to us. You see, the soul withers quickly down there, and full restoration becomes more and more difficult."

"But not impossible?"

"Not impossible because it has happened, but the desire has to be there, and that's precisely what was missing and why they never availed themselves of life in the light."

"There would be 'weeping and gnashing of teeth' when they find themselves in darkness. Surely they would desire—"

"The weeping comes later, after the sentencing, when they're thrown into the pit of isolation and darkness at the bottom of this globe[1] along with Satan and his band. Of course if Satan wins the trial, then everyone goes free. That's why the sentencing for everyone is on hold. Everyone knows this instinctively, which is why Satan has always had most of the world on his side."

"But those currently living in the nether world could migrate into the light if they had a skillful leader. Is that true?"

"Yes. But they're not in total darkness or discomfort where they are a present. Indeed, life is easy for them, and they make dwellings for themselves with little effort because the rarity of spirit is balanced by simplicity in everything, which is the reason for their comfort. So with no pain they think they have nothing to gain. Nevertheless, as with almost everything, there are exceptions, but you must not think of that. You have been assigned to bring Earl to the light, and you must not let him die in blindness."

"If the Spirit of God cannot move him, who am I? Am I in the place of the Spirit of God?"

"He has chosen to use you, Leila, so you need not doubt your ability to influence Ichabod Samson. Not only do you love him more than anyone else, but you believe in him. This is why you were chosen. But you may fail, for there is no human coercion that can save a soul. You must count the cost before you begin. This is what it means to serve God; you experience what he experiences in your own finite way, and it will draw you closer to him."

"I'm not prepared for this, Pastor Murphy."

"I think you are. If Earl dies in his blindness—"

"I will go and find him. I will plead with him until he gives in and lets me bring him back with me to the light!"

---

1. The terrestrial image of this is the lake of fire.

I chabod made his mark every day at the homeless shelter by taking on more than his share of cleaning and laundry and kitchen duty. In the afternoons he hobbled over to the information ministry building and dropped in to see Chester who always took time to visit. Mostly they talked about the place out west where we had all once lived. Chester was keenly interested in every detail of the events that had transpired since he was abruptly removed because, as Samson told me, he was sorry to have missed the opportunity to publish the news. They reminisced about pleasant times too, especially the Monday sailing races on the lake.

Samson was itching to find his niche in this strange new world and get his teeth into something more challenging than housework. His primary purpose in visiting Chester was to judge the likelihood of getting that special assignment which had been mentioned on his first visit, for if that was not going to work out for him, he needed to be looking for a family to join that would give him an opportunity for employment. He hesitated asking Chester about it, assuming that everything was being done that could be done and that his old boss would tell him if it was not going to work out. On his third visit Chester had another idea:

"How long would it take you to build a boat like *Wind Chaser*?"

It was a ludicrous question considering the circumstances, but Samson played along: "A couple of months, maybe."

Chester looked at him fondly and smiled. "I believe it. But we need to find you a shop and some materials."

Samson laughed. He knew it was a game of imagination. They could both wish for it to be real, but they both knew that in his present condition and without the right collection of materials, parts, and tools it would not be possible. "Those boats moored here on the river—do you know any of their owners?" he asked his old sailing opponent.

"Yes, and I might get use of one. I've looked them over carefully, but none of them appeal to me like *Wind Chaser* and her sisters did. I think you know what I mean. After you've loved a boat you never forget her."

"I didn't know you were a romantic," teased Ichabod. "You seemed to love winning more than anything, whether it was a game of chess or a sailboat race or cornering the local news."

"Haven't you noticed I've changed?"

"Yes, of course. The old Chester Matthew never took time to reminisce or fantasize—unless it was about fishing. And yes, there is the obvious: your glow of health and—what is it?—there's something like mirth that you try to keep hidden."

"That's known as joy, son. It's in the air of heaven and clings to one even when under the stiffness of one's materialized body. Frankly, I wish I could share it with you. ... Well, I know how you loved working on those boats, so I thought you might like to get into that again."

"Are you telling me you were serious?"

"We can do almost anything here if we approach it the right way. Would it be more efficient to build two at once than to build them one after the other?"

"Not unless I could avoid making mistakes."

"You'll be surprised, if you haven't noticed already, at how well things go compared to the old world where whenever there was a chance that something could go wrong it did. Here there is no chance—not that there ever was then, exactly, but it seemed that way."

"Tell me plainly, Chester. Are you serious about me building sailboats?"

"Yes, I am, and I've received a go-ahead for it. How you'll accomplish it I was not told, but I have no doubt that you'll succeed. On the other side of the river is Clark Regional Airport. It's not in use at present. Find space in a vacant hangar where you can set up your boat shop. If you help them with house building up there, you can scrounge for materials at the same time."

"Is it far? Will I have a place to stay? And what will I do for transportation?"

"It's ten, maybe twelve miles north of here. You take the Lincoln bridge in Louisville and stay on highway 31. Nearest town is Sellersburg. Few people have personal vehicles, but hitchhiking is easy. Until you find a place to stay up there you'll have to commute. Unfortunately, I have no budget for this project. Never fear: you find whatever you need in this world."

Thus began a new chapter in Ichabod's life. He went back to the homeless shelter and made the sign that he would show to passing drivers the next morning. "SELLERSBURG" is all it said. Then in case he would need to hitch a ride back at the end of the day, he put "LOUISVILLE" on the other side.

Chester was right: almost immediately after Ichabod held up his sign, a pickup truck pulled over.

"Where's Sellersburg?" the driver shouted.

"Actually, I need to get to Clark Regional Airport."

"That's where I'm going. Climb in if you can."

With some difficulty Ichabod got the door open and dragged himself onto the running board and into the cab.

"Do you know much about this airport?" Earl asked.

"Yes and no. I've never been there, but I have information about it—or what it used to be. My name's BJ, by the way."

"Ichabod is what I'm called."

"The glory has departed, eh? Well, things always work out in this world. I'm guessing you're an exceptional."

"Yes, and I'm exceptionally lucky that you stopped for me."

"What takes you to JVY?"

"I was given an assignment that has nothing to do with aircraft. My boss wants me to set up shop in a hangar and build a couple of wooden sailboats."

"The building that housed one of the FBOs is reported to be in good condition. They had a maintenance shop that might have some tools you could make use of. Yes, I know, you'll need woodworking tools, but there might be some of those too."

"What is *your* mission at the airport, BJ?"

"I'm surveying airports, bridges, and dams in this area. You see the leaning piers under the John F. Kennedy Memorial bridge over there? I've recommended that it be condemned. It was built in 1963 to withstand earthquakes, but the ground shifted under the south pier which forced the whole structure out of alignment. This is the Abraham Lincoln bridge we're on now. It was built in 2015 and should have suffered a similar fate, but it was miraculously preserved, which is good because the next bridge upstream is the Lewis and Clark, and if we had to go that way it would add 25 miles to our trip this morning. That one's in good shape too, by the way. It's a cable-stayed structure that was completed about the same time this one was. Eventually they'll all have to be replaced, of course. None of these bridges were built to last a thousand years, and I think they'll all be needed."

"How many bridges have you surveyed?"

"On the Ohio, starting downstream from here, I've looked at the Glover Cary at Owensboro. The main span buckled on that one, and it'll have to be replaced. It was built in 1940. Next upstream, the Natcher bridge is intact. It's another cable-stayed bridge, built in 2002. The suspended roadway on the Lincoln Trail Bridge at Cannelton is broken in several places. The south approach to the Mauckport bridge is down, and the span is unstable. It's official name is the Matthew E. Welsh Bridge, named after the Indiana governor famous for increasing taxes. It was built in 1966. The Sherman Minton, a steel arch suspension bridge collapsed because they used T1 steel when it was built in 1961. The Kentucky and Indiana Railroad Terminal Bridge appears to be in good shape even though it was built in 1912. The Ohio Falls Louisiana and Indiana Railroad Bridge is intact, fortunately. It's an even older one, built in 1870. Before 1918 it had a swing span, now a lift span. The Clark Memorial Bridge in Louisville is intact, which is fortunate for you if you sail at that end of the pond. That's a Warren truss built in 1929. Then the Kennedy Bridge, which used the Warren truss as well but didn't fare as well."

"Obviously the dam here is doing its job making this wonderful pool that I'm looking forward to sailing on."

"It's over 70 miles from here up to the Markland dam. Yes, the MacAlpine dam was well preserved. Even the hydroelectric plant came through."

"Is that the source of our electricity?"

"Right. The Ohio Falls Generating Station was solidly built in the 1920's and upgraded several times. It can put out a hundred megawatts, which is adequate for this area right now."

"I noticed as we drove through part of old Louisville that there was no evidence of buildings ever having been there. Or was that not where the city stood."

"I wasn't here personally when the cleanup began, but I understand that everything was either buried or recycled."

"With so much destruction having taken place, I'm surprised that enough heavy machinery was available to do the cleanup."

"It was done with primitive tools, Ichabod."

"That's amazing. How many years did it take?"

"Not many years, just many thousands of slaves."

"Slaves? On new earth?"

"Right. They were the ones who took the mark of the beast so they could participate in the economy, which gave them an advantage in surviving the tribulation. But here in the kingdom the mark worked just the opposite and prevented them from buying and selling. They had to submit to forced labor to stay alive. All or nearly all of them have died out by now. They were called beasties. The relatively few who came through *without* the mark of the beast and yet were living in dangerous urban areas were rounded up and kept in Israel. The beasties were kept in Egypt."

"How were they rounded up? It sounds supernatural."

"It was. Angels got them out of the war zones before bringing down the judgment on the nations that had made trouble for Israel."

"There must have been huge refugee camps in Israel and Egypt."

"Exactly. It was a lot like when the children of Israel were maintained by miracles on their wilderness march."

"Then did the angels direct the cleanup?"

"That's right. I don't think human task masters could have done it."

"How did they move people around?"

"Tell me how you got here, and I'll know the answer to that."

"I'm wondering if the mark of the beast was their eternal doom. Do you know if the beasties regretted their decisions?"

"No, I don't know. But I'm sure the hard labor at least was independent of that; otherwise who wouldn't express repentance to escape the consequences of siding with the beast."

Clark Regional Airport is hard to miss since it borders on highway **31**. They arrived there directly.

BJ pushed the main gate open easily, as it was unlocked. They found the hangars all standing. No meteorites had fallen on them, and fires had not scorched the buildings, thanks to the lack of trees in the area. Earthquake damage to the runways and taxiways was minimal. The cleanup crews of the Ohio Beasties Regiment had swept up the ash.

"Apparently nothing is going on here," Ichabod remarked.

"All airports, including the hangars and buildings and their contents, belong to the Kingdom Aviation Administration," BJ informed him. "But few aircraft are in operation now partly because the world has taken a big step backwards in technology. Most advanced aircraft were torn down and buried. However, some older planes, especially those without essential electronics— antiques really—were spared. I expect to find some of them here."

"I was wondering about digital devices making it through the tribulation. Is that why there are so few automobiles?"

"That's right. Any car you see that looks new has had its engine reworked or replaced with one from an old vehicle. Digital controls are a thing of the future because most electronic devices and all their manufacturing facilities were destroyed."

"That pretty well shut everything down, didn't it?"

"Everything. Much of it had been disabled in the tribulation, but within nations that had been hostile or unfriendly to Israel it was all destroyed. Here in the USA the judgment was directed at certain areas, including the technology centers. The information and entertainment industries and their technology base had become wholly-owned subsidiaries of hell."

"Where does that leave communication services?"

"Cities have local telephone wires with manual switching. Most of them are very primitive. There's no commercial radio."

"The satellites are down, I suppose."

"Right. The heavens got cleaned up too."

"Then how do cities communicate with the rest of the world?"

"Long distance communications go through heaven."

"Oh. ... Are you serious?"

"There's a new heaven that's synchronized with this earth, you know. Communication in real time goes on with it constantly."

"No, I didn't know. Like a parallel universe? That changes everything."

"It's definitely not a parallel universe. It's a heaven adapted to life of this earth."

"All right, so they have magic devices that look something like pocket phones that tap into signals in another dimension. Is that what you're telling me?"

"No, there are no personal devices. There are locations where you go to get connected. In that sense it's something like an old-fashioned phone booth, but there's no visible enclosure. You might think of it as a beam of light from heaven, but that's not literally true either."

"You said digital electronics are a thing of the future."

"There's nothing inherently evil in digital technology. It just got off to a bad start and became Satan's tool, and then Satan destroyed it. But the potential for it, which is part of creation, will always be there. However, I doubt that it will ever become as pervasive as it was. We have adequate spiritual lines of communication, and we get news in heaven every night."

"How does that work? I mean, news in heaven isn't the same as news about what's going on here, is it?"

"In heaven you tune into anything you want to find out about just by asking around."

"But how does that do us any good?"

"I thought you knew. Some of us spend every night up there."

"Are you telling me you're an angel?"

"No, I'm a glorified human. My home is actually in heaven. I work down here during the day."

"I didn't know glorified people were from heaven. Then at the end of the day do you simply vanish?"

"We have to be in a certain place to undergo the translation."

"Another phone booth sort of thing?"

"There are hotels where certain rooms connect with heaven. That prevents inconvenient or disruptive appearances and disappearances. It's called the Jacob's Ladder effect."

"What happens if you can't make it to a ladder? Or don't you have to go up every night?"

"I once stayed down for three straight days, but glorified bodies need to breathe the air of heaven. It's like the refreshment you get from sleep. We don't sleep here or in heaven either, but spending a night in heaven has a similar effect on us."

"The people I meet here that I knew in the old world look younger and more vibrant than they ever did. But I never suspected they went to heaven every night for maintenance. It's hard to believe, but I feel it's impossible to disbelieve you, somehow."

"Well, it's been a long road to get here, but that part is almost forgotten. The old life doesn't seem very significant any more."

"I imagine that some manufacturing must be going on. But everything depended on computers, so how does that work if all the equipment became useless—or as you say, destroyed?"

"In rural areas all over the world primitive tools and methods were still in use. Such places were preserved, and their methods were replicated. Suddenly, obscure craftsmen were called upon to bootstrap the world's economy, and they became heroes."

"I suppose because they were self sufficient they never were tempted to worship the beast."

"Yes, and they were more resilient too, being energy independent. Large numbers of them survived the tribulation. Actually, most of them had learned of Jesus and would have been loyal to him anyway. They remembered he said the last would be first."

"I'm puzzled about one thing, BJ. You said the MacAlpine hydro plant was preserved. Doesn't it depend on computers?"

"It's known as the Ohio Falls Generating Station. No, it did not depend on computers in any fundamental way because it dates back to the 1920s. Of course it was upgraded with a modern control system, but the EMP hardening project restored mechanical controls for backup purposes. There's no grid as yet, which makes the operation pretty simple. You're fortunate to have power. Many areas of the country have to depend on small generators."

"What happened to the nuclear plants?"

"They were shut down and made harmless by angels."

"Is that to be permanent? What are the plans for energy in the future?"

"Geothermal. Fissures from earthquakes and bombardment by meteors opened up more hot spots than anyone knew existed."

"What about oil and gas?"

"There's always that too, though a lot of the natural gas got burned off during the tribulation. Something has to be done about those steam vents anyway, so they come first."

"What are you burning in this rig?"

"Bio diesel, which can be made quite simply."

"It smells like it."

"I'll stop here, and we'll have a look."

After driving around and quickly surveying the many hangars and miscellaneous buildings, they had stopped at the door of one of the large hangars where BJ expected to find a maintenance shop. The original lock on the door had been removed, allowing them free entrance. The large bay, which normally would be servicing several aircraft, was entirely vacant. The machine shop had been stripped of its electronic components, which rendered the tools inoperative.

"This isn't quite what you need," BJ noted. "This field serviced private and corporate jets mostly, but there were small planes here too—obviously, with so many small hangars. Somewhere we'll find a nice collection of old tools."

"I know exactly what you mean. There was one of those at Sorek. I don't know how he got his C150 in and out of it. He collected tools, fishing gear, kayaks—everything you can imagine."

"Was his name Larry Peters?"

Earl smiled and shook his head. "I should have known you wouldn't be a complete stranger."

"Claudia Nice called me out there once to do an annual on her plane."

"I remember hearing your name. Do you recognize the name Evelyn Newton?"

"Yeah. I did a little extra maintenance on that government jet for her so she could get baptized the day before we departed."

"Well, I can't tell you how much trouble that caused me. Have you run into her either here or in heaven?"

"In heaven briefly. She interceded for me for delaying that plane. I'll put the word out that Ichabod ... what's the rest of your name? Or I should ask, what's the name she would recognize?"

"I'm glad you asked, BJ. My real name is Kenneth Clark, but I went by Earl, my middle name. Ichabod came after the accident that messed up my body because I needed a disguise to keep from being arrested for opposing the Reorganization—and another minor thing that I could blame Evelyn for. You're the only person I've told this to. One other reason I need to maintain this disguise is I need to avoid disappointing another dear person who is a friend of Evelyn's."

"All right. I'll keep your secret as well as I can. I don't see any reason why Evelyn would need to ask me about you."

"I hope you're right. But her friend might. I hope .... Never mind, let's look in some of these hangars."

They did find what they were looking for, and it was very like Larry Peter's hangar at Sorek Valley. There was an antique C172 in it that they had to push to another hangar before they could get to the back where most of the tools were stashed. Although many were very old and generally rusty, that suited Ichabod well, for he knew he could repair and sharpen them. He needed a larger space for the boat shop, however, and they found one close by in a much larger hangar in the facing row.

"This is better than anything I expected to find," said Ichabod.

"Before you get too excited, I need to get permission to use these spaces for something that isn't aviation related."

"How long will that take?"

"Tomorrow or the day after tomorrow I'll have an answer."

On the way back across the river BJ asked about Claudia Nice. He said he had seen the gutted fuselage of her personal jet at the field in Salem Oregon and wondered how it had gotten there. Earl confirmed that she had not been taken in the Rapture, and as far as he knew, she had planned to leave town on her boat; so the remains of her plane should still be at Sorek.

"Is it possible that she somehow got to the airport undetected and flew her plane out?" BJ suggested.

"It's possible. ... But I thought you were assigned to *this* area."

"I was temporarily assigned to survey bridges and dams here on the Ohio, but my regular work is inspecting smaller airports west of the Mississippi. However, since I was in this area, they gave me Clark Regional."

"Will you be going on to look at another field after tomorrow?"

"No, I won't finish Clark tomorrow, so I'll be going back the day after. This is the only airfield I'm doing outside my territory."

"Do you have more bridges to survey?"

"No, that project is complete. I'll be going to Boise next and surveying a couple of airports from there."

"How will you get there from here?"

"From heaven it's easy. Any Jacob's Ladder worldwide is accessible. It's like putting all the airports in the world together."

"Sounds awful. I picture a vast network of corridors."

"No. Forget that picture."

"Is it like an elevator where you step into the car and tap in the code for your destination?"

"That's not a bad analogy."

"How long do you have to wait in line for the elevator?"

"Not long. There are many of them throughout the rings where we live. It's seldom crowded, really."

"What are the rings?"

"That's what we call the streets. They're laid out in concentric circles."

"Give me some idea of the size. How many houses are on a street? Say on the outermost ring."

"*A lot* is all I can say. On the ring where I live it takes me about an hour to walk five minutes."

"I take it you're referring to the angular distance between numbers on the face of a clock."

"That's right. It would take me twelve hours to walk completely around the Hay Street ring."

"Hay Street? Are there farms up in heaven?"

"Ha! ... *Hay* is the sixth letter in the Hebrew alphabet."

"How far do you have to go to get to the nearest elevator? Is there transportation? Do you walk or fly or what?"

"Everyone walks. We don't have wings. In heaven you have a spirit body that looks about the same as the materialized forms you see here. It takes me five minutes, and if I get to the station early, I find a vacant booth—or elevator as you say—right away."

"Where do you have breakfast?"

"We don't eat physical food there. When I get here in the morning I'm not hungry. Around the middle of the day I might have something, but I can take it or leave it.

"So tomorrow evening you go up there and arrive near your dwelling place; and then in the morning you get in the same elevator, and it takes you to Idaho?"

"You've got it."

•••

The next day BJ picked Ichabod up at the homeless shelter and took him back across the river. They drove past Clark airport a little way, intending to scout for possible sources of lumber around Sellersburg. A flatbed truck drew their attention because it had "Clark Lumber" painted on the door. It was parked by a house that was in the process of being rebuilt.

"Wait here and I'll find out where they get their lumber." BJ leaped out and jogged to the door of the house.

A minute later he came back with a man whom Ichabod thought he recognized. It was Ken Martin, in fact.

"This is my new friend Ichabod Samson."

Curiously, he did not mention Ken Martin's name (some mannerism convinced Earl it was Ken), which left Earl in the awkward position of having to feign ignorance. But he could not do it. (Had BJ—who was grinning—violated the trust to keep Ichabod's true identity secret?)

"Ken Martin," said Ken Martin as he offered his hand through the open window of the truck in which Earl was still sitting.

Ichabod paused a moment. "Earl Clark," he said.

"I used to know an Earl Clark. Wait! You *are* Kenneth Earl Clark! ... You've been through hard times, son. I was hoping I'd find you here. What have you been doing?"

"I'm working for Chester Mathew, as always. BJ is helping me get set up to build a couple of sailboats for him."

Ken grinned and shook his head.

"Ken and I used to sail together regularly," Earl informed BJ.

"We'll get you some boat lumber somehow," said Ken. "The lumber outfit which that truck belongs to handled more than common construction materials. You might find some suitable boards there. Where are you living?"

"I'm homeless at present—staying at the shelter in Louisville. I've been here only a few days."

"Then you must join our family!"

"I'd like that. Of course I'll have to clear it with Chester."

"Aah! He's not the boss of the world as far as I know."

"How about I go back to the airport," BJ interrupted, "and work on my survey. I'll swing by here this afternoon and see if you need a ride back to the city."

I know Ken was overjoyed to be reunited with Earl, and I say that carefully because I know the joy of heaven that Ken experiences every day. I'm sure he felt Earl's pain, but pain is incapable of spoiling this quality of joy. I know Earl was delighted to see Ken's bright eyes and hear his sharp wit. Ken said his dementia was a foggy nightmare that had faded away at the sunrise.

They both had many questions to ask and answer. Earl said he was surprised at how Ken was barely interested in what happened after he left—compared to Chester's intense curiosity. I thought it was natural for the newsman since his interest in heaven was a very late development whereas Ken had learned early in life to care less for earthly matters as he anticipated life in heaven.

Ken insisted that he would bring the matter up with Hunter right away and get approval for Earl to become a member.

Earl involuntarily stiffened at hearing that name. "Is he still crazy about gold?" he asked Ken.

"You wouldn't know him. He's off the chart on the humility scale, yet he has a way with bossing the naturals. They love him."

"It sounds like he's glorified too. I knew he got baptized."

"Yes, he is. We leave Hyacinth in charge of the family when we're not there. You wouldn't know her either. She's half the woman she was on the outside but inside she's a weighty saint."

"I do recall that she had turned around. She was a changed person when I came out of hiding. Where is Luke?"

"Luke? He oversees the medical staff in Louisville. I see him occasionally, and I'm sure he could get you in for repairs once you're a member of the family."

"Where is Sookie?"

"Sookie is in heaven. Most of our people are. Only certain ones are 'betweens' at this time: the ones in management roles mostly.

"How many are in the family?"

"Thirty-three right now, counting the children. There are three nuclear families, all of them naturals. The rest are resurrected."

"Where do they all live?"

"Ours and another family use the St. Paul School building."

"Do you have to go back to Louisville every night?"

"Yes, normally Hunter and I do. The electric truck doesn't have the range since the battery is weak, so we thumb a ride on 65. It doesn't take long, and it's a great way to meet people."

"If I were to join your family, what would my job be?"

"We're chartered for residential house-building, so we could make good use of your carpentry skills."

"Framing houses?"

"Some of that, but there's interior joinery."

"Do you get all your lumber from the lumber outfit the truck belongs to?"

"That's a problem we currently have. We've used all of those stocks, so we're having to patch together materials from buildings that have been condemned. The yard has sawing and milling equipment and even a drying kiln, and we've brought in logs from trees that were felled during the storms. But I need someone who can run the mill. I think you could do it."

"Maybe—if I had the time. I'm slow getting around, and I have little lifting ability with just one arm."

"You *have* lost a bit of that muscle mass you had when you were bulked up for your Samson role."

"I'm surprised you remember that."

"I was more aware of things than it appeared. Have you encountered Delilah yet?"

"No. I wouldn't want to disappoint her."

"Well, you never know. I hope you'll think about joining us. I'm surprised Chester didn't send you to us in the first place. Isn't housing more important than recreational boating? ... On the other hand, I understand. I'll be next in line after Chester to go sailing with you, if you don't mind."

"Do you have any other plan to get fresh lumber?"

"No, the yard here in Sellersburg is the only plan. I'm expected to bring it up and into production, and I thought perhaps you were part of the plan. I know you're handicapped at the moment, but I don't see that as being permanent. You would have help, of course. And you could build your boats there."

"BJ is inquiring about permission to set up shop at the airport. Would you be willing to let me use your truck to haul materials? I might have to scrounge for things like you're doing."

"Where would you live? You can't stay at the shelter forever. How if I rebuild the office at the yard and include living quarters for you. You could still be part of the family, and you wouldn't have to see much of Hunter. Of course the mill would have to be productive beyond what you need for your project."

"You have to realize I'm only mortal, Ken, and my stamina isn't like yours. I'm afraid I would have to devote a hundred per-cent of my energy to the business of the mill and the yard."

"I do see your point, son, and I have to agree that you may be right. Let's wait a day or so. There will be a solution."

"I do miss the shop at the Beach House."

"The Beach House is still standing. Did you know that?"

"It was when I left—however long ago that was."

"And there are settlers living in the south end."

"That's good to hear, because it was entirely leveled and no one was living there when Melchior sent me off into the future."

"You got the leveling off to a good start from what I hear."

"You're looking at the result on my left side."

"I understand Hunter's gold mine saved your life."

"Are there no secrets here?"

"I've been back. It's easy because there's a Jacob's Ladder con-necting to the attic of the Beach House."

"Who's living at the Beach House now?"

"Enid and Ernie are there enjoying power from the old hydro plant, thanks to Harold Foster. He needed electricity at the air-port where his family business makes power modules for planes. There's one in our truck; it uses batteries from a derelict car."

• • •

The next morning Samson caught a ride with Louis—yes, Louis the mayor of Louisville. On the way to the airport they discussed Samson's invitation to join the Martin family. Louis was of the opinion that Samson should join because he felt that another offer would not come his way soon.

"Do you know Chester Matthew at the Information Ministry?" Ichabod asked the mayor.

"I met him once but have had no occasion to get to know him, really."

"He hinted that he might have an assignment for me."

"Have you told him about this invitation in Sellersburg yet?"

"No. Well, you see, Chess has fond memories of the sailboat races we had on Monday afternoons, and he wants me to make that happen here."

"I think I see. Everything here has to be better than it was in the old world—a lot better. That's what we're all working for. But I'm constantly prioritizing projects so we can get there as soon as possible, and ... I'm assuming he wants you to find suitable boats. Have you looked at what we have in the marina?"

"Chester has. He didn't find a sailboat he liked. He wants me to build the same type we had on the lake at home."

"So he wants you to get started now because it will take you some years. I'm guessing you built the boats that you used to sail."

"I did, and it was a perfect setup there for doing it."

"Hmm. He must have sent you to Sellersburg for a reason. Does the Martin Construction Family have what you need?"

"They're in the residential construction business. Ken Martin would get me set up with a shop, but I'd have to run the mill, and I'm afraid it would leave me no time for boat building."

"We don't allow fear here. You can be excused because you're a natural human, but I assure you, if you find yourself between two glorified friends you have nothing to fear."

"Ken seemed to think the problems would shake out in a few days. ... Oh! Can we take 31? I need to stop at the airport."

Earl had not asked Louis whether he was stopping at Sellersburg or going farther on route **65**, but if the airport was out of his way, it was only slightly so since highway **31** nearly parallels the freeway and reconnects with it three miles past the airport.

Louis let him off at the hangar where the old tools were found, which Earl called "Larry Peter's hangar" since the former owner was unknown. Later Earl found an old logbook belonging to Peter Lawrence, but he never bothered to change the hangar's name. Then he went across to the larger hangar and opened the door so BJ would know he was there if he drove by. Exploring it more thoroughly, he found a space partitioned off and equipped with a kitchen and a lounging area. He could live there, he thought.

The airport was quiet. Since the runways were closed he was not expecting activity. Apparently he was the only one present. As midday approached he became certain that he should have waited for BJ at the shelter because no definite plan had been mentioned. He had just assumed that if BJ had more work to do at the airport, he would meet him there and find out about permission to use the hangar. He had not told anyone at the shelter where he was going, which he realized was a mistake.

Earl had decided to make his way back to the road and try to get a ride to the place where he had met Ken Martin yesterday when BJ's truck swung around the corner and onto the taxiway between the two rows of hangars. Someone else was with him.

The truck came to a halt, and the passenger, whom Samson recognized immediately, leaped out.

"Homer! When did you get here?"

"Just now. I mean just today. My dad gave me leave."

BJ explained: "I was talking to Chester Matthew when Officer Headworthy brought him in. The arrangements have been made. We were just up talking to Ken Martin. Homer will be your partner again. He's contracted with the Martin family, and you'll be helping him run the lumber yard. Chester had stipulated that building two sailboats was to remain top priority for you. Ken agreed to that as long as you help Homer manage the yard."

Samson Boat Co.

Chapter Eight

"Limpy, you will have to move. ... Good girl. Now give me a paw on this strake, will you? ... Oh, I'm just teasing. You can go play with your mouse."

"*Meow.*"

Limpy leaped from the bench on which Ichabod Samson was building his first boat since leaving the old world. Having constructed four of them to this same design in his prior life, the procedure was familiar, but there were other differences besides having a cat to keep him company and get in his way.

Of course having only one good hand was a major handicap. Another was the lack of a source of suitable fasteners, which required much scrounging and improvising. Added to that was a scarcity of proper tools and equipment. He knew when he embarked on this project that it would be a challenge, but the opportunity to be a pioneer, so to speak, where supports are largely lacking, had a certain attraction for Ichabod.

Nevertheless, it is doubtful that he would have felt the same contentment about similar circumstances under the old dispensation. Difficulties used to crop up frequently for no good reason. They never did anymore. To his amazement things had been coming together and working out much better than they should according to his past experiences.[1]

Samson lifted one end of the slender plank to its approximate position on the frame, and while holding it there with his left shoulder, he picked up a makeshift clamp which he jockeyed into place with the fingers of his right hand and managed to tighten the screw without it falling off. Shifting to the stern end of the inverted skeleton of the hull, he raised the other end of the long strip and by the same method fastened it temporarily to a frame at that end. He would not have been surprised had it dropped out

---

1. This eliminates a foremost leg of story telling. In addition to plots, characters, and settings, readers expect struggles with or against unrighteous elements. Truly evil happenings of any substance are hard to find anymore. Much like Samson Boat Co., which consisted solely of Ichabod Samson and his one employee, a stray cat, we have to limp along with benign material where nothing goes very much wrong for very long.

of the first clamp after that much rotation, but it did not—almost as if an unseen hand had been holding it for him. He understood that demons had been rounded up and put in a pen somewhere, but to have instead helpful spirits about was a bonus that still seemed too good to be true.

The hangar doors stood wide open, letting in plenty of light along with pleasant drafts of summer air. Limpy had taken a position near the middle of the opening, just outside the track on which the doors ran, sitting on her haunches and half dozing in the warm sun. Suddenly she got up, stretched, and proceeded in casual hops to the right, maintaining all the dignity of a cat in spite of her truncated left front leg. Her casual manner made it appear that she had decided to take a little walk when in fact she had seen someone approaching and was going to meet him.

This was confirmed to Samson's ear by the sound of footsteps pausing for a moment at the meeting of man and cat. Presently, the visitor strode into full view with Limpy galloping behind him. He stopped just outside the doorway, peering from the outdoor brightness into the relatively dim interior of the building.

"Looks like you could use another hand right now," said BJ, walking toward Ichabod's bench.

"The more the merrier," Earl replied. "I could have sworn there was another hand floating around here a minute ago. Have you noticed that things sometimes go better than they did in former times?"

"More and more so. Are you just now noticing that? The devil is bound and his demons are too, which cleared the air for helpful sprites. But they're a bonus. It's not everyone that they favor."

"It takes longer for some of us to believe even when the evidence is close at hand," said Earl. "Now I need to get this plank clamped with its upper edge just below those marks and the vertical scribe aligning with this side of the frame."

"Are these the best clamps you could come up with?"

"So far. I was anxious to get started and didn't take time to make anything decent."

"I discovered an assortment of better tools last time I was here. I forgot to tell you. They're in H8 at the end of this row. Have you looked over there? There's no lock on the door. In fact, that's why I'm here—one reason, anyway."

"No, I'm not privy to legal information, so how much property I've a right to use is beyond me. I've been playing it safe and haven't been snooping around."

"It's a problem for everybody," said BJ. "Everything belongs to the King, really, but his policies are lenient because right now there's not enough supervision to go around. I happened to meet the previous owner of H8, and as far as he knows there are no plans to use any of his stuff. He's expecting a call to supervise the building of a new machine shop and small manufacturing facility in Louisville, so he will have access to everything in the tool barn over there."

"The tool barn?"

"Yeah. He said it's like a giant tool store. Anything serviceable that they pulled out of the ruins has been collected under one roof —just to get things started. Better tools and equipment will be available before too long. ... Okay, how's this?"

"It looks right from here. Clamp it there if you can, and I'll reposition this end."

"Where's your drill, Ichabod?"

"I've been using that thing."

"That old hand drill? It takes two hands at least."

"Want me to show you?"

"I would be surprised if there isn't a functioning power drill in H8 that we could borrow. By the way, you have permission to use this space."

"Speaking of power ...." Samson was straining to identify some unusual noises.

"I was expecting that," said BJ. "Wait. ... No, that's not an airplane engine."

"It sounds like a classic motorcycle to me—or two. Or it could be several."

BJ stepped outside the hangar to see what could be seen of the source of the noise. Limpy, having taken up her former station as receptionist, stood up on all three and went to rub against BJ's leg.

"There's a gang of motorcyclists going by," BJ announced.

"I haven't seen or heard a genuine motorcycle in a very long time," said Samson."

"First I've seen in this world—other than the electrics," BJ shouted. "It's a sweet sound, isn't it? I had assumed all the bikes would be electric from now on." He walked back into the hangar, leaving Limpy alone at her post. "At first I thought it was an airplane engine only because I'm expecting one."

"So you're getting your runway tested with a real landing!"

"There's one supposed to come in sometime this afternoon. I thought I had better warn you. That's another reason I'm here. It's your flight examiner."

"But I don't have a plane to fly yet."

"This is short notice, so I think the purpose is not to do any testing today. You can meet the examiner and maybe schedule an appointment far enough ahead to give us time to get at least one of these abandoned planes checked out."

"Did you tell them about the 172 we found?"

"Yes, and that's why we got a quick response. A limited amount of air travel is decreed, partly to keep from losing pilot skills which will be needed in the future. The 172 is good for that and useful too with its decent range. So they're trying to get all the well preserved C172s with mechanical panels back into service."

"What do you know about plans to get production of new aircraft set up?"

"Nothing major is scheduled as far as I know. Even when it begins, production is going to be limited to small aircraft at first. Just what size that goes up to I'm not sure. But word has it that there will be no airliners or large cargo planes."

"So people will have to travel by land or stay put? What about transporting goods?"

"Rail is coming back in a big way for freight, and passenger trains too. Of course glorifieds use the Hermon hotel chain for travel anyway."

"Hermon hotels? Tell me about it, BJ."

"There's one across the river. It's where we all go to spend the night—in heaven, you know."

"You mentioned having to go back up the ladder every night. And Ken Martin told me a little about it."

"Well.... It's nothing to brag about, Ichabod."

"You don't mean it isn't good up there."

"Oh, it's good; I just don't know how I would begin to describe it. One must be careful. Bragging is actually painful."

"Is it hard to make the transition?"

"Yes, I'll have to say it is."

"Because things are so different, or what?"

"Actually the pace of time is different there. It's like you can do a lot more in a day."

"I thought heaven is where you rest and get rejuvenated?"

"Rest? Well, it's hard to say. There isn't that distinction between resting and not resting."

"What do you do there?"

"We enjoy God and the people in whom he dwells."

"But what does that mean? Is it one-on-one, or is it strictly a corporate thing?"

"Well, again I can't translate it into worldly terms because there's no such distinction. It seems like it's all about the people, but then I think, no, it's the spirit, but that isn't right either because we're together in fellowship with God—actually *in God*, which is a metaphor here but there it's real—or I should say the *family* of God because others are part of it, but I'm afraid that's a rather hollow image when I hear myself say it."

"In the Bible I read references to the throne of God, and bizarre beings around it. Have you seen God that way?"

"New heaven didn't exist when the Bible was written, but it reflects the same thing. Everyone is offering their crowns to praise

God, and some of us are rather bizarre beings. The scene would overwhelm a non-glorified human brain."

"Okay, there are millions up there, right? Is it like a big choir of glorified people and angels around the throne—everybody singing praises?"

"The angels don't sing. People do, but I never saw a big choir or a big crowd of people. The way it's arranged you mostly see the people closest to you."

"How many?"

"It's something like the way churches used to be. I mean in terms of the people you see. It's like you hang out with people in a local church, but that isn't a good comparison either. It's way more fun—so much of the Spirit. We sing partly because the angels can't get enough of it. They love it; it makes them light up!"

"So you can't meet just anyone you want to?"

"You can in theory, but you can't just go barging through any-where anytime you like. Basically, you're motivated by listening and obeying, not satisfying you own wishes—come to think of it you don't have any, or else they're not interesting in comparison with Yahweh's wishes for you."

"Is it like little individual communities, or is it mansions, or what?"

"It depends, Ichabod. I've only seen two dwelling places out-side of my own fellowship—the ones located on either side of us—and they're both very different."

"It doesn't make sense. On the one hand you say the scene is large and overwhelming, and on the other hand you say you've only been in three houses."

"As I mentioned before, the dwelling places are on the rim and the hub is like the throne of God. So you can go directly to the throne and not see many houses or much of the city's vastness."

"What about the Hermon hotels? Where do they fit into that layout?"

"When you check into the hotel you get a key to a room that turns out to be your dwelling place in heaven."

"Instantly? You just open the door and you're there?"

"No. You sit down at the desk, which has something like a crystal ball on it. You stare at yourself in it and it's like you become the image, but really you were an image and you become the real person and you find yourself in your dwelling place in heaven. But not every Jacob's Ladder is exactly like that."

"Then to come back to earth it's just the reverse of that?"

"Almost, but there are no hotels up there. You step into a booth and it's like virtual reality. That's what this universe is, really—like a simulation from heaven's point of view."

"I get it. There's just about that much difference between heaven and earth—reality and virtual reality."

"Yes and no. Earth is a realization of a permanent ideal and so is new heaven, but new heaven is clean—unmarked by evil."

"How is life in heaven so much different?"

"I can't tell you, Ichabod. ... There's a brightness. But it's not that. Can you imagine the Lord—it's like he's everywhere—in everyone. They're all ... beautiful! You just want to ... behold! But there is so much to do."

"Do you mean physically beautiful? Do their bodies look something like human bodies only more vivid somehow?"

"Evelyn was like a little glimpse of what people are like up there. She had some of that sort of radiance."

"I had a date with her. I know what you mean. It was her spirit. She was enchanting, but it wasn't just her looks and her personality. You would never say she was glamorous—nothing like that; that would be an insult. She was humble, even playful—yet noble at the same time. It was devastating."

"No kidding."

"But I would not want it to be known that I said that."

"What does it matter now?"

"Look at me. I wasn't torn up then. What would she think of me now? I know it would make her sad, and I don't want to do that. I wouldn't want to grieve her in any way."

"Are you sure it isn't your ... what shall we say?"

"Go ahead and say it. I may not be glorifiable material, but I'm far enough along to keep from being offended by anything."

"That's pretty far along."

"Try me, BJ. It's my pride, right?"

"Of course."

"Right. So there it is. What comes of that?"

"I think there's a remedy now for everything. It will come in time."

Earl paused to listen. "There's those bikes again. Sounds like they're heading our way."

The roar of motorcycle engines reverberated off the metal walls of the hangars. Limpy galloped back in and jumped up onto the workbench next to her boss. One, two, three ... seven motorcycles paraded before the hangar door, their engines rumbling between spasmodic blasts. The riders were dressed in blue denim with red bandannas tied around their heads in lieu of helmets. They circled around and lined up to the right side slightly out of view and cut their engines. BJ went out to meet them.

"Is there an Ichabod Samson somewhere around here?" asked the chief rider who evidently had been glorified.

"That's him in the hangar," replied BJ. "Nice bikes you guys have there. Where did you get them?"

"We put them together from bits and pieces we found when we were helping salvage things from rubble in what used to be Pittsburgh. My name's Franky, by the way, and these are my glorified buddies. Milt—" Milt standing by his bike raised his hand. "Blink —" Having some trouble the kick stand, Blink looked up and smiled at BJ. "Mule over there on the Indian. Chub—" "Glad to meet you, BJ." "Red—wouldn't you know he had to have a red bike. And that's Buck there on the Harley."

"What are you fellows doing—just touring the country?" BJ asked.

"We're on a mission: we're building boardwalks on city waterfronts along the river, wherever there's a Hermon hotel not far away," Franky replied. "We've been working our way downstream; we got here this morning, and we're lookin' for fuel. Someone told us we might have better luck getting gas in Sellers-burg, and when we got here someone suggested we go find Icha-bod Samson at the airport as he has connections in town and may know where there's some gasoline waiting for a worthy cause."

"Did you fellows get training in boardwalks?" BJ asked.

"Milt is our master carpenter. I got leadership and healing arts somehow. Blink got trained in structural engineering. Mule spe-cialized in means of moving heavy objects. Chub is a chemical engineer with a minor in materials science. Red is a machinist, but he can do anything. And Buck—what are you, Buck? I forgot."

"He's a mechanic if I ever saw one," said BJ.

"Motorcycles!" said Buck.

"Yeah, you're right," said Franky. "Buck is fantastic with engines. Every bike here owes its existence to him. Mind if I go in and talk to Ichabod?"

"No. Go ahead. I don't man the reception desk; the cat does."

Franky walked into the hangar where Ichabod had remained at his project.

"Nice! ... Sailboat?"

"Someday."

"Have you built them before?"

"Yeah."

"My name's Franky. ... Ichabod. That's an unusual name. What does it mean?"

"The glory has departed."

"You must be an exceptional. Where are you from?"

"Northwest."

"I am too. Pacific Northwest?"

"Yeah."

"I'd tell you the name of the town I used to hang out in, but I can't remember it for some reason. Been here long?"

"No, just about three months."

"Samson. ... There's something about that name. I see you're left hand is lame."

"Yeah, my whole left side got crushed. But that was the old world. Everything feels better here."

Franky reached out with both hands and grabbed Samson's right arm.

"You haven't seen Ms. Evans, have you? ..."

"No."

"So you know who I mean!"

Ichabod was silent and pulled his arm away.

"You know who I mean, don't you? ... Pamela!"

Ichabod was silent.

"We all owe her our lives. But there's someone else I want to thank, and I never thought I'd find him."

"He's dead, Franky."

Franky looked into Earl's eye.

"This is Clark Airport, isn't it?"

"Yes, Franky, it is."

Franky threw both his arms around Ichabod.

"Does that left arm hurt?"

"Not much."

"I'm sorry. It was a good arm. A very good arm. I know."

Franky wrapped both his hands gently around Ichabod's left arm and bowed his head. From outside there came the sound of a light aircraft in the area.

"That might be your examiner," BJ shouted into the hangar.

Ichabod broke loose from Franky and walked to the hangar door and stood next to BJ. Franky came out behind him and joined the other cyclists near their bikes. They all searched the sky in the direction from which the sound came, looking for the plane.

"There it is," said BJ, pointing to the sky on the right.

"I see it," said Buck.

"Where?" said Mule.

"Right there," said Buck.

"I see it," said Red. "Just a speck."

"Where? ... I still can't see it,"

"See that white puffy cloud in the shape of a heart?" said Red.

"Okay; I see it now, just below the heart," said Chub.

"What color is it?" asked Blink.

"It's still too far away to determine the color," said BJ.

They all waited in silence.

Ichabod said, "Sounds like a Cessna 150."

"Could be," said BJ. "But I have a hunch it's a 152 Aerobat."

"Did they tell you that?" Samson asked him.

"No. But I think I know the plane."

"Just by the sound, huh?"

"I think so."

"It's yellow!" exclaimed Blink.

"Appears to be," said BJ.

"It's not the Aerobat, then?"

"Maybe not. There's no way to tell from this distance—unless she does some aerobatics. It looks just like a 152."

"She?"

"Yeah, if it's who I think it is. Only thing is, her Aerobat was red and white. It needed new paint, though, so maybe they found some yellow paint somewhere."

"I guess there aren't too many Aeorbats flying," said Ichabod.

"I'm sure it's the only one. It sounds like her plane."

"I take it you worked on it," said Ichabod.

"Yeah," replied BJ. "It took a lot of work."

The plane had become much nearer, flying a thousand feet above the ground not far beyond the far side of the runway.

"There you go .... It's an Aerobat," said Ichabod.

"I'll tell you in just a moment if it's who I think it is," said BJ.

"Nice barrel roll!" Samson exclaimed.

"She's showing off," said BJ. "Now watch as she comes out of it. ... It's her! That little wiggle at the end is her signature."

"Wow! And spiraling to a landing, it looks like," said Samson. "I never could master that."

"We'll see how she comes out of it," said BJ.

"Beautiful!" exclaimed Samson. "And she greases it on. ... So you know this lady?"

"She's one of my favorite people. I knew her in the old world too."

The plane turned off the runway mid field and taxied toward them, made a smart turn into the hangar alley and stopped near them. The plane was yellow with a Tweety-Bird painted on its black vertical fin. The pilot stepped out, smiling.

"BJ!" she exclaimed. "I didn't expect to see you here! Who is your friend there?"

"This is your student, Ichabod Samson."

"Hi. I'm Judy."

"These fellows by the motorcycles have just happened by," said BJ. "They're on a boardwalk-building mission from Pittsburgh. Franky, I'll let you introduce your gang to Judy."

After the introductions Franky said:

"You wouldn't be giving plane rides to just anyone, would you?"

"Give me a ride on the back of your bike and I'll take you up for a spin."

"That's a deal, honey!"

"You might be getting more than you bargained for, Franky," said BJ. "Do you know what a spin is in an airplane?"

"If I'm with her, I won't care what it is," declared Franky.

"I'll get you fellows fixed up with some gas," said BJ. "Follow me."

As BJ walked back the way he had come the bikers quickly mounted their machines, started their engines, and trailed after him. As soon as the noise had died out, Judy approached Samson and held out her hand.

"I know you used to fly a lot," she said, "but that was before your arm got injured. Have you considered modifying a plane to make it easier to manage the controls with one hand?"

Ichabod stood without answering. He was opening and closing his left hand.

Finally he said: "It was almost useless until just a few minutes ago. ... Franky fixed my hand!"

I t was not the first time Samson had been picked up by Lazar Manipi. On this occasion Lazar had been to Sellersburg for an inspection assignment and was on his way back to the city when he felt compelled to turn off the freeway at Clarksville. He was not surprised at finding Ichabod there, needing a ride into Louisville.[1]

Lazar had developed a fondness for Ichabod in spite of the fact that his most difficult assignment was to monitor Samson's activities in Clarksville. You will not be surprised to learn that Lazar was employed by the Louisville housing authority in the reconstruction planning department where he was responsible for enforcing compliance with building codes and regulations.

Samson had not thought it necessary to apply for a permit or file a report before undertaking projects in Clarksville. He worked among unregistered naturals, survivors of many disasters, (some of whom were crippled too) who were attempting to eke out a living in that area. This was bleak and unclaimed territory where cleanup had been incomplete, leaving damaged buildings, some of which were in hazardous conditions.

Since no official family or trading authority existed in or near Clarksville, food had to be grown, caught, and killed locally, and the yield varied by the season. No one went hungry for very long, however, thanks to a family in New Albany that delivered donations regularly and sometimes traded with "wealthy" Clarksville individuals for game.

Samson donated his time and talents to help these unregistered survivors reclaim dwellings from damaged structures and improve the ones they had. He knew this was not the approved approach to rebuilding and that whatever they manged to put together would be replaced with new construction in due time. But these were tribulation veterans whose families had lived in Clarksville for generations, who did not trust dispensations from Louisville and were satisfied to be on their own.

---

1. We have skipped ahead three years. Earl's first boat had been completed ar d launched.

It was all Samson could do to keep from laughing every time he caught Lazar MacDonald (he still thought of his old surname) snooping around projects he had undertaken. He felt not the slightest resentment toward the man, and he wanted to reveal his identity and share the irony, but so far he had resisted that temptation, knowing that Lazar would not be able to keep the secret. He came close to it one time when he called Lazar a "walking wonder," which strongly suggested that Samson knew his history.

Two days each week Samson enjoyed working alongside Steve Antinanco, who was one of the New Albany missionaries. Even though Steve was glorified, he looked up to Ichabod for a reason he could not quite comprehend. Their conversation as they worked together often concerned flying light aircraft. Steve was particularly interested in the fact that Ichabod knew of a C172 at Clark Regional that had been singled out for restoration. But that was not what primarily drew him to exceptional Mr. Samson. There was that about Ichabod that reminded him of Earl Clark in the old world, who had been his mentor in carpentry and his flight instructor.

Of course Earl recognized Steve Airheart. One day he asked him about his surname.

"It means 'eagle of the sun' in Mapuche.

"Is that a native American language?"

"Yes, and a people living in South America."

"Are you related to them, somehow?"

"Not in the old world, but in heaven I've been befriended by a Mapuche tribe, and they gave me this name."

"Are there many of them up there?"

"Yes, there was a large evangelical Christian presence in Chile among the Mapuche."

"Is there a universal language that you speak in heaven, or have you learned the Mapuche language?"

Steve laughed. "It's really simple," he said. "Everyone speaks a form of Hebrew almost all the time. But we haven't forgotten our native languages."

Lazar dropped Samson off near the city marina and then drove around the block to the parking lot next to the ASA building. He parked his government car and went up to the planning department on the second floor.

Samson had come to town to take advantage of the pleasant weather after last night's rainstorm, which meant he would be out on the river sailing *Wind Chaser* if at all possible. But the first thing he found to do as he limped toward the dock from the curb where Lazar had let him out was lending a hand moving large rocks that had been unloaded from a truck. The rocks were being used to build a boundry wall for the river-facing edge of a new garden located upstream from the marina parking lot. Evidently no boulder-handling equipment was available, because two husky men were attempting to heft the rocks manually. Samson was able to lend two hands since the bones and ligaments in his left arm had been perfectly restored by Dr. Franky. His work in Clarksville, where he often spent whole days not just organizing and directing but also physically lifting and handling materials, had restored strength in his arms. Thus Samson was able to move rocks that had resisted the combined efforts of the workers.

With dusty hands and a sweaty face he went from there to *Wind Chaser's* float, with an eye on the weather, hoping to take her out for a sail on the river if a favorable wind should come up.

He was crouching in the cockpit, mopping the last of the rainwater with a sponge and squeezing it overboard when he was reminded of the "environmental" law in the old world which required that rainwater be disposed of in a shoreside facility. A particular occasion stood out in his mind in that regard: he was visited by the head of the organization responsible for enforcing that regulation. He remembered well what she said when she caught him emptying the rainwater-soaked sponge overboard: "It's an insulting rule. I'll ignore it too even though they're watching us with telephoto video." Then she took the sponge and finished the job for him while he stepped up onto the cabin top, removed and stowed the mainsail cover, and rigged the halyard.

This recollection put Samson in a melancholy mood. He did not want to think about that incident or what happened next. She had come to participate in his sailing class, having never sailed before in her life. The other students present on that Saturday afternoon had received instruction in his shore school a week earlier, but Leila Labaki had missed the school, and so he took her with him in the instructor's boat, expecting that she could pick up some practical knowledge by observing.

Well, observe I did, I must say. In a short time I was doing all the work, sailing Wind Chaser *myself with minimal coaching and advising the students in the other two boats while Earl sat back admiring his* protege.

Yes, this vessel Samson had launched on the Ohio River was of the same design and named after the original *Wind Chaser*.

But at that moment he did not want to think about her at all, for he was not prepared to encounter her on earth. He had done what he could for her in the old life. He knew she was a blessed citizen of heaven now, with a new immortal body while he was trapped in broken mortal flesh. In the old life she had been perfect in his eyes. Now she had moved on to a kind of perfection he could not fully comprehend—a body of youthful vigor and also of an ageless quality. Partly he was pleased about that because he would never have to worry about her welfare. But since she lived in a world he had no ability to experience, the fundamental distress of missing her fellowship had to remain unresolved. He was still of that natural mind where the appearance of impossibility eclipsed any hope of a different future that might be better.

"With her talents, she would have duties on earth that might bring her here," he murmured darkly, shuddering at the pain he would cause her if she saw his disfigured face. Another possible reason that she might show up, he theorized, was that although the glorified saints were morally flawless, visiting earth was an obligation they had to endure in order to be reminded of the results of disobedience—which remained visible everywhere.

Realistically it's unlikely. ... Unless she comes looking for me.

Yes, *very unlikely*, he thought, because she would be too occupied with her new life and relationships for that. ... And would he even recognize her should their paths happen to cross? She would not recognize him unless she knew of his particular deformities, which he prayed she would never discover.

There were only seven—or eight or nine—people who knew the dual identity of Earl Clark and Ichabod Samson. The only one of them who might possibly reveal it to others was Karen Martin. Although Karen had kept his secret before, she might think it was safe by now to look into medical services for him.

Ichabod had thought through this many times. The one reasonable possibility was that I might look up his records in heaven. But according to what he had learned from BJ, the intelligence system in heaven was not accessible: there was no technology available to regular residents of heaven for collecting and disseminating information. So he counted on there being no record available to me of what had happened to Earl Clark.

Overall, however, it was little comfort to him to know that I would never have to know him as a cripple with a disfigured face. But little is not nothing. To be on opposite sides of mortality would be distressful to both of us, and for that reason he could be a little comforted for his marred appearance. It was as good an insurance against that awkward eventuality as he could desire.

But there is that which had formerly been called chance, and there is no escaping it as long as one is alive. Chance did not bother him in the old life after the Rapture when there was no possibility of our meeting. Those were dark days when waves of disappointment followed one right after another, difficulty upon difficulty, and it kept all his faculties busy trying to render some significant service to the withering community against multiple obstacles. But this new life was the opposite of that. There was plenty of time for the inconceivable to become conceivable—even likely. Chance might march me out on the dock even as he bailed rainwater. Then what would he do? How could he ignore me? How could he remain a stranger?

Although he had told himself that he must never let me know, in order to save me from a degree of disappointment that he thought should not exist on new earth, did he have the power to do it? If we should meet, would I compel him to reveal his secret? At the bottom of his heart he hoped I would do just that, but his reason told him he must not let it happen; he must deny his heart and perpetuate its pain for my sake. He was determined to do it.

Enough of the rainwater had been bailed, and he was thinking he must get away from the boat and its association with memories that had suddenly assaulted him with such disturbing intensity.

For the sake of my sanity I must stop thinking about her.

Of course there was nothing new and exceptional about the intensity. The void I had left when I disappeared had tried to close itself immediately: it had given him the strength to snap the wristbands and bring my building tumbling down upon him. Certainly today's pain had to be less than that.

"One more squeeze and that will be it," he muttered. "I'll take you out another day," he promised *Wind Chaser*.

The sound of footsteps on the deck behind him caught his attention. Two people were walking out on the float.

Most likely it's visitors looking at boats. If it's her, she will see the name. Why do I moor Wind Chaser with her name showing?

• • •

It happened by "chance" that I was in Louisville on that day.[1] I was there to meet the ASA Executive Officer at the Louisville office—as a courtesy. There was no business that required my presence. Communication by the "telephone" of heaven had met all our needs. He had invited me to see the restored waterfront of which he was particularly proud. (No, that was not justifiable.)

As I toured the Louisville ASA building I overheard part of a conversation between Lazar Manipi and another enforcement officer. The two of them were standing by a window, and Lazar

---

1. Yes, of course we will meet. If I were the author of a romance, I would not disappoint you. Few authors would. It happens like this in stories all the time, especially in happy stories, and our millennium tale qualifies as one of those. Of course there are sad things in all stories, and Ichabod is an efficient supplier of sadness. Now we shall see whether my meeting with him turns out to be satisfactory or sets things up for exceptional glory in the end.

was pointing down at the waterfront. I was mildly surprised to see Lazar there, but not too surprised that he was in the same position as when he worked for me. I knew it was him not by his face, because he was looking the other way; it was not his voice alone, though it did resemble Lazar MacDonald's voice to some degree— it was definitely without strain and more pleasant than it had been in the old life. The way he spoke had some of the sameness, but there was much new there too. It was simply that there was nothing about him that could not possibly be Lazar. When he turned around and saw me, he beamed at his old boss.

"Why not come with me, and I'll give you a tour of the waterfront," Lazar said. "There's a man I need to see, and he's down there right now. I brought him into town just an hour ago, and I see his boat still tied at the dock, so he must be down there somewhere. Maybe I can catch him and ask him to share with me what additional plans he has for his renovation efforts in Clarksville. At least I need to get some information about it into the system."

"I thought you said you gave him a ride into town. Didn't you mention it to him then?" I asked.

"No, I didn't want to bring up business while giving him a ride. It didn't seem right to hit him with that when I was doing him a good turn. I'm not even sure I have the nerve to confront him now, but if you're with me, it will give me more confidence."

My host took Lazar's suggestion in good humor and gave us leave to explore the waterfront. For me it was a chance to renew my acquaintance with Lazar and remake my impression of him now as my glorified brother. But I had another thought as well.

"That's him on the dock, walking out to his sailboat."

"Is he badly—"

"Yes, his left side was hurt in some accident of which we have no information. It's not quite as bad as it was at first. His left arm is good now; it *was* useless. Somehow that got repaired, but we have no record of it. I remember when he started building that boat. He could only use his right hand. By the time it was finished both hands seemed to be fine."

"I'm glad. It makes sailing easier if you have two hands."

As we watched him, the sailor stepped gingerly into the cockpit of his boat.

"But you see his left leg doesn't bend very well."

"Oh ... that would make it difficult."

"He manages pretty well. I've seen him out there with one or two crippled people. I guess he feels more comfortable in their company."

All we could see of Lazar's target at that moment was head and shoulders as he bent down to lift a floorboard.

"This may seem silly, but I've been procrastinating because I really like Ichabod. I didn't want to seem to be critical of what he was doing in Clarksville, yet we do need to have a record of the condition and availability of housing, and it would simplify things greatly if he—"

Lazar stopped his monologue as he realized that I was not listening but intently watching the man whose hand had reached over the side of the boat, squeezing water out of a sponge.

"I'll wait here until he finishes bailing," said Lazer.

"Do you remember how bailing rainwater used to be illegal?" I asked him.

"No. ... Really?"

"There were so many regulations no one could know them all. This reminds me of the time when I took that sailing class and got to be in the boat with Earl Clark. He was mopping up rainwater with a sponge just like that."

"He must be almost through. ... I'll go out and ask him if he will consider giving us reports. I don't expect it will take more than a couple of minutes. If you will excuse me, I'll be right back."

"I'll go with you."

I followed Lazar out onto the dock but stopped a few feet short of the boat's berth and let him go on ahead. Though having heard the footsteps, Ichabod did not turn to look until Lazar stopped and was almost standing over him. Then he glanced up to see who it was.

"Hi, Ichabod. It's me again. I'm really sorry to bother you here. But if you'll bear with me, I'm supposed to have gotten you set up to help us keep track of the housing situation up in Clarksville. Could we have a little meeting sometime and figure out a format you could use to keep us updated?"

Out of the corner of his right eye Ichabod noticed that there was another person standing on the dock. He turned his head, and I saw his face for the first time. I was visibly shocked, as everyone was at first; he was used to that. But I startled him because he recognized me.

It's her! She is definitely glorified. … But maybe it isn't her.

He told me later it was not so much my face, for though I bore a strong resemblance to my former self. There was something unmistakable about my stance and mannerism.

I diverted my gaze, dropping my eyes from the shocking face of the man I dared not think of as Samson and down to the transom of his boat where I read the name painted there.

"Oh! Your boat is named *Wind Chaser!*" I blurted out.

It's her.

"Let me introduce you," said Lazar. "This is Leila Lolomi, visiting us from ASA headquarters at Appleton. I was showing her the work we have nearly completed on the waterfront. Leila, this is my good friend Ichabod Samson."

"I'm sorry," I said, looking at Lazar. "I didn't mean to intrude into your conversation. Please go ahead. I'll wait on shore."

With that I turned and walked away, barely able to think.

"It won't be a big burden, I promise," continued Lazar. "We do appreciate what you are doing in Clarksville."

"Yeah. Sure," said Ichabod.

Samson's eyes followed me for a moment. *Obviously she's not interested in me anymore—if she* did *recognize me.*

"Any time," he added.

Or was it the shock and she needs time to get over it?

"Sure. Whatever," Samson repeated absently.

She won't look this way again.

"All right," said Lazar. "I appreciate that. I'll stop in with some forms you can use next time I go up that way."

Lazar thanked him and left to join me. I had stopped looking his way. We continued our walk.

Ichabod did not want to have me catch him looking at me, but of course he sneaked a peak. Lazar was doing the talking, and I was not looking back.

Samson told me later, "The land on which you walked suddenly had more to do with you than *Wind Chaser* ever did, and suddenly the boat was my refuge. I decided to try to sail across the river even in the light wind. I hurriedly removed the mains'l cover, stowed it, attached the halyard, and then scrambled out onto the dock as quickly as was possible. I untied the mooring lines, and pushed the dock away with my good leg. At that moment there was not enough breeze to make it worth raising the sail, so I had to use the oars."

• • •

I had been silent as Lazar pointed out the work that was nearly completed to bring the waterfront up to the first stage of renovation; I was listening but was not paying close attention. None of it interested me in the least at that moment.

Finally, I asked him:

"Was your conversation with Ichabod successful?"

"He was in a receptive mood. It shouldn't be a problem now."

"How long has he been here?"

"About three years. He's one of the exceptionals. He just showed up one day."

"Did you say he built that sailboat himself?"

"Yes—in an abandoned hangar at the Clark airport."

"Lazar, do you know what his name means? ... Ichabod. Do you know what that means?"

"I'm not sure."

"It means the glory has departed."

The glory has departed, Samson. I'm so sorry you believe that. If I could cry I would: these glorified bodies aren't all they were cracked up to be.

114

A Pleasant Place

Chapter Ten

Within the holy city in new heaven are many pleasant places. There is no equivalent on earth because our senses in heaven are different. Beauty is everywhere, perceived as much by your spirit as by your eyes. Or you might say there is a spiritual dimension of beauty which pervades everything. The primary impression you get of people is due to their inner spirit; but even buildings and streets have an inner aspect and a glow. While everything is comprised of spirit-material, there is a living Spirit within everything as well, which is "visible"—Spirit being perceived by the Spirit.

On earth we have a great variety of living plants that clothe the hills and the valleys, often with great beauty and majesty. In the holy city the inner Spirit clothes all its inanimate structures with an architectural splendor and majesty. The earth below has its dynamic moods and its complex geologic and organic splendor. The glory of heaven is of a different order, more suited to the eternal Spirit than to earth's mortal cycles—cycles of life and death.

As I said, there is no way to describe heaven in earthly terms that makes a lot of sense. The inner Spirit is like energy, but he doesn't really belong to the person or thing in which he dwells. He flows from God, he's received, and he makes everything glorious!

Far outside the walls of the city there is only the material spirit, and things are drab in comparison—so I am told. I have never ventured that far myself. But I have heard there are wonders to be explored out there.

What is beauty? What makes one thing more beautiful than another? There is no rule, of course. Beauty is in the eye of the beholder, we always said. And so it is in the holy city. I think everyone agrees that what frames the scene or the figure is all-important, and that applies to time as well as space. One's sense of beauty can easily be blunted by an abundance of scenes that would be better appreciated in isolation. This is true whether the objects are clustered too closely in either time or space. This is obvious and elementary to an artist or a photographer. I mention it because the superlatives one hears about heaven will conjure up an impression of one's senses being over stimulated. In fact, no such imbalance ever occurs.

The point I want to make is that heaven is very well designed for the pleasure of our spiritual selves, and beauty is often very subtle. I say again, "pleasant" is a better word than "beautiful" to describe it. I do not say "peaceful" because that sounds like it could put one to sleep. No one sleeps in heaven! I do not say "stimulating" because that sounds like an imbalance in the other direction. On earth, "pleasant" is limited by circumstances and spoiled by lack of motivation. In heaven the circumstances are always propitious, and the Spirit's energy never wanes.

Nowhere is "pleasantness" more constant than in the interactions between people. The primary reason for this is that within and near the walls of the holy city there is no doubt or fear anywhere. Love flourishes unceasingly in the absence of its foes. On earth you can never get or give very much love. You have heard that streets in heaven are paved with gold. That is certainly a metaphor. My interpretation is that love paves the streets. There is none of that cold shiny metal in heaven, but love is abundant.

I have written all these preliminary words because I am about to tell those of you who are readers of Claudia's books about a meeting I had with some of your old friends. I needed to describe the environment in which the meeting occurred, but there are no physical parallels, and I think I've failed. I could have borrowed earthly images such as a seaside setting under gently rustling palm trees on a sunny afternoon where I met some of your friends as they came by the bench where I was sitting. But then you would have a false picture although the effect of the pleasant setting would be a partial approximation—but a poor one at that. So forget the earthly scene and do the best you can with "pleasant."

And remember that the area around the walls of heaven's holy city is enormous. There are actually nations within it because you don't cease to be who you are when you come here.

The first friend of yours I had the honor of meeting on that day—it was Sabbath, which allowed me to spend it in heaven—was Laura. I had not seen her since two days before the Rapture. You will remember earlier in that week we had met in the park by the lake. The second and last time I saw her was when she and little Emmett came up to my office along with Veronica Sweet.

I remember being captivated by her happy countenance when I first saw her that day in the park. You know her: now what would be her demeanor in heaven, do you think? I will leave that to your imagination, but for my part when I saw her face that Sabbath day, I rejoiced and wanted to dance. And that was before she noticed me, for several other people were close by.

When she saw me she lit up like an angel—not literally (you know angels *do* light up)—but she gave out a little scream and rushed to embrace me as if I were the one person she had been looking for that day—and maybe I was.

Immediately after we exchanged a few words of happy reunion I asked her about the children.

"They're both here!" she exclaimed. "I see Emmett almost every day and Emma most every weekend."

"I've heard Emma has important work to do on earth. Have you ... seen Veronica?"

"Veronica is not here. But she trusted the Lord would bring her through the tribulation, and he did, and she never took the mark. She's living in a family overseen by Emma and Valentine."

I wanted to ask Laura about her parents. As you know, I had been part of the reason she was able to visit them the day before the Rapture. I hesitated a moment, but Laura read my question without me saying it. She told me that her father had survived without the mark and was later saved. Her mother took the mark, which made her sick, and she did not survive the tribulation.

"I'm sorry about your mother," I said. "There may be hope for her still."

"Oh, but I'm not the one chosen to go meet her, and I don't know who it could be," Laura said without the least trace of worry.

"And how is your grandmother?"

"Did Veronica tell you about my grandmother?"

"No, I think you did."

Laura laughed. "I was going to. She's here! She even got permission to go down to see my father before he fell asleep. And I want to thank you, my dear friend, for making it possible for me to visit them. I promise to repay you with my love for ever and ever. Have you seen Mr. Samson? He's the one I need to thank first and foremost. I wouldn't be here if it were not for him."

"And neither would I!"

"Oh!" Laura exclaimed, because Emmett had appeared during the time we were talking.

I had noticed the lad approaching with a man in tow whom I assumed might be his father. Emmett grabbed his Aunt Laura's arm and pointed to the man, who stood back and seemed to be shy. He was wearing a crown.

"This is Felix!" said Emmett. "You remember Felix! But he wasn't Felix, really, his real name is Paul."

Paul hastily removed the circlet from his head and hid it within his robe. "Emmett insisted I put it on," he said and bowed to Laura.

"This is my friend Leila. She's a busy ruler on earth."

"Emmett told me about you. He was very impressed the first time he met you. I haven't told him, though, that you almost had me shot or at least arrested."

"Earl failed me on that one," I said with a smile. Paul caught my meaning and laughed then bowed.

"How is Earl, do you know?" Paul asked. "I owe him my crown."

I knew what he meant (and I think you do too), but the others did not. "Yes. He's an exceptional in the Louisville area."

"Several of your people are in that area, I understand," Paul replied.

"Yes. ... Yes they are," Then, addressing Emmett, I asked, "How did you get to know Paul?"

As he hesitated, Laura answered for him: "He came by where Emmett and I were waiting for you in the park. It was on Tuesday, the day after you and I met, and I was there hoping you would come by again."

"That was foolish Felix," said Paul, "and Emmett sensed I was up to no good. I think you both did."

"And so did Franky!" Emmett added.

"I mean, here," I said to Emmett. "You're a young man now, and you were a little boy back them. Did Paul recognize you, or did you remember him?"

"We hadn't met until five minutes ago," Paul answered. "We were standing right over there."

"I knew it was him," said Emmett, "and I was surprised, and I said, 'Why are *you* here?' And he just showed me his soul-winner crown. Then I saw aunt Laura and I wanted her to see it."

"You must have more story to tell than I know, Paul," I said.

"In brief it is this: That very night I was visited by two gentlemen who prayed for my release from bondage—that and, yes, there's more to the story. Anyway, the next day I felt compelled to explain the way to heaven to as many people as I possibly could."

"How did you do it?" Emmett asked earnestly.

"Well, I began a lecture series from the book of Romans."

"What's that?" Emmett asked.

"It's a rather long letter written by Paul the apostle and addressed to Christians in ancient Rome. ... It's in the Bible."

"And then did they learn about King Jesus?"

"Most of them did. All I did was go over the letter with them."

"Would you show me how to do that?"

"I'm going down tomorrow to start a Bible school. If you would like to go with me, I'll make the arrangements."

Paul then turned to Laura. "Forgive me, I overheard you saying your mother died without the Savior. If you will send me, I'll go look for her and meet her on your behalf."

"Oh, are you the one chosen to meet her?"

"I could be."

"Oh. ... I thought it was very difficult."

"It is difficult. I've been there twice. It is very difficult. But I will go for you if you send me."

"I couldn't put you through that!"

"No, but the option is yours. If you decide to send me, I will know."

"Oh! Here's Emma and Valentine!" Laura exclaimed. "This is my friend Leila, and Emmett's friend Paul the evangelist."

"Yes, we were talking with Emmett before Paul came along," said Emma. "We didn't want to interrupt your conversation, so we waited."

"And we know about Leila Lalomi," said Valentine. "May I have the honor of receiving a hug from you?"

"And the two of you are quite famous down on earth," I said.

"We're handling it, somehow," said Emma.

"What is the population of Los Angeles by now?" I asked.

"Still nothing like it was before the tribulation, of course," Emma replied.

"There hasn't been a census, but we estimate half a million," said Valentine.

"Is that within the old LA boundary?" I asked.

"Yes. The metropolis area is not being used at all yet," Emma answered, and she looked too fresh and honest to be a politician.

"There is so much more to dispose of still," Valentine added.

"Come along with me now, Emmett, if you like, and we shall see about getting you certified for an introductory earth descent. Oh, here's Sookie!"

Sookie rushed to Paul and threw her arms around him. "Thank you for talking to me and giving me that poem."

"Sookie, do you know these folks?"

"One of them I do," she said, staring at me. "Leila, forgive me for being the brat I was."

"You're a lovely girl, Sookie. I always thought you were. I do forgive you. How could I not forgive you? Did you attend Paul's lectures?"

"All he did was give me a poem by George MacDonald."

"He's here! I've seen him," Paul announced.

"George MacDonald? How did you recognize him?"

"There was a long line of people waiting to meet some renowned person. I asked someone in the line who it was, and he showed me a new book by George MacDonald. Normally, you have to make a reservation years in advance to visit a famous person; otherwise, if you see someone like that you're expected to allow them space and not speak to them unless they speak to you first. In this case MacDonald was signing his latest book, which everyone in line had a copy of."

"Has he written many books?" Sookie asked.

"Oh, thousands by now, I suppose. He got here before the Rapture, somehow."

She clapped her hands. "I would like to read them someday."

"If you ladies will excuse us, Emmett and I have some important business to attend to."

"And so do we," said Emma.

As they walked away, I turned to Laura and said, "I wasn't happy when Samson let him go. But he knew to do the right thing. I wonder who else is here because of those lectures in Romans."

"I've been looking for him. Have you seen Earl?" Sookie asked.

"Yes. Once. Very briefly. But I didn't speak to him."

"I can't imagine that," she said with a smile I knew well.

"I think he was in hiding, so I respected that."

"Earl in hiding? I can't imagine that either."

I proposed that we sit down on a bench that was near us. We had been standing near the side of a wide street (a walkway, actually since there are no wheels for human locomotion in heaven). Sookie sat on my left and Laura on my right.

"Earl was badly injured," I said solemnly. "I think, in fact I know, he doesn't want anyone to feel sorry for him."

"He doesn't want to disappoint you," said Laura. "Am I right?"

"I think you are right."

"So did he know it was you?" Sookie asked.

"I'm sure he did, but I knew he didn't want me to know it."

"Did he think you didn't recognize him?" Sookie pressed.

"No. He knew I did. But he wanted to pretend that I didn't."

"That so he could imagine you were not disappointed?"

"Yes, I think so. Then I could pretend he was someone else."

"Are his injuries so bad that he can't be helped medically?" Laura asked.

"I believe he can be helped," I said. "I inquired about that. He arrived as an exceptional, which means there is no record of him, and he is not part of a family. The medical people have no way of verifying that he belongs there and has not strayed from his family somewhere."

"If you will excuse me," said Sookie, "I have a prayer meeting to attend over in the emerald chapel. Several friends of Claudia Nice meet to pray for her. She is in jail, in poor health, in a great deal of pain, and she has little time to give up her grudge against Al Cypher before she dies, and if she does surrender she will be here in the end; otherwise we will never see her again. If she had not hired me to serve at the Green Broccoli, I never would have met Felix—Paul, I mean—and he would not have given me that poem, and I would be down there with her."

"Do you know where Al Cypher is and what he's doing?" I asked Sookie.

"He's the chaplain at the jail in Salem where Claudia is serving for selling a painting of a castle that she said was her creation but really was a copy of one that Harrietta Foster had painted, and she will not be released until she returns the last cent. The sort of art she was famous for became rubbish in the kingdom of heaven, and she found she couldn't paint anything else that was original. I must go now, or they'll be out looking for me."

"Could you have imagined that Emma would be capable of administering a great city like LA?" I said to Laura.

"Not by herself, but when I saw that she and Valentine were soul mates I thought they could do anything if they had the opportunity to work together."

"Were you surprised when you learned that they had been trained for city government?"

"I really was, but the training they received worked marvelously. It was a special course for diarchies. They graduated with honors and were rewarded the equivalent of ten cities."

"I'm a little surprised that heaven would sponsor a diarchy. Because I report to the King, I'm not really a monarch, though it may appear to some of my subordinates that I am. Our chain of command is simple and it works perfectly. But I don't know how a co-regency would be an advantage at the second level."

"I think it's because they were inseparable."

"Well, the magnitude of the reward that they received is generally given to someone who has been very productive in the former life. Those girls had no time to be productive."

"I see what you mean. They had no qualification for what they received, unless it was being soul mates, and I have read through the Bible seven times since I have been here, and I have seen nothing like that. But I think it's coming to me now. It's because they consult with each other and they get things right without needing to wait for orders. And the King is pleased with that."

"From my point of view that's really daring. I wouldn't trust my own wisdom that well."

"I know that if we serve the King, and we are perfectly obedient to him and his Law, we may become part of the evidence for the goodness of creation. Is that why you feel it is daring to make decisions on your own?"

"Yes, exactly."

"Now if Emma and Valentine with their shared wisdom are perfectly obedient to the law and by their divine training promote a city government that is perfectly obedient to the law, will that not be ten cities worth of evidence of the good creation?"

"Yes, I can see that."

"And here's something to add to it: since the devil's suit is over the question of free will, the value of any exhibit depends on the exercise of free will in it."

"I see that now too," I said. "If I still had a sinful bone in my body, I would be envious."

"Of course that's ridiculous."

"Of course it is," I echoed. "How could I begin to envy having a soul mate when I know nothing about it."

"I meant being envious of the reward of ruling over LA."

"Oh, my dear Laura, you are so right. It would be impossible for anyone to envy *that* assignment."

"Emma told me the challenges are enormous, and if it weren't for the angelic police force, order would be impossible."

"Yes, I knew about that. LA isn't quite self-sustaining yet."

"'At last Los Angeles is living up to its name,' Emma said. She told me there had been discussions about whether the city should be resurrected or left as a rural area or even made a wilderness."

"Yes, I got involved in that. The unmarked population that needed to be moved was unusually large since they had prepared to survive the tribulation. But what do you do with anti-Zionists?"

Contrary to our current topic, we both had Samson on our minds. "I'm not feeling at peace about Mr. Samson," Laura said.

"Neither am I," was my reply. "How can I say this? ... It's awkward not being able to be sad. If he only knew that fact about us."

"Either way it spells difficulty for him," Laura pointed out. "I could almost be sad, and I would cry for him if I could."

"I will see that he gets medical attention," I promised.

"It occurs to me that our Maker loves to see his creatures fulfilling the roles they were made for."

"Yes," I agreed. "He must see mistakes differently than we do."

"And obstacles and handicaps too," Laura added.

"One thing I know for sure about Samson is that he was brought here for a purpose," I asserted. "He will fulfill that, and I know I fit into it somehow."

"But isn't it lamentable that he can't be an exhibit in the trial?"

"Worse than lamentable if he doesn't apply for servant-hood," I said.

Laura bowed her head, and we said no more about him.

Chapter Eleven

With no assignment having come through from Chester at the Ministry of Information, Samson had time to work on his second boat—again in the hangar at the airport—in addition to helping with housing needs in Clarksville. Having two good hands, thanks to Dr. Franky, he was able to work much more efficiently, especially when Homer spent late afternoons with him bringing materials and food.

After the renovation was completed the airport became a rather lonely place again. But then BJ dropped in. Being on leave for two weeks, he flew in with Harold Foster. Harold was building flight time on a converted 206,[1] which left the next morning with a fully charged battery, taking away Homer and leaving BJ.

"I think I know the answer," said Samson as he and BJ watched the surprisingly quiet plane lift off after using a quarter of runway 14, "but why did you spend three days to travel by air in a plane with limited range and uncertain fueling when you could have come in no time by way of new heaven?"

"You're right. Of course it's more fun."

"But isn't it sacrilegious to say that even if it's true?"

"That's an oxymoron, Samson. Anyway, why shouldn't it be more fun?"

"Because heaven is better according to what you told me. Isn't that true? You could have spent three whole days there."

"Heaven is pleasant, but earth is in transition right now, and that makes things here very interesting. And challenging. Maybe I'm lacking spiritual refinement, but some of us are equipped to carry on the King's business down here."

"Have you any word about my airman examination?"

"Your examiner will be here on the 19th—in one week."

Because Samson and Steve were eager to get their pilot certifications—if they had an airplane—that would be good news.

---

1. Harold's design converts petroleum-fueled aircraft to electric battery power using batteries and motors taken from useless automobiles (due to their damaged digital components). Harold designs and manufactures the motor speed controllers.

BJ said he would see about making the 172 airworthy by then, although it had low compression on three of its cylinders when it had been tested. He would pull all four cylinders and make repairs, which could be done in as little as a day.

They found the pistons in poor condition, which could not be justified by the log book's entry at the last inspection. BJ said they might get by if he lapped the valves and honed the cylinders without replacing two cracked rings, but he would not recommend that. They spent the rest of the day searching unsuccessfully for the parts they needed.

In one of the hangars they found a 1972 Cessna 150 in fine condition with a panel that had not been upgraded. The owner evidently had been changing the oil and never returned to finish the job. The log book was on the workbench next to the plane.

"Donald Miller. Let me see if I can find out where he is when I go home tonight," said BJ.

"There's a Don Miller in Sellersburg," Samson offered. "He could be the same one."

"He's a natural, right? How could he abandon this little bird for twenty years? Look, here's the last logbook entry."

"True. He is a natural, and not the natural pilot type really."

"The owner was here after the Rapture. Something else took him suddenly. If he's alive on earth, I don't think he would mind if we finish his oil change."

"Cosmetically she's a cream puff," said Samson.

"Let me check the compression. There's only a hundred hours since the last major overhaul, but there could be corrosion inside, and we may still have to pull the cylinders."

Though not perfect, the compression was promising, so they went ahead and prepared the plane for testing. After replacing the fuel, adding oil, servicing the battery, and inflating the tires they got the engine started.

Since BJ was indestructible, in theory at least, he took the revived Cessna up and for the initial test flight. Then they went up together, staying within gliding distance of the airport.

"How much aviation gas do we have?" Samson asked BJ as they circled the field.

"Fortunately the av-gas tank here is above ground. I'm not sure how much is in it, but there was plenty of pressure when I cracked the drain valve to let the water out."

"You say fortunately because the pumps are out of service?"

"Right. The fuel situation at this airport has yet to be resolved. The pumps are tied into a payment network that no longer exists."

"What happens when all the fuel gets used up?"

"I asked the same question and haven't gotten an answer yet. But a plan must be in the works; otherwise they wouldn't be renovating airports."

"Could it be the plan is to go all electric?"

"I don't think so."

"What about air traffic control?"

"ATC doesn't exist, and may never be used again. My eyesight is as good as radar, and I can communicate with other glorified pilots without radio."

"If all pilots will have to be glorified, that leaves me out."

"You're exceptional, Ichabod."

"But isn't the mechanical flying machine a clumsy way of getting around for a person with a glorified body? It seems it should be the other way around: why prevent naturals from using the machines they have invented?"

"We're not that detached from our past. I can't imagine letting go of aviation."

"But I mean, naturals have even more reason to enjoy flying."

"You'd be amazed at the number of would-be pilots there are in heaven."

"All right. Contact Steve Airheart and tell him we've got a 150 in the air."

"Ha. It isn't that easy. He'd have to be listening."

"Okay, let's fly over Sellersburg. If he's down here today and hears airplane noise he will be listening."

"Good idea. You take it. You know where he's likely to be."

The next day was the 19th. BJ and Steve Antinanco were at Samson's hangar early in anticipation of Judy's arrival. She landed about noon in her yellow aerobat and taxied to the hangar. Samson had arranged chairs for everyone as he knew Judy would have a few questions for the candidates before the flight exam. I know it sounds strange to your ears if you are a natural human, but no one was interested in lunch but Samson. He lied and said he was not hungry.

Judy queried Ichabod first: "What's the minimum visibility distance you need, VFR?"

"Three miles."

"Do you agree, Steve?"

"Five miles above ten thousand feet MSL and one mile in class G, below one thousand two hundred feet AGL."

"You taught him well, Ichabod. What about cloud distance?"

"Five hundred below, one thousand above."

"Why is frost on the wings hazardous, Steve?"

"Spoils smooth airflow across wings."

"Which? ..."

"Which reduces lift."

"What's the first sign of carburetor ice, Ichabod?"

"A drop in RPM."

"In an emergency landing, you should keep your airspeed constant. Is that true, Steve?"

"Yes."

"Can you tell me why?"

"I'm trying to pick out a spot to land, right?"

"Right. Then once you've picked your spot ..."

"The problem is setting up an approach."

"Okay, instructor. Why is a constant airspeed helpful at that point?"

"Constant airspeed means constant rate of descent, so you can take that rate divided into your altitude AGL and get the time to touchdown, which will stay good if you hold the airspeed, and that allows you to time your downwind."

"Is that what you advised Steve to do when you were training him, Ichabod?"

"I probably told him: in a case where you have plenty of altitude, you can avoid wasting it by doing a little calculating."

"No, he told me to go out and practice picking a spot and setting up power-off landings."

"Okay, we'll see how well you practiced it when you take your check ride."

Samson went first. He made Judy promise not to make him do a power-failure simulation right after takeoff. Generally she was pretty easy on him, he said.

Steve said she really put him through the paces; he got to demonstrate everything including power-on and power-off stalls. She asked him if he would like to try a spin. He did, and in his exhilaration afterwards he asked her if she would teach him to do aerobatic maneuvers. Judy laughed. "Not in this little buggy."

When they got back to the hangar and she was reviewing their performances, she explained about the aerobatics.

"Belinda taught me to do rolls and loops, which are really simple beginner's maneuvers. I got tired hanging out with my former husband who spends all his time in heaven writing history."

"Who is Belinda?" Steve asked.

"Belinda manages the national flight school. I ran into her in heaven and began hanging out with her down here since we had been friends in our former lives. That's when she pressed me into taking flight lessons."

BJ stood up. "Who is this?"

A robust woman, obviously an aging natural, stood in the hangar doorway.

"I'm looking for Judge Samson," she said, peering into the shadowy interior of the hangar. "There you are. We have an issue with our neighbors. They're complaining about the noise that some of our naturals have been making."

"This is Hyacinth, by the way," said Steve Airheart. "She's an officer in the Martin family."

"Not only the Martin family. I keep the peace in the neighborhood," Hyacinth declared.

"Wait until we get more airplanes flying out of here," said Steve. "You haven't heard noise yet."

"I was going to mention that too. One flew over yesterday and then today it came back and was circling and doing irregular things. I know in the former world we tolerated airplane noise. But now we're supposed to have the perfect world. I thought we were through with being obsessed with machines. Why should we have to tolerate airplanes at all?"

"I see your point," said Judy.

"This is Judy, by the way," said Steve. "She's a flight examiner working for the kingdom."

"I can't promise there will be no airplane noise from now on," Judy continued, "but we will mark out areas for practice maneuvers that are away from residential areas."

"You haven't answered my question." said Hyacinth. "Why should there be any airplanes at all? What benefit is there to naturals who don't have the privilege of flying? What do you say, Judge Samson?"

"I don't know where you got that 'Judge' idea," said Ichabod. "Samson in the Bible was a judge in Israel, but I'm nobody special."

"Yes he is," said Judy. "He's exceptional, so I wouldn't put any limitations on him. From what I've observed in the little time I've gotten to know him is that he's more like Samson of old than he will admit."

"All right, if you want me to be your judge, we'll have a court hearing on this matter. Can you being the individuals who are concerned about this to the airport? How many do you think will want to come?"

"There's one in particular. If he knows there's going to be a decision made, he'll come and bring a few more, but not very many, I'm sure. If there's more than a half dozen willing to testify, I'd be surprised."

"Good. Tomorrow is Sabbath. Bring them or have them come at 6:30 tomorrow evening. We'll meet in the vacant hangar across the way."

After Hyacinth had left, Judy said she would have to be on her schedule and asked permission to take on fuel.

"Stay put. I'll bring the fuel truck over," said BJ.

"Ichabod, can you tell me about the boat you're building? Is it a sailboat? It looks like one. Did you design it yourself?"

"It's a replica of one I built back in the old days. It won't be quite as nice because materials are limited here. But I think she'll sail well enough."

"He knows what he's talking about," said Steve. "This is the second one he's built."

"Why do you need two?" Judy asked.

"My boss wants two of the same design so we can have races."

"That will be a lot of fun for you. Which do you like better, sailing or flying?"

"I like sailing best."

"Me too. I used to sail. Could you take me out sometime?"

"I would be honored. But there's a lady who would be hurt if she happened to see me sailing with you."

"Obviously she's a natural who hasn't been sanctified much."

"No, she's glorified."

"Then she couldn't be hurt that way."

"You're right, but she would want to go sailing with me if she could, and I'm not going to let her."

"That's funny. Why not?"

"Because she doesn't know who I am."

"You're a riddle, Ichabod. Why did Hyacinth call you Samson?"

"Samson is my name, and you've given me an idea: riddles! That's what I'll do. When I hold court on the noise issue tomorrow I'll give them a riddle to answer. It won't be an obvious one: they'll have to search their Bibles for the answer. Whoever answers the riddle correctly gets an airplane ride."

"I can see that working," said Steven Airheart. "I volunteer to provide the rides. We can do it over again in a week and so on until all the noise complainers have had their turn."

"You will find there are more than six complainers at that rate," Judy predicted.

"That's fine with me as long as the fuel holds out."

Just then BJ reappeared, saying, "Tweety Bird's topped off."

"Thank you; I appreciate it. While you were away these nuts came up with a plan to use up all your fuel," Judy informed him. "They want to give every noise complainer in the county a joyride and drain your avgas supply dry."

"I don't see any problem with that," BJ replied. "If the King's fuel makes people happy, it's all credit to the King."

"It will be interesting when the tank runs dry, though," said Steve. "Will they be happy to never see or hear airplanes in the sky, or will they miss them?"

"Let me know how it comes out," said Judy. "I have to leave now. I'm going to hop over to Blue Grass where there's a student waiting for a checkride, and I'm going to be late!"

"I'm thinking this could turn into a way to get some of those unsaved naturals interested in studying the Bible," said Ichabod.

"What will you do if nobody answers the riddle?" Airheart asked.

"Another thing you can do, Steve, is when they pressure you during the week, you can tell them where to look in the Bible."

"Then there will likely be more than one with the answer."

"In that case we'll put the names in a hat and draw one, and I'll break any tie among the others with another riddle."

"Do you have one for tomorrow?"

"I've got a day to work on it."

"What if that vocal complainer is an aerophobe?"

"That's the weakness of the plan," Ichabod admitted.

"Not really," said BJ. "Embarrassment is on our side."

"I've got one," said Samson: "Who was bound by lies and blinded by love?"

Leila Revisits Louisville
Chapter Twelve

My first encounter with Samson had answered many questions, but ignorance in this matter had been much easier to live with, for if knowledge of his location and physical condition were all I was to be given, I was at some level a failure, because I was desperate to know more, and sanctified souls are not supposed to succumb to desires of the flesh. How could it even be, since I have no flesh?

In other and better words, my heart was pulling me back to Louisville, but I had no business going there again at that time. You may want to tell me, "Pray about it!" But you must remember that we have a promise that anything we ask of the Father in the name of Jesus will be granted. When you believe that, it puts more responsibility on you than you may be prepared to handle. If you are weak in your faith, there is nothing to worry about, but if you really believe, then be prepared to deal with unforeseen consequences.

I was desperate, and I may have been foolish, but I prayed for another opportunity to travel to Louisville and speak with Samson.

• • •

Ichabod was still ignoring Lazar's request that he comply with the reporting requirements for what he was doing in Clarksville. Lazar was increasingly concerned that Stan, his boss, would ask him why he had not been performing consistent oversight in that area. It suddenly occurred to him that this was similar to the experience he had had in the former world with Earl Clark, and he wondered why he had missed the obvious: Ichabod Samson *was* Earl Clark. That explained the odd behavior of Ms. Lolomi on the marina dock and her questions about Ichabod afterward.

Now, why had Earl Clark changed his name to Ichabod? That, coupled with his altered appearance, would keep him from connecting with acquaintances from the old earth, which is one of the joys of living on or visiting new earth.

As Lazar thought back on that encounter at the marina, it was clear that Earl was embarrassed because his disguise had failed to deceive me. From there Lazar leaped ahead, skipping over such questions as whether I would want to respect his disguise, and coming to reason simply that Samson would be more respectful of authority if whatever differences he had with me could be settled. With that theory filling his imagination as a viable solution, Lazar requested a meeting to discuss the noncompliance issue with Ichabod.

Lazar, along with one other inspector, attended the meeting with Stan, which was to be brief. Lazar presented his his plan:

"I have reason to believe that there is some issue between Leila Lolomi and Ichabod Samson which only causes trouble and is not worthy of new earth. What makes that important to this department is that Ichabod will be more cooperative with authority in general if he is on peaceful terms with Ms. Lolomi."

"That's a big 'if,' young man," said Stan. "And what makes you think Ms. Lolomi would take time away from her primary responsibilities for a minor thing like that."

"I'm not sure that she would. But we could present the invitation without any pressure and see what happens."

"So you want me to tell her that you've tried everything to get Samson to follow instructions, and maybe she would be more effective in persuading him to be a good citizen of the kingdom."

"No, just tell her that if she will come here, I will arrange for her to have a meeting with Samson."

"And what if she doesn't agree to come right away? Then do I tell her to forget it?"

"I have a strong feeling that she will be happy to come again. I'm not sure why I feel that way. It came on suddenly when I was thinking back to the brief encounter they had when she was here."

"How do you know Samson will be happy about seeing her? Maybe he will resent your sticking your nose into his private affairs."

"That's a risk I'm willing to take."

"All right. Although I think you should reconcile this directly with Mr. Samson, I'll test your intuition, Lazar. In the old world I wouldn't have risked going off on a tangent like this, but recently I'm learning to obey my heart, and it's telling me to go ahead. I'll let you know when I get an answer."

"If you speak to her directly, you can easily test my intuition: if she agrees without hesitation it'll prove that my idea is sound."

"Yes, of course. The invitation will be presented as depending entirely on her interest, with no pressure at all."

That was on a Friday afternoon. I was home for Sabbath, and I stayed in heaven on Sunday. That afternoon I happened to encounter Stan who was on his way to a the opening performance of another "Samson and Delilah" ballet.

"You're not going?" he exclaimed. "I would have thought you would be first in line to get a ticket, young lady."

"No, I'm sure the dancing will be lovely, but I doubt that the story would make sense to me. I wrote my own version, you know."

"Oh, I know. Well, my date canceled. Come with me and see."

"That's kind of you, sir, but I need time to pray and plan for next week."

"'Take no thought for tomorrow,' I would have said in my old moralizing way. But on this occasion there's a reason to take thought for tomorrow. I've got an important message for you. Come with me and I'll share it with you while we're waiting for the show to start."

"Can't you tell me now?"

"Yes, I could, but you know how all things work together for good. So consider this: the message I have for you is not disconnected from the main characters in this ballet. It's funny how that idea just came to me, because I'm usually skeptical about the significance of things that can be construed by a creative mind to be divine appointments."

I held my ground for a bit longer, but Stan was adamant. I suspected this was the answer to my prayer. "All right," I said.

The next day I was in Louisville. I had gone to my office in Appleton that morning. I had to cancel three meetings that were scheduled for the afternoon. I let Stan know when I would be at the Hermon Hotel in Louisville. He sent Lazar to pick me up.

"I can't tell you how much I appreciate you're coming today," Lazar was saying. "Did Stan tell you what this is about?"

"He told me everything he knew, I'm sure, and probably a little more. I got the impression that you think I have a magic charm that will make your job easier."

"Yes I do; I really do. I've figured out that Ichabod is actually Earl Clark."

"Did you tell Stan that?"

"No. I didn't dare to."

"Good. Let's keep it to ourselves. Do you know where Earl is right now?"

"Not for certain, but unless he's gotten a ride with someone else, he's across the river in Indiana, either at the Clark County airport or working in Clarksville. I'll swing by the office and let Stan know you're here before we take off."

"He knows I'm here. He sent you to pick me up."

"I'll be all right. I'm just a little nervous, but I don't know why."

"If you can drive us across the river, then let's go. I don't have all the time in the world."

"I appreciate that you would spend any time at all on this."

After we got on the bridge Lazar shared with me his theory about why Samson was trying to hide his identity.

"Obviously, Ichabod thinks it is best if nobody acknowledges that Earl Clark received those injuries."

"You say, 'if nobody acknowledges.' In other words, knowing he is wounded is less of an evil thing than saying or acting as though it is true. Is that what you think?"

"That's what I mean. But I think he's trying to protect us—you in particular—and not himself."

"Explain what you mean."

"Take it a step back then a step forward. First, ask the question, 'Is he content being a cripple after living the life of the strong man as he did?' No, of course not. It has to be painful mentally and emotionally. Now take it a step forward: 'Why doesn't he want you to be reminding him of what he once was?' It's because he knows it would be hard on you to be doing that to him—just as much or more than it would be hard on him directly."

"I do see what you mean. You think he's content to let his disguise stand as a fictional cloak to insulate me from entering into his anguish. I'm not sure how that can be fair."

"Isn't it true that delicate things in life are commonly kept behind curtains?"

"In this case Samson's physical condition is delicate only in your mind, Lazar. Do you know what happened to him—how he was injured?"

"No."

"I think I do after watching the ballet yesterday. Samson brought the pagan temple down on himself, and it killed him. Our temple almost killed my Samson. He too wanted to die."

"Do you think he wanted you to think he had died?"

"I think he didn't want to disappoint me."

"I hope you have some idea about how you're going to resolve this."

"I don't. All I can do is be there and give him an opportunity to let down his guard. Just the fact that I've come back to visit him will tell him something."

"You're an authority figure now. If he's committed a crime that he hasn't paid for, maybe he feels vulnerable."

"That's not new. It's always been that way. You should know."

"I can see how he would think that continuing your friendship with him would be too difficult for you. Even if you convinced him that his deformity could never keep you from wanting to visit him, your future is unlimited, and his—"

"Yes, he is mortal. I've thought about that a great deal. But only his body will die, not his soul."

"Then when will these saved naturals get new bodies? It seems nobody has an answer to that question."

"There is an answer, but I can't go into it now. In the mean time I want to have his injuries taken care of properly if he will let me."

"You *do* know he's an exceptional—"

"Yes, he's as exceptional as Samson was, or *is*, I should say. Without credentials it's almost impossible to get competent medical care. But there must be a way. There's always a way. I know his present body will be healed."

"Maybe you can tell him that following all the rules to the last jot and tittle will improve his standing in the system."

"But he's not in the system, Lazar. How do you record his compliance or noncompliance?"

"That's a good question. I've never had occasion to record compliance, and I haven't attempted to put down anything for noncompliance yet."

"Do you have any evidence that his work has been substandard? ... No? ... Then why do you need him to fill out forms?"

"I don't, really. But Stan expects it."

"Maybe I could talk to Stan about that, so your purpose for calling me down here will not go unmet."

"Could you? That will make my life easier."

"Of course. I did it before, remember?"

"But Stan wasn't my boss then."

"I gave him my afternoon. He owes me a favor."

"I've a strong feeling that we'll find him at the airport, so I'm going to turn off here on **31** which will save a little time. If he's not at his hangar, we'll have to backtrack to Clarksville, and then there's no telling where we'll find him in Clarksville. But this being Monday I think he will be at his hangar working on his sailboat—or rather Chester Matthew's sailboat, as I understand it."

When we arrived at the airport Lazar admitted that he did not know in which building we would find Samson's boat shop.

"Look for a hangar door that's not tightly closed."

He drove slowly in front of a long building and eight individual hangar doors. We came to the end without seeing an open one. Around on the other side of the same building eight more doors marked eight hangars, and facing it on the other side of the driveway stood an identical building with eight doors facing us. All were tightly closed. I had assumed from Lazar's talk about Ichabod that he had been here and would know in which building we would find him. Heaven has not improved some people as much as we might wish it had.

"Don't lose heart; there's the other side of this one too." Lazar muttered as he rounded the end and proceeded on the pavement between that and yet another building with hangar doors.

But here we were presented with something very different: one of the doors was wide open, and a small, high-winged, blue-and-white airplane was parked near it—the same kind, as far as I could tell, in which he once took me for a sunset flight.

Lazar parked clear of the plane, and we walked to the wide-open doorway. He reintroduced me to Ichabod, telling him I had requested that he bring me to speak with him.

"Is that your airplane?" I asked Samson.

"I have access to it."

"May I ask you where you lived in the former world?"

"In a small town that isn't anymore."

"Because it was destroyed by the beastly regime?"

"Yes. ... This is Limpy. Say hello to Ms. Lolomi."

"*Meow.*"

"He's precious. Or is it a 'she'?"

"She's a she."

"That's so awful that the town was destroyed. Were you injured at that time?"

"No. Before."

"I believe I lived there too. Did you know Earl Clark?"

"I've heard the name."

"I wish I knew where he was."

"So do I."

"I have a vacation coming up. We should go looking for him. An airplane would be perfect. I would need air transportation because I'm limited by needing to be near one of those hotels every night."

Earl looked down at the cat. "What would you think of that, Limpy? No one would be here to feed you milk and cheese. You don't like grass. What would you do?"

"*Meow.*"

"You'd be lonely. Yes, I think you would."

Lazar spoke up: "I'll take care of Limpy for you while you're away."

The cat, seeming to disapprove of that, limped to the door and greeted two women, both of them vaguely familiar to me.

"Oh, hello, Leila!" said the older of the two.

I knew then she was Hyacinth Fuller, the police officer, slimmed down considerably. She gave me the impression that she had not come to visit; however, she explained her friend to me.

"This is Mellonie. She came with the correct answer to Judge Samson's riddle last week and she's here for the airplane ride."

Then turning to Earl she announced, "Judge, you get the honor of being the pilot today because Airheart couldn't get his act together."

"I'm so excited that I get to fly with you, sir!" gushed Mellonie. "And, Leila! Do you remember me at the Fitness Center when Earl Clark helped me learn to use the treadmill?"

I recognized her voice, and I thought her face bore some resemblance, but otherwise I would not have guessed she was the same Mellonie who back then would not have fit into the cockpit.

"Have you flown in small planes much?" I asked her.

"No. This is my first time."

"Excuse me, folks, I have to fulfill a court order. ... Where would you like to go?" Earl asked his admiring passenger as they walked out to the waiting airplane.

"I need to get back," said Lazar.

"So do I. Does God have a sense of humor, or what?"

Lolomi Lodge
Chapter Thirteen

This chapter includes material written by my dear friend Flo to whom I am indebted for that turning point in my life when I fell out of love with corridors of power in the nation's capital and into the spell of a western canyon, a rustic ranch, the family who ran it, and especially Flo who recommended a book that I read during the time she cared for me when I was ill.

But I missed my opportunity to go back. An administrative position can consume one's days as relentlessly in a lazy little town as anywhere else. While I often thought of booking a week's vacation in that lovely spot, I waited too long. Flo came to me one day looking for a job because the canyon where her home was located had been designated a wilderness reserve: her family who owned the ranch had been evicted with little compensation; the buildings had been dismantled; and the canyon had been left to the bears, the wolves, the coyote, and the deer.

Flo and I often reminisced about that place. Yes, even as we walked in a park in new heaven where gold-tipped grass that never needs mowing glows like emeralds and the bejeweled flowers that never wilt stand in beds of diamonds. We mentioned the warm fire on misty mornings, the riding trails and our favorite horses, and the waterfalls cascading down steep canyon walls.

Heaven is beautiful, and the angels glory in it, but we who are still human even in glorified bodies have an enduring affinity for the earth of whose dust we were originally made. Being near to Yeshua in the heavenly way is satisfying beyond measure, but even our King spends days on the earth. He must like it: he made it. So likewise when we descend to our places of service in the lower world we are still not separated from his worlds.

"Do you ever wish we could go back to Lolomi?" Flo asked me in a wistful tone that meant she was not confident that her feelings were entirely justified.

"Maybe we can," I said with a rush of infinite possibility that sometimes comes upon one breathing divine air.

From that spark of nostalgia came a new Lolomi!

We submitted our idea to Jerusalem, and it came to Prince Solomon's attention. He understood perfectly how and why we felt as we did, and moreover he was looking for an excuse to build something—at least that is what I think. Within a few months the road going up to Flo's canyon had been restored, a new lodge in the same style of Lolomi only larger with more rooms for guests had been constructed, a barn, a stable, and a corral had been built, and Flo had been appointed manager. There was one novel feature: one of the bedrooms on the upper floor was for transitioning to and from heaven, not for sleeping.

We had thought there would be no kitchen or any of the complications that food entails, and sanitary facilities would not be needed. So while it would be genuinely earthy, it would be exclusively like heaven. But Prince Solomon was thinking ahead. What we got instead was a guest-ready ranch including an ample dining room, a fully equipped kitchen, livestock, and a well-stocked pantry.

Flo wanted as many of heaven's saints as possible to experience Lolomi, so she made up a schedule, allocating week-long stays covering an entire year. Of course each week had to be punctuated by nightly returns to heaven; but otherwise it would be a genuine experience, lacking only the drive on the winding road.

There was little interest at first. The announcements Flo posted on bulletin boards had to compete with heaven's events and activities that were well understood. "What is this? A vacation on earth? How absurd. That's where I go to work!" I overheard someone saying.

Flo contacted a few friends whom she believed she could rely on to test this revolutionary kind of vacation. She scheduled the first week a month ahead, and as soon as four had signed up, she asked Prince Solomon for four horses. He responded immediately, arranging for six horses and a pony. The only regret he had doing this project was that he could not experience the ranch himself. He predicted it would become a great success in time.

Ellery Paine volunteered to take care of the horses. He had no regular duties on earth that would prevent him from spending every day at the ranch, and he was more than happy to do so, for he loved horses.

Pamela and Philip Evans were intrigued by the possibilities of Lolomi, and they too committed to be involved full time, which delighted Ellery. Philip pointed out that among the many natural people involved in rebuilding of the road, constructing the buildings, and transporting the horses there would likely be someone who would take unlawful advantage of the remote location. We needed to have someone on the premises around the clock. Philip consulted Adam Murphy about the problem, and Adam mentioned Rhoda the Ranger. Flo located Rhoda who said she would love to stand night watches and return to heaven during the day only when she ran out of breath, which would not be too soon.

Ellery told Jolene, the nurse who attended him the week before the Rapture, and Jolene told Jocosa about the ranch. They both wanted him to put in a good word for them. Neither one had regular duties on earth; they would make themselves useful at the ranch. Jolene wanted to know if there might be occasions when medical skill would needed. Of course she knew the answer, but it seemed she was hopeful and somewhat serious, because it was a question nobody knew a definite answer to: was it at all possible for a glorified body to sustain injury?

Jocosa begged to be put in charge of the cows and chickens.

In retrospect, our initial concept was woefully short-sighted. We thought Lolomi would be our exclusive vacation spot: for a week or two we would forsake heaven's jeweled city and escape to enjoy this organic jewel of the earth. It began much like that, but within a year we had guests coming from earth, not just heaven.

Pamela and Philip had that greater vision from the beginning, and though they were silent about it at first, they eventually brought to Flo's attention Lolomi's potential as a place for troubled boys to find joy in life and experience the love of their Savior. Far from diminishing our good times, each boy added to our joy.

Now, here is Flo's introduction and sketch of the start of a typical week at Lolomi:

From the beginning the spread looked awesome. A whole lot more was there than I ever dreamed of or even thought was possible. Solomon sure made his mark with the stable and barn and orchards. They even brought up apple and pear trees with fruit on them. Just for the looks, I thought, because a glorified body never craves fruit as far as I know. But that was before I found out that the Spirit of God had more ways to use this place than I ever thought of.

Here is what it was like after things got moving along well. I'm thinking of one particular Monday morning when I arrived about daybreak, a little earlier than usual. When I came down the stairs Rhoda was at her table by the window playing Solitaire.

I stepped outside for just a moment to check the weather. The stars were still bright in the canyon sky because it would be a while yet before we would see the sun, but it meant the sky was clear. It would be a perfect day by the weather.

When I came back inside Rhoda was shuffling the deck. "Where did you get those cards?" I asked her.

"I found them here the day after the workers left. I checked the regulations and there's nothing either for or against Solitaire. I keep them hidden away from the boys, of course."

"Well, I don't blame you. You've got the loneliest job in the world as far as I'm able to tell."

"It only lasts a few hours. Did you see that Ellery is here? He's out there with the horses already—came down a half hour ago."

"How did it go in the bunk house?"

"I checked every hour, as usual. They were worn out from the hike yesterday."

At that moment Pamela and Philip came bouncing down the stairs, fresh from heaven and full of energy.

"Good morning you beautiful saints," was Pamela's greeting. "How are the boys?"

"Still asleep," said Rhoda. "Tuckered out from yesterday. They said you and Philip took them up that trail over on the north wall."

"Are Jolene and Jocosa in the kitchen?" Philip asked.

Rhoda laughed. "Turn around. They came close behind you."

"I'll go rouse the gang," said Philip. "Put the coffee on for me today, will you, Jocosa?"

"When did Philip start drinking coffee?" Rhoda wanted to know.

"A guest from earth brought us some coffee as a gift," I explained. "It's hard to come by, you know. Philip doesn't drink it. He just likes to smell it."

"Well, I can't keep up when I'm gone half the day."

After breakfast Pamela took the boys to the chapel where her former pupils Skyler and Amber were waiting with a Bible quiz and a lesson they had prepared.

"Who wrote Proverbs in the Bible?" Skyler asked the class. ... "Does anyone know?"

"Proverbs was written by Solomon," said Salim.

"*Prince* Solomon. Was he a prince when he wrote Proverbs, Salim?"

"That was a long time ago because the Bible is thousands of years old."

"Was he King David's son?" Amber prompted.

"Yes, I think so."

"That's right, so he was a prince at that time too."

Naiche posed the dilemma: "Is he thousands of years old?"

"That's a good question," Amber said. "Sister Pamela knows."

"I'm sure he remembers things from thousands of years ago."

Amber turned to Skyler. "What do you say, teacher?"

"I like Sister Pamela's answer."

"If he forgets, he can look in the Bible," Naiche suggested.

Andre offered a solution: "If you're born in a certain year, you can find out how old you are by subtracting it from this year,"

"Well, that's usually true," said Skyler. "What year was Prince Solomon born, Amber?"

Amber turned to Pamela. "Wasn't it a thousand BC?"

"That's right."

"Solomon's older than three thousand years then," said Naiche.

"I think, Naiche, we have to say his life was interrupted, and years went by that didn't count for him," said Amber.

"But the proverbs he wrote are over three thousand years old. How could he be younger than what he wrote?" persisted Naiche.

"God inspired the Bible, so he inspired Proverbs, so it was like God really wrote Proverbs, and God is a lot older than Prince Solomon could ever be," Andre reasoned.

"It really doesn't matter how old they are, because the proverbs never grow old," Amber pointed out.

"And Prince Solomon won't grow old any more because he's been resurrected," Chizoba noted.

"He will be older, but he won't look older," Salim pointed out.

"Is that true?" inquired Naiche, but no one was listening.

"Have you all found Proverbs in your Bibles?" Amber asked the class. "Turn to chapter two. Would you like to read the first six verses, Andre?""

> *My son, if you will receive my words*
> *and lay up my commandments within you,*
> *so as to incline your ear unto wisdom*
> *and apply your heart to understanding;*
> *Yes, if you cry after discernment*
> *and lift up your voice for understanding;*
> *if you seek her as silver*
> *and search for her as for hidden treasure,*
> *then you will understand the fear of Yahweh*
> *and find the knowledge of God.*
> *For Yahweh gives wisdom;*
> *from his mouth comes knowledge and understanding.*

"What is wisdom?" Amber asked the class. "Look at verse six."

"Wisdom is knowledge and understanding," said Salim.

"Why isn't knowledge by itself wisdom?"

"You have to know what something you know means."

"What it really means, not what someone says it means," Naiche added.

"How do you know what something means?" Amber asked him.

"That's what wisdom is for," Naiche replied.

"Wasn't Solomon the wisest man in the world?" Chizoba asked.

"He prayed for wisdom and God gave it to him," Jamal replied.

"If all he had to do to become wise was to pray for wisdom, why does he say it's like hidden treasure that you have to search for?" Andre asked.

"It was a dream: Solomon awoke, and behold it was a dream," said Naiche.

"You have to believe there's treasure before you will search for it," said Jamal. "I think he believed his dream."

"What does 'cry after discernment' mean?" Chizoba wondered.

"You have to take the whole verse. The two parts of the verse go together," Skyler hinted.

"'Lift up your voice for understanding' sounds like praying," Salim suggested.

"So Solomon believed God had given him understanding, and he cried out: 'You gave it to me, now where is it?'" Naiche mocked.

"What is the fear of Yahweh?" asked Salim.

"Look at the rest of the verse: it's knowing God," said Naiche.

"It's really knowing God and how almighty he is," said Skyler.

"Verse six says Yahweh gives wisdom, and it comes out of his mouth. What does that mean?" Amber asked the class.

"It's like the first verse says to receive his words and lay up his commandments within you," Andre answered.

"Where do we find Yahweh's words and commandments?"

"In the Bible," Salim answered.

"By reading the Bible?"

"You have to seek and search for wisdom when you read the Bible," Naiche answered.

"And incline your ear: listen for the wisdom in what you read," said Amber. "And don't forget the second part: apply your heart to understand. ... Ellery and Jocosa! Come join us. I see you have your Bible, Ellery. Do you have something to contribute to our study in Proverbs?

"Proverbs! That's my favorite. Did you read this one? It's in chapter sixteen, verse twenty: 'He who gives heed unto the word will find good; and happy is he who trusts Yahweh.' Can somebody tell me what it means to give heed to the word?"

"It means pay attention to it," said Salim.

"How do you pay attention to it, Salim?"

"It means do what it says," Naiche interjected.

"Both your answers are right: pay attention to what it says and then do what it says. By the way, what is the word?"

"It's the Bible," replied Salim.

"It's all the words in the Bible," said Naiche.

"Be careful about that," said Ellery. "Some of the words in the Bible are not addressed to everyone."

"That's why you have to pay attention and find out who the words are there for," said Salim.

"Then what is the result?"

"He finds good."

"Okay, now we have to look at the second part of the verse also because they go together. See, it tells us what the first part means by 'good.' What is it?"

"He finds happiness," said Salim.

"It also tells us more about heeding the word."

"You have to trust Yahweh before you can really do what the word says," said Chizoba.

"Are you ready to trust God? What happens if you trust him?"

"You will be happy," said Chizoba.

"Ellery, I know of a time when you forgot to trust God," said Jocosa. "Do you know what I'm referring to?"

"Yes I do. Go ahead. I'm not proud."

"No, you're not proud, Ellery. That's why everyone loves you."

"You all should know from your history studies that there was a time when things were much different," said Ellery. "All around the world things were much different than today."

"That was before Prince Solomon came back," said Naiche

"And before King Jesus came back!" said Amber.

"Yes, the world had been waiting for Christ Jesus to come and rule the world as he said he would," Ellery continued. "But not all the people in the world believed he would return. Then there came a big surprise when it was announced that the translation of living Christians to heaven—and the beginning of resurrection—was to take place in exactly one week. The ones who heard the announcement were church leaders like the preacher in my church. Everyone who attended church that day heard the announcement."

"But Ellery stayed home," Jocosa reported. "He was fearful of the operation on his knee the next day which put him in a bad mood. Can you imagine Ellery being in a bad mood?"

"That's right. I was."

"The surgeon didn't know either, or else he didn't believe, and before we knew it Ellery had gotten an artificial knee and had to spend the week before his Rapture to heaven in the hospital."

"I was in a lot of pain, but the worst of it was Jocosa—and it seemed like everyone else in the hospital—thought it was funny."

"No, it really wasn't funny. We were all sorry that you had to go through with that major operation, but it was ironical: because you skipped church you didn't know to cancel the surgery that you really didn't want anyway and it turned out that you didn't need."

"I had to agree. The joke was on me. But you all made it worse because you couldn't stop laughing which made me laugh too."

"We were all so excited about going to heaven in a few days that almost anything could make us laugh."

"What was my mistake? ... It was fear. I was fearful of the oper-ation. Why was I fearful? Well, I didn't give heed to the word on that Sunday morning, so I missed finding out about the good thing that was coming. But regardless of that I wasn't happy because I wasn't trusting the Lord. So I had to spend the entire week in pain getting used to a metal knee joint which I didn't need."

"Do you still have it?" asked Naiche.

"No. Glorified bodies don't have any metal parts."

"What happened to it?" Naiche persisted.

"I'm not sure. What did you decide, Jocosa?"

"The Rapture was a grand miracle. Nothing but a little dust was left behind when we disappeared and reappeared in new heaven."

At that juncture the bell rang for lunch, and Jocosa waved goodbye and hurried out the door.

"Will there be another Rapture for us?" Chizoba asked.

"No. That was a very special event like the great flood in Noah's day was a one-time event," Pamela explained. "Class is dismissed!"

"What will happen to us when we die?" Salim asked her.

"If you trust Jesus, he will keep you from all harm and someday you will receive a glorified body."

Jocosa was in the dining room completing the table settings and Philip was helping Jolene in the kitchen as the boys and I arrived at our places with clean hands. Presently, Amber, Skyler, and Pamela joined us.

Pamela previously had coached Jamal and announced that he would offer a prayer of thanksgiving for the meal.

"We thank you, Father, for providing food for our bodies and souls today. And I thank you for these new friends and bringing me to Lolomi Ranch. ... Amen."

"What are we having for dessert?" Naiche asked immediately.

"We don't serve dessert for lunch," Philip informed him. "And it's not guaranteed that we'll get dessert after supper."

"You could pray for dessert," said Chizoba seriously.

"I tried praying for dessert before, and it didn't work," Naiche said.

"What did you pray for? Chocolate pie?" Andre goaded.

"God won't answer a prayer for something that's not good for us," said Jamal.

"Don't you think an apple is good? That's what I prayed for," Naiche said.

"Sometimes God answers with something that's better," said Skyler.

"What's better than an apple?" argued Naiche.

"Isn't this meal a whole lot better than an apple? And don't forget everything you ate for breakfast," Amber admonished.

"I wasn't talking about that. I asked God for dessert now, and what Mr. Evans said seems to be my answer. It's *no*. Period."

"There's apple trees in the orchard, but the apples aren't very big, and they're probably not ripe yet," Andre reported.

"Sometimes the answer you get is *wait*," Amber suggested.

Naiche laughed.

"I mean as a general principle, not pertaining to your dessert prayer," she clarified.

"No, that's fine," said Naiche, "I'll wait," and he laughed again.

"Someone's here," Jamal announced.

"Who is it?" Naiche demanded.

"I don't know. Some tall man walked by the window."

Adam Murphy appeared in the doorway with a large red apple in his hand, saying: "Did someone ask for an apple?"

"He did!" several said, pointing to Naiche.

"Here you are, son. It was the only ripe one. It's too early to be ripe, but there it was."

"It's not for me," said Naiche. "It's a mistake. I really didn't pray for an apple."

"Well, it's yours. It's surely a gift from God."

"It's so big. ... Can I share it?"

"Yes you may share it," said Pamela. "Take it to the kitchen and ask Sister Jolene to cut it in five pieces for you."

After lunch comes R&D—rest and private devotion time—until two o'clock. No walking or talking is allowed during that hour. On the first day this is really difficult, and this was the first time these boys had experienced this discipline—except Salim who had been here before. (They came in yesterday afternoon, had an early dinner and went with Philip and Pamela on a hike.)

The bell rings for Chore Time at two o'clock. Each person—not just the boys—gets assigned to a particular task. Ellery takes two boys to help him clean the barn. Philip takes one boy to collect and cut firewood. Flo takes two or more to help in the garden—weeding this time of year. Jocosa and Jolene would be busy with the chickens and cows. Skyler and Amber clean the floors and restrooms in the lodge, and they do it cheerfully and well.

Then comes recreation time. Ellery and I take two for horseback riding. The horses are gentle with children, which makes it easy and safe. Skyler and Amber conduct horseshoe games. Philip and Pamela lead a short hike.

After the evening meal we meet in the chapel again where Pamela leads vespers with singing and sharing.

Chizoba was silent during the singing. At the end of the service he raised his hand. "Is that man who brought the apple still here?" he asked Pamela.

"I don't think he is here right now. He's very busy in heaven, but he volunteered to take care of the orchard here at Lolomi, so he appears from time to time."

"I wanted to thank him. If you see him, could you tell him?"

On my way upstairs to "Jacob's ladder" I met Rhoda coming down for the night.

"Oh, you poor thing!" she said. I must have looked every bit as tired as I felt. "Can you make it up to the room on your own, or do you need a tow?"

The next morning when I came down thoroughly revived, Rhoda was there with her Solitaire cards.

"I can't tell that you've lost any of your energy, Rhoda," I said.

"I have, actually. It was an unusual night."

"Tell me about it. Are the boys okay?"

"They're fine. Someone didn't close the hen house door securely, and a coyote got it open."

"Well, I know exactly what that sounds like."

"The noise woke Salim, who came to get me, but I was already on the scene. The gunshot must have woken the others."

"Did you kill the coyote?"

"No. It was hard to see him clearly by starlight. He got away with one chicken."

Pamela and Philip had come down and overheard our conversation.

"Doesn't the Bible say the lion will lie down with the lamb?" Rhoda asked Pamela.

"Yes, but it doesn't promise that the coyote will lie peacefully beside the hen."

"That critter must be from the old stock," I said. "But I don't mind having some of them around. It reminds me of the old ranch. Things are pretty easy compared to the way it was then."

That is how Flo concluded her sketch of a Monday at Lolomi. It fits into my story perfectly, since my vacation had been delayed a day. I met Rhoda on the stairway. She seemed to be in a hurry to get back to heaven. We exchanged greetings, and that was all.

This was a day I certainly did not want to miss, because we had planned an overnight camping trip on horseback. I went out to the stable where Flo had gone already. Ellery was there, of course. I had gotten in a little riding experience in the few times I had been able to visit Lolomi, so I had no apprehension.

How would we be able to spend a night away from heaven, you might ask? The answer is we were not sure but were willing to experiment. I had stretched my stay on earth before, up to about twenty hours, and certainly some had gone longer than that. We would spend the night at a higher altitude where the air is closer to that of heaven—we had told each other. But there was no scientific basis for that. We knew that whatever happened it would not kill us, and angels would come to take us home if necessary.

Ellery was quite concerned that it might happen, and he had an idea: "Let Salim go with you on the pony. He is an accomplished rider." Salim had a special place at the ranch. He was there full time, while the other boys were there for the week.[1]

Philip, Pamela, Flo, and myself expected to be joined by Adam and Evelyn. Since we were all from heaven we needed no food, but with Salim along there would be meals to plan; and to make him feel comfortable we would all join Salim and the horses in partaking of earthly food. "You'll be surprised at how good beans taste when they're baked in the coals of a campfire," Flo told me.

I had a feeling that Adam would go immediately to his orchard, so I told Flo I would go and make sure he would not keep us waiting too long, because he loved his trees so much that he tended to lose track of time. Indeed, I found him there carefully examining the apple trees. He said he was still curious about how that one apple he found yesterday had gotten to be so large.

"Here's an exceptionally large one, Adam," came a familiar voice from behind us. Evelyn had arrived, and knowing where she would find Adam she came stealthily to the apple grove. "May I pick it?"

"Go ahead, Eve. We have permission this time. It's harmless. Give it to Leila; she can give it to Salim for lunch."

"How did you know Salim is going with us?" I asked Adam.

"Going with us? What do you mean?"

"Didn't I tell you?" Evelyn asked him. "Today is the day of our overnight camping adventure on horseback."

---

1. I had adopted Salim and given him that privilege.

"Well, yes you did, but I thought it was yesterday, and when I got here late and found everyone at lunch I assumed it had been called off because it was an outrageous idea. Leila, do you mean everyone is ready to go, and you were waiting for us?"

"Almost. The plan was for six of us from heaven because there are six horses. Now we've added Salim who has his own pony. Right now they're getting together some food and equipment for a campfire tonight."

Flo was anxious that we get started because she knew the trail and how long it would take to get to the top of the ridge where she had in mind a fine spot to camp near a stream with grass nearby for the horses, and it would not do to arrive after it became too dark to see well.

"I haven't tried it myself, but I've heard that we see about as well down here at night as we do in bright sunlight," I said.

"That's a heaven-legend," said Flo, "perpetrated by those whose imaginations substitute theory for experience."

"I wouldn't be frightened in the dark—at least I think I've gotten over that. Of course we don't want to frighten Salim."

"Yes, and I wouldn't want to test the horses on a narrow trail after dark," Flo added.

"Are there coyotes up there?" I asked Flo on a whim. "I still remember that night when they chased me out of the woods with their shrill cries."

"Could be. We just lost a chicken to one of the old breed. Rhoda shot at it, but it was dark and it got away. So there's our proof that we don't see well at night."

"Can we get some of the new kind to guard our campsite?"

"I reckon that's a good idea. Ask Adam."

Flo took the lead, followed by Salim on the pony, then me on my new Baxter, then Evelyn followed by Adam, then Pamela, and finally Philip bringing up the rear. Ellery was left in charge at the ranch, with Jocosa and Jolene. (Skyler and Amber had stayed home in heaven that day.) We followed a lively little stream of crystal clear water that flows down from the head of the canyon.

The sky was mostly clear and the air was warming pleasantly as we approached noon. We saw several deer. They seemed more intelligent—more circumspect and deliberate in their motions—than those I had observed in the old earth.

We stopped for lunch in a place with grass for the horses. Salim loosened up and admitted he was enjoying himself. Jolene had packed a cheese sandwich and cookies for him. I gave him the apple. I stayed by Salim while the others nibbled on cookies and strolled around. There were bees about which ignored us, but the butterflies were friendly in that spot, which delighted Salim when they would land on his outstretched palm. Adam discovered a new kind of berry bush. The fruit, somewhat like a raspberry, was soft and came off easily. He tasted it and declared it edible, so we all had a taste. Salim liked them very much and was still picking and eating them when Flo brought him his pony.

We all remounted and followed Flo in the same order, crossing the shallow stream and heading toward the south side of the canyon. If Flo was following a trail, it was invisible to me. She had been there many times—and I had been there once—but that was many years ago in the old life. During the intervening years when the canyon was closed to humans no riders would have been there to keep the trail fresh, but in the tribulation period and since then riders might have gone this way.

Nevertheless, Flo did not hesitate until we came quite close to the canyon wall. She stopped and turned her horse to face us.

"This is different than what it was," she said. "I was a little bit afraid that the earthquakes might have caused slides that are now blocking the trail. It seems that's what happened here. But there's another way. We have to backtrack a little."

With that, Flo did a "U" turn. We followed her back along the southern side of the canyon, weaving among trees and uneven ground where there was no trail. After perhaps half an hour we came to a break in the canyon wall where it met an arm that rose gradually to the south. Flo seemed to find a trail there as well—or what had been there and lived permanently in her memory.

By a generally easy incline we reached the plateau in spite of more than one rock slide we had to circumvent.

The place we came to on the canyon rim was not what I remembered; it was not the same as the spot where we camped when I was there in the flesh many years ago. But it was a good place because there was water and grass for the horses. Really, we had no choice, because there was no time to go looking for a better location. Fortunately, the wind was very light.

The most suitable area for the horses was out of sight of the spot we preferred to camp, so someone would have to spend the night with the horses.

There was no time to waste. Flo gathered up twigs and pine needles for a fire starter and went to work with flint and steel. Philip took Salim and the hatchet to procure dry branches of suitable lengths. It was not long before they had tongues of flame licking the larger sticks, and soon the fire was making coals. I supervised Salim as he made biscuit dough. We placed the dough in a covered pan and set it near the fire, rotating it often. Pamela put dried beans and water and seasonings in another pot—no pork!—and suspended it directly over the coals.

Meanwhile, Adam and Evelyn had gone to explore the immediate area. When they returned they were not alone. A large wolf walked between them as if he were a well trained pet. We could see very easily that he was of the new-earth breed by the look of intelligence in his eyes.

"He came to guard us and the horses tonight," Adam said. "Beautiful, isn't he? I wish I knew his name."

I believe the animal understood what Adam had said, for he wagged his tail like a dog and seemed to be very pleased with our company.

"What will he eat?" Salim asked.

"He eats grass like the horses, as far as I know," said Adam. "But offer him a biscuit."

The food was delicious, somehow. We all had a bite of biscuit and a little of the beans, except Salim who ate heartily.

After the fire had burned down the smoke forced Salim to stand and take a few steps away. Philip offered to take him and climb the nearby ridge because the sky in the west was showing sunset colors and they would have a better view from there. Flo and Pamela joined them, while Adam, Evelyn, and I huddled around the fire, for the air had become chilly. Our eyes were not much bothered by the smoke, but energy is energy and we needed to conserve what remained in bodies meant for heaven. The glowing embers held my gaze as I remembered a dream.

"Earl would love to be here," I said, forgetting that my companions would have no reason to think of him in connection with Lolomi.

"Oh? Did he know about the original Lolomi?" Evelyn guessed.

"Yes, not the one Flo's parents built: the original. The original Lolomi lodge was in a different canyon somewhere in the southeast. How much of it was real and how much was an invention of Zane Grey's mind, Earl and I couldn't decide. When I described in detail what I experienced, he knew exactly how I felt, because he had read the book too, and he was able to imagine Lolomi as I had experienced it. So that's why I say Earl would love to be here."

"Did you chose your new name?" Evelyn asked me.

"I had a dream the night before the Rapture. I dreamed of a heavenly Lolomi Lodge that I entered magically through a door that had my name on it: *Leila Lolomi.* Both of you were there. Flo was there. My horse Baxter was there. Salim was there, and he was presented to me as a son. When at the Rapture training camp I was called Lolomi instead of Labaki, I liked it of course."

"Was Earl in your dream?" Adam asked me.

"No. I wasn't thinking of him at that moment because, well, Jesus was there. But Earl was in the dream at the beginning."

"We're all wedded to King Yeshua now, but that doesn't make Earl's absence seem fair," Evelyn said.

"He's officially an exceptional man," said Adam. "It's not an error or an accident. Earl was called out of the past as we were, and though there was no formal school for him, he will succeed."

"Tell me more," I said. "I seem to have an enduring connection with him. Am I destined to play a role in his future?"

"Earl was called to fulfill a high purpose. That's all we have been able to find out. But the implication is that he will be doing something that will please King Yeshua."

"We think of you as our daughter," said Eve, "so we are always looking out for you, which is how we know something about your connection with Earl."

"Oh! Do you know all about my dream? You and Adam adopted me with Yeshua's blessing."

"I believe your dream was inspired," said Adam. "Essentially it predicted today, did it not? Such were the dreams of the prophets which found their way into history."

"This feels like a dream to me," I said. "Like I'm asleep dreaming about having come home. Heaven is home, of course. Maybe it's because Earl isn't there. I can imagine him being here, but not there. I wonder where he is right now."

"One doesn't need to be a prophet to predict that he will be looking for you," said Evelyn.

"I've nearly forgotten the stars," Adam remarked, leaning back. "It will be a treat when it gets darker. Even now new stars are appearing every moment."

Then suddenly an angel appeared as if floating down in the updraft of the fire. He apologized for interrupting our cozy fellowship, but he had a word for Adam:

"You omitted signing out for this overnight. If it was an oversight, and you are not here against your will, I will correct the record for you."

"Yes, it was an oversight. Thank you for watching over me."

After the angel departed, Evelyn turned to Adam: "I recall that you often cited Murphy's Law to explain how things went wrong if there was any chance that something could go wrong. The assumption was that Murphy's Law was part of nature in the fallen world. Have you considered that you yourself may have been enforcing Murphy's Law?"

Having escaped from Babylon (after losing Lucy to the Rapture), to Moscow (where his dog was stolen from him), and finally having been sent back to his own country, Larry Link worked for United Express in Redmond long enough to save for a taxi ride home, only to find that his town had been evacuated and destroyed. His house was a heap of ashes. The Beach House alone remained unscathed, as if it had been invisible to the enemy.[1]

Enid and Ernie, the couple who had valued a cruise vacation more than the Rapture (but now had faith that the Beach House would keep them from harm during the tribulation), were the residents when Larry arrived. Enid, who claimed that an angel had predicted that she would become mayor, generously took Larry in along with "Brother" Ned, one of the few survivors.

This town[2] suffered no further damage during the height of heaven's outpouring of wrath. There were no damaging earthquakes, and no plague spoiled the lake upon which they depended for water and fish. Their greatest tribulation was being unable to buy food and household supplies; they had no transportation for such distances nor had they any means of communication.

Thanks to their Bible studies, they patiently endured their isolation, believing it would end in a few years. But while they trusted that their remote location (plus the fact that the town had been officially vacated) would keep them from being noticed by the beast of Revelation 13, they could not be certain that their refuge would last until the arrival of the armies of heaven.

"We can't buy or sell anything anyway, so why should the mark of the beast be forced on us?" Larry reasoned.

They were ever conscious of the possibility of being seen when they ventured into the ruins and were therefore cautious. Nevertheless, they found useful items that had not been destroyed which supplemented their limited equipment at the Beach House.

---

1. This venerable structure, located on the bay north of town, was completed in 1930 by pioneer Joe Martin and his son Ephraim.
2. It had been my town as well.

When they saw Christ return (as everyone did) they knew the tribulation had ended: dark clouds suddenly covered the sky with flashes of lightning, and an image of a rider on a white horse swept over their heads from east to west. Then the sky cleared.

The omen drove every doubt out of mind: this was the event of the ages. Never before in human history had it been possible to celebrate without reservation, for every day, in every corner of the earth, there had been groaning in anticipation of this since Eden.

What did Ernie and Enid, Larry, and Bro. Ned do in response? Were they speechless? Did they shout for joy? I cannot say for certain. But certainly they had no reason to fear the beast now, so they boldly strove to rid their land of rubble.

Day after day they worked more hours—as much time as could be spared after the chores of living—because they expected that resurrections would soon be manifesting everywhere, and they wanted to be in positions of leadership and not regarded as inferior citizens even if their physical bodies were inferior. I cannot blame them if they felt they might be treated as slaves if they did not assert themselves. While they stood on the promise of eternal life as disciples of Christ, they thought the only passages in Scripture that might apply to their temporal treatment in the company of resurrected saints were those that urged diligence on the part of slaves and the expectation of just treatment by their masters.

But to make a significant dent in the ruins would take months at the rate they were going, and to complete the cleanup by hand —let alone rebuild anything—even in a lifetime was unthinkable. Yet what else were they to do? They were unaware that supernatural forces were at work and that angels were involved in other places where cities had been devastated or condemned. Our town had always been set apart to the point of seeming nonexistent, so even if Mayor Enid had known about the divine plan for cleansing the earth, she would not believe she had the right to petition for any sort of priority. So they slogged on to show themselves approved. In truth they were slaves of their old-world assumptions.

Unusual precipitation both in frequency and intensity prevented them from working, sometimes for days, but the washing away of soot and ashes more than made up for the loss of their efforts on those days. Whether due to the rain or changes in the soil or some new feature of the new earth, aggressive green shoots pushed up through the rubble with relentless force, even splitting concrete. These were plants of a kind never seen before; they were in no way noxious to the touch and were easily cut, yet when dried they made acceptable fuel for the stove, even giving off a pleasant aroma. As these changes were noticed, they began to appreciate that an invisible hand was working with them.

As weeks of the slaving work became months, they made noticeable progress in clearing obstacles from the streets. While that was their priority, they continued to explore the ruins for salvageable items. Anything that could serve as a tool or become part of a tool was especially prized: things such as shovel blades, axe heads, and saw blades—even without the wooden and plastic handles. You can imagine their delight when they found a steel cabinet in a basement that contained four brooms in good condition— because the bristles on the brooms from the Beach House had been worn down to stubs.

Despite these encouraging signs that suggested a new supernatural element in the natural order, they had to wonder what had gone wrong, because surely this was not how the new earth was meant to be enjoyed. What were they not doing that they should be doing? The return of Christ was supposed to make the earth seem like heaven. Were they missing everything because they were in the wrong place? Or were the benefits only for the resurrected, not for those who had lived through the tribulation?

"I would give anything to see a five-minute news report about what's going on in Jerusalem right now," Larry Link said one day, leaning on his shovel.

It was a warm day, and they were all weary of sweeping and scraping.

"Let's go for a swim," Bro. Ned suggested.

At that moment, as if some listening ear in the heavens had dispatched aerial supervision, the hum of a single-engine airplane came out of the west. They stood, listening and wondering. Angels they would have welcomed, but no one had prepared them to expect machines in the air over new earth. The noise gradually increased then burst upon them like a clap of thunder as a vintage Cessna 206 came low across the hill and out over the lake where it wheeled around in a steep bank, cut its power to a whisper and quickly disappeared over the hill.

"It's landing at the airport!" Larry exclaimed, tossing his shovel aside. "I'm going to find out what's going on in this world." He left the others standing in awe and wonder as he took off running down Main Street toward Hill Street.

"I'm glad to see Larry is making good use of my street sweeping," Bro. Ned remarked dryly.

"It sounds like the plane landed successfully," Enid noted while Ernie muttered, "I figured the enemy bombed the runway."

"Let's be cautious," said Ned. "I'm going back to the house."

Larry slowed to a walk as he climbed Hill Street and then ran down the other side. He crossed the highway, but before he reached the airport he met Harold Foster walking toward him.

This was Larry's first encounter with a glorified person. He beheld a glorifying result of the Rapture that he had never contemplated, yet he was sure he was looking at Harold Foster. Harold's voice soon confirmed he was not an apparition.

Before Larry could ask Harold about happenings elsewhere on earth Harold began rattling off plans for developing his business. He mentioned the demand for aircraft and the universal destruction of digital devices that put most vehicles out of service. Then he explained that certain electric motors were uncomplicated and many storage batteries were usable but useless without charging equipment. In automotive applications the controller between the battery and the motor had to adjust torque smoothly and also operate in braking mode as a charger. But on an airplane the controller's duties were less, so it could be much simpler.

"You won't find anyone here who wants to buy an airplane," Larry interrupted him.

"I understand you're in a little bit of recession right now," Harold returned in like humor. "But things will get better."

"That's good. Now tell me why you're here," Larry demanded.

"I want to put our town on the map. ... You're laughing. Do you think that's incredible? I've been in Bellingham, and I've seen what can happen in a short time."

"Tell me about it."

"I've designed a controller that uses old technology. There was a time when electric trolleys and diesel locomotives operated without electronics. Their speed controls were very simple, so it can be done. I was glad to find the runway here at Sorek in good condition and my old hangar standing, because I want to make the controllers here. First I'll convert that 206 you saw and then sell similar controllers and also offer consultation for doing 206 conversions to electric. Suitable motors can be found, and batteries are available at no cost from vehicles that have been abandoned. All things work together for good, Larry."

During that conversation they were walking back the way Larry had come. Although Harold had gotten a glimpse of the ruins on his fly-over, he was speechless as they trudged down Hill Street. On Main Street they walked in silence beside the ruins until at its end they found Ernie trying to pry apart charred structural members of what had been the Lakeview Restaurant.

"Harold, is that you?" Ernie said. "I though it would be. But you're looking so good. I can't believe it's you!"

"Well, Ernie, I can't say I'm sorry you missed the Rapture because we all have our parts to play in God's great plan. Larry tells me you've been working like this since day one."

"Even before that. We've been doing whatever we found we could do."

"I'm going to sit Harold down and have him tell us everything he knows about what's going on in Bellingham," Larry declared, "—and anywhere else he knows about. You don't want to miss it."

Harold and Ernie followed Larry to the Beach House by way of the shoreline path, crossing Gold Creek on the footbridge they had built.[1] Once at the house, Larry demanded they sit down, forego small talk, and find out from Harold what was going on in Bellingham and beyond. But Enid and Ned kept remarking about Harold's glowing health, which I think is something Larry would have been more interested in if he had thought of Lucy.

Harold told them about the conditions in Bellingham, the cleanup, and the building of dwelling places for the resurrected. He explained the two kinds of immortal people: those taken in the Rapture like himself being heaven dwellers, visiting earth when needed, and those resurrected from death being permanently at home on earth. Before the first resurrected family arrived, the glorifieds had prepared a dwelling place for them.

This was too much for Ernie: "Now wait a minute," he said, "Jesus promised he was going to build a dwelling place for us, and it was going to be in his Father's house."

"Actually, that was a promise to his disciples, not everyone," countered Bro. Ned.

Harold then told them about the precision planning required to bring people from the point of physical death to resurrected life on earth. In heaven—original heaven, not new heaven—the immediate presence of the Father sanctified each spirit, making him or her compatible with the new body they would inhabit on earth. The family arrangements were determined there as well.

He explained that on a preset day and hour the materialization of twenty-four fifty-member families takes place in each of the marriage banquet halls in Jerusalem. One week later, each of the twenty-four families in the banquet hall transitions to its permanent dwelling place in a miraculous moment. This may be considered the moment of resurrection, for it is the beginning of resurrected life with a definite calling in the Savior's kingdom.

---

1. Joe Martin put in a bridge at that location strong enough to take horses and wagons before he built the Beach House, because it greatly shortened the distance to town. This bridge that Enid had the boys build was wide enough for one person. (The original bridge was removed before my time at the FSA in compliance with the regulation that prohibited humans from going near the creek.)

"How many families are in Bellingham now?" Larry asked.

"Four at present. The first to come was a construction company—they all have building construction as a vocation. It took a few of us from new heaven several weeks to build their fifty-room mansion to meet the deadline—and *then* it wasn't finished. The family members had recent experience with similar construction, so they would have finished it themselves, but it was more urgent for them to get another building put up for the next family—which has agriculture and fishing experience. Then came a family with expertise in transportation—I'm involved with that one as an overseer—and the fourth family is full of educators."

"How long did it take for the first family to eventually finish their building?" Larry asked.

"It still lacks some details like showers and interior doors. Finding hardware and plumbing items is a problem because the factories are gone, so now supplies must be local. To remedy that, the technology department at the new university is teaching old ways of making things—methods that require minimum capital."

"Can the students be regular people like me?" Larry inquired.

"Anyone can apply. We have a mixture of naturals and resurrected students. We're limited on space until we get new buildings. We're using part of the old high school campus temporarily."

"Weren't the buildings in Bellingham ruined?" Ned asked. "I thought the bowls of wrath ruined just about everything in places where there was anything to ruin. We only escaped the worst of it here because this town got destroyed early."

"Quakes took down tall buildings, and the ensuing tsunamis washed things out into the bay. Then when our King arrived he decreed that angels would organize a cleanup."

"If it was organized by angels, who did the work?" Ernie asked.

"The survivors had fled the city, trying to find refuge in the farmlands. The vast majority—those who bore the mark of the beast—found they could buy neither food nor shelter. The angels took advantage of that by luring them back to the ruins with manna—food from heaven—and forced them to carry out orders."

"What became of them after that?" Ned pursued. "Were they integrated back into the general population?"

"No. Those who survived years of forced labor were taken to other areas where cleanup had not been started—areas not scheduled for rebuilding at present. For some of them it was going back home, but not to live."

"I thought you said all modern vehicles went out of service because of the electronics," Larry said. "Then how were the cleanup crews taken to other areas?"

"Angels took them directly. Angels can do that. It's not their preferred method, but they transport people when necessary."

"Then did they get set free at some point?" Ned asked.

"No, because they could not buy or sell with the mark of the beast on them. They all died early either from the hard labor or from starvation if they got stranded without daily manna."

"I understand Solomon is the prince in charge," said Enid. "How does he justify such cruelty?"

"He always had forced labor going for his kingdom," Harold continued. "I suppose he sees nothing wrong with it. But think of it this way: when those folks took the mark of the beast, they decided to worship the devil. So their lot is like Satan's. They made their choice and were generally not repentant; they were angry about the treatment they were getting. Enforcing law and order among naturals who refused the devil's mark is difficult enough without the sworn enemies of the law wreaking havoc."

"Now the Rapture makes sense," Larry declared.

"Tell them what you mean, Larry."

"Okay. What a letdown it would be if you expected a mansion prepared just for you and then you were told you had to build it yourself! Even if you're a builder and like putting up buildings, it would be a shock to find yourself standing out in the rain on your first day in what you supposed was heaven. The Rapture to new heaven solved that problem because the glorifieds don't need dwelling places on earth. So they're available to build mansions for the builders."

Ned asked, "If each family specializes in some activity, like builders, for example, and they come with experience, don't they have different ways of doing things?"

"That's not so much of a difficulty with people who are members of the body of Yeshua first and members of the family second. But still, if the members come from different times with different ways of doing things, they're faced with the need to work out standards, which could take weeks and months before they begin to contribute to the economy. So, for the sake of efficiency at least, the family members are drawn from the same period."

"But," Enid interrupted, "if they hire naturals to do some of the work, don't they have to be from the years just before the Rapture? Otherwise, they wouldn't even understand modern speech."

"Yes, as late as possible, and getting fifty modern builders from a place the size of Bellingham was not possible, so we included resurrectees who had lived in surrounding areas."

"Doesn't that put those areas at a disadvantage?" Larry asked.

"Yes, they're left to the local naturals who will eventually migrate to places where they can find employment. The plan is to resurrect certain cities and leave others in their graves until later."

"Then what about the saints from *earlier* times?" asked Ned. "They can't be left in heaven without resurrected bodies forever!"

"No, they're resurrected with their contemporaries in places where they can preserve their time-period's culture. In fact, I think that's what will happen here in this town."

"Do you mean old-timers like Joe Martin will show up?"

"I think so."

"How will you build a mansion here in this desolate place?" asked Ernie. "There's no materials and no tools."

"That's not a problem. They settled here because they're pioneers at heart. There's nothing they like better than building things from scratch. That's heaven to them. Put them in a nice mansion and they'd be out building cabins in the woods. Give a pioneer an axe and a hammer and he'll build anything."

"Well, we've got the axe head and the hammer," said Ernie.

Enid was wondering: "If you bring in resurrected folks from other areas, the naturals might resent being a minority. I know in Bellingham, Christians weren't appreciated, to put it mildly."

"How many of those who disliked Christians would have refused the mark? Not many. But there are those libertarian types who are opposed to regulated morality. They would have left if they had transportation. But they're not the adventuresome types, and they rather like being where they can complain. That's another reason powered vehicles have been made rare; it keeps rebels on a short leash and prevents them from organizing."

"From what you said it sounds like resurrected saints run the local government, which leaves naturals like us out," said Ned.

"The laws and the entire governmental system come from above; no legitimate legislation goes on at the local level, so that eliminates one kind of contention among citizens since complaints have to be directed to Jerusalem. The laws which every citizen is expected to know and obey are handed down from heaven while the local judiciary is made up of elders from the families. Administrative responsibility for appointing magistrates is in the hands of glorified overseers. Naturals tend to treat us like angels."

Then Enid ventured to ask, "What is heaven like?"

"I could not begin to tell you in the time I have left today. On another day maybe I could answer your questions about new heaven. But I must tell you that I need to go back up tonight, or an angel will come for me, and that would leave my airplane here with no way for me to get to it because the nearest place that connects with new heaven is in Bellingham."

Larry wanted to know more about that, so he walked with Harold back to the airport, asking, among other things, "Why does your portal to heaven have to be restricted to one place?"

"Think about how disruptive it would be if people from heaven could materialize anywhere."

"Disruptive? It would be spooky!"

"Also, if there were no limitations there might be collisions, which could injure someone."

"That makes sense. ... You said Joe Martin might show up and there's a Joseph Martin in your transportation company. He isn't the same Joe Martin that built the Beach House, is he?"

"He's the same man, Larry. He really is. It took me awhile to accept that, but I believe he's genuine. He was born a century before anyone else in the family."

"How does he get along? It must be a culture shock for him."

"Joe is still a very practical man and always will be. He likes to be doing things—building things, repairing things. He likes work, and likes to be busy. Having work to do is heaven to him. Most of those born a century later are programmed to think of heaven as eternal retirement, so Joe gets his pick of the jobs he wants to do, and the others look on him like he's a living history lesson."

"What kind of transportation is available in Bellingham?"

"I assume you mean vehicles. We have bicycles, buggies, a vintage fire truck, and one ancient diesel van. There's a limited amount of fuel in storage tanks, which we're saving for emergencies, but we have one young man who makes bio diesel, and he's been successful in getting the van run on it."

"Does your family include any professional drivers?"

"No, because they haven't been resurrected yet. The resurrection of motorized vehicles has to come first."

"I can understand that. But I wouldn't mind learning to drive a buggy, though I've never been around horses. ... How do the wealthy—that is formerly rich—people like living in the same mansion with common people?"

"Those types are in with the education family where there's no manual labor and they can claim whatever status they like."

"So who operates your bikes and buggies if most of your transportation company aren't keen on it?"

"The naturals need jobs to survive. We have managers (who are not very good managers because they're inexperienced), but they hire local naturals to run the vehicles."

"I can see it would be a test for naturals. But are resurrected folks being tested too?"

"They are, but they don't know they are. The educators are supposed to be offering a course that teaches the great purposes of this millennial kingdom. I've heard they're not happy with the textbook Jerusalem sent them, so something needs to be done about that."

"You seem to see things more clearly than they do. Are the glorified different in that respect?"

"We went through an intensive sanctification process on this earth before we were graduated to glorification. On the other hand, while their route to resurrection included sanctification, it was far removed from the stresses of this earth, so it was rather academic, and consequently their sanctification needs challenges before it becomes fully developed."

"It just occurred to me why Joe Martin was included in your family. He would know more about horses and buggies than anyone from the later generation or even the naturals."

"That's right. And where do you suppose we got the wagons and carriages?"

"I suppose Joe Martin built them."

"He also trains riders and drivers. They're all naturals. Some of them lived here in our town before it was destroyed."

The next day Harold came back and he brought Joe Martin with him. As the two of them walked along Main Street, Joe reminisced about what had been there when the mine was in operation and the town was prosperous. There were no later buildings there to tempt his curiosity as he remembered former days.

"But it was not all good," he said. "I left for a few years, you know, and when I got back the pioneering was over. There was no glory if you worked in the mine or in the woods. Drinking and gambling and fighting consumed what little spirit those men had left in them after their day's work. I dream of what it will be like if we're all sanctified souls living here, doing honest work and blessing our neighbors. We could be nearly independent of the world if we live like they did in the early days before the investors came in and built the railroad."

Harold had a purpose in bringing Joe with him. He wanted to investigate the possibility of using the hydroelectric plant that was built by the mining company. It had been in use until late century when the town was connected to the grid—which went down during the tribulation because it depended on digital-electronic controls. Joe had worked at the local plant briefly as an operator.

When Harold and Joe reached Park Street they found the tiny population at work.

"When I heard your plane come in I thought you were bringin' in a crew in to help us," said Ernie.

"This is the man who built the house you're living in, Ernie. I told you about Joe Martin, and here he is. I've told him about all of you. Joe, I would like to introduce you to Ernie's wife, Enid, who was declared by an angel to be our mayor. Ned over there is the man with the shovel, and Larry Link is the guy with the grin."

"Very pleased to meet you ma'am—and all of you," said Joe.

"It must be heartbreaking to see what happened to your town," said Enid.

"Yes, but I have a vision of its glorious future," Joe declared.

"I hope you fellows have a vision for getting these ruins cleaned up," said Ernie, "'cause we've a long ways to go. Nobody wants to build somethin' new with it looking like it does now."

"Unfortunately, this town is not one of the places where reconstruction had been planned, as I told you yesterday," said Harold. "So it was not on the list of locales to be cleaned up immediately. But we have advocates in high places. You can expect reinforcements within a week, Ernie.

"Now, I want to have Joe look at the old hydro plant," Harold continued. "If we can bring it up, the Beach House might have electricity before you thought it was possible."

"The power line from the plant to town used to run along Beach House Road," said Joe. "Is it still there?"

"It was still in use until the bombing raid," Ernie replied.

Enid added: "It brought power to Beach House Road from the other direction until Karen Martin's house was bombed."

"The whole region lost its power, so that didn't matter," Ernie pointed out.

"There's a power line crossing mountain highway," Ned reminded them. "Is that where it went to the old electric plant?"

"That's right," said Harold. "There was a road to it off Mountain Highway. It's grown over now, but there's a decent trail."

"It's not very far from the Beach House," said Joe Martin. "When I worked there as a night operator it took me less than half an hour to walk the distance."

"We don't have a lot of time today, so if we're going to do anything when we get there, we need to be hustling," said Harold. "Larry, I'd like you to come with us if that's all right with Mayor Enid."

When they arrived at the old power plant they found the penstock, the Pelton wheel, and the generator intact. The only vandalism had been committed by birds. Harold examined what he could see of the wires. He said the insulation was in fine condition. Evidently, the generator had been overhauled to serve as backup power after it had been taken out of service. After inspecting the mechanical governor, Joe said all it needed was oil. He told Larry to see about opening the gate valve on the penstock while he checked the oil sump. After vigorously cranking the oil pump by hand, Harold reported that the governor lever was able to move the spear that regulated flow in the nozzle. Larry had not been able to turn the rusty wheel on the gate valve by hand, but he found a bar that gave him enough leverage, and sooner than they would have thought possible the flywheel began turning. As the turbine gained efficiency the generator gradually came up to speed, and the lights in the room came on.

"There isn't time to do any more today," Harold said. "Shall we leave it running, Joe?"

"I don't see why not. In all the time I was here as operator there were no breakdowns, and that was when the curse was in effect."

(By the way, the old power plant is still running today.)

On the walk back, Joe offered Larry a job in Bellingham as the delivery van driver. Harold assured Larry that he would be flying several men in tomorrow to repair the power lines and perform the cleanup. Larry was skeptical and curious about how such a massive amount of work could be done by the six men—the capacity of Harold's airplane—in a day.

"It will not be done in a day, but Enid and Ernie will be relieved of their burden," said Harold. "You will find driving in Bellingham a challenge, but I believe you can do it."

Larry accepted the job. He stopped at the Beach House, stuffed a few belongings into his pack, and went with Harold and Joe back to the airport.

"Someday when you retire you can come back here and live in the Beach House," Joe promised him.

The next morning Harold flew in with five glorified men: Ken Martin, Philip Evans, Harold's fellow engineer Jim, and Archie the architect. The fifth name I have not found. It could be Geoffrey the plumber who appeared in Philip's dream. Four of them had lived in the town until the Rapture.

Since Harold's primary concern was restoring electricity at the airport, they pursued that project first. Airport electricity was supplied via the power line that ran along the highway, which originally had been fed from the north by the hydro plant. That line was dead, as was expected, because there was no power coming in from the defunct grid. They switched off the connection to the south then hiked up to Four Corners, checking the utility poles and wires along the way. From Four Corners the lines to the old plant were carried on utility poles along Mountain Highway. If the generator which they had started up yesterday was still going, those lines should be live, and they would only have to engage switches on the poles—which they were able to accomplish.

That meant that Don's Cycle at Four Corners should have power. The door was not locked. Inside they found six electric motorbikes plugged in and charging, all with digital controls.

"Murphy's Law is turned on its head!" Harold exclaimed.

As they waited for the motorbikes to finish their charging cycles, Harold addressed his work crew:

"I know you're eager to try out these bikes because we have nothing like them in heaven. Now, I was wondering: what's the reason for that? Do any of you have an idea?"

"It couldn't be because they're too much fun," Ken said with a grin, and he answered his quip with a laugh because they were all anxious to prove exactly that.

"Bikes would be useless in heaven because we're never in a hurry to go anywhere," Archie pointed out.

"That's only because we haven't the means," Jim muttered.

"I never thought about it, but have you ever tried to hurry when you're up there, Jim?"

"It's not what people do, because it would mean something had not worked out just right," Philip postulated.

"Come to think of it, Philip," said Archie, "you're right. Nobody needs to run for exercise, so that's what it would mean."

"I can't imagine someone jogging in heaven," said Jim. "It would be like running up and down the aisles during a performance of the Hallelujah Chorus."

"I never even tried to walk fast up there," Philip testified.

"No, and I never had reason to," Archie added. "I'm not sure these glorified bodies are designed for running or jogging."

"Maybe we're not made to balance on bikes, either," said Jim.

"Go ahead, somebody," Harold urged. "See if you can run. ... Jim, give it a try. ... All right, I'll do it. ... Hey, guys! It's easy!"

One by one they followed Harold's lead, Archie first and Jim last, circling the Crossroads Chapel building across the street.[1]

"This doesn't mean it will work in heaven," said Philip. "You know we're slightly different there."

"Probably we'll never know," said Jim.

"Now let's try the bikes," Harold proposed. "I believe they're ready to go."

And so they were.

---

1. This, as I have heard it told, was when these guys discovered the joy of glorified running.

In order to save time, two of them, Harold and Ken, rode back down the highway to verify that electric power was available at the airport while the others went east on Mountain Highway to see about restoring power to the Beach House. They agreed to meet in town on Lake Way at or near Park Avenue.

Although they expected that glorified bodies would not be subject to electrocution, as a precaution Jim and Archie rode to the power station to switch off the line to Beach House Road. On the service trail they zoomed past a black bear with cubs.

They discovered what they might have noticed before: there was only one line out, and if Four Corners had power, it was hot. So they turned around and sped back to warn the others but had to stop for the bears because the mother was blocking the road, which really was little more than a trail. Obviously she was fearless, but evidently she was curious though meaning no harm.

"It was a mistake to stop," said Archie as he was telling about the event later. "The mother had no control over her cubs. They were pawing the wheels and trying to climb aboard my bike."

Philip and the other fellow found nothing wrong with the power line where it crossed Mountain Highway at Shore Drive, and all looked well on Beach House Road until they came to the ruins of the Martin residence.

"I'm glad Ken went with Harold to the airport," Philip said.

"Yes, it's incredibly unfair what they did there," said the other fellow.

"Since the power line is already severed here, there's nothing we need to do right now," Philip announced.

"Right. The end is hanging high enough."

"Now we ride back and meet Jim and Archie. These bikes are great, aren't they?"

At Mountain highway the two teams met.

"It's safe to power up this line now," Philip said.

"Look up!" said Jim. "There's only one set of wires from the plant, and Four Corners branches off here. All we have to do is close the switch here and you'll have power at the Beach House."

Philip stopped at the Beach House to make sure there would be no surprises when the power came on. Enid thought she was seeing a ghost when she answered his knock at the front door.

"Enid, my dear, don't be afraid. I'm Philip Evans, the same Philip you used to know, just made a little brighter. I lived in this house once a long time ago. Did you know that? Would you mind if we turned the electricity on?"

"You must be here with Harold Foster. He promised he would send us help."

"Yes, your town hasn't been forgotten."

"I know they got the old power plant going again yesterday. If we could have electricity, it would be like heaven. I'll be forever grateful."

"All right. I won't argue about that. I'll go back to the garage where the main panel is, and if no one has messed with the wiring, your lights should come on and all your outlets should be working again. Go around and check for anything that looks or sounds or smells unusual."

"Will I get an invoice? We have very little money."

"The electricity, like the water that powers the generator, is free."

"What's going to happen now?" Enid asked him. "Harold said to expect good things."

"I agree with Harold. One reason is I had an elaborate dream the night before the Rapture in which Harold and I and Ken Martin and some others were given instructions about rebuilding the town—because in my dream it had been destroyed like it is now. Harold brought some of us in today, so it looks like we'll be starting soon. Where is Ernie? Is he in town?"

"Yes, he goes every day but Sunday digging for things we can use. Brother Ned is with him."

"I'll see him there then. Can I get through this way, or do I have to go back out to Deer Drive? I've got a motorbike."

"You can get through on foot. We built a temporary bridge across the creek. I think it will hold a motorbike."

Philip took the shorter route, speeding across the creek and following the well-trodden trail which the Beach-House residents had been using to go to and from what used to be the downtown area. Then continuing on Lake Street to Park Avenue, he arrived at the prearranged meeting place ahead of the other members of the team who were coming by the longer route.

This was the first ground-level view of the ruins that Harold's crew had seen, and Philip was certainly dismayed as he compared what he was seeing to the image he imagined from his dream. The others too seemed to be stunned by the results of the cruel demolition by fire.

"I estimate it would take a thousand slaves some months to haul away and bury this much rubble," said Archie.

"Maybe now is not the time," Philip said. "I had a dream on the Saturday night before the Rapture. We were all here—I think on this very spot, even—and Jesus was instructing us about rebuilding, and he showed us the layout of the reconstructed town. He mentioned bringing in trucks and equipment from the city to make it happen. Is there any plan for that, Harold?"

"I don't think so, because this is not one of the locations where resurrections are going to take place."

"Mansion Row up there, if it could be reconstructed, would be a natural place for them to come to," Ken noted with a grin.

"Well, my dream *started* to come true," said Philip, "but not perfectly. It was accurate about who would be here and that Harold would bring us in by plane. We were told in the dream to go to Bob's Cycle to get transportation, but there was nothing about the old hydro plant supplying electricity."

Archie asked, "Aren't dreams usually like that? If there's any truth in them it's only partial."

"We know that's not *always* the case," said Harold. "Dreams have come true absolutely."

"Does partial mean the rest happens someday?" Archie asked.

"Not unless you're a prophet," said Harold.

"I'm not a prophet," said Philip, "so don't hold me to it."

Jim: "Are we on our own, then? What resources do we have?"

"You've got us," said Ernie, who with Ned had been digging nearby in the ruins of the Gallery. "What's the plan?"

"Ernie, you've got electricity at the beach House," Philip said.

"Hooray! What's next?"

"The town may have to wait," Harold confessed. "Is there anything going on in the valley?"

Ned: "Someone's living in one of the farmhouses down there."

Ernie: "Like Joe Martin was saying, we need resurrected citizens with the pioneer spirit willing to start from scratch."

"We'll work on that," Harold promised. "It's time we got back to the airport. Here, take this bike, Ernie. I'll ride behind Philip. You can get it recharged at Bob's Cycle."

"Did Bob give you permission to use those bikes?" Ned asked.

"No, but the King did," Philip replied.

That evening when they were back in heaven, Harold met with Adam Murphy about the problem and Joe Martin's solution. "There's nothing a sanctified pioneer can't do," Adam agreed; and he sent to Jerusalem for pioneers from the early days to be resurrected and left to make their own dwelling places. "If angels could bring tarps and leave them in the park, it would be something they could accept as tokens of dwelling places," Adam suggested.

When Harold learned that the second part of Adam's request had been rejected, he said he would get donations from people who had lived there more recently and fly them in.

Ernie and Ned took their collection of axe heads and crosscut saw blades and knives and nails and left them on Park Street.

When the resurrectees came, they found themselves standing (or sitting or lying if they were very young) by the graves which had been their resting places—where they might even find their names on markers. It was an exceptional manner of resurrection, but it matched their sensible expectations.

There were joyful reunions when recognition came, for in spite of the dates on their gravestones, the elders appeared to be in the prime of life and looked no older than their adult children.

They had a fine view of the lake, and looking down over the city streets there were no structures to wonder about. The evidence of destruction by fire was not surprising. They expected it.

What were they wearing? you might ask, for in that setting heavenly garments such as angels are thought to wear would be incongruous. Perhaps you have questioned the kind of clothing our glorified bodies wear when we transit between heaven and earth. If robes are worn on the streets in heaven, do they become different clothes when we set foot on earth? If the answer is "yes," does it not seem like gratuitous magic? Are we thereby pasting together two things that are fundamentally irreconcilable?

Some had said glorified bodies must emit light with infinite variations as cinema images do, not merely reflecting light as real objects do. When you meet someone in heaven whom you want to hug, how will it be hugging a light beam?

Well, let me enlighten you about the attire worn in heaven. Or, first, I should ask you what purpose clothing would serve. Why would any clothing be needed in heaven? Our first parents wore no clothing when they were innocent. Would not our innocence in heaven eliminate the need for clothing?

When more than two people who are enlightened and free get together, clothing does more than conceal infrastructure. When we are able to freely choose our clothing—not being coerced by an occasion or convention or lack of means—what we wear gives an instant impression of our character without a word being spoken.

Clothing is what distinguishes humans from animals. Animals do not care so much about the personalities of other animals, or if they do, the parameters are few.

When I finally got admitted into new heaven, I was the same person and I wore the same clothes. Just as the new body I was granted was an improved copy of the one I lived in on earth, the clothes were of an improved substance, and I must say very comfortable. Do I have a selection of outfits to wear in heaven? I do. The women I know would not believe it was heaven if they could not choose from a variety of clothing.

What about the industry needed to produce garments? Where is that located? The principle is this: when the evils are taken out, whatever remains that is good and holy finds a place in heaven.

No, white robes are symbols of being "clothed in righteousness," which is a metaphor. Metaphors do not clothe you.

So no essential change of clothes is necessary when moving between new heaven and earth. I cannot say what happens at the microscopic level, but the cloth seems the same on earth as it does in heaven only not quite as comfortable.

Now, realize that our pioneers have not come from new heaven. They are newly resurrected, newly minted manifestations of their heritage. If that miracle cannot go so far as to render them well clothed according to their purposes and customs and characters, then it had not been thought through very well at all. And, as we keep learning, every provision was waiting to be discovered.

They caught fish for food and made proper tools. They made use of items from the ruins such as wire and hinges. They felled scorched trees, scraped away charred bark, split logs, and built cabins. Ernie came out to Park Street, introducing himself and trying to explain the tarps, which they had little use for. He had brought a few tools from Earl's shop, but they were prejudiced against modern tools. They knew from reading Revelation that civilization had gone mad, and they wanted no part of it. With his aged face and worn clothes, they took Ernie for an unsanctified vagrant. Since he had been there first, they said they would gladly leave him alone and stay away from the Beach House.

The pioneers explored the valley and befriended farmers. They traded fish for meat and eventually acquired horses.

When they got around to cleaning the hillside, the foliage had broken up large pieces of concrete. They cut rebar and shoved the fragments into basements. They planted trees.

After much debate they made a law that excluded motorbikes. Harold still made much use of motorbikes, going by way of Four Corners. He flew less, because he had successfully petitioned to have a Jacob's Ladder installed in the Beach House attic.

Larry Link Retires
Chapter Fifteen

While busy with her weekday assignment in Louisville and her literary pursuit in heaven, Lucy Link took time out of each day to remember Larry and pray for him. She did not know whether he had gotten out of Babylon before its destruction, but she had an unaccountable hunch that he had lost Junior in Russia, which gave her hope that he might miss her and be glad to see her should they meet again.

How close she came to learning of Larry's mishap in Russia when Samson visited Carmen's parole office! If he had not been masquerading as Ichabod, he would have informed Lucy and let her know that Larry had returned home.

It did not occur to her to search heaven for others who might have heard from him. Lucy belonged to a circle of friends who had been patients of Dr. Carmen Hayrab, patients who had prayed for the salvation of their dentist and spoken about the meaning of life. Lucy had gotten to know them well in training and had been graduated to heaven in the same class. Those members who had assignments on earth were all located near Louisville, and in heaven they shared a dwelling place. Lucy thought it very unlikely that she would encounter anyone else whom she had known in the past life, for she had yet to discover that chance in new heaven and even on new earth is full of purpose.

But chance does not tolerate neglect by a person of unfulfilled promise, and so it was that when Lucy had gone to find Ichabod after he had missed his bi-weekly appointment, she encountered Harold Foster at Clark Regional airport. She learned from Harold that Larry was unemployed and living at the Beach House. She suggested that Larry could be the driver they needed for the van in Bellingham, and Harold carried the suggestion to Joe Martin. Then, as you know, Joe arranged for Larry to work with them on the hydroelectric plant preliminary to offering him the job.

Larry drove the diesel van for Joe's company, and though he was a natural he lived with the transportation family as well.

On his seven-year anniversary of employment by the transportation company, Joe Martin prompted Larry to take early retirement and return to the town he had called home, for the Beach House had no permanent resident and he wanted someone to maintain it.

Although Larry was not eager to retire, he would never oppose Joe Martin—not only because Joe was his boss but also because he considered Joe his best friend. If Joe Martin needed him to maintain the Martin Beach House, Larry said he would consider it a privilege.

Was this the answer to Larry's prayer that he find a living environment in which he would not be regarded merely as a specimen of physical degeneration? His apparent seniority counted for nothing in the company of saints who had risen above gray hair and wrinkles. This was a common problem whenever naturals and resurrected folks were required to live and work in close proximity and why glorified supervision was necessary for maintaining peace on earth.

Or was it an answer to another of Lucy's prayers?

Larry packed up his belongings and Joe drove him in a buggy to BLI on the day of the week when Harold Foster was most likely to fly in for supplies. Usually Harold would be heading back soon after getting what he needed, and this was the expedient Joe made use of whenever he wanted to visit his home town, for mechanized transportation over many miles in that direction was not available.

Joe was surprised to find not Harold's antique aircraft but a light plane which he had never seen before at the fuel pump. The solo pilot said he knew the town's location and that he would be happy to take Larry and his baggage to his destination immediately. This may seem odd and unnecessary, but Joe urged Larry to accept the offer. Can you guess who that generous man was? I have spent a whole chapter getting around to telling you. Yes, by divine chance it was Ichabod Samson. He had come to Bellingham to investigate a report of heretical teaching at the college.

Samson told me Larry looked shockingly advanced in age: so much older than he appeared to be at their last meeting, which was when they both lived at the Beach House—Samson briefly, Larry for several years—during the tribulation period.

Their conversation during the flight included this:

"After we found out that Melchior sent you to the future, we had a baptism right there on the beach. Claudia and I both got baptized along with Karen. Did you know that?"

"No. Is it too late to congratulate you now?"

"I'm still trusting King Jesus, if that's what you mean."

"Do you know the whereabouts of Claudia and Karen?"

"No. They sailed away on Claudia's yacht, which has to be on the lake somewhere since there's no outlet."

"I doubt that Claudia's jet is still at the airport."

"I don't know about that because the hangar is locked."

"Don't be too surprised if Claudia shows up at the Beach House. But I'm forgetting: she would be in her late eighties or early nineties by now if she's still alive."

"What's going to happen to us, Earl? Can we still go to heaven when we die? Or do we have to pass the Judgment first?"

"The Judgment, yes. That's my understanding."

"That's where the books get opened and all our deeds get exposed, right?"

"That might be right. I don't think the Bible says for sure. If we trust Jesus Christ's sacrifice for the erasure of our sins, then we must be forgiven. I don't see a time limit on that. But *are we still able* to trust him for saving us from the penalty of sin when he's ruling over us as King? When we're forced to bow down to him it's not the same as acknowledging our need to be forgiven."

"Why should a few days make such a big difference? I could be in a glorified body if I had dropped that nonsense about finding heaven on earth like Lucy told me to."

"The Rapture warning was clear and unmistakable, yet we ignored it. Is there something we're ignoring now, Larry? That's what concerns me."

"But you're exceptional, Earl. You got pulled right past the beast and into the kingdom. You must know why they did that and what special things you're supposed to be doing here."

"I haven't figured it out yet. No one has told me anything. I'm here on this mission only because of Chester Matthew's kindness. He doesn't know either why I was made an exception."

"You were always exceptional, Earl. You could have asked anyone in town and they would have said you were exceptional."

"Yes, but what they didn't know was that I was a spy for the government—not a good spy, because I was ignoring my duty, but that made it worse. I was a long way from being a saint, and even now after acknowledging my sins I'm not what anyone would call a sanctified saint."

"Those resurrected folks definitely have that on us," said Larry. "I thought they were acting pious, like people used to do in church. But they can't help it. That's just the way they are."

"And that's the trouble with us, Larry. We missed out on sanctification. I don't see how we'll get it unless we get it in this life before we die."

"O for purgatory, blessed purgatory," Larry moaned.

"Now, you won't be surprised when I tell you I have an ulterior motive in giving you this lift, will you? But first, tell me about my boats. Were they still floating last time you were there?"

"Yes, and I bailed rainwater many times. But I haven't been to the Beach House in seven years."

"Ernie is there. Do you think he would be looking after them?"

"I'm sure he would, but I heard he's no longer there."

"Here's what you must do to pay me for taking you back home, Larry. Look after the boats as best you can, and give special attention to *Wind Chaser*."

After letting Larry Link out and wishing him well, Samson returned to Bellingham while Larry walked up Hill Street as he had done the day after the town was destroyed. This time the shock of what he saw when he looked down toward the lake was almost as great.

There was nothing on First Avenue or on Lake Way north of Hill Street—no buildings were there at all. What had been the center of town was now abandoned. On First Avenue south of Hill Street stood low buildings and store fronts that might have been built for the set of an old-west movie. On the level property where the school and athletic fields had been were small, single-story dwellings built of logs or crudely sawn lumber, none of them painted. The hillside above was green, shrouded in bushes and small trees. Farther south, as far as he could see toward Market Street, the buildings were of the same rough construction. Apparently, the pioneers of Joe Martin's generation were satisfied with what they could build and improvise from local resources.

Larry walked down Hill Street that was now a path between plants that had pushed up through the pavement, thinking that he would find out why they had failed to improve their building methods. He knew electric power was available, but there was no evidence that they were making use of it.

A number of people were about. They seemed to be happy and cordial to one another but they avoided him. He assumed it was his aged looks. They were all resurrected folks and none of them looked older than thirty. Finally, he struck up a conversation with a smiling young lady who had been brave enough or charitable enough to greet him.

"I lived here once," Larry informed her. "I had a house up there near the top of the hill on what was Seventh Avenue. Do you know Joe Martin?"

"Yes. Everybody knows Joe Martin."

"He sent me here to live in the Beach House. I'm assuming it's vacant now. Did you know the folks that lived there when you came?"

"I knew *of* them. Enid died last winter. Ernie and another man who lived there left after that."

"Did they fly out with Harold? Do you know Harold Foster?"

"I know there's a family living over there. We're not interested in those things."

"Do you make use of electricity?"

"No. We've decided to keep life simple here, even if we have to work harder than if we used electricity."

"Why not use it just for lights?"

"Some are for that, but we voted it down. I remember how it was when the town got started with the mine. We had electric lights then and a lot of other things that made life easier in some ways. But we know what it led to, and we're not going to get started on that again."

"I see your point. But the world is different now. They're not going to let technology dominate everything."

"We're making sure of that."

"Do you really think you can remain isolated for hundreds of years?"

"No, not really. But until we're told to do differently we will."

"Well, it's been nice talking to you. My name's Larry."

"My name is Lillian. Are you Larry Link?"

"I'm afraid so."

"Your wife was here looking for you just an hour ago. She said she would wait for you at the Beach House."

Larry was speechless, naturally. He had known this would be a possibility but had put it out of his mind. He knew the Beach House had become connected with new heaven and the Fosters used it almost daily. He asked himself why he had no apprehension at all about seeing the Fosters. The answer was because he owed them nothing and therefore they allowed him some dignity. Lucy would have to be gracious, of course. No, not have-to; she *would* be gracious. What did he have to offer in return? Nothing: she was not the debtor. There was nothing to forgive her of. Was she seeking an apology from him? No, glorified people were not like that. Then why had she taken time away from heaven to meet him? She must have a reason, he thought. Was it possible that she missed him? That would be something else altogether—beyond gracious. Did he miss her? It was a question he had put away long ago along with its negative answer. But the answer was a lie.

Larry walked slowly, reluctantly, dreading to find out what moral exercises Lucy had planned for him. He imagined that Joe Martin, Earl Clark, and Harold Foster were all in on it. They represented three levels of human development superior to himself—even Earl Clark, being an exceptional, was his superior.

After trudging through what used to be the vibrant heart of town, now a deserted wilderness, he was comforted to find the Beach House looking the same as it always had. He walked down the side path toward the beach and then paused before turning toward the back door.

He tried to imagine how she would look. As a glorified woman she would be more beautiful than ever. How could he face her who had been his wife, now a glorious emissary of new heaven? Her charity would ignore his wrinkles while he would be compelled to praise her beauty and ask her forgiveness. Should he bow before her with his face to the floor?

She must have known his mind, for she made herself his debtor by her first words, which were not even polite: she remarked about his aged appearance. "The spots and wrinkles on your face make you look like an old man, Larry."

So incongruous to the occasion was Lucy's remark that Larry laughed involuntarily, and in that moment he knew he loved her.

Then she said, very soberly, "I would trade places with you if I could, Larry. It's true. But I didn't know it until I saw you just now."

Larry could only stare at her in wonderment until she said, "It's your house, I know, but come, sit down with me." She turned, and he nervously followed her into the living room. He wanted to embrace her, but she was an angel in his eyes, and he thought he should ask her permission, but that seemed inappropriate.

"Let me make a fire in the fireplace," he said, noticing that someone had left kindling ready to be ignited. It would give him a minute to think. But the room was not cold, and Lucy did not give him time to think.

"Did you meet Lillian?" she asked.

"Yes. She told me you were here."

"Did she give you the reason for their rustic policy?"

"She did. I understand it. ... Do you like it?"

"They're too isolated to be of benefit either to themselves or the kingdom. I have to be concerned about that because I've been appointed to be their overseer."

"I thought Harold Foster had that assignment. I know he's a transportation overseer in Bellingham, but he's out here so much. Why can't he do both?"

"He might have served as overseer here as well, but his activity at the airport is not appreciated. They fancy themselves a resurrection of preindustrial civilization, which they believe they must perpetuate because ease promotes luxury which is idolatry. I've learned from Harold that they have no money; they keep handwritten ledgers. They would not be able to live so simply if they had unsanctified naturals living among them, and they know that, which explains their reluctance to associate with mortals living in the Beach House."

"How are you going to survive on your own, Larry?"

"I'll do what I did when I lived here during the tribulation. This to me is essentially an extension of the tribulation."

Lucy laughed. "May I be part of your tribulation?"

"I'm sorry. I didn't put two and two together. As overseer do you intend to come here often?"

"More often to start with. I must teach the big picture and get them ready to accept responsibility. After that I will still be checking in from time to time—if that's all right with you."

"Yes, of course."

"I want to make sure they treat you well."

"I think they will. They trade with farms in the valley. As long as I can catch fish, I'll have something to trade."

"What about in winter. The lake freezes sometimes."

"After the ice thickens I can still catch fish. It's the in-between times that I'm pretty much reduced to potatoes and carrots."

"I'll not let that happen. You were a bit younger then. With proper planning the population will become chronologically integrated. Having a good balance of naturals among them, you will fit right in. That will force these pioneers to get serious about looking to Jerusalem for direction."

"I hope I live to see it."

"I checked the pantry. Harrietta brought in a few things this morning. Would you like me to make us lunch? ... Larry?"

"I ... I guess so if this is what heaven is like."

"You said that so well, Larry. Yes, we're in a little bit of heaven right now."

"But I thought glorified people don't eat. Harold feeds his airplane, but he never takes in food for himself, as far as I know."

"We don't have to take in food on earth, but we can if there's a special occasion that calls for it. If you will let me fix us a little meal I'll be very pleased to eat along with you."

"Lucy, I'm sorry I didn't look for the good in you and learn to love you until now. You weren't any different then. I was too wrapped up in my dog to really know you."

"Oh, I *was* different then. I never forgave you then. Now I enjoy forgiving you, and I ask you to forgive me for playing the boss. I was pretty bossy. You knew that."

"I really wasted my life, didn't I? There's hardly anything left of it now. Will anything good happen to me when I die? But this isn't the time to be talking like that."

"There will be a good time to discuss everything on another day. There's bread and crackers and cheese and honey and blueberry jam and yogurt and eggs and milk and mayonnaise and lettuce in the refrigerator. Do you still like egg sandwiches?"

"If you could make one like you used to do, I will know that you love me. ... Lucy?"

"Yes, Larry."

"This is a miracle, isn't it?"

"Do you mean a gift from God?"

"Yes, that's what I mean now."

"Do you believe he loves you, Larry?"

"Yes, I understand now why he gave me you. ... What can I do to be more faithful to him? Because I don't know why I'm here, really. Is it only naturals who feel this way?"

"Yes, according to what I've observed it is. When you were driving for Joe Martin's company, did you consider that you were driving for the King?"

"No, I didn't think past Joe Martin. I wanted his company to prosper, so I went the extra mile to please everyone."

"Now that you're retired from that, another assignment will come along, and if I know Larry Link, you will do it well and still look for more."

"Earl Clark gave me one: I'm going to be maintaining his sailboats. If Joe was serving the King and I was serving Joe's company, then I was serving God too, so that's good to realize. But Earl doesn't know why he's here either."

"Does that mean he isn't serving King Jesus?"

"Well, he's on some kind of assignment having to do with keeping education in line."

"God is looking for people who are proven faithful to him because the devil doesn't believe it's possible. That's why records are being kept."

"Do you know what that reminds me of, Lucy? We read from the Bible every day when I was living with Joe Martin's family."

"Job?"

"Exactly!"

"Looking back, can you see that you were being tested during those seven years in Bellingham?"

"Nothing ever went wrong with that old diesel truck. It was amazing. It smelled like fried potatoes. Naturals would sometimes get impatient with me, but it was nothing like the old days here in this town, which at that time I thought were easy but now seem sometimes difficult as I look back. If you mean was I being tested with temptation, I was, but it was repulsive to me. Why would I crucify Jesus over again?"

Joe Martin was waiting for Samson when he landed and taxied to the fuel dispenser. Most likely Joe had not gone anywhere because Earl had promised to return in forty minutes or less, and Joe was concerned about the dwindling reserve of aviation fuel.

"From here I'm supposed to go to Boise," said the pilot as he checked fuel levels in the wings. "Looks like I've enough unless there's a strong headwind."

"Go ahead and top it off," said the fuel boss. "Then I'm shutting off the supply."

Joe understood Samson's purpose in being there, and on their way to the college campus he warned him not to expect much of the teaching staff.

"Resurrected educators are in short supply," he explained, "and there are none among the pool of glorified servants that we have access to. So don't be surprised if you encounter a natural delivering a lecture."

"I can't object; I'm one myself," said Samson. "I'm assuming lectures are open to the public."

"They are. The seating is for registered students, however."

As Samson explored the campus—which consisted of three buildings, one of them under construction—he noticed that natural students did not mix with resurrected saints, or so it appeared at first, but he concluded that compassion for imperfect bodies was lacking among the resurrected, as if the naturals were intruders marring the perfection of heaven. He tried to catch talk that was critical of the scholastic substance the natural students had been exposed to, which might lead to something worth investigating. But everything that reached his ears was social banter.

He was looking for a chance to audit a lecture because the report that had brought him there, while it lacked detail, was based on a submitted complaint that a lecture was heard in which an errant interpretation of hell had been presented as the truth.

Samson's hope was rewarded when following a group of young mortals moving toward one of the buildings he found posted inside an announcement of a lecture scheduled for that hour:

Morality in the Workplace:
accommodating conflicting views
Lecture by Ward Howard

"Joe wasn't kidding," Samson muttered, seeing there was no "Prof." or "Dr." before the speaker's name. His conclusion that credentials were lacking was confirmed by the biographical note which stated that Mr. Howard had taught a course in "principles of personnel management" at a junior college in San Francisco.

Though a speech on the advertised subject was unlikely to be heretical in any important sense, Samson decided to look into the lecture hall since he was tired of walking and guessed that the number of students that had been drawn in was insufficient to fill all the seats. He was right. Though it was a few minutes past the hour, most of the seating was bare.

Obviously the lecturer was mortal, for he looked to be about eighty years of age. Samson concluded that he was likely seeing the same Ward Howard whom he had known as "Howie."

The lecture was proceeding somewhat like this:

> The next question I would like to address is: Is breaking company rules grounds for termination? Yes or no. Or *should* it be grounds for termination.

> If your answer is "Yes," it's like the view of sin that it ultimately leads to death. Not to put it in theological terms at all, I mean simply as an analogy: you're fired from your job, your life's blood, and you're no longer on the payroll; you're dead as far as company business is concerned.

> If your answer is "No," it's like the view of sin that leads ultimately to reconciliation. There may be disciplinary measures taken, but they are not fatal. Under this policy there will always be a way to correct or remedy or forgive the transgression. Employees are the company's most valuable resource, so keeping a transgressing employee on the payroll is the better choice.

Logically, there is a third possibility, but it's only an imaginary possibility because it's utterly unrealistic: instead of termination or reconciliation, lock the employee in a prison with nothing to do and with no possibility of ever being let go or being restored but rather being tortured day and night. Besides being nonsensical, it's unrealistic because there is no such prison owned by any company, for it would be utterly inhumane and would ruin the reputation of the company, not to mention that it would be illegal because it would be cruel and obviously unusual.

Likewise, the doctrine of eternal captivity in hell is unrealistic and a complete negation of reality. Where is there an inescapable place which exposes the damned person to continuous torture where there is no death and no possibility of reconciliation? Let me give you five reasons—and there are many more—why there could never be such a place and why this teaching is false.

First, the Bible says the wages of sin is death. That I can understand, though I don't agree with it. It says the wages of sin is *death*—that means end-of-life—not continuous, unending life in hell.

Second, the English word "eternal" in the Bible quite often doesn't mean what you think it means because it's a translation of a word in the original language which doesn't have an exact English equivalent. "Eternal" is generally in reference to an age with an implicit end, not endless time as we think of eternity. So eternal damnation really doesn't mean "without end."

Third, hell is said to be a place of continuous fire, yet fire must consume or there will be no more fire. So being immersed in everlasting fire without being consumed by it is simply a contradiction and therefore cannot be true.

Fourth, how could you—or anyone—enjoy heaven while knowing of a friend or family member who is not only missing out on the pleasures you are experiencing but they're being relentlessly tortured in hell?

And Fifth, the Bible says God will be all in all, which precludes there being anything like a permanent hell.

Samson took down those five points, and to satisfy himself, as well as to prove to anyone reading his report that they were not only invalid arguments but intentionally deceptive, he sketched a rebuttal for each one.

1. "Death" in "The wages of sin is death" is set against "life" in "the free gift of God is eternal life in Christ Jesus." Mr. Howard was inconsistent in representing this "death" as a termination when in the context it means a continuation. As life with Christ is ongoing, so death without Christ is an ongoing condition. But primarily the verse is about receiving life: death is the spiritual malady for which the gift of life is the cure.

2. While the word translated "eternal" may refer to an "age," the context defines what "age" means; it can refer to "the age to come," which is forever. Mr. Howard forgot to mention that.

3. Obviously, the fire of hell is no ordinary fire. Mr. Howard seems to think that God must use only things that we encounter in our present experience; or to put it another way, that the word "fire" can only refer to the chemical reaction known to him.

4. I will not accuse Mr. Howard of being disingenuous on this one, because it seems that few people know the right answer. The answer is obvious once you understand that sin has no place in the holiness of God and yet sin originates out of his gift of freedom. If rebellion might happen again, how can there be peace in heaven even after Satan is out of the way? Only when your freedom is anchored in Christ are you safe to have around heaven. But we know that even then there is danger because Satan rebelled out of the blue. The battle to eradicate sin has cost Christ his blood, and that must not be forgotten. But do we hate sin enough?

5. More real than the horror of hell is the horror of sin. So lest sin be forgotten, heaven must keep hell on display. Apparently Mr. Howard would accept the annihilation of sinners as a better way to combat evil, not realizing that he would be recommending the truly impossible. An employee can be terminated, but our spirits cannot be terminated because spirits, which are not physical matter, exist outside the domain of time, and "termination" is a time word.

Samson had heard enough to convict Howie, so he did not stay for the rest of the lecture. On exiting the building he was thankful to find Joe Martin waiting, for if he had to wait an hour for his ride, Mr. Howard would stop and ask him why he had left early. Now all that was left for him to do was turn in the report, and if justice was as swift as it was reputed to be, Howie would soon find out which method of dealing with transgressors applies to him. Certainly he would lose his qualification to be an educator, but he wondered what the court would add to that.

"Any luck?" Joe asked as Samson climbed up into the buggy.

"I caught the renegade lecturer. Here's the report. Give it to Harold Foster and have him transmit it to Chester Matthew."

"You're not going to fly to Boise this late in the day, are you? Why don't you stay with us tonight at the transportation dwelling. Have some dinner, get a good night's rest, a good breakfast, and leave refreshed in the morning?"

The barometer was high and steady and clear skies the next day were assured, so Samson agreed it was the prudent thing to do. But as it turned out that next morning he wished he had followed his original plan and not lingered in Bellingham.

Everyone at dinner had heard about Ichabod Samson the exceptional, so they were cordial but more inquisitive than he would have liked. There was a discussion about fuel and aviation gasoline in particular and questions about running antique engines, such as the one in Samson's airplane, on modern automotive fuel of which there was a good supply in underground tanks. Everyone agreed that it would be possible with modified hoses and carburetors if the fuel could be refreshed and some of its additives removed. No one knew when new engines would be developed and manufactured, but all believed that the physical possibilities that had enabled runaway technology were in the plan of God and someday would be implemented in a better way.

The next morning at breakfast Harold came with dreadful news for Samson: Ward Howard was to stand trial in Salem and Samson was to take him there immediately. A marshal with Mr.

Howard in his custody was there in an official carriage drawn by two horses, waiting to take the prisoner and the pilot to the airport. When informed of this, Samson felt compelled to leave the table with his breakfast half eaten. If he had hated this duty the moment it was thrust upon him, now he despised the system that caused it. The overseers who had allowed him immense freedom were now treating him as a slave.

That word "slave" shocked him as he begrudged his present circumstance because it reminded him of the duty that he had once believed was essential to being a Christian and the whole purpose of the millennial kingdom. Was he excepted from being a reliable "bond-servant" of Christ? No. He was being tested.

Howie might have harbored hostility toward his accuser at that point but for the fact that he was terrified of air travel, and the fear of being in a shaky machine high in the sky eclipsed every other emotion. Samson was unsure about interpreting Howie's silence and stone-faced demeanor until, as an experiment, he told the prisoner that he had never had occasion to land at Salem before and he was not sure what to look for, so it might take longer to find it, and he hoped there would be enough fuel. Howie's aerophobia was confirmed then as his voice failed him.

Samson strapped his passenger in and gave him instructions about what to do in case of an emergency landing, which he regretted after seeing Howie's near-panic reaction.

The nonstop flight was smooth, and the beautiful scenery would have delighted a guilt-free person, but poor Howie was petrified, and no audible utterance emerged from his mouth during the entire two-hour flight.

At Salem an old rusty car[1] was waiting at the gate for the accused. Samson by that time had thought more about Howie and was feeling a bit of compassion toward him. He helped the old man out of the plane and handed him off to the marshal.

A sign at the fuel pumps said fuel was not available, but enough remained in the plane for the two-hour flight to Boise.

---

1. The elegant horse-drawn carriage in Bellingham was a product of Joe Martin's industry.

In contrast to Bellingham and Salem, KBOI had been a busy passenger hub before the tribulation and coming of the kingdom shut it down. Samson had no information about the condition of the runways; he assumed that since heaven was aware of his mission there would be a place where he could set down his C172.

After landing he taxied ten minutes before he found human activity at one of the hangars. It turned out that someone was working on a plane similar to his. This was a resurrected man, not a mortal. His name was Bill. He had owned that very plane in his former life, and it had not been flown in sixty years. He was skeptical when Samson refused to reveal the purpose of his mission, saying it was official business of the crown; nevertheless, he was eager to hear how this crippled pilot with one eye had gotten his plane back into service.

Bill offered to take Samson into town. He drove an electric golf cart that he had modified such that it attained a speed of 30 miles per hour on a level road.

"How far do you need to go?" he asked Samson.

"How far is the university?"

"Not far. Less than four miles, I guess."

"If you're sure your rig will make it with two bodies aboard and still get you back here or wherever you're going—"

"It hasn't failed me yet. Let's give it a try."

The driver was quite familiar with Boise, having lived in the area his entire life, both before and after he was resurrected. He answered Samson's questions freely without asking why he needed to know.

"I assume there are Mormon survivors here."

"Yes, because they refused to obey the beast."

"Are they holding to their beliefs?"

"Some are. I don't know if any still believe New Jerusalem will be in Missouri—or how serious they are if they do."

"They're not going to die out, I suppose."

"The new-earth generation of Mormons are into their teens, so it looks like they're here for the millennium."

197

Bill followed Vista Avenue north from the airport as far as Platt Gardens where a new exit off to the east had been devised.

"As you can see, there's more repair work to be done," said the driver. "But I want to show you one miracle building that survived the quake and all the tremors. It's the Stueckle Sky Center adjacent to the stadium. It has to be a miracle because it consists of four stories with massive amounts of glass."

"I saw the building when I was here—well, a number of years ago. I've lost track of time."

"Then you'll be interested in this: not only did the structure come through with zero damage, the electronic systems inside the building kept working."

"That's truly exceptional. There must be a reason for it. Maybe you don't know how fortunate you are here. Louisville, where I'm based, got shaken so badly they're rebuilding on a different site. Who was Stueckle? Did you know him?"

"Duane Stueckle. I didn't know him before, but he's resurrected, he's here now, and I've met him. He was and is an entrepreneur, and he's still very generous with his time and talents."

"That may explain it. ... I see you have electrical power here. Most places are struggling with makeshift generators."

"We're on hydroelectric power, you know. Some of the dams were up for renewal of their federal licenses, which they anticipated would be denied, so they deferred modernization. They kept running because they don't depend on computers."

"There's the Stueckle Sky Center," said Samson, pointing to it.

"Right, and this is B Plaza in front of it. Look, there's a kid standing on a park bench trying to get everyone's attention without a bullhorn. That's one of the blessings that comes from having no digital electronics—all the bullhorns are useless."

"This is perfect, Bill, if you could let me off here. I expect to be flying out tomorrow morning if I can get fuel. If you're at your hangar I may see you before I leave."

"I hope everything works out for your mission, Ichabod, whatever it is; and good luck with the fuel."

The crowd in B Plaza was indicative of a rally having just ended or one about to begin. College-age naturals were clustered randomly, talking loudly, and mostly ignoring the orator on the bench. Though the young speaker was almost shouting, Samson had to get near to hear what he was saying.

> If we don't act now, we'll lose our salvation! The whole teaching of the church hangs on New Jerusalem. Do we believe it? If we believe it, we'll act on it. If we don't believe it, what do we believe? We have to live what we believe. That's what Mormon salvation rests on. So if we're for New Jerusalem in Missouri, we need to be there and prove our faith so the Lord can act. Are we the people of the promise or are we not? If we are not, we prove it by staying home. If we are the chosen and this is the promised land, we'll march to Missouri and establish Jerusalem. The hour is late! We have waited almost too long. We need to begin the long march now! Some of us have made preparations. What are we waiting for! Tomorrow or next week we must set out for New Jerusalem! ...

This rhetoric fit the description of the Mormon unrest that Samson had been sent to investigate, but judging from this crowd the momentum to rebel did not exist. Nevertheless, he moved slowly, working his way among the clusters and listening for serious talk about the Mormon New Jerusalem.

Because he had eaten little that day and none since breakfast, an idea came to Samson's mind that food might be available in the Stueckle Sky Center. He walked across the street and went in the door at the street level. There was nothing about food there, but the elevators were working, and inside one he found a directory. Without thinking much about the kind of food service that was indicated and being curious about the architecture, he asked for the top floor where parties were hosted.

He found the doors to the Skyline Room closed, but on hearing a familiar voice inside he daringly opened a door. ... Why had there been no sign announcing an event taking place? Tables set for food were arranged around the room with a hundred or so guests listening to my presentation. Yes, I was the speaker.

When I saw him—I knew it was Samson instantly—I did something very rash because it was the only thing I could do to keep him from leaving: I stopped in mid sentence, interrupting my speech on security, and I said:

"A dear friend of mine has arrived, and I would like to introduce him to you. Ichabod, please come up to the head table where there's an extra seat next to Duane. This is Ichabod Samson, ladies and gentlemen. He's an exceptional mortal in many ways. He piloted his airplane here today from Bellingham, Washington by way of Salem, Oregon on official business. If you get a chance to talk to him, ask him about it. I would call him a heresy hunter. Please come in, Ichabod; don't feel like you're crashing the party. As far as I'm concerned you're an honored guest."

I thought he might make some excuse and refuse to enter or just turn and leave. It would take courage to limp in among those beautiful people. But not only that, it was within his power to embarrass me and thereby let me know he was determined to maintain his compassionate isolation.

When he did not turn away but hobbled in with his long hair and shaggy beard and patch over one eye, I revealed my exceptional love for him, for I had tears to dry. I thought I was losing my sanctity because glorified eyes do not water. I needed a handkerchief, which was embarrassing, but I did not care.

I stumbled through the remainder of my speech outlining a new security policy applying to areas with growing Mormon populations. Then I took my seat on the other side of Duane Stueckle at the head table, where I had little to do as Duane gave all his attention to Samson, and I had no food.

Finally, Duane turned to me, saying, "I understand that you believe Ichabod is able to find your friend Earl Clark and that you once proposed that the two of you go looking for him. He will be staying with me tonight, and tomorrow I'll take him to the airport and get him the fuel he needs. He would like you to go with him."

I agreed, of course. Had I set a trap? What do *you* think?

We decided the first place to look was where I used to live.

Chapter Seventeen

The intercom did not work well in Ichabod's airplane or else it was the headset he gave me. I could hear him when he spoke, but he did not seem to hear me very well.

He followed highway **84** for the first hour then continued on in a northwest heading after that, checking the chart on his lap against the terrain. He was not in a talkative mood, and I was so absorbed in what I could see—my eyes are sharp like an eagle's—that I neglected to make better use of the time. I was looking down on Moses Lake when I managed to ask him if he had been reading the Bible.

"No. Not since I was pulled out of the old world. There I had a copy that had belonged to someone you might know. I'm hoping to find it again. I have read all of it more than once."

"You must have studied some of its books more than others. What are your favorites?"

"Revelation was the first book I read, and then Job got me to thinking about the big picture. And Ezekiel too. Of course all the New Testament establishes Jesus in one's mind—wherever he's allowed to go. I feel accepted by him."

"I'm glad you're an exceptional."

"It's weird to have Larry Link be older than I am, but neither of us will be alive many more years."

"There's always hope."

"What do you mean by that?"

"I mean you have heaven to look forward to."

"Do you know that for certain? I can't find where the Bible is clear about the future of those who miss the first resurrection. Do I have the second resurrection and the great-white-throne judgment to look forward to?"

"If your name is in the book of life, there's nothing to fear."

"Why then will the other book be opened?'

"When your life ends here you will be in heaven, and then you will certainly learn more about it."

We were into the Cascade Mountains by then, and there were some clouds. He seemed to be uncertain of our position. He was studying the chart and trying to compare it to what he saw. Once he had to turn around and go back to find another pass. I prayed for our safety. Finally we got through under the clouds. We were farther south than the route he had plotted would have taken us, but the terrain was familiar to him, and he folded up the chart.

There was no air traffic, of course, but when the lake came into view I was thinking of the time Earl took me flying and taught me the radio protocol for announcing positions to other pilots. He never used the radio, which like the rest of the plane looked worn. That everything worked so well should not have been surprising.

Homer was there, greeting Samson whom he addressed as Ichabod. I'm sure he was surprised to see me. He looked puzzled, so I said I was searching for Earl Clark. Then he looked even more puzzled. He suggested that I go up to the site of the FSA building and see the monument to Earl Clark that was still there.

Homer lead us to the hangar that served as the home of the Foster Aircraft Company. It was much less than I had imagined from what they had told me. They all looked bright and happy in their earthly personas. Only Hannah was missing. Homer said he would go and have her bring the horse and buggy. I learned that Hannah had been accepted by the pioneers and had gotten them to teach her horseback riding and driving the buggy. She was crazy about horses, Homer said. She spent more time with the pioneers than with her family's business, which her parents did not object to because the tension between the old timers and the moderns had been virtually eliminated by Hannah's diplomacy.

Harold answered Ichabod's questions about his plans for the future of the business.

"There's more demand for these controllers than we can fulfill. We're working six days a week trying to keep up."

"I keep telling him we need to raise the prices," said Harrietta.

"She's right, and if she were still my wife I'd have to do it."

"Pretend she's your wife, and then do it," Holly said.

"I *am* his wife," Harrietta declared. "He just doesn't want to admit it."

"Of course. Glorified people don't marry," said Holly. "I know that better than anyone."

"It's a matter of attitude," Harrietta said. "I'm so proud of Harold it wouldn't be right not to be his wife, though it makes him uncomfortable. He got so used to the way I used to treat him, and now I'm making up for it."

"It's not clear that it would be good to increase the price," Harold explained. "I'm ready and willing to be obedient to any directive that comes down from Jerusalem, but so far I've received none. This entire business is my idea. I've never applied for or received approval from higher-up."

I turned to Harrietta and asked, "Are you doing any painting down here?"

"No. Someday I will. My 'Castle in the Clouds' painting exhausted my artistic interest, and I haven't gotten it back yet. There are opportunities in heaven, but nothing that I would do would last long."

"I know. I've seen would-be artists making paintings that fade away in a day," I said.

"It has to be that way or every wall in heaven would be plastered with amateur artwork since many people have nothing to do that interests them much—or have no other way to be expressive."

"Did your 'Castle in the Clouds' survive when they destroyed the town?"

"It did because Claudia had given it to Enid who loved it. It's hanging on a wall in the Beach House right now. I think Claudia was jealous of my talent, though it really was only that one painting that was worth anything—I think because the subject was a dream of heaven that I was inspired by when I painted it. Claudia, of course, only painted what I would call scenes from hell because that's where the money was."

"I'm not even sure that aviation will be allowed, ultimately," said Harold, returning to his subject.

"Why would our Creator have made it possible if he didn't want us to build flying machines?" Harrietta argued.

"You keep saying that," said Holly. "Maybe Ms. Lolomi can find out for us."

"The reason I wanted to get something going here was to give our town an economic base like it once had," said Harold. "But the residents are content with their horse and buggy. I'm sure no one would want to be employed building airplane parts."

"Lucy Link says there are plans to resurrect the later generations. That will change everything, won't it?"

"I hope so," said Harold.

"That's why they're officially silent about our work," said Harrietta. "The town has to be ready for it."

"Is Hannah with you today?" I asked Harrietta.

"She came down with us this morning, then she was off to see her friends in town."

"Is it her friends, or is it the horse?" said Holly.

"Hannah has gotten in with the pioneers. They like her."

"They like her because she likes their horse."

"Have they only one horse?" I asked.

"One horse and one rickety buggy," Holly replied. "They have a wagon that the horse pulls sometimes too."

"She's here right now," said Homer who had heard familiar sounds coming from outside. "And it sounds like she's brought the buggy."

"She saw your airplane land and guessed that someone will need a ride," said Holly.

"They're here looking for Earl Clark," Homer told Hannah. "Why don't you take them up to the FSA site?"

Hannah had brought not a buggy but a wagon with a seat on it. It was not a large wagon. The seat was barely wide enough for the three of us. She sat in the middle with the horse's reigns in her hands, and we on either side of her held tightly to the sides of the seat. There were no springs to soften the ride. Hannah thought nothing of it, and the jolts did not hurt me. But poor Ichabod!

Going up Hill Street, Samson and I got out and walked to make it easier on the horse. Then we got back aboard and rode northward on Ridge Avenue, past the ruins of the hospital and the fitness center to the FSA site which was free of debris, discounting the top of the building protruding out of the pit into which it had sunk before the town was destroyed. The monument in remembrance of Earl Clark which Homer had constructed was there.

This was my first experience at ground level seeing what had become of my building. The roof was level with the surrounding pavement. My old office suite was down there not very far from the edge. I had known that the foundation was strengthened by pillars going down into the old mine cavern; but surely that depth was less than the height of the building, which meant that much of the lower structure supporting the floor levels had collapsed.

"Is it still a mystery how this happened?" I asked Samson as we walked toward the monument.

"There are theories," is all he said.

"It says that Earl Clark was in the building when it collapsed," Hannah noted, pointing to the plaque on the monument.

"So that was his grave—buried alive?" I said, staring at the ruins. "Or did he escape?"

"They found one outlet from the mine where he could have come out," Hannah informed us. "It's down there in the basement of the house where Sookie Martin lived. She told me about her dad digging a shaft down to a mine tunnel."

"Do you think he got out?" I asked Hannah.

"You could ask Homer."

Samson had stepped back. I turned to look, and he was facing away. I knew that being there was painful for him, and I chastised myself for agreeing that we go there.

"We'd like to visit the beach House next," I told Hannah.

We rode back to Hill Street, walked down to First Avenue, then climbed onto the wagon and rode to the end of Lake Way. Samson and I walked the trail to Beach House Road, past the ruins of Karen Martin's house, Samson hobbling along in silence.

We found Larry Link preparing dinner and tomorrow's meals ahead of time,[1] for Sabbath began soon after sundown. He invited Samson and me both to spend Sabbath with him this evening and tomorrow. I accepted. Samson nodded his assent. I would not join them for dinner but wait for the Fosters whom I was sure would be arriving before dark, for there was no other place to transition to heaven. I just then realized that Samson did not know that I knew about Jacob's Ladder at the Beach House and thought that I was expecting him to take me to Bellingham. Otherwise, why would I not have gone by way of the ladder instead of riding in his noisy flying machine?

Voices and footsteps on the front porch announced the arrival of four of the Fosters. Holly explained to me that they had come by way of Four Corners because it was relatively level and easier on the horse; and now Hannah was returning the horse by the waterfront trail, the wagon remaining on Beach House Road.

"I'm afraid she'll not get back before dark," said Harrietta.

"It wouldn't be the first time," Holly argued.

"But this is Sabbath, and she'll have to climb the ladder by herself."

It turned out Hannah did come in, exhausted, shortly before six o'clock. You might picture her as being sweaty and out of breath. She was neither. Glorified bodies do not burn oxygen, and though we get warm with exercise, our muscles and joints are efficient enough that cooling is unnecessary.

They took their leave, one by one, ascending the stairs to the second floor and from there by a narrow stairway to the attic. Promising to return in the morning, I followed them.

When I came back down next morning, Larry and Samson, having finished breakfast, were still at the table talking about canoeing on the lake. Two days ago Larry had paddled a few miles south, following the shoreline, and had discovered Claudia's yacht, sunk, laying on her side, clearly visible in the clear water.

"That's very sad," said Samson. "No one loved her much."

---

1. According to Lucy's instruction.

Samson and I moved to the living room while Larry took care of the dishes. This would be the first Sabbath I had observed on earth. In heaven we had Sabbath worship meetings in our local areas. I thought about teaching them one or two songs from heaven. No, that would not be fair to Samson who's voice since his injury was not conducive to pleasant song. I asked him if he had a suggestion about how we might spend the day. He stood up, went to a bookcase, pulled out a volume of essays, and began paging through them.

Larry came in and sat down. It was obvious that he had something on his mind. He was looking at Harrietta's painting of the castle in heaven when he said, "I wonder if I'll ever see new heaven?"

"I would think so, at the rate you're going," said Samson.

"I may look like I'm on my last leg, but didn't I paddle your canoe for hours, and am I not none the worse for it?"

"No, that's not what I meant," said Samson. "I was referring to your observance of Sabbath."

"Because I washed dishes? He's kidding, isn't he?"

"I think so. How shall we spend this Sabbath day, Larry?"

"We could read from the Bible. ... You know what? Your Bible is here, Leila. Did you know that?"

"I received a hint that it might be here. Is that it on the shelf?"

"That's it. Ichabod was using it last time he was here. Do they use the Bible in heaven?"

"Yes. Constantly."

"What part? Because it's all about trouble on earth from cover to cover."

"In heaven it's applied differently. And remember we're not to the end of Revelation yet. Satan is bound, but he will be released and his argument against his Creator must be settled before he's permanently banished from heaven. You're right that most of the Bible is about troubles on earth and human failings, things that heaven is virtually free of. When you read of those things from the comfort and security of heaven you realize how blessed you are."

"Is that what it takes to feel blessed?"

"No, of course not. But history is the foundation of blessing whether we're thinking about it every moment or not. Without the history of where we've been, we could blindly go there again. In fact, we *would* go there again. Remember Eve in the Garden? How foolish she was in her practical ignorance. She and Adam didn't know how close they stood to the abyss."

"Sure, but suppose there was no serpent in the garden. There would be no incentive to disobey, and so history would be much different, right?"

"What do you say, Ichabod?"

"Satan was a glorious creature at first. If he could become a serpent, then I think anyone could."

"Oh. ... That sends a shiver up my spine," Larry said. "That's why the Bible is the eternal word of God. I get it now."

"That's not the most relevant part, though," Ichabod added. "Am I right, Leila?"

"Yes. The story of Jesus is the foundation of new heaven, and there are depths in it that we discover every day. The amazing thing is, it's all there in the Bible if you read every word carefully and think clearly, which is rarely done on earth. The Bible was designed for revealing Christ in eternity."

"I thought it was becoming obsolete," Larry said. "So I need to be reading Scripture every day, would you say?"

"Don't stop reading until you find something new every day. Or find something to meditate on. At least make that your goal. Then if you want to improve your brain, start memorizing whole chapters."

"Would you read something from your Bible for us now?" Larry asked, handing the book to me.

It was the moment in my life where the two halves of it clicked together. I was not there in that room for some time, but I do not know for how long. When I looked down at the book on my lap it seemed I was looking at the whole universe. It had fallen open at Psalm 91.

"Psalm ninety-one begins by poetically stating the position and testimony of every true believer."

1   He who dwells in the shelter of the Most High,
     who abides in the shadow of the Almighty,

2   will say of Yahweh, "He is my refuge and my fortress;
     my God in whom I trust."

"Is this trust based on a promise? The next verse seems to say it is based on experience. At least that's the way we take it in heaven."

3   For he will deliver you from the snare of the hunter
     and from the deadly pestilence.

"Note that it's insurance of *deliverance* from ensnarement by man and nature, not insulation from it ever happening.

Then comes a most remarkable verse where a poetic couplet of comfort is followed by an extra line that explains how the insurance policy works:"

4   He will cover you with his pinions,
     and under his wings you will take refuge;
     his truth is your shield and protection.

"Jesus said his truth will set you free. How is his truth our shield? It deflects fear of the unknown."

5   You will not fear terrors at night
     nor arrows that fly during the day;

6   You will not fear pestilence that stalks in darkness
     nor destruction that wastes at noonday.

"Next the poem speaks prophetically directly to our Lord. This was fulfilled when he came and defeated his enemies:"

7   Though a thousand fall at your side
     and ten thousand at your right hand,
     it will not come near you.

8   You will only look on with your eyes
     and see the reward of the wicked.

"The psalmist breaks out in an exclamation of praise for the victor and goes on to describe him as being invincible."

9   "For you, O Yahweh, are my refuge!"
     You have made the Most High your habitation.

10   No evil will befall you,
      neither will any plague come near your tent.

11   For he will give his angels charge over you,
      to keep you in all your ways.

12   They will bear you up in their hands,
      lest you dash your foot against a stone.

13   You will tread upon the lion and adder:
      the young lion and the serpent you will trample under foot.

"Finally, the poem switches to Yahweh's voice, describing his Son from an earthly point of view."

14   Because he has set his love upon me, I will deliver him:
      I will set him on high, because he has known my name.

15   He will call upon me, and I will answer him;
      I will be with him in trouble:
      I will deliver him, and honor him.

16   With long life will I satisfy him,
      and show him my salvation.

"What does that last line, 'show him my salvation,' mean?"

"Never try to interpret one line of a couplet on its own, Larry; take both lines of verse sixteen together to see what it means."

"So it refers to the thousand years of this present age?"

"Yes, and the wonderful purpose of this age in which heaven is saved from being threatened by its enemies."

"Okay, that's cool. Now I have a psalm for you. This was Ernie's Bible, and he had it marked. It's number 82."

1   God stands in the congregation of God;
      He judges among the gods.

"Who are *the gods*?" Larry asked me.

"From our point of view on earth they are like high ranking angels, created by God like Satan was created. Elsewhere in the Bible they are called Sons of God. In heaven this is made more clear, and this psalm is often on my mind because peace in heaven as well as on earth is not certain while Satan and these divine 'judges' are able to rule the nations. Presently during this trial period they are ineffective because their leader is in prison while Jesus Son of David reigns along with Prince Solomon."

"That makes sense because the next three verses sound like a king telling the judges that he appointed to shape up."

2   How long will you judge unjustly
      and respect the persons of the wicked?

3   Judge the poor and fatherless;
      do justice to the afflicted and destitute.

4   Protect the poor and needy;
      deliver them out of the hand of the wicked.

"But why did God tolerate bad angels ruling over the nations?"

"They challenged God's standard of righteousness as being unnecessary, so in order to show they were wrong before condemning them to hell for rebellion he gave them a chance to prove they could rule by a lesser standard. The result was verse five."

5   They know not, neither do they understand;
      they walk to and fro in darkness.
      All the foundations of the earth are shaken.

"I get it. They're to be stripped of their divine privilege but not until it's made clear to everyone that they're unworthy."

6   I said, you are gods,
      and all of you are sons of the Most High.

7   Nevertheless, you will die like men
      and fall like one of the princes.

Samson objected: "In John chapter ten when Jesus quoted verse six, it seems he applied it to human judges, not angels."

"Could you find that verse and read it?" I asked, handing my Bible to him.

"They were about to stone Jesus. Then in John ten thirty-four and thirty-five he says, *Is it not written in your law, 'I said, you are gods'? If he called them gods to whom the word of God came (and the Scripture cannot be broken) ....*"

"Jesus put himself in the category of those to whom the word of God came," I said. "That's not really an interpretation, is it?"

"No, it just makes one pause. They couldn't throw stones while trying to process what he said at the same time."

"I've got it here," Larry added. "They weren't buying what he said. They tried to grab him but he got away."

"Now please read the last verse of Psalm 82, Ichabod."

8   Arise, O God, judge the earth,
       for you will inherit all the nations.

"That verse really says it all," I argued. "Because if we respect its context, the only interpretation of the 'gods' is that they had been given dominion over the nations. The psalmist is looking ahead, and he is anxious to see the day where we are now."

"It's like a prophecy, and we're seeing the fulfillment," Larry declared. ... "What is that book you were thumbing through, Ichabod?"

"It's a curious little volume of poems and essays. There's one here that intrigues me. It's somebody's yacht talking. The title is, 'Songs of a Lonely Sailing Yacht'.

"Let's hear it. ... Is that all right with you, Leila?"

"If Ichabod will read it."

> I long for your touch on my helm and the fragrance of your oils in my cabin. Wine parties do nothing for me.
>
> But I have neither! I am abandoned; no reveling in my saloon, no wine on my deck. They've let my brightwork turn dull and become dry. It awaits your anointing!
>
> I know why every new yacht desires to sail under your flag. Your name is like fragrant oil, like the finest perfume. I hope you have not forgotten me. Day and night I listen for you. Come, draw up my anchor and let us run before the wind!
>
> (The king once had me in his royal marina.)
>
> *We all rejoice in the king. Rightly do they adore him.*
>
> I am dusty but still lovely, O daughters of the royal city. Do not stare at my faded sails and spars; the sun has been looking harshly upon me since they took away my covers. My keeper's sons have been rough with me. They rented me to friends who are not sailors. They used me for their parties. They abused me. They did not keep me up.
>
> Tell me, you whose feet my sole adores: where do you send your fleet; where do you have them harbor after their long days at sea? Why should I be kept apart, never allowed to sail with your companions? Why was I sent away after you became king?

If you do not know, O most beautiful of vessels, follow my sails and see where they anchor at night. I have not forgotten you, my love. I think of you as a schooner among shrimp boats. Your frames are of acacia wood set in floors of silver, and your spars we shall overlay with gold.

We shall make for you ornaments of gold, studded with silver.

I remember the day when I leaped wave to wave, leaving streaks of white in my wake. The king was at my helm! He is a crimson sky at sunset and a steady breeze by night. He is to me the fragrance of myrrh in my cabin.

Behold, you are beautiful, my love; you are beautiful even in the dark of night when your moonlit sails sweep the sky, or when anchored on a peaceful bay with your port lights glowing like eyes.

I dream of you being with me. Our couch is the sea, the beams of the moon are the beams of our house, and our rafters are constellations.

Am I not your lily of the sea?

As a lily among kelp, so is my love among the royal yachts.

As a varnished mast among checked spars, so is my beloved among young sailors.

Those were days of great delight when he moored me alongside his dock, and his feet were sweet to my sole. He entered me in the yacht parade, and his banner over me was love.

Sustain me with sweet promises; refresh me with words, for I cry for you in my dreams. ... *His right hand grasps my helm, holding my head to the wind, and his left hand adjusts my sheets.*

I adjure you, O daughters of the royal city, for the sake of vessels whose skippers love the sea, do not stir up his desire to sail upon them if he is not delighted with them.

What do I hear? Is it the voice of my beloved? Has he come leaping over mountains, bounding over hills? (He is like a gazelle or a young stag.) Is that him standing afar on the shore? Does he look at me through his glass?

I hear my beloved singing to me:

213

Up with your anchor, my beautiful ship;
now sail away with me.
The winter is past, the storms are gone,
the days are sunny at last.
The season of singing of birds has come,
and flowers do flourish ashore.
Up with your anchor, my beautiful one;
now sail away with me.
O my dove, in that secret pass
to the islands off the coast,
let me see the sun on your jib;
let me hear the wind in your rig
whose humming is music to me.
(We must avoid those foxes,
those noisy little speedboats
that spoil our rendezvous.)

Shall we not cruise tonight among the islands until the day breathes and the shadows flee? Be a skipper who misses his craft! Come back to me tonight!

In my dream I sought him whom my sole loves; I sought him but found him not. I said I will slip my moorings and ghost along the waterfront, by the docks and the marinas, and I will seek him whom my sole loves. I sought him but found him not. The watchman hailed me, and I said, "Have you seen him whom my sole loves?" Shortly afterward as I drifted along I found him whom my sole loves. I took him aboard and would not let him leave me until he sailed me under the stars to the exact location at which my designer conceived me, that he would be so inspired.

I adjure you, O daughters of the city, for the sake of vessels whose skippers love the sea, stir not up his desire to sail them if he is not thoroughly delighted with them.

What is this coming up from the desert country like columns of smoke? Behold, it is the motorcade of our king! Sixty escorts are with him, all of them armed.

(The king had his limousine specially made. Its roof is silver, its doors are gold, its seats are of royal purple. The interior leather we fashioned ourselves; we inlaid with our love.)

Remember, O daughters of the city, remember the king as he was when his mother crowned him, on the day of the gladness of his heart, before his name was poured out abroad. Is he happier now? Is he? He is with me!

Behold, you are beautiful, my love; indeed, you are delightful. Your ports are eyes of peace, peeking over your toe-rail. The planks of your deck nestle like ripples under a gentle breeze. Your bobstay is like a silver blade as it slices bounding waves. The line of your stem arcs forward like a dew-laden lily's stem. The sweep of your sheer is a fabulous curve—and more, much more I could say!

You captivate me, my perfect one, but beware: it's not me alone who loves you. I see a hundred flags from clubs of renown fluttering like gulls about your mast.

In your cabin a cozy berth awaits me, I know. Until the day breathes and the shadows flee we shall lie under the mountain of myrrh and the hill of frankincense.

Yes, you are altogether beautiful, my love; there is no flaw in you. Come with me from exile, my ship; come with me from your harbor in the wilds. You captured my heart, my yacht, my pride; you captured my heart after one glance at the rake of your masts. How much better than wine is a nap in your berth. Oh, how I prefer the fragrance of your woodwork to the smell of diesel fuel!

A secret garden is my ship, my pride, a spring locked, a fountain sealed. Your ways are an orchard of pomegranates with choicest fruits and spices, a garden fountain, a well of living water, and flowing streams from the north.

Awake, O north wind, and come O southern breeze! Blow upon my beloved that her aroma may come to me.

Rather, let my beloved come to his beloved—come to his garden and enjoy his choicest fruits! My days are reserved for him since he has shown me his love.

I sailed my garden, my ship, my pride—I buried her rail, I did—and never a reef did she keep in her sail. I ate the honeycomb with my honey; I drank my wine with my milk.

Eat, friends of the bride; drink, and be drunk with love!

I slept, but my heart was awake. I heard a voice calling! My beloved has come, I said. He has come for me!

Open for me, my ship, my dove, my perfect one; my head is wet and my locks are damp with the dew of night.

My sole was encumbered by sails in bags. How could I clear them away? I was not ready! My beloved put his hand on the latch, and my heart thrilled within me. I scrambled to open to my beloved, and I found my latch dripping with myrrh from his hand on the handle of the bolt. When I opened to my beloved, he had turned away, and he was gone. My sole had failed me in the moment at which he called for me.

I flew in my dream to the city and sought him but found him not. I called him. He gave no answer. But the harbor patrol found me. They rammed into me and scuffed me badly when they came aboard. They took away the ensign of my beloved—those watchmen over the royal city.

I adjure you, O daughters of the royal city, if you find my beloved, tell him I am sick with love.

What is your beloved more than another beloved, O most beautiful among sailing craft? What is your beloved more than your young sailors, that you thus adjure us?

Among ten thousand you'll know him:
he's handsome, sturdy, and trim.
His head, you know, is meant for
a crown of the finest gold.
His locks, oh, how shiny and wavy,
are black as a raven and full.
His eyes are quick yet mild
like doves swimming in milk.
His beard is a garden of spices,
sweet-smelling and carefully kept.
The arms that are strong and golden
wear bands of colorful jewels.
His waistcoat like polished ivory
is adorned with gems of blue.
His legs are strong as pillars
of marble in bases of gold.
His mouth speaks words of wisdom,
still true after all has been told.

He's the choicest cedar in Lebanon,
this man whom I welcome aboard.
This man is my beloved,
and this man is my friend,
O daughters of the royal city.

Where has your beloved gone, O most beautiful among yachts? Where has your beloved turned that we may seek him with you?

My beloved has gone down to his marina, to the royal harbor, to meet the visiting yachts and pick his favorites. I am my beloved's and he is mine, yet he has others too.

You are my delight, my love, lovely as the royal city, awesome as an armada with banners. I had to turn your noble stern away from me, for you overwhelmed me. Your sails are like a flock of geese, winging northward in the sky. Your decks are halves of golden mangoes glowing under the sun.

There are sixty look-alike luxury yachts, eighty noisy cruisers, and numberless newbie boats in my collection; but you, my dove, my favored one, are the only one of your kind; perfect you were in your designer's eyes. When the newer vessels saw you they called you blessed; the classic yachts and cruisers praised you too: "Who is this whose sails have silently appeared like the dawn of a day?" they said. "She is beautiful as the moon, swift as the breeze, awesome as an armada with banners!"

I was curious, and I inquired about the island of the nut orchard, to see whether the yachts of the prince had been launched. Before I was aware, I found myself desiring to be among them, those yachts of his kinsman, my prince.

Return, O estranged one, return that we may look upon you. Why should you tarry for your beloved? Are you Helen? Do you think he will wage war for you?

I love your forefoot, even when entwined in seaweed, O noble daughter! Your buttocks by the shipwright's art follow perfect lines. Your stateroom, warm and spacious, is the kind that seamen adore. Your bowsprit is an ivory pulpit for watching porpoises play.

A king is held captive in your cockpit, each sheet and halyard at his hand. But you never mind keeping our course yourself when I dive below for a raisin cake or something else. When we come to rest at the end of the day your sails slide smoothly down, and the wind flows evenly over you to hold your anchor true.

Yes, my sails come down smoothly for my beloved, gliding over clips and reefs. I am my beloved's, and his desire is for me.

Now, my beloved, I have in mind greater pleasure for you: When you come again, we shall moor near the coastal towns, and from there we shall go early to sea in order to find fair winds. Then I will show you my love while the steady breeze holds our course and keeps my canvas full. Later we shall visit every harbor, unfrequented bays as well as anchorages where fine boats gather.

Oh, that the royal yacht were my brother. If I found my brother here in my moorage, I would bring him alongside, and none would despise me. I would take you aboard, and I would give you spiced wine to drink, and you would stay with me for the comfort of my nectar. Then in the morning we would slip away. *His right hand on my helm keeps my head to the wind, and his left hand holds my sheet.*

I adjure you, O daughters of the royal city: do not stir up his desire to sail those other yachts if he is not delighted to do so.

Oh, my master and king, someday I will come out of exile with you being my pilot. For under a starry sky at sea it was I who claimed you when your mother conceived you. Then when at sea she labored for you, my seal was fixed on your heart.

Jealousy is as fierce as the grave, but love is stronger than death. If the flame of my love is the flame of the Lord, it will never be cold. Lonely days will not quench my love, nor will winter storms cause despair.

If another sailor were to lavish even all his wealth upon me, I would utterly despise him.

We have a little boat, and she has as yet no cabin on her for a king. What shall we do for this sister on the day she is put up for sale?

If she repels young sailors, build on her a silver cabin. If she attracts them, let her cabin be boards of cedar.

I despised the young sailors, but my stateroom's berth is fine, and the king found peace in me.

The king had a marina in a large city. He let it out to a keeper who returned for the rentals a thousand pieces of silver. My marina is myself. The king may keep their thousands and pay my keepers two hundred.

O you who dwell in the country where only your tugboat brothers hear your voice ... Let **me** hear it!

I cry for you each night! Come back to your garden of spices soon, for I have flooded my sole with my tears!

"Who wrote that?" I asked Larry.

"Why? Is it blasphemy?"

"There's no author indicated," Samson volunteered.

"Why did you ask if it's blasphemy, Larry?"

"Well, because Solomon is so strict about laws. I know who wrote it, but she doesn't need more trouble, from what I hear."

"I don't see why you think Solomon wouldn't like it," Samson said. "He might like it better than the original."

"Are the Songs of Solomon used in heaven?" Larry asked me.

"Yes. I can't tell you why, though. I mean, such songs speak for themselves, and trying to explain them adds what doesn't belong to them."

"So why do you think Solomon might like Cl— ... might like that author's takeoff?"

"I think he would never have let it be in the Bible if it had been up to him. But what do I know about such things? I do know about the love of boats, however, and that's an inexplicable thing too. Back when Jesus lived in Galilee, he used boats many times. He was a carpenter. I've wondered if he ever built a boat. Surely as a child he would have crafted a small one at least."

"It amazes me that he slept during a storm while sailors panicked. Of course he could walk on water, so there was no danger."

"You can look at it that way, Larry, but I think when waves rock you to sleep it's because you love being on the boat."

I took my leave before the end of Sabbath so I could attend the Havdalah with my family in heaven.

Perhaps you have wondered how new heaven could be synchronized with all the time zones on earth at once. The zones exist in heaven too. The top of the "ladder" in heaven and the foot on earth are in the same time zone. Distances are shorter around the city, of course. It would be like living near the north pole on earth.

Before I left I promised Samson I would meet him in Salem on Monday. He needed to be there for Ward Howard's heresy trial.

The Foster family would not be coming down Sunday morning. Samson could have spent Sunday at the Beach House, but he had been watching the barometer and decided to fly to Bellingham if possible, spend Sunday night with Joe Martin's family, and fly out Monday morning with full fuel tanks because he knew fuel was unavailable in Salem.

But that meant he was on his own getting to the airport. If Larry had walked with him they would have taken the shorter route through town, and Larry offered to do so, but since he had said previously that he always went fishing on Sundays, Samson insisted that he needed the exercise and did not mind hiking by way of Four Corners. Larry then urged him to take the motorbike, but Samson refused the offer because Larry would be without transportation until he walked to the airport to retrieve it. The bike was smaller than the others and not intended for two riders.

But after Samson had walked up the driveway he reevaluated his options. According to what he had heard from Larry about the pioneers' ignorance of the real world, he assumed that walking alone with an obvious limp would make him a spectacle. They were all whole, healthy, resurrected folks who were well satisfied with what they believed was heaven. They accepted Larry because he merely bore signs of old age, but it would be a shock to them to realize that a painful relic of tribulation infested heaven. Was the naïve theology embraced by a whole community of so little value that it could be justly disturbed for lessening one man's brief discomfort? He thought not and borrowed Larry's bike.

The Meeting in Salem
Chapter Eighteen

Everything went according to plan. Samson was able to fly out below broken low clouds on Sunday. Monday morning Joe allowed him to refuel his plane once more. And at exactly noon on Monday he had landed at Salem, taxied to transient parking, and tied down the airplane's wings and tail. He was not clear on the date of the trial, but he knew it could not take place without his presence. He hoped that someone—not me—would be there to meet him: someone from a Salem family where he could get meals and spend the night. (I had told Karen he would be there at noon. How did I know? It feels like it was a lucky guess, but I think it was not. I just knew.)

So Samson, from a distance, saw someone—a woman—waiting for him at the gate. She did not have the fresh look of a glorified person, so she could not be his Delilah. As he hobbled toward the gate he observed that she knew him. But who was she? Karen, possibly? Yes, she had to be Karen Martin looking decades older than when he saw her last.

Karen's plan was to take him to the baseball training camp being run by Victoria Martin where they could get some lunch. Karen was driving an ancient diesel pickup truck which belonged to the construction family she worked for. I had seen it, and I had ridden in it. It was terribly noisy and smelly too.

The camp was held at Judson Middle School which was not far from the airport and would have been an easy drive if more roads were open—because there was little traffic.

Being one of the few people who knew Ichabod's true identity, Karen had thought carefully about how to introduce him to Victoria, for as the starting pitcher for the Herne Hornets, Victoria had known Earl Clark when he managed the Lakeside Leaders ball team. She would not try to make it a secret that Ichabod was interested in baseball, but she would be vague about his home town. Victoria, however, had talked to me in heaven that morning as we were both in line to descend to earth on the same ladder which landed us in the newly built Hermon Hotel in Salem. So she was expecting a special visitor.

When Karen and Ichabod arrived at the school the players were enjoying free time after having finished their lunch. Some were throwing and catching. Most were still at the table talking and laughing. I had warned Victoria about Ichabod's appearance so she would not have to reset any expectation. But I think she was very curious about his obvious importance to us.

"Ichabod flew in from Bellingham this morning. He's here to be a witness in a trial taking place at the courthouse this afternoon," said Karen. "He used to manage a youth team."

"Was that in Bellingham?" Victoria asked.

"Not too far from there," Ichabod replied.

"Do you know the Fosters?—Harold Foster?"

"Yes, Harold is well known in Bellingham. He's overseer at Bellingham's construction family."

"I was wondering because Harold is involved with airplanes. Have you been to his shop where they're making parts for electric motors?"

"I was there on Friday."

"Have you met Homer Foster?"

"Yes, and he knows you well, I believe."

"Did he tell you we were on opposing teams, both of us starting pitchers?"

"I understand you are unique in the history of baseball for hitting a Homer yet not making it to first base."

They all laughed, though for Victoria it was a hackneyed quip.

"Victoria played for the Herne Hornets," I said. "Three of her glorified teammates are here helping with the camp."

"Isabella and Amelia Young and Sonya Stern," Victoria added as if Ichabod would know their names, and I believe she had that possibility in mind.

"Are all your players here today naturals?" Ichabod asked.

"No, in fact, we have three glorifieds participating with us each week."

"Aren't the glorified players intrinsically superior to the natural kids mentally and physically?"

"No, there are naturals that are, well, naturals at baseball. The glorified kids are more uniform in their abilities and not as versatile as natural humans. The glorified players have the advantage of not being as susceptible to injury. They don't bruise and they don't bleed because our bodies are grounded in another dimension. But they tire more quickly."

"Why do they come to earth for baseball? I thought heaven would have pleasures to suit everyone. I know baseball had become unwholesome and never was anything like holy, but if managed by honest men and played with sincere souls, I think it would exercise like nothing else certain abilities that God included in the human design, and so it would be in heaven."

"I don't have an answer to that. It sounds reasonable. All I know is that there are no spectator sports in heaven. No field is large enough for baseball. And these glorified children that are participating in the camp this week have no desire to apply their training in heaven. All the young folk in heaven want to come down to earth, but not to play. They want to evangelize the natural children, and in order to be accepted to come down even for one week they have to take a year-long evangelism course and pass the final exam with a perfect score."

Neither Karen nor Ichabod had heard this before. It changed the atmosphere. They both glanced at the youngsters and easily picked out three shining faces. Samson said he saw halos and wondered why he had not noticed the difference before. The joy and beauty which Victoria and her three helpers possessed was at the modest level we are all trained to manifest when on earth. The children had no such inhibitions.

Victoria ended the awkward pause: "Isn't it amazing that Homer got his own private Rapture?"

"You knew you would find him," Ichabod said, which prompted her to serve him a penetrating look.

"Ichabod did too," Karen said. "But not in heaven."

"Oh! Ichabod, you're an exceptional! I never had the privilege of meeting one before, but I knew somehow that you were different."

"It means you never know what to expect," said Karen.

"I think Homer is like that too. I would like it if he helped me run the camp. In heaven I have no authority to make him do anything, unfortunately. He could come down with me now because he's no longer needed at that lumber mill, and he's got nothing better to do on earth than tag along with his old family."

"That's ideal, isn't it?" Karen said.

"No, that's unusual. But I don't think it will last forever. What they are doing is not a project of the crown; it's Harold's brain-child, and he's providing a temporary solution to the lack of usable aircraft. My prayer is that when we get our assignments Homer and I will not be far apart. If it has nothing to do with baseball, that will be fine with me as long as I get to see Homer."

"Why wouldn't it be baseball?" Karen asked. "If baseball isn't in the plan then why are we setting up that field?"

"I'm not saying spectator sports on earth aren't in the plan; it's just that the balance of my body and spirit is much different now. It's difficult to explain."

After the meeting with Victoria there was still time before Ichabod needed to be at the courthouse for Ward Howard's pretrial hearing. Karen took him to her work site where she was supervising the construction of spectator stands. Since it was not easy for Samson to walk, they sat in the truck and talked.

"How is your diesel fuel supply?" Ichabod inquired.

"Good. We got a tank car of automotive diesel last month."

"Is there any word on gasoline?"

"Yes. The word is it isn't available yet. Do you have enough in your plane to get you to where you're going next?"

"Until I get further instructions I don't know where I'm going next."

"There's a spare bedroom at my house. Claudia has moved out temporarily. Or it could be permanent."

"I heard someone say things were not going well for her."

"She's in prison. We call it the rod of iron. She got convicted of copying another artist's work and selling it."

"That surprises me. I thought she was creative in her artistic work."

"So did she until she tried a new subject. She discovered that the genius in her creativity was narrow, and of course she would not want to turn out what had made her famous in the past. She still had her skill with paint but no inspiration. I suggested that she try something along the lines of what Harrietta Foster had done in that painting of the castle in the sky that hangs on the front-room wall at the Beach House."

"I always liked it. For me it changed the atmosphere of that room where I had spent many evenings alone. I never understood why Claudia didn't like it."

"You didn't? Well, it goes with being an artist."

"So that's what she copied—copied it entirely from memory? She must have studied it intently."

"She said she didn't intend to copy it but only use it for inspiration. When I saw it, I told her, 'Claudia, that's Harrietta's castle exactly.' She said no, it was maybe close but not exactly the same."

"Is there a law against that? Did she make money with it?"

"That was her mistake. I told her to just donate it, but she was poor—we both were poor. By the end of the tribulation we had lost everything and were starving. The friends we thought were Christians gave up and got the mark. We were part of a micro economy which ended at that point because the penalty for sharing with unmarked friends was death. You wouldn't know about that. How did you earn the privilege of skipping past the worst times? Melchior told Claudia you had been summoned for some special purpose."

"Whatever that purpose was perhaps doesn't exist anymore, because no one has told me what I was summoned for. Wouldn't you think someone would have met me right away to tell me what to do or where to go to find out what I was called for?"

"Is there anything that you could do to prepare for being used in some special way? Maybe you're on trial and they're waiting to see if you will make yourself as presentable as you can."

"Like getting my hair cut?

"I don't think it's you. It's not the manly look you once had."

"Well, nothing can restore what I was."

"Don't say that. You have friends here, and medical services are available if you know the right people."

"It appears to me this is a dangerous place. How did they know about Harrietta's painting?"

"What happened was an angel was both places and saw both paintings. I mean, we built the Hermon Hotel and the angel that set up the Jacob's ladder also did the ladder at the Beach House."

"You're saying Claudia sold it to the hotel?"

"Yes, it seemed the perfect place for it."

"And now she's in prison?"

"She has to pay Harrietta the price she sold it for. I didn't have much to lend her, and she had spent all the proceeds of the sale on paints and canvas and brushes (things impossible to find in this town). So she's behind bars until she's able to pay the last penny."

"How was it that you and Claudia came to Salem? I thought you were in a good place at the Beach House."

"It was by Melchior's advice."

"Claudia went to see Melchior?"

"She did. She used the last bit of charge in your electric car."

"And she made it back on her own?"

"Yes, she came back on Homer's motorcycle."

"I heard that her plane was here and in pretty bad shape, so I expected to find her here. Why did *you* leave your Beach House?"

"As I said, it was by Melchior's advice. I wanted to get away from the ruined town and forget the disaster we were living with. Also Ernie and Enid were not prepared to host more than themselves in the Beach House. Larry and Ned pulled their weight, but Claudia and me not so much."

"Larry told me he found where Claudia's sailing yacht lies."

"Lies at anchor or—"

"At anchor, yes, but on the bottom—under water."

"It was a moonlit night that we made our escape and sailed her down to that cove Claudia knew about which is close enough to the highway that we could sneak back to the airport. It was a beautiful night but sad. Claudia promised her she would be back."

"I think Claudia knew in the back of her mind that she would never get back. If she hadn't had that little jet, she would not have taken you so far that you couldn't get back. I knew it was too much airplane for her and would get her into trouble someday."

"It never will again."

"From what I heard it will never fly again."

"It's completely ruined. When the beast turned directed energy weapons on aircraft, her poor plane was hit extra hard."

"I thought most of the damage was caused by the sun's massive coronal ejection event that accompanied Jesus' return."

"You would think that. There were earthquakes and fires from the CME, but those of us who lived through the transition saw it all. The beast started it. I was here, like I said, when directed energy defenses were turned on us. After ruining the airport they rolled through Salem, burning buildings and frying vehicles."

"They thought they were making recovery impossible."

"Can you imagine the devil being that foolish?"

"Well, I can imagine since he knew how effective digital technology had become in controlling earth, he didn't want to leave such power in the hands of his enemy."

"I suppose he never expected heaven would drop ladders to put modern sanctified intelligence into the world," Karen said.

"That's because he never believed the Rapture would supply the bodies. ... Now, we have some time before the trial. Can we visit Claudia? Is the prison far?"

"She's in what used to be a jail, and it's in the courthouse. It's all we have for a prison, but it's sufficient. There's little crime because the penalties are stiff. I need to visit her today anyway."

On their way to the jail Samson asked Karen about me. He wanted to know whether she had seen me today. I'm not sure what she said exactly. He told me it was an evasive answer.

Claudia was in a cell by herself with dozens of pencils that needed sharpening. She earned the prisoner's minimum wage, which in her case was a penny for each proverb she copied. She was dependent on visitors to bring her sharpened pencils because she had no sharpener and blades were not allowed in her cell. Every day, regardless of how much her fingers ached, she wore down the leads of all the pencils in her possession. Karen had brought a bag of sharpened pencils which she exchanged for as many dull ones, passing them a few at a time between the bars in the cell door.

Claudia was glad to see Earl. She wanted to know where he had been and especially about common acquaintances. He nearly told her about her sunken sailing yacht. She would want to know —had a right to know—but as he hesitated she was agreeing with Karen that he would be wise to take advantage of the medical services available in Salem. First, however, he needed to have his tresses cut. Though Samson did not agree with them, he did not argue. Since I had promised to meet him in Salem, he suspected that I was behind the prodding. They had to cut the visit short in order to be on time for the pretrial hearing which took place in the same building.

Howie was brought in by a kingdom marshal. Samson was relieved that the marshal was not someone he knew, because that would be so bizarre that he would have to doubt that reality was real. But when the judge came in it reached that point. He doubted his eyes. Karen had neglected to tell him that Ward Howard's former "significant other" was a judge in Salem.

Samson knew that Betty Rice had disappeared at the Rapture. He had come to expect meeting people from his former life with improbable frequency as if the kingdom of God were a fairy tale; but the irony in this one forced him to excuse himself so he could leave the room and let it sink in without embarrassing Karen.

The most insanely judgmental anti-Christian person he had ever met was now an officer in the kingdom of God! She was completely transformed. Every time he had seen her about town she had been in her wheelchair, a pitiful creature, wearing the same brightly-colored sweater and complaining about something. He knew this was the same person, but how he knew he did not know. She stood tall, graced by the robe of an officer in the service of the King of kings. He had to recover quickly; he was being called to testify about Ward Howard's heretical teaching.

Karen came to find him. "What are you doing?" she said. "You're supposed to be in there testifying about your evidence!"

At that point Samson would rather have dropped the charge than be an actor in what seemed a comedy skit. He could not begin to imagine Howie's state of mind, but he believed it would be penalty enough even if the charge were dismissed.

For Karen's sake Earl pulled himself together, returned to the courtroom, and listened as the judge read notes he had taken during Ward's speech and submitted to heaven. The judge then, in a kindly voice, asked her former "significant other" to state whether or not the evidence was a true record of what he had said.

"I agree that I said that," Howie stated, "but I disagree that there was any harm in it, because it was a similitude, simply a parallel that one might casually apply in the field of theology where there is similar debate on the necessity of termination. I was speaking on the subject of employee relations and policies for ensuring the welfare of both employee the employer. The lecture was all about applying experience from the former world for the benefit of new business leaders in this world who have no experience dealing with the complexities that often arise when someone is found to be performing at a level which is unsuitable to the employer and/or other employees in the organization."

"Thank you, Mr. Howard. You may catch your breath. The witness will now explain to the court why, if he thinks Mr. Howard's statements during his lecture promoted heresy, they would be taken as a theological position on the question of damnation."

"It was in all seriousness that Mr. Ward laid out those five points arguing against a literal lake of fire," Samson began. "As proof I submit that what he claims was an inconsequential digression, he also maintains was logically linked to the subject of his lecture in order to justify having said it. Yet I fail to see anything but a contrived connection to his subject of employer/employee relations. Therefore, he intended that heresy to be taken seriously, quite independently of the subject of his lecture."

"Thank you, Mr. Samson. Now, Howie, you surely remember what we both believed in the old days before I saw the light while you preferred darkness. Is there any difference between that and what you espoused in your lecture?"

"Your honor, I spun off that metaphor because I thought it was clever."

"Please answer the court's question, Howie. Have you changed your belief?"

"Whether it is a belief or not I question even in my own mind."

"Why did you say it if it wasn't your belief? Do you still go around saying nonsensical things, making yourself—I can't say 'fool.' ... I must say making yourself sound like an idiot. Or do you have a more serious purpose now in what you say?"

"I would have to go back and examine the factors that came to play when it occurred to me there was a parallel between righteous employers firing errant employees and the Creator throwing sinful creatures into the fire. It's quite possible that I may have been somewhat serious on a day when I was confused about everything and didn't know it."

At that point the hearing was over because the judge declared that an opinion on Howie's sanity would be necessary. Howie was ushered back to his jail cell by the marshal while Samson stared in wonder at the judge. He wanted to honor her glorification and thank her for the speedy hearing and confirm that he had done his part and would see no more of Howie, but Karen was suddenly acting impatiently. She took Samson to the Hermon Hotel where a room had been reserved for him.

I t seemed that Karen was more abrupt than her usual self when she left Samson at the curb outside the Hermon hotel. She had given him instructions: the room, being reserved and paid for, he needed only to check in at the counter in the lobby.

As he walked into the building he was surprised by Leila.

No. ... I must do this chapter in first person.

On his way in he was met by me.

"I've taken care of everything, Ichabod," I said. "And I have a few things to tell you before I go back tonight."

"Karen told me I needed to check in," he replied guardedly. "Have you taken care of that too?"

"Everything is arranged. Come talk with me for a little while."

I led him to a nook in the lobby where the seating was arranged for two.

"I must tell you about this man I've met," I said, trying not to smile. "His name is Samson. I mean he's the original Samson—the one who appears in the Bible. I see him often. Delilah is there too."

I easily read the puzzled expression on Ichabod's face. *Why are you telling me this?* his eyes asked, though he said nothing.

"Samson is an interesting person," I continued brightly. "I wish you could meet him."

I had planned to say more, but he didn't seem to be interested in hearing more. I waited. He had to say something, but he only stared inquiringly at me. I didn't expect this to be difficult.

Finally, when he saw I wasn't wavering from my purpose, he responded with a reasonable question:

"Did you meet him in heaven?—or where is he located?"

"He works in Dan, a territory in Israel. But when I see him it's in Jerusalem where he goes often to visit Delilah. She lives in Sorek, a settlement southwest of Jerusalem, but she spends a few days each month in Zion."

"Do they travel much—outside of Israel, I mean?" he inquired.

"No, not anymore. Back in the beginning, before the rebellions were put down, Samson did. I've heard stories. He's quite famous, as you would expect. One story has it that he uprooted a mountain and cast it into the sea. Delilah told me it really happened."

"Uprooted a literal mountain?"

"I don't think she meant a literal mountain. I didn't ask her, but I think she meant something of political prominence somewhere in the world. Perhaps it was a government building or perhaps the chief executive within it or perhaps both."

He nodded. He wasn't sure I wasn't making this up.

"What's your impression of Delilah?" he asked.

"Delilah is a delightful person. She and I have become good friends."

I knew he wanted to ask me why I was telling him these things, and I saw he was about to do so. So I cut it short and told him, "I see a certain likeness of Samson in you. Is it all right if I start calling you Samson—as if it were your first name? It's what I called Earl sometimes."

He laughed politely and shook his head. "I'm not worthy to be compared to him." He folded his arms.

"How about if I call you Earl then."

"Oh? ... Are you giving up hope of finding him?"

This was the moment I had long anticipated, and suddenly I realized I was not ready for it. What I had to say would change everything, and I had no assurance that it would be a change for the better. Indeed, at that moment I felt that the change would not be what I had imagined it to be. But I couldn't go back; he knew what I meant.

"I have found him," I whispered.

He smiled reassuringly. "You knew all the time, didn't you?"

"I never doubted that we would meet again," I said. "Clearly you didn't want me to know, so I respected your secret even though it wasn't a secret."

Earl shook his head. "So why did you insist that we keep looking for me if you knew you had already found me?"

"That was the only way I could keep from acknowledging your secret. I thought you didn't want me to see how badly Earl was hurt, and that gave me a way to prove that I didn't love you less. Besides, I needed a reason to be with you."

He must have known this, but to hear me say it destroyed the posture of defense he had so long maintained. I realized too late that it was also cruel, for it emphasized the mortality that separated his body from mine.

Earl only looked at the floor. It must have been his mixed feelings that muted him. I knew he had reason to be concerned about the legality of what we were doing, so for something to say I mentioned one of the reasons I had been able to spend time with him.

"To enlist the help of an earthling in searching for a lost person is permitted. I checked with Evelyn. She gave me permission."

After I said that I realized that I had only given him grounds for more confusion, or I should say less ground on which to make his exceptional stand in which self determination is tolerated and expected more than it is for most of us.

"But you weren't serious about the search," he said.

"No one ever stopped me."

"They must have known you were stretching it out."

"I'm sure they did."

"Will I have to pay for it?" he asked very seriously.

"It was my doing, and my judgment account is closed."

"I'm not innocent, though. It's scary to me."

"Fear not, Samson. Evelyn loves you as much as I do, and she always gets her way."

I think Earl thought I was being a little facetious at that point. "How can you be sure? She isn't the savior."

"You do know who she is—"

"Eve? You don't mean the first Eve."

"Yes, as a type, and she personifies more than Eve. She intercedes for all Eve's children."

"I guess I had better get in line or I'll never get a reward," he said, perhaps to little purpose.

"Earl, I am your reward. And yes, it is time."

"I'm having a little difficulty believing this. Did Evelyn give you this assignment?"

"Oh, no. I thought we were friends."

"At one time we almost were, but I was wary because, well, you worked for a higher power, for one thing. And you still do."

"Yes, I do, and I'm committed to my job absolutely. What was the other thing?"

"You were falling in love with me."

"And I did, and I am in love with you, but now you have nothing to fear on that account because I'm married—yes to that higher Power."

"Then you must be here on an assignment."

"There's a reason I'm here that I don't fully understand. You're exceptional, and it's been granted to me to spend time with you and become part of your exception. No one is excluded from the domain of the higher powers. That includes you and your career, and it involves me. If I had not found you, I don't know what I would have done."

"How can you be an exceptional? I thought you were a citizen of heaven?"

"Yes, I am, and thus it is not possible for me to be sad for very long, which I'm sure is part of the reason I'm here. There's no exception for that, so I have become exceptional in order to join you in your sorrow."

"You defy logic," Delilah.

"No, it's better for me to spend one hour with you than a whole day in heaven."

He shook his head. I don't think he thought I was serious.

"In my condition I'm a poor sight for you," he said very sadly.

"Earl, if I notice your disfigurement at all, I see your sacrifice for me."

"You were already gone. It was my fury against Cypher; that's all."

"Yes, but thanks to you and Evelyn I was included."

"Even as a child you were included, am I not correct?"

"What became of me was preordained, but you loved me first; remember that."

"Must I tell you that you have never left my thoughts?"

It was my turn to doubt the sincerity of words, but I didn't. I had the advantage of being able to see into another soul, and I knew he spoke his heart.

"Someday you will have to move on to another place, and you will have other company," I said.

It sounds heartless as I hear myself saying it now, but he knew what I meant and he knew I had something to offer him that would either forestall that day or make it easier for him to bear.

"I wanted to ask you how many years I have," he said.

"How am I to know? Mortals guard their secret."

"Then why are you here? You have a plan."

"I want you to be whole so that the years you have will be more enjoyable. Will you trust me?"

"Go ahead. It was inevitable that this day would come."

The hotel has only the one upper floor, reached by a stairway. "Let us go up to your room."

As we climbed the stairs, I outlined my plan: "We have scheduled several operations. Tomorrow morning will be the first, and if it's successful you will have sight in both your eyes."

"Where?"

"Right here in Salem."

"Oh. I thought you were taking me with you to heaven. If you've become an exceptional, I thought you could have an exception of that kind made for me."

"I would if that were possible. We'll have to take it a step at a time. ... Here is your room."

"I thought the rooms in this hotel were for transiting to heaven," he said. I know he meant that to mean he would not object if we took that step sooner.

"Some are. Most are not. Yours is a little different. It has a special purpose tonight."

I opened the door, which has no lock on the outside, and he followed me in. I had a rush of emotion at that point, which caught me off guard. It must have been the association of being alone with him in a hotel room—the association of that with the thrill of the first night of marriage, which I never experienced ... but here I was somehow experiencing it! I'm not sure what he felt, but I know he was keenly aware of the physical gulf between us. And of course he was on his guard because he didn't know why I wanted to be with him in his room.

Before he could ask me I told him:

"I promised that you would meet their requirements at the clinic. I'm going to cut your hair."

He must have suspected this. "All right, Delilah. But are you sure this will turn out the way you expect it to?"

"Everything will work out fine. Everything depends on who you know. Nothing else matters."

"That's like it always has been on this earth. We used to call it corruption."

"Remember, we're under the regime of our blessed benign King where the channels that always became corrupt during demon rule are now in the hands of righteous servants."

"But there are strict rules, isn't that so?"

"Strict? Yes, to someone whose heart isn't owned by the King. But no, if guarding your estate is no longer your concern."

"Tell me about heaven. What I've gathered I find hard to fit into a clear picture. What do people do? I assume there's as much difference in people as there was in their lives on earth. How are the differences handled? I assume everyone is happy?"

"Yes, everyone is happy as to their assignment and purpose," I answered, knowing that it would be impossible to answer his question in general. But I could give him examples, I thought, with enough explanation to satisfy earthly reason.

"Heaven is different things to different people," I began. "What heaven is to you depends largely on where you were in sanctification when you left your mortal body. For example, some of Yahweh's most faithful servants seldom examined their lives critically, always pressing forward to the high calling in Christ. So when they alight on a street of heaven they're suddenly at loose ends because there's no higher calling than simply being in heaven—according to all they can imagine. They are justly proud of their service, but they find no immediate reward or recognition presented to them. When they go looking to find the reason for this they always come to Memory Lane. Yes, there is a Memory Lane in heaven for those who need it. And there is no going back once you start down that terrible road. When someone faints before reaching the end, an angel carries them to the Hall of Memories. This is a large, soundproof building for people who have crying to do. I spent only a short time there because, fortunately, I had already done a good bit of crying as a mortal—the kind that comes with honest repentance. For saints who haven't faced their past and worked through the pain in it, they have this opportunity, and it's the fulfillment of crying for them."

Earl was shaking his head in disbelief as I tried to explain this, and he spoke his objection: "I'm sure I've heard it said there will be no crying up there. Doesn't the Bible say that?"

"No, it doesn't. Isaiah wrote that there will no longer be heard in Jerusalem the voice of weeping and the sound of crying. His reference was Jerusalem on earth, and it's not strictly true, of course. Comparatively, it's true on earth now because of the wise government that fosters peace. But humans do and should cry on occasion—except with glorified eyes you almost never shed tears."

"I remember reading in Revelation," he want on, still shaking his head, "that God will wipe away every tear. Now are you going to tell me that the crying place up there serves that purpose?"

Earl, dear, you comprehend so well, I thought. But I went on: "Isaiah in another place says the same thing. There are times and places for crying even in heaven, but there is joyful resolution too, and because of that, the crying is not forgotten! In fact, there is a permanent record of tears along with the joy. What the Bible does say is that those who sow in tears shall reap with joyful shouting, but it is not tied to any particular time and place. It's a principle which works even in heaven, though less often than on earth."

Earl said nothing for a moment, and I was sorry I had started with that relatively unimportant subject.

"Does everyone go through that crying discipline to some degree?" he asked.

"No. Unfortunately for some, they do not. Instead, their discipline toward practical sanctification becomes more severe."

"What? Are there rebels in heaven?"

"No. Rebels are not admitted. These people are harmless as to their intentions when they arrive after training. They're legally sinless and righteous, which is why they got admitted, but their conduct lacks that practical sanctity which would make them fit for the common areas in heaven. They don't join into heaven's society and modes of worship well, but neither is there a reason for them to be condemned. So their souls undergo a sort of pruning which makes them incapable of becoming restless."

"That makes sense. You wouldn't want a man like me wandering the golden streets with no boats to build or planes to fly or drains to fix."

"Seriously, restlessness in an incompletely sanctified soul is not only unpleasant to himself and others, but his presence is a potential danger to the peace of heaven," I explained.

"I think I see what you mean. Then what's done about it? What did you mean by pruning?"

"I'll give you an example. Here's a person who is devoted to sports—as well as being observant regarding religious duties. This person has no business in hell, but there is a deficit of interest in the business of heaven. Heaven for this soul would not be a happy experience without games. So that's precisely the arrangement that's made for him by our merciful Savior."

"For all eternity? Wouldn't boredom set in after, say, a million or so tennis games. There are only so many variations."

"The pruning takes care of that: the soul's memory receives a heavenly truncation—without any objection, for there was no anticipation of remembering things in heaven. Now only the last game is remembered. So every tennis match is new and exciting."

Earl looked incredulous. "Is that the end of it? It seems that the wisdom of heaven could nourish that poor soul and bring forth a shoot of new growth that would open a new vista that would excite him more than the game ever did."

"I'm pretty sure you're right about that and that new growth happens in some cases. But I do know that there are entire levels in New Jerusalem covered with playing fields. I visited one, and I tell you the excitement and exuberant joy was a real testimony to the variety of modes that the design of the human being is capable of manifesting.

"I'll give you another example. Here is someone who possesses the gift of creativity to an exemplary extent. The exercise of her creative talent is what feeds her soul, and through long practice on earth she comes to heaven still powerful in that regard. But she respects her Creator and realizes that she's only a sub-creator. She is not prideful at all about it. There would be nothing for her to do in hell, and since she gives some of her time to true religion, she is of no immediate threat to heaven. What would you do with a person like that if you were a judge in heaven?"

"In what way does she get pruned, in other words? Well, if she creates things, it isn't like a game that can be played over and over. Her creations, I suppose, would have to be controlled some-how. But if they could be virtual…. She might be used to doing that anyway."

"We don't have many whose creations are essentially remak-ing the world as a virtual model, because that kind of work tends to the dark side. Hell fits their tastes better, so we'll not consider them. The righteous architects and artists who are addicted to their craft are similarly cured by turning off their memory beyond a certain point, so every idea seems new to them and they never become restless."

"On and on forever?"

"It could well be for a long time, anyway."

"And that's heaven to them? Do they communicate with each other?"

"Oh, yes. It's like a separate universe. They put on shows and lectures and seminars—the same ones over and over, of course."

"Are all the arts treated that way?"

"No. There is an appreciation and display of art everywhere. But there is a purpose in all of the sanctioned art because the artists see the big picture and are helping to ensure the peace of New Jerusalem in their own way."

"I'm starting to get the big picture myself: Being made in the image of God means we have a tendency to act like God, which should be a flashing red light to every human being. But we're not made to be constantly aware of that danger because it would shut us down like a terrible nagging pain. So we're free to do our own thing; and almost invariably we turn out liking ourselves better than we like God."

"Or loving someone or something else better than we love God, which leads to conflict as well," I added.

"But isn't everyone who is made in the image of God subject to misdirecting their love at some point?"

"It's possible to reach a point where one's love is a pure image of God's love directed back to him. This is where being in Christ takes you if it works well. But, yes, as a practical matter heaven has to accommodate saints like me who are not there yet."

"How is that done? On earth in the old days they had a surveillance and deterrence system that was supposed to keep the peace. In theory it could work well if administered to maximize freedom."

"That's exactly what we have in heaven."

Earl shook his head again. "I guessed that, not because I thought it could be true. Is it really? I don't see how it would lead to the freedom and happiness that heaven is supposed to have."

"Heaven has always surveilled earth, don't you know? There were never any secrets, really. Why should it be any different in new heaven?"

"Because nothing much is done about it on earth, as far as I can tell."

"But records were being kept and are being kept. Surely you are aware of that."

"Well, yes, but I thought the freedom bought by the blood of Christ did away with all such records."

"No, only their interpretation."

"Okay, then why do memories cause crying?"

"Not simply because of faulty interpretation, if that's what you're suggesting. Even correct interpretation of memories is very often painful. The harm we have caused simply by being who we are is a double-edged sword that can slay any amount of bliss or joy the first time we remember it. For example, you might see someone going down the wide road to ruin in life because you said something that you intended to be recommending the right road, but the way you said it or the way it was taken was harmful and therefore had the opposite effect."

"Leila, tell me honestly. Do you like heaven?"

"Oh yes. Everyone does. The love of God is palpable so much more than on earth. Where that love is there is joy and peace. So you're wondering why there should be any down side at all. It comes back to the divine essence of human nature which can swell to a degree of love and joy *in itself* that brings about conflict."

"So with super surveillance such swelling gets put down before it spreads: is that how peace is kept?"

"That's the last safeguard, as far as I know. But the atmosphere of heaven is like a blanket of bliss imposed on everyone. While it doesn't interfere with normal cognition as if it were an intoxication, it occupies the mind in such a way that individual ambition becomes less attractive."

"What do you mean by atmosphere? Is this literally something you breathe like a heavenly intoxicant?"

"I think so. But also it's the sound: the music. Everywhere there is song and music. And you've never seen such flash mobs!"

"You've said hell suits some people better than heaven would. Were you speaking euphemistically?"

"Yes, I was."

"Do you know what hell is, actually?"

"Yes."

"Are you free to talk about it?"

I hesitated to answer, and before I had made up my mind about how to begin he asked:

"In heaven are they aware of people suffering in hell?"

"No, because no one is there yet—assuming you mean the place prepared for the devil and his angels and not just the grave."

"I see. It's not an acute issue right now. I'm just wondering how life in heaven could be joyful when there's awareness of, say, family members suffering isolation and torment—is it torment?"

"I think you know. What do the scriptures say?"

"Fire sounds like torment. Gnashing of teeth certainly does."

"We have something to contemplate that's much worse than hellfire, Earl. There has been war in heaven, and it's not quite over yet. Do you realize that?"

"Yes, I've read Revelation. It ends well for the redeemed, but the credentials for passing that final judgment are impossible."

"You're missing my point. You weren't here when Christ and heaven's angels warred against the opposition. If you weren't enraged by evil, the slaughter was sickening. Either way it was sickening to see this beautiful creation abused. And do you know that the issue hasn't been resolved yet? That's the sad thing. Who wants eternal fighting against God?"

"I hear your passion, Leila."

"If opposition to God's sovereign rule doesn't break your heart, then you're part of it: you're in league with devils. The Father tolerates that now as he develops the Son's bride, but the day is coming when Satan and his spoil will be put away without pity, and all we in the Bride will rejoice to see the divorce of self reliant spirits and champions of independence who followed their own light into darkness."

"I understand that spirits aren't composed of matter and therefore must live indefinitely. So I see the necessity of isolating those factors that might make heaven unpleasant. But isn't there an evangelistic outreach from heaven to make a way out for those unfortunates who belatedly see the light after the deadline?"

"They have no eyes to see the light, Earl. Otherwise they wouldn't have died in rebellion."

"We were all blind once, isn't that true?"

"Yes, but the human spirit is not eternal in all its capacities. Experience in the flesh substantially and permanently shapes the spirit. There's an indelible stamp of experience on every spirit which very often leaves it with organs for seeing darkness where it was meant to see light."

"How does that happen in most cases? Is it the work of the devil or does it happen by neglect and carelessness."

"Those causes are all the same. Neglect and carelessness are not neutral.

"In other words, the devil fills every void?"

"Not currently, but yes, the demons had infested the world and manipulated mankind to blind his spirit to goodness and open his eyes to evil. Everything on earth was contaminated."

"That explains my reaction when reading those passages in Revelation where they fell down—they were always falling down—so when I judged their radical demonstrations of allegiance as being unnecessary I was blind to the goodness of it."

"You would do the same if you got so near to God whether you liked doing it or not. But for true saints it's pure pleasure. However, attaining that devotion always and everywhere is only possible when your hatred of sin stands in the way of glorifying anything or anyone, including yourself."

"I think it is a miracle that anyone attains to that."

"It *would* be a miracle, but it cannot be, don't you see? The investment the Father has in creating free beings would be ruined if we were sanctified apart from our will by miracles. Yes, the Atonement was a miracle. So was Creation."

"I understand you're now glorified, but you look the same, except for the slight glow, as you did in your human flesh before the Rapture blew you away—or is there a significant difference?"

"Yes, the significant difference is what you could call the infrastructure. In heaven we appear just as we do when we visit earth. But beneath our skin is a different construction that's more suited to heaven. Your natural body is the dust of earth held together by a complex of living and dying cells and organisms, and it gradually wears out over time. Heaven's version of the human body looks nearly the same on the outside, but inside it works on a principle which we share with angels. It's much simpler because we don't have the ability to procreate, and our energy doesn't come from digesting food."

"Why is it that you still look as though you were meant to bear children—I'm not objecting, you understand."

"Yes, but the purpose is different. Simply put, our bodies in heaven honor our lives on earth to a very significant, though sometimes limited, extent. We're not exact replicas of our original incarnation. Defects are left behind, for one thing."

"Well, it sounds uninspiring to me. If heaven is platonic, it must be dull. Is there any drama at all?"

"We lack the worst of drama but we gain the best of human intercourse. The difference is astounding."

"You've lost me. Give me an example."

"Have you ever met a person who is genuinely more interested in getting to know you than in wanting to be appreciated by you?"

"I know the type. They're generally unintelligent and have limited understanding."

"Now imagine that person being intelligent and perceptive."

"There's no such person on earth."

"I won't say we're all like that, but it's not rare up there. Add to it exquisite communication skill, and what do you get?"

"It's hard for me to imagine because I'm not like that at all."

"What you get is a blessing from the Spirit of God as you study and learn the mind of another. And, I must add, communing with the opposite sex in the absence of the competitive instinct and without having to suppress unruly infrastructure is a joy and a wonder that I think must be nearly unattainable in this world."

"Yet there is a potential for jealousy in that, is there not?"

"Yes, but greatly mitigated because there's strong overarching love and unlimited time."

"I assume there's no gossip. How does everyone speak the truth all the time? In this world it's difficult for various reasons."

"Untruths and even minor slights don't come out well in heaven. They evaporate. There's nothing to support a lie, not even someone's poor memory because there are no poor memories."

"So fiction is out—no plays, dramas, literature?"

"Not so. Art is another matter, and yes, drama is an art form which by its nature is fictional. All the arts are well represented, and storytelling is quite popular."

"Don't tell me you're running your Samson-and-Delilah play."

"I'm not because the Samson in my play isn't there."

"Nor is he here. What about work? Some of us would get bored to death if we had no way to be productive."

"Yes, there's work for everyone. Horticulture and agriculture you might consider work, though that term isn't used."

"I thought you said there's no eating in heaven."

"I said we don't get our energy from eating. But meals are important because we're still essentially human, and there is plea-sure and social value in eating—and the expression of the culinary arts is important too, of course. But there are no gluttons."

"Now let me understand. If this mirrors what people do on earth, crops are grown and harvested, and edible parts are pre-pared to be tasty. Then what becomes of what you swallow?"

"It's magic, Earl. The celestial stomach disappears what goes into it. This is what delights some people more than anything, though we actually swallow very little."

"It sounds to me like a less-than-real existence mimicking real earth. What's the soil like?"

"Here on earth many crops are grown without soil, you know."

"By the way, does the heaven you're telling me about match the description in Revelation: the huge city with walls and gates?"

"I wouldn't say it's a direct 'match.' The picture in Revelation chapter twenty-one is an icon, really. It touches significant features in those few written words. And, yes, there are walls—"

"So what's the purpose of walls without enemies?"

"The walls define a special space. At present New Jerusalem has no enemies, but not everyone lives within the walls of the city. You remember the nations are mentioned?"

"I remember there's a river and trees on its banks with leaves for healing the nations."

"I don't have time tonight to tell you everything I know. In brief, the best way to visualize heaven is to imagine a planet in space with the north pole at the center of New Jerusalem—but without the solar effects of climate. Most of the surface of the planet is outside the walls, and most of the inhabitants live outside the walls in areas representing the earthly nations. The farther you are from the walls the fewer privileges you have."

"Is the throne of God at the center of the city?"

"No, because this is not the original heaven. It was created to compliment new earth, so it's days are synchronized with the twenty-four hour days on earth. The original abode of Father God is another heaven independent of this creation and creation's time, of course. But people can go there too!"

"Have you seen God?"

"Yes, every sanctified face in heaven is the face of God."

"All right. That's as much as I can handle right now. Do what you have to do," he said. Then, looking around the room, he asked, "Where are your barber tools?"

"Delilah told me how to do it. First I will make seven braids. If you sit in the recliner chair and lean back slightly—"

I was a bit surprised that he offered no resistance. "Thank you," I said. "That's good. Now just relax. This will take a little while. I want to make it look nice. We don't need it too short, just so it's not hanging below your shoulders."

B right sunlight was filtering through the curtains when Samson, still in the haircut chair, was awakened by loud knocking on the door of his room in the Salem Hermon Hotel. (He fell asleep before I had quite finished cutting his hair, so I left quietly, went to my own room and ascended to heaven.) Karen had sent for him because it was late and he had not appeared in the lobby. The hour of the surgery was at hand. Earl had no time for breakfast or even a shower. Karen rushed him to the eye clinic, got him checked in, and sat down in the waiting room. She had gotten permission to take the day off and was prepared to wait all day if necessary.

Hours later when the doctor finally came to speak to her he was extremely apologetic. It was bad news. Nothing could be done. The damage to the eye was such that it could not be repaired. But the worst part was that the good eye had been prepared for surgery by mistake; an exploratory incision had been made behind it, and the optic nerve had been damaged. He held out little hope that Earl would ever see again.

Karen couldn't believe it. When it became obvious that this was the surgeon who had done the damage, she was furious. She told me she wanted to strangle the miserable man and blow up the incompetent clinic. What was to be done?

The doctor told her he could get Earl admitted to the best eye clinic in the world. He said if anything could be done to partially restore Earl's eyesight, it would be there or nowhere.[1]

"Then do it!" Karen barked. "How soon can you get him in?"

"As soon as he can get there."

"Where? Where is this place? How long will it take to get there?"

"It will take some time. We'll arrange transportation so there will be no expense for Mr. Samson."

---

1. Ironically, if Earl had taken advantage of the more advanced technology that was available in the old world, he probably could have had his eyesight restored.

"I need to know specifically. He'll need an escort. Whether it's me or someone else, I need to know how and when and where he will be traveling."

"My clinic will arrange train transportation and will also pay for someone to escort him as far as Newport. From there—"

"As far as Newport?"

"Yes, Newport, Rhode Island."

"Where is this clinic located?"

"The clinic is in Israel. Excuse me, please; Ichabod will be out shortly."

The physician turned and left Karen speechless and stunned by his incredible report. She returned to the chair where she had been waiting, wiping away tears with her hands.

An hour later Earl came out, assisted by a staff worker. He wore dark glasses that did not completely hide the bandages over his eyes, and he carried a red-tipped blind cane. Karen had to restrain herself: she wanted to cry and curse and scream at the clinic all at once. But realizing that Earl needed her at that moment more than ever, she bravely went to him, took his other arm and told him how sorry she was.

Earl shook his head slightly but said nothing in response.

The attendant handed Karen an envelope. "Take this to the train station and get your reservation," she said. "It's good for one round trip plus one one-way coach to Providence. It also contains a voucher for passage from Newport to Haifa on any of the king's ships. There is a letter from the doctor that will get Mr. Samson into the eye clinic, which is located in Haifa."

Karen told Earl's attendant to stay with him while she brought her truck to the entrance. She could not get him away from that dreadful place fast enough and she prayed for mercy.

From the clinic they went straight to the train station in Salem. Leaving Earl in the truck, she went inside to see about making the reservation. She was told that space was available on the train scheduled to come through at 10:10 PM that same day. The next possibility was a week later.

Her decision was easy because on the way to the station Earl had told her he wanted to take the first train that had seats available, and he hoped it would be that same day. So she got the tickets.

Next they had to find an escort for Earl, and there was very little time for it. Karen wanted to be Earl's escort herself, but she knew she would not be allowed to leave her job for a trip that could take her away for up to two weeks. She would have to find someone who was willing and able to take a vacation on short notice.

Earl suggested that they get Howie Howard. Not that he cared for Howie's company, but that the judge might agree to have it be his penalty while on parole. Earl felt he could make the journey sufficiently uncomfortable for Howie, and that it would serve a penal purpose.

Karen agreed that it was worth a try, so she took Earl to the courthouse where Howie was being detained, and they got right in to see Judge Rice.

Earl was not prepared for the reaction he got from this glorified judge. She would not know the part he played in her former life or that he had been the reporter who had saved her daughter's chocolate-chip cookies, but the horror of learning he had been blinded by that particular doctor at the Salem eye clinic caused her to leave the room briefly. When she returned she gave away that she knew who he was, and she had some reassuring words for Earl, who gave her permission to call him by his real name.

Judge Betty Rice thought Earl's idea sounded reasonable enough, and it would save her from having to arrange for Howie's psychological evaluation immediately. To ensure that he would return, she stamped "parolee" on his card and wrote in the date he was to return. Howie was notified of his temporary release for work-duty parole beginning at nine o'clock that night.

Next, Karen took Earl to the airport, for he needed to get his pack from his airplane. He insisted on walking out to the plane, which brought about his first encounter with sidewalk steps since becoming blind. Karen held his left arm tightly while directing his every step as he probed the walkway with his cane. I know she was absolutely heartbroken, and she would forever be sorry she had pressured him into going for surgery. In the old world, Earl had resisted her pressure to see the doctors, and now with me adding my voice to hers, he had given in. But I think at that point she felt it was largely her fault. I believe it was my fault if it was anyone's, because I cut his hair, and if I had not done that he would not have been allowed into that clinic.

He told Karen to find a hangar for the plane if possible in case he got his eyesight back, and to have me be responsible for paying whatever rent was required for the space, which I was more than happy to do, and I believed at the time it was his way of saying he had forgiven me.

Then Karen took him to the company dwelling place where she was welcomed as a guest once per month, and they had a fine dinner prepared by the culinary staff. One of the men helped Earl with his personal needs. He had to be guided and assisted every moment, for he had none of the skills that a blind person needs to navigate, especially within an unfamiliar space.

When it was revealed that he was an exceptional, he became the center of the conversation. Karen sat next to him, helping him with his food. There was talk about the doctor at the Salem eye clinic. This was not his first botched operation, and they were concerned that it should be reported. The chain of command went up through the local health official who was glorified, a very nice man, but some doubted his competence; and exactly how this incident was to be reported no one knew for sure except that the mayor of the city should be notified. Several of them volunteered to write a letter to the mayor. Karen said she would visit the mayor in person, with or without the letter.

At 7:30 they left in order to be at the courthouse to get Howie before the eight o'clock closing time for visitors. He was not ready. He made a fuss about not having enough underwear, etc. Finally, they got him out and squeezed him into Karen's truck.

When Howie saw Ichabod's helpless condition, he was not as sympathetic as one might expect. This was the man who had accused him of promoting a heretical view of the the lake of fire which had never been a marginal view and never considered heretical in the former world. He was not aware that only literal biblical interpretations were acceptable under Solomon's rules.

While Howie did not dispute having crossed the line into disobedience and had made an excuse for it, he believed that Ichabod had definitely crossed the line at some time; otherwise, he would not be suffering this total loss of his eyesight which was explicable only as a penalty for something he needed to confess.

The train arrived on time. They boarded to find that Earl and Howie had been assigned seats in separate cars. When the conductor understood their special need, she relocated the passenger who had been assigned to the seat next to Earl.

This was the last time Karen saw Earl partly because she was older than he at that point, though in the past they had been close to the same age. But it was her grief and her dissatisfaction with her lot in life that ruined her health.

I determined to follow up with Karen, and I did so the next day, returning to Salem unannounced because I wanted to surprise her. I set my arrival at the Hermon Hotel for midday and took the hotel's taxi from there to Karen's job site. It was shortly after noon when I arrived. I found her in coveralls, surveying the bleacher seats she had been painting that morning.

Karen did not seem to be surprised when I came stealing around the corner. She had brought a sandwich in a paper bag and offered me half of it, which I accepted because I thought it symbolized the part I had played in causing Earl's blinding and that she was taking half of the responsibility.

We found a place to sit away from the other workers. As I expected, Karen was depressed almost beyond words. I coaxed her to share her grief—without mentioning Earl directly.

"Tell me honestly how you feel about life in the kingdom," I said—an opening for her to go in any direction, I thought.

She remained silent. It appeared that she was ether wary of that topic or lacked energy for it, so I narrowed my inquiry and substituted a simple statement for the question.

"You have been employed by a very good family," I said.

I expected this would get a comment from her, at least, but instead she answered my original question.

"If this is the age of peace and prosperity everyone yearned for under the reign of the King in Jerusalem, I say we were deceived by all the preachers and teachers."

I agreed. "They failed to take into account that binding the devil wouldn't eradicate human imperfection."

"I have no problems with the people I've met and work with here. I'm just not appreciating the culture. Some people are happy, but for my part, I was much better off in the old world."

I knew exactly what she meant. Images awakened in my memory of the life we both had enjoyed in our little town.

As you may know, Karen Martin along with her husband, Ken, owned the only construction business in town. After Ken's health deteriorated to the point where he was unable to work, I persuaded Karen to undertake one more project, which she completed just before the Rapture. But she was aided immensely by Earl who helped her solve problems every day.

"I would have had this entire stand painted in one afternoon," she said.

Recalling the robot she used for applying the siding on the Burns house, I said, "Using a robot, I presume."

Karen grunted and nodded. "I don't enjoy painting with a brush. It's hard for me to go back to these primitive methods. I'm a very poor robot."

"I would turn that around and say your robot is a very poor Karen Martin."

"The worst thing is that I'm not in charge anymore. I was always the boss; even when Ken was involved I was the boss, pretty much. Now I'm classed as a laborer with no chance to advance because I'm a mortal human! I could get this project done better and quicker than the manager here is capable of doing. He knows how to manage people, but he has had no hands-on experience in construction or the construction business."

"Perhaps that's deliberate because they purposely kept back technology that had become unmanageable."

Karen just shook her head. "I know if Ken were here they would have put him in charge. But that wouldn't be any better for me. In fact, it would be worse for me and my arthritic joints while ageless Ken flits about like a teenager."

"There's a body like that waiting for you in heaven, Karen."

"Heaven for me is back where we came from. Is there any hope for our town's future? Is it being resettled?"

"Yes, it is partially resettled. I've been back there."

"I must go back. I will go back as soon as I've fulfilled my seven years here. Earl will take me back. If Claudia is free by then, she'll go too. By then we will have found some aviation fuel for Earl's plane."

"Don't get your hopes up. The town is not one that has been chosen for reconstruction. Little has changed since you were there."

"But you said it's been resettled."

"Some of it has, but mostly it's still in ruins. The settlement is in the south end, south of Hill Street."

"Who is there? They must be former residents. If it hasn't been designated for reconstruction they must be naturals, and I'm sure we would know many of them."

"You're right, they are former residents. But they're resurrectees, not naturals."

"All of them?"

"Yes, I believe so. They call themselves pioneers because they go back to the days before the mine was developed."

"Is that the plan, then?"

"I don't believe it's the ultimate plan. For now it brings those folks to a resurrection experience that's all they hoped for. They learned about heaven from Ephraim Martin's preaching."

"Did you visit the Beach House by any chance?"

"Yes. It looks just the same."

"Then we have a place to stay because I'm the legal owner."

"All real estate belongs to the crown, you know."

"So I wouldn't necessarily be welcome in my own home?"

"Private property had become a fiction even then, you remember—strictly speaking I mean. The FSA had a right to take it for any reason if we decided it would serve the public good. Of course with Earl Clark living there—"

"Who's living there now?"

"Larry Link is keeping the place up for Joe Martin."

"Joe Martin, the man who built the Beach House?"

"Yes, the one you inherited it from. But he retains stewardship of it, and now you will need permission from him to live there."

"So were those happy days of freedom a mirage? I don't believe that. Those days were real. And this ... this is, I don't know what this is. When Earl showed up he was a ray of sunshine. But now he's gone, and we're all worse off for his being here."

"I'll keep you informed. Miracles do happen," I said.

"If not, he'll need someone to care for him."

"I'm sure that will be arranged."

"Well, regardless of the outcome he'll be returning to Salem because his airplane is here."

"Let us pray that he will be able to fly again."

Karen seemed not to hear that. She went on:

"If there's any convalescent time in store for him, I'd be more than happy to be his caregiver. I've done it before, and I would do it again without hesitation."

"Then with your experience you know he's unmanageable. He's very independent minded."

"He never turned me down if I wanted him to do anything. I would ask him to help me with some problem or difficulty we were having on the Burns house and he always came through and solved the problem for me, even when he had to take time away from his own work and risk the wrath of his boss."

"Yes, he can be cooperative too. That whole project was my idea in the first place, and Earl helped me get it organized."

"Don't forget, I've spent far more time with Earl than you have. Before you came to town he worked very close with me and Ken when we were building the Fitness Center."

"And I'm glad you did, because that's where I met Earl."

"You went there pretending to be interested in physical exercise and maintaining your health when you were really interested in him, isn't that right?"

"Yes, but—"

"I know because I've heard reports that none of the women could get close to him on the days you were there."

"Yes, but it was his plan that I meet him."

"That was so soon after you came that he didn't have the slightest idea who you were when you showed up one morning."

"Not so. Earl told me that he met me much earlier, before I had any notion of moving here."

"Well, it's a mystery to me that he suddenly fell in love with you. But the way things are now I don't believe it could still be true."

"If you go by his actions, you're right. The day he got here he determined to masquerade as one whose glory had departed."

"I know all about that. He was the same way when he was living with me. He didn't want to disappoint you. So how is it now that he's let down his disguise and the two of you have been traveling together?"

"It wasn't the two of us exactly. I was with Ichabod, going about looking for Earl. It wasn't until the other night at the hotel when I cut his hair that he told me his secret."

"Give me a break, Leila. Am I supposed to believe that? You had to know Ichabod Samson was really Earl Clark."

"Of course I did. I was playing along with his desire to keep his secret from me. It was his solution to the conflict in his mind. He couldn't bear having me be disappointed in his physical condition. It wasn't vanity so much as his misplaced sympathy for me."

"Now he knows that you know, obviously. But he must have known that at some point before you cut his hair. And now—does he have any reason to still prefer you in any way?"

"I don't know."

"Well, I presume he hasn't had an opportunity yet in this world to live with someone who doesn't disappear every night."

"We don't know yet what will become of him in Israel. There are possibilities. He may appeal to the King, and then—"

"Wouldn't that be wonderful. Then you and Earl could continue where you left off."

"That could never happen."

"Why not? Your friendship with him was always platonic, was it not?"

"I mean because we were adversaries. We didn't intend to be, and we didn't want to be, but so we were, and that wouldn't be heavenly if it were to continue. Heaven is organized to eliminate conflicts without limiting the expression of individual personalities, and that requires distance. I might never encounter Earl in heaven."

"Well, he and I get along very well. Even in stressful circumstances like when he lived in my basement. So if the choice were his, why wouldn't he choose me and remain a mortal? Actually, he owes it to me. I've done far more for him than you have."

"A much better plan would be for both of you to get together in heaven."

"Ultimately, I suppose that's true. But I still have a few years left, and I want to spend them here if I can. You glorifieds are really out of place here. Those that are resurrected are the ones who have it made. The old saints and even Jesus Christ himself enjoy resurrected bodies, isn't that right? If this world is inferior to heaven, then why are they here twenty-four seven?"

"Earth is in a transition period, Karen; remember that. At the end everyone moves out. The resurrected have all been saved and will transition to heaven. But many in the natural flesh fail to realize that in this dispensation obedience is being tested."

On the Train

Chapter Twenty-One

Soon after the lights of the city of Salem had receded, Ward Howard leaned back in his recliner seat and fell asleep. But not for long. He was awakened when Ichabod Samson suddenly began talking:

"Let the day I was born perish. Let deep darkness and the shadow of death have it. Let the light of that day be eclipsed and let thick darkness seize its night."

Jolted out of his slumber, Ward momentarily forgot where he was and why he was aboard a train. He awoke to something more dreamlike than a dream: the man who sat beside him and spoke those words was the same who had charged him with a crime and now was blind—indeed had been blinded that very day—and they were traveling together because the accused had been sentenced to act as chaperon and custodian of his accuser.

Having missed the first sentence of Ichabod's odd utterance, Ward assumed that the outburst railed against the dark night, for it was mostly black outside and there was little to see. But the blind man was facing forward, not looking out the window.

"Yes, let that night be silent and empty," Ichabod rambled on. "Let no joyful sound be heard in it, and let the stars of its twilight be dark. And when dawn comes let it see no light, neither let it behold the eyelids of the morning. Cursed be that day because it did not close the doors of my mother's womb, nor did it shut trouble from my eyes. Why did I not die right out of the womb and give up the ghost when my mother bore me?"

"If you're asking me, I haven't a clue," Ward Howard interrupted. Then he waited to see what would come next. Perhaps this manner of talk was not unusual from a man newly blinded.

"For then I would have slept and been at rest—along with the untimely births of infants who never saw light. Why is light ever given to him who is in misery, and why is life given to the bitter soul who longs for death. For the thing which I feared has come upon me."

"Will it grieve you if someone like me ventures to communicate with you?" Ward asked, mocking his seat-mate's lyrical manner of speaking. "But who can restrain himself from pointing out your fault?—certainly not the one you have abused. Look, you instructed me, but now with the hardship of blindness touching you, it is you who are troubled and in need of instruction. Is not the mending of your ways your only hope? I ask you, can you remember anyone who perished for being innocent? According to what I have seen, those who sow trouble reap the same. You might say by the breath of God they perish, and by the blast of his anger they are consumed. Can mortal man be a better judge of justice than God? Affliction never comes up out of the dust, Ichabod Samson, though it is said that man is born to trouble as the sparks fly upward. If I believed in God like you claim to, I would seek God, and to God I would present my cause. Does he not have the reputation of doing great things?—marvelous things? Things without number he does. He lifts up those who are low, and those who mourn he carries to safety. He frustrates the devices of the crafty so their hands cannot carry out their plans. He confounds the wise in their own craftiness, and the counsel of the cunning ones he frustrates: they encounter darkness in the daytime and grope at noonday as if it were night. Happy is the man whom God corrects! Therefore, see that you do not despise the chastening of the Almighty. He makes sore, but then he binds up; he wounds, but then his hands make whole. So confess to him and see if he will deliver you out of half a dozen troubles; yes, even in seven or more trials he will allow no evil to touch you, and you will come to your grave at a full age. This is what the wise have discovered, and so it must be. Listen to my advice, and believe it for your good."

Whether or not Samson had heard and taken in any of this monologue Ward Howard could hardly tell, for no speech was forthcoming from the reputedly righteous man suddenly stricken by God, who had just said he hated the day he was born. Only the rhythmic clatter of carriage wheels on steel rails answered the argument Howie had proudly plagiarized from Job's comforter.

On the Train

The train would avoid the coastal route; instead of using the tracks that would lead it south to San Francisco before turning east, it would bypass that desolate area, the ruins of which lay in dangerous fissures that continued to spew smoke and ash. Indeed, it would avoid touching California altogether, making its first brief night stop at Bend then going on to Boise and Twin Falls. From there it would skirt the ruins of Salt Lake City on new rails, expecting to continue on to the south; but a signal would warn of a landslide north of Provo, causing it to divert and use the northern loop that goes by way of Evanston rather than through Grand Junction. It would arrive at Cheyenne about noon the next day.

Because technology had been severely set back, the railroad's rolling stock were antiques extracted from railroad museums, and the personnel operating this millennial line were railroad buffs who had invested years in the museums and had often been criticized for neglecting religious duties. This passenger train aboard which Samson and Ward Howard had begun their transcontinental journey was pulled by two beautifully restored, 20th-century, electronics-free diesel-electric locomotives.

Unfortunately, our travelers were not privileged to be in a sleeper car, and their lately acquired tickets gave them no access to a better place to spend long days and nights. They remained in their seats that first night, and before long the swaying carriage and clacketing wheels had put them both to sleep.

Samson could not tell whether it was day or night when he awoke from a dream in which he had relived the sailing event where I was there in the boat with him, braced across the cockpit and holding the helm to maintain a good angle of heel. I was leaving him little to do but admire the success of his instructions, for it was my first time aboard a sailboat of any kind. The pitching of the little craft on that sunny day as she skipped across foaming waves and the shaking of her close-hauled sails gave way to the swaying of the railroad carriage and the noise of wheels and tracks—and blackness, unending blackness.

"Oh that my vexation were weighed and my calamity laid in the balances!" Samson blurted aloud, startling Ward again.

Morning light, which Samson could not see, was in the sky.

"For it would be heavier than the sand of the seas," he continued. "Perhaps my words have been rash, but the arrow of the Almighty is within me, and my spirit has drunk its poison. Can that which has no savor be eaten without salt? Is there any taste in the white of an egg? Life is loathsome food to me."

"Then you'll not like the breakfast they brought us," said Ward. "In front of you is a plate of eggs and toast. Reach out and pull the serving tray toward you. Here, let me salt your egg."

"Oh that I might have my request," moaned miserable, sightless Samson. "And that God would grant the thing I long for. Oh that it would please God to crush me, that he would let loose his hand and cut off my life!"

"Have some food and maybe you'll feel better," Ward growled, alarmed by the persistent death wish of the blind man.

"What is my end that I should be patient? Is it not that I'm helpless and that wisdom has been driven quite from me? Teach me, and I'll hold my peace. Cause me to understand wherein I have erred. But your reproof—what did it reprove? Do you think it fair to reprove my words, seeing that the speeches of one who is desperate are like wind? I'm bound to have weeks of misery, and wearisome nights are appointed to me. When shall I arise and the night be gone? My eyes are no good now and may never see light again. Therefore, I will not restrain my mouth; I will speak in the anguish of my spirit; I will complain in the bitterness of my soul."

"How long will you say these things?" Ward broke in. "How long will the words of your mouth be a mighty wind? Does God pervert justice? Does the Almighty disregard righteousness? If you would seek God diligently and make your supplication to the Almighty, surely he will restore wholeness in your life. Can the rush grow without mud? Can the flag grow without water? While yet green it withers sooner than any plant. So are the paths of all who forget God. Though God will not cast away a perfect man, neither will he uphold evildoers. So perhaps there is hope for you, Ichabod Samson. When you turn away from evil he will fill your mouth with laughter and your lips with shouting."

"Honestly, I know all this," Samson shot back. "But how can any man be blameless with God? If one attempted to reason with him, he would not make a correct argument even once in a thousand years. When God goes after someone, who can dissuade him? Who has the right to ask him, 'What are you doing?' How could I answer him and choose words to impress him? Even if I were righteous I could never have an acceptable response. If I were to call and he were to answer me, I would never believe that he had accepted my words, because he breaks me in his fury and multiplies my hurts without cause. If I were to attempt to present a complaint, he would not allow me to take a breath but would leave me full of bitterness. If I were to show some strength—but he is mighty! And if my cause is just, who will pay any attention to me? Though I be however righteous, my own mouth would condemn me; if I conducted myself with perfection, it would prove me perverse. I may or may not be blameless, but I do not care about myself; I despise my life. From now on my days will pass swifter than a runner; they will slip away unremembered, for they will see no good. They pass by like paper ships, swift as an eagle swooping on its prey. If I say, 'I will forget my complaint, I will put off my sad countenance and be of good cheer,' it's no use because my sorrows have already condemned me: I know he won't hold me innocent of them. Why then do I labor in vain? For he isn't a man, as I am, that I could answer him, that we could come together in judgment. There's no umpire between us who might lay his hand upon us both. Let him take his rod away from me, and let not his terror make me afraid; then I would speak and not fear him, for right now I'm not confident in myself. My soul is weary of my life, and I'll give free course to my complaint; I'll speak in the bitterness of my soul. I'll say to God: 'Is it good to you that you should oppress, that you should despise the work of your hands? Your hands have framed me and fashioned my body, yet you destroy me. You've clothed me with skin and flesh and knit me together with bones and sinews. You've granted me life and loving-kindness, and your presence has preserved my spirit. If I be wicked, woe unto me; and if I be righteous, still I'll not lift up my head, being filled with shame according to my affliction. You renew your witnesses against me and increase your indignation upon me: changes hit me and warfare is upon me. For what reason did you bring me out of the womb? Had I given up the ghost and no eye had seen me, I would have been as though I had never been; I should have been carried from the womb to the grave. Aren't my days few now? Cease then, and let me alone, that I may take a little comfort before I go where I'll not return, to the land of darkness and of the shadow of death, the land dark as midnight, without any order.'"

"This is Cheyenne," Ward announced. "I'm going to get out of this wretched car and stretch my legs and maybe find something for lunch in the station—something that's better than what we've been getting on board. We have three hours before the train departs. You can stay here or come with me, whichever you like."

Samson responded by taking his cane in hand, rising from his seat, and following Ward to the door of the coach. That much was well practiced. But descending the train-car steps was something new and not easy because everything he touched was unfamiliar, and it took some time.

Once on the platform, Ward took Ichabod's arm and marched him into the station. Almost immediately he was hailed by a man who had followed them though the door.

"Excuse me. Are you Ward Howard?"

"I'm one of them. ... Do I know you?"

"You used to know me. I worked in the same building with you, if I'm not mistaken. I was in the Child Weight department."

"Brutus? ... You're not Brutus .... You *are* Brutus!"

"Yes, a shadow of my former self, we might say."

"You look perfect. How did you lose ...? Oh, you've been glorified. But I didn't know—"

"Thanks to our blessed boss, I went and heard the message and got baptized almost at the last hour."

"I wasn't so fortunate. I ignored her recommendation, and I've paid for it dearly. I've had to struggle to survive ever since. But I'm not complaining—right, Ichabod? Brutus, this is Ichabod Samson. He recently lost his eyesight, so I'm taking two weeks off to help him travel across the country to see an eye doctor."

"That's very good of you. Well, you're in good hands, Ichabod."

Ward Howard grinned—so I assume, don't you? "Were you on the Millennium Flyer, Brutus? We call it the Millennium Crawler. Oh, of course not; you have a more efficient way to get from point A to point B."

"That's true. I'm here to inspect the restaurant. It's operated by someone you know. You remember Margaret at the Lakeview, I'm sure."

"Margaret is here? That's astounding! I'll never get used to the small-world phenomenon. I was going to see about a meal. Is it as good as the Lakeview was?"

"Oh, I'm sure it is. Margaret is first rate. I'll tell her you're here."

The restaurant was crowded by that time, and they stood in line while Brutus went to do his inspection. After half an hour he returned with Margaret, who said she had a table for them and led them to a booth.

Ward slid in and let Samson have the outside while Margaret sat next to Brutus and across from Samson.

"Before we order anything, I want to know if the kitchen passed your inspection," said Ward.

"Just one small violation is all. It's nothing to be concerned about," replied the inspector.

"Well, I *am* concerned about it," said Margaret.

"Are you going to let us know what it is?" Ward pressed.

"We could, but we don't have to because it's already been fixed," Brutus replied. "And since no one's health was endangered there's no follow-up required."

"I can't check everything every day," said Margaret. "They're all pretty reliable, better than I had in the old world, but no one is perfect. I have to assume that they've spent enough time on the cleanup because I'm not here at that hour. One day I'll stay late and surprise them."

"Do you miss the electronic kitchen?" Ward asked her.

"No. Definitely not. Everything takes longer, but the work is more satisfying. Everyone says that. And I think the food tastes better and is more healthful."

"What do you say about that?" Ward prompted Brutus.

"Personally, I don't indulge in it."

"Oh, yes, of course. Your food is from out of this world. How did you get your job? I thought being a "between" was a reward given out to those who invested their talents exceptionally well—like being evangelists."

"Mine isn't a very glorious assignment, of course."

"But how did you find time to make any investment in heaven if you joined the church only two days before it left the earth?"

"I had the same question. In my youth I was an active member of the church, and it turned out that the faith I had back then counted. When I went for baptism on the day before the parousia, I hoped for that, but I wanted to end my silence, at least, and I felt much better afterward. I'm constantly amazed at the grace I have received."

"You'll get used to it," Ward declared with the air of an authority on the subject.

"I hope not," Brutus replied. "I expect to live with this amazement forever."

"That's interesting to me," said Ward. "Because I would think being in a continuous state of amazement would blunt your initiative and impair your ability to live life to your full potential and solve problems creatively."

"Well, you might be right. Maybe it does, but it's the perfect mindset for the work I do."

"I can't imagine it's all that rewarding," said Ward.

"Being faithful is all the reward I need."

"That's the way I feel too," said Margaret. "There are many benefits, but the fact that I can be faithful in this job gives me all the freedom I could desire."

"That doesn't make theological sense to me, and I teach theology," said Ward, and he glanced over at Ichabod to see his reaction, but there was none. "Fine, if you've reached your potential, but Yahweh has been known to strike some who are less than what he expects." He glanced at his seatmate again, but Ichabod remained inexpressive and silent.

A server brought them handwritten menus.

"I'll read the lunch menu for you, Ichabod," said Ward.

"I'm not hungry," growled the blind man.

"Personally, I wouldn't recommend the Steam Engine Soup, but some seem to like it, so I keep it on the menu," Margaret advised.

"Hmm. That sounds interesting," said Ward. "What's in it?"

"You don't want to know."

"She will tell you, of course," said Brutus.

"I think I'll play it safe and have the mutton pie," said Ward.

"Are you sure you don't want anything? Something to drink, Ichabod?"

Samson shook his bowed head slightly.

Someone summoned Margaret about then, and she excused herself, leaving Brutus exclusively to Ward.

"There must be thousands of commercial kitchens you can't reach in a day from a Hermon hotel. How do you get to them all?"

"Oh, we deputize regular folks who report to us."

"How do you ensure their honesty? Couldn't someone say he inspected a certain eating establishment when in fact the operator paid him to falsify the report?"

"As supervisors we come with a kind of perception that easily detects lies, and they all know that. The system works quite well."

"I see. It's because there's no corruption at the top."

"That's exactly right."

After that, Samson paid no attention to the conversation between Ward and Brutus, and they ignored him.

Back on the train, Ward was eager to answer Samson's last rant, and he started in immediately:

"Shouldn't a man full of talk be judged? Do you think your boasting forces me to hold my peace? When you mock God, may no one shame you? You say, 'My doctrine is pure, and I'm clean in God's eyes.' But oh that God would speak and open his lips against you, that he would show you the secrets of wisdom, for he is rich in understanding. Can you by searching learn about God? Can you find out everything about the Almighty? It being high as heaven, what can you do? And being deeper than sheol, what can you know? When he passes judgment on everything, who can hinder him? For he knows false men; he sees iniquity even when he doesn't attend to it. But vain man is void of understanding; yes, man is born a wild donkey's colt. Now, if you set your heart aright and stretch out your hands toward him, and if iniquity be in your hand you put it far away and not let unrighteousness dwell in your house, then surely you'll lift up your face without spot; yes, you'll be steadfast and have no fear: for you will forget your misery; you will remember it as waters that have passed by, and your life will be clearer than the noonday; though there be darkness, it will be as the morning. And you will be secure because there is hope; yes, you will search and find and take your rest in safety. And when you lie down, none will make you afraid. Though many pursue you, the eyes of the wicked will fail, and they will have no way to flee, and their hope will be the giving up of the ghost."

Samson answered this outrage indignantly:

"No doubt wisdom will die with you. But I have understanding as well; truly, who doesn't know such things? There is contempt for misfortune in the thoughts of one who is at ease. Notice that when God breaks something down it cannot be built again; when he shuts a man up, there can be no escape. Yes, I would speak to the Almighty; I would like to reason with God. But you, you're a forger of lies. Oh that you would hold your peace altogether, and that would be your wisdom! Would you speak for God, and talk deceitfully for him? Would you represent his face? Would you argue for God? Would it be good if he cross examined you? Or do you intend to deceive him as one deceives a man? He will surely reprove you if you represent him without his approval. Doesn't his majesty make you fearful, and the dread of him weigh upon you? Your well-known sayings are proverbs of ashes, fragile as clay. Hold your peace that I may speak, and let come to me what will. Why should I not take my life in my hand? Look, he may slay me, for I have no hope; nevertheless, I will maintain my ways before him. There is hope for a tree if it be cut down that it will sprout again and its tender shoots not end though its root grow old in the earth and its stock die in the ground; yet the scent of water will cause it to bud and put forth boughs like a new plant. But when man dies he is laid low; yes, when man gives up the ghost where is he? Waters recede from the lake, and the river goes down and dries up. Likewise man lies down and rises not until the heavens are no more. He will not be roused out of his sleep, but his soul mourns."

Ward apparently had had enough of such banter and became quiet as he sat watching the scenery go by. He had been in the window seat since Cheyenne, so he was not looking past Samson anymore who, unable to look anywhere, invariably faced the back of the seat in front of him.

Without the dialog going on there was nothing for Samson to attend to other than the clatter of the wheels and his sorrowful thoughts. After drifting in and out of light sleep he apparently fell into a deep slumber during which he dreamed that he had arrived at the eye clinic in Israel alone—somehow he had gotten there without an escort—to find that Ward had sent a letter ahead telling them of his unworthiness, which caused them to cancel his appointment. To right this injustice he appealed to the throne in Jerusalem. (How he got there was not detailed in the dream.) He presented his case to the King, arguing that he had been blinded through no fault of his own.

When there was a delay at the station in Gettysburg, Samson was not inclined to leave the train, so Ward left him alone.

"Earl, I came to cheer you up!" It was a familiar voice. It was Evelyn. She sat down beside him. "Leila wanted to be here, but she was not sure how you would receive her, so she sent me."

"That was kind of her. Does she know what I'm going through?"

"She has taken responsibility for you like a guardian angel. She called for this train to pause. The passengers and the conductors are wondering what the train is waiting for. The engineers only know they received an order to wait one hour. If you will allow her to help you get to the ship, which docks at Newport, she will meet you at the end of the rail line in Providence.

"Close by where we are right now is Rogers Park. If you will come with me, I will take you for a little walk. Someone else you know is there doing what he always does. We might listen to him for a little while. You will find him refreshing after Howie."

Samson knew the speaker was Felix not by his voice but by the simple way he put words together. His subject was the power and glory of forgiveness. Samson did not take it well. It compounded what he needed to forgive me for.

He was terribly aloof when I met him at the station in Providence. While on the ferry to Newport I tried to be his eyes. He received my descriptions with little comment.

At the top of the boarding ramp to the ship Samson was met by the steward whom we had assigned to him for the duration of the voyage. I said my goodbye at that point. He seemed depressed, and I don't think it was because he would miss me.

I was very sorry for Samson—for Earl. My old Earl was in him somewhere, I was sure of that. I wept as I walked back down the boarding ramp. Glorified bodies are not constructed to weep, but mine surely did on that occasion. I stood watching until the ship departed. The day was foggy, and it faded quickly into the mist.

I had two weeks to wait before meeting him at the end of his voyage. I thought he would need me then, at least.

On the Ship

Chapter Twenty-Two

When the steward introduced himself as Alvin, the sound of his voice was familiar to Samson. But if Alvin was who he sounded like, Ichabod was not eager to reveal his identity to him. And he didn't. He avoided friendly conversation that might lead to questions he would not want to answer and feelings he would not want to face.

After the first day aboard the ship, Samson was able to find his way between his stateroom and the dining room, which gave Alvin more freedom to do other things. At mealtime the servers carefully described each plate as it was set down before him, which was all he needed. He always sat at the same table, and though it could seat two, no one joined him until one day a lovely voice asked if she might sit across from him. He had no clue as to her appearance, whether she was tall or short, young or old, thin or stout. But if her voice was indicative, she was beautiful.

She said her name was Lydia. She had been on the same cross-continental train, and it was there that she had first taken notice of him. Now she wondered if he would like someone to talk to since he seemed to be alone—and she was alone. He told her she was very kind to offer to sit at his table.

Samson learned that Lydia's mission was to meet someone—anyone—who appeared in the Bible. As a writer of biblical stories, she had the hopeful idea that she would make her work more authentic if she could interview someone who knew about details which writers of her genre normally had to improvise.

"I'm even daring to hope that I might be fortunate enough to see King Yeshua," she said. "Oh! I'm very sorry, Ichabod! ... You wouldn't be able to see him in your present condition. I hope and pray those bandages aren't permanent and that they come off soon. But if—God forbid—they are permanent, I will still be your friend."

It seemed to Samson that she was trying to compensate for some insensitivity to his condition, so he didn't take her seriously.

"I was blinded in the house of my friend," he stated dryly.

"Do you mean literally? Or are you making an allusion to Scripture?"

"It's nearly literal. My friend sent me to this eye doctor who botched the job."

"That's awful. I'm so sorry. ... The surgeon didn't cut your hair too, did he? I don't know if you know it, but someone botched your haircut."

"She cut it."

"Your friend cut your hair?

"Yeah. I didn't have a chance to look at it before they took me to the eye clinic."

"Your hair must have been quite long from the looks of it."

"It was."

"Long hair used to be common on men where I come from. I've cut hair more than once, and I could give you a trim that would even it out nicely. One thing I had in mind as I decided to come over and visit you was, *Though I can't do anything about his eyes, I could make his hair look nice.*"

"Do they sell baseball caps on this ship?"

"Possibly there's one somewhere."

"If you could steer me toward it, I'd buy it and save you the trouble."

"I think you'd still want a trim around the edges. I'll find you a baseball cap too."

"Are you having lunch?" he inquired of his table mate, for he couldn't be sure that she had not brought food with her.

"I was here for lunch earlier. ... So what about that haircut after you're through here."

"Do you have a pair of scissors?"

"No, but I have a very sharp knife. It takes longer, but I've cut hair with a knife before."

"Maybe there's a barber shop on board."

"Maybe there is. Or maybe we could find some scissors to borrow."

Samson made no reply. It was awkward facing another person when there was no face to see, but he had to assume that she found some value in observing his face, though she was seeing nothing but patches behind his dark glasses. While he finished his lunch she talked about her plan to seek out resurrected saints. She knew they must be different from people who had never died.

She took his arm and they went in search of a store where they might buy him a hat. The ship was not up to the standards of a luxury cruise liner or even a large ferry boat. But they did find a small shop and a baseball cap. Samson insisted that he did not need both hat and haircut. Lydia finally accepted that.

Again without asking his permission she guided him around that deck. He was grateful for that bit of exercise. As they passed a lounge area with windows looking outside, she asked,

"Would you like me to tell you what there is to see?"

"We must be well out of sight of land by now."

"There's nothing to see. At present I don't see another vessel even. The sea is gray and calm. You know it's calm as well as I do because our feet tell us that, but now you know it's gray too. ... There's plenty of room in this lounge. In fact, the couple that was sitting here just left. Let's sit down, and you can tell me more about your ordeal. I suspect there's a story behind it. Obviously your friend wasn't qualified to cut hair. She didn't do it without your permission, did she?"

"Not quite, but close."

"It sounds like there was some pressure."

"She had been pleading for me to get the surgery. Then she set up this appointment with the eye doctor without my knowledge, and like clinics everywhere, you have to meet standards. When I found out what she had done, I reluctantly agreed to go through with it, and by then there was no time for a haircut."

"So she cut your hair in a hurry?"

"She cut it in my hotel room. She's a new-heaven person, and she left right after that."

"Her name isn't Delilah, is it? Just kidding of course."

"No, but mine's Samson."

"Oh! That's marvelous! I mean, whenever I encounter an echo out of Scripture I like to imagine there's some reason for it. The Samson story is dear to my heart because I did an adaptation of it. Samson loved her, but things didn't work out. If your friend's name is even close to Delilah, I'll know there's a reason for sure."

"Go ahead and guess."

"Delilah ... Lilah. Is that it? Lilah ... Leila?"

"Leila."

"Would she be here if she could?"

"I don't know. After what she did, I don't know."

"If she's glorified, her intentions must have been good."

"Maybe she was following orders."

"So does the Almighty have a hand in this, do you think?"

"It feels like it. I'm an exceptional to start with—"

"I've heard the term, but I don't know what an exceptional is."

"I skipped over a few years to get here from the old world. Why, I don't know, and how, I'm not sure. I was told it was a summons, but I haven't found anyone who knows what I was summoned for. That's all I know. Another exceptional would tell you something different, for all I know."

"Did it ever occur to you that you were summoned by the crown and this is the means by—"

"No, it never occurred to me. If that's the case, I shudder to think what I'm being summoned for. I was doing my own thing, pretty much, until this total blindness hit me. I don't know how many rules I've broken. I thought I was getting along with nearly everyone, and I actually had an assignment that I was fulfilling. But suddenly I was struck with this cruel injury that may not be treatable. I would argue that I got singled out for exceptional infliction."

"Why are you going to Haifa?"

"There's an eye surgeon there who's supposed to be the best in the world. It's my only hope, I'm told."

"Don't you believe in miracles?"

"Only as a last resort."

"Isn't your glorified friend, Leila, a walking miracle?"

"That's fine for her. But for me, and I think you too—don't we have to live with whatever the natural order presents us with? Have you seen any miracles?"

"My people often talked about them. I think it's a miracle that I got this far, but to someone else it would seem like a natural course of events—or mostly natural."

"Where are you from?"

"My people were in the Sitka area, and some still are—Sitka, Alaska, you know. I was born shortly after the Rapture took place. My parents became believers right after the Rapture. They knew everything, and they had participated in our gatherings of disciples, but secretly they doubted everything, clinging to the stories from before the evangelists camped among us. I'm a full blooded Tlingit—what they used to call an indigenous American."

Samson from then on pictured her with black hair and dark eyes, but he had to let her voice and her words define her face.

"The miracle you mentioned—tell me about that," he said.

"Surviving the tribulation was a miracle. I think everyone who lived through it calls it a miracle. Yet in Southeast Alaska the wet weather and melting glaciers saved us from the worst heat. There were fires, but not everywhere. The outflow from glaciers kept the inside passages from being poisoned and we continued to get good fish, which is partly how we survived. Also, we possessed knowledge handed down from our ancestors about edible plants and hunting methods that we put to good use. No one ever took the mark because we were not at the mercy of the government. The city of Sitka got locked down, but natives simply moved out into the forest to places we had prepared in advance."

"How did you get here? I mean how did you travel?"

"I came down by kayak and got on the train at Everett, Washington."

"You paddled a kayak all that way?"

"Yes. I'm not the only one who did it."

"Then you boarded a train that took you all the way to Providence? You said it was a miracle."

"The fact that I made the kayak trip was. For me that was a miracle. I was alone almost the entire way."

"Did you start out with others?"

"No. When I said I wasn't the only one, I meant others had paddled the inside passage before I did. The miracle was really when I was met by a native woman as soon as I landed on the bank of a slough just north of Everett at high tide. She said she had been waiting for me. She had a large canoe and said she would take me to the train station. I hadn't told her where I wanted to go; she just knew, and she had a train pass for me."

"How did you know to land at that particular spot north of Everett?"

"I didn't know. I had no chart. I was tired and needed to rest."

"Then she paddled the canoe into town? Or did she take you some other way?"

"She took me another way. I don't know how she did it. It was instantaneous. Instantly, I was at the train station and she was nowhere."

"You and your backpack, I presume."

"Yes, she had told me to put it on and get in her canoe."

"Will someone meet you in Haifa?"

"Not that I know of, but I wouldn't be surprised. I have a feeling that this is where I'm supposed to be and what I'm supposed to be doing."

"Aren't you a member of a family back home?"

"No. If you mean a millennium family, no; they hadn't gotten organized yet when I left."

"So you're running around loose like I am—or was."

"I don't feel like I'm independent, though. Someone is directing me. I think someone must be watching over you too."

"Maybe so, but they've made a poor job of it."

"That man who was with you on the train—at least you had someone to help you get around."

"I should be grateful for that, I know. But he was a poor comforter. He insisted that I'm being punished for some wrongdoing. A man can take only so much of that."

"At Gettysburg you were met by the most beautiful woman. Was that Leila?"

"No. She was another former friend."

"She must be glorified too."

"She is. Leila sent her because she couldn't be there herself."

"And who was that nice looking woman on the pier at Newport who saw you off?"

"That was Leila."

"Did you know she was crying?"

"No."

"I thought it was strange for a glorified person."

"I suppose she regrets what she did."

"I wouldn't think that real saints ever make mistakes. I could tell that she loves you."

"Real saints aren't supposed to cry either, are they?"

"I was very surprised to see it. But now we know they do cry sometimes. Will she meet you in Haifa?"

"That's possible. She said she would, but she might have been too busy to meet the train at Gettysburg. So I'm not counting on it. She has important responsibilities. I'm not supposed to be one of them."

"Well, if no one is there for you in Haifa, I'll either take you to the clinic or whatever you have to do. I'll stay with you and make sure that you're not alone. That would be awful to be blind in a strange place. Who knows? Maybe that's why I'm here. I wanted to meet a biblical character, and here you are. You say your name is Samson, but you sound like Job to me. I mean that for good humor. You can't see me smiling, but I was. I'm not good at laughing, but sometimes I try to smile. I'll try to remember to tell you when I do."

"Don't be concerned about that too much. I could hear your smile in your voice. ... Well, fair enough; I've been complaining, which I don't think Samson ever did, or if he did it was soon followed by action. But I'm not to be compared to either of them, of course."

"You can complain all you like, and I won't be anything like Job's miserable comforters."

"You comfort me more than you know. It gives me relief not to worry about that steward who has been assigned to me. I never know where he is, if he's watching me or what."

"I talked to Alvin. He seems like a nice old gentleman."

"Then he's not who I was afraid he was."

"I see him right now. He's been watching us."

"Perhaps he has nothing else to do."

"He's one of the marine guards, you know. Now he's leaving."

"Is he in uniform?"

"Yes."

"It really doesn't worry me, Lydia. I'm sure he doesn't know me."

"Well, I'm curious myself. I'll find out."

"You're a regular detective, aren't you?"

"I've written too many mystery stories."

"No, I think you've written one too few."

"I do keep on the lookout for unusual things that may become part of a story."

"Am I one of them?"

"I'm smiling. I mean really smiling, I'm sure."

"Have I found you out?"

"Maybe you have. But really I just like you."

"Women always have. I'd assumed it was my looks."

"I like it about you that you can't see my looks."

"Oh, I can see you well enough."

"Do you have some vision, then?"

"No. Just nothing. It's awful. But your voice is sunlight to me, and so I'm sure your face is beautiful. That's how I see you."

Lydia fell silent for a for seconds.

"Even your silence is beautiful," he said.

"How many women have you beguiled in your life?"

"Did I hear a smile?"

"No. I'm just testing you."

"Then you need an answer."

She was silent again and seemed to be waiting for an answer.

"I try to keep my feelings from causing trouble," he said.

"And women are always trouble, isn't that right?"

"Yes, of course. But not many are much trouble."

"Not like Leila?"

"That's right. But you already know that story. Yes, I was married once in the old world when I was young and unwise in the ways of women."

"Then you became wise, and Leila still causes you trouble."

"You can call me Samson. She does. But not always."

"It's too bad she's glorified. ... No, I'm sorry, I shouldn't have said that. There's more to your face than your eyes."

"It's really too bad we're *not* glorified, isn't it?"

"I don't know the answer to that because there are places they can't go and places we can't go. And if heaven is so wonderful, why do they come here at all? And if earth is so wonderful, why do we dream of heaven?"

"I'll have to be honest with you, Lydia. What matters is not the place but who's in the place. Do you know what I mean?"

"No, not really. I miss my folks, but I like adventure."

"When you get to be my age, you'll have had enough of that."

"I'm not much younger than you. In fact, I may be older."

"Then your kayak journey really was a miracle."

"This will be my last journey, I'm sure. No, I'm not sure because there could be another miracle."

"Do you have any children?"

"No natural ones because the kind of man I could get would be too much for me to handle. But I helped raise my older brothers."

"Are they still living in Sitka?"

"The tribulation made drunkards of them, and they both died of it."

"I'm sorry."

"I could name several reasons why I left. You know I had a strange feeling about you when I saw you on the train, and then to find you on my ship .... As I said, this may be the truest reason I left home."

"We must expect Leila to be there at the end of this voyage."

"Do you have any choice in the matter?"

"No."

"So you're not very upset with her?"

"That doesn't matter. I chose her, and she won't let me forget."

"It sounds like you're her slave."

"For a little while. Then she'll find someone else to torment."

"I think you'll be surprised."

"Why? Do you have some inside information?"

"Just what you told me. You said you were summoned. And you're exceptional as a result. Surely you have an exceptional calling."

"Maybe this is it. You're more important than you knew. Perhaps I'm here to serve you, and not the other way around. If I could, it would make me happy, because I feel useless for the first time in my life."

"I'll accept that. The way you can serve me is to let me be your caretaker. I have an uncanny way of knowing what's inside a person, and I'll show you where your blind spots are. Yes, some of us Indians have gifts of intuition that are not what you expect."

• • •

The morning of the tenth day out the weather was sunny but still cool on deck where Lydia was guiding Samson on their daily walk.

"Do you smell land?" she asked him.

"I think so. I've been thinking it's about time we rounded Gibraltar."

"I believe I'm seeing where it lays by the look of the sky. It will be coming up soon. Let's go up to the forward lounge and see if there's a place for us where we can see ahead."

It had become as though Samson shared Lydia's eyes. She described everything to him and did it well with the skill of a writer—so well that he left off complaining about being blind. They found two good seats up in the forward lounge, which was unusual fortune on a clear day and more so as they were approaching land after being at sea for ten days.

"If you won't miss me for fifteen minutes, and if you'll save my seat, I'll be right back," said Lydia.

"I'm not going anywhere," said Samson.

There was little danger of someone else taking Lydia's seat because the two were always seen together and Samson's dependence on her was obvious. But someone did take her seat soon after she left. It was Alvin.

"Who are you?" Samson demanded.

"Alvin, your official caretaker."

"I thought so. Give me my cane."

"You're not leaving, are you?"

"No. Lydia will be back shortly."

"Not necessarily. That's up to you."

Samson grunted. *I thought I could trust her.* "What do you have to say for yourself, Cypher?"

"I'm sorry for the despicable things I did to you."

"Who else have you confessed to?"

"Everyone concerned. Especially God."

"Have you talked to Claudia?"

"Yes. I was a jail counselor in Salem where she is paying her debt. She has forgiven me."

"Do you remember Paul Christian a.k.a. Felix?"

"I heard about him, but I never actually met him."

"He's become quite the preacher. I took in one of his sermons in Gettysburg when I was passing through on the way east. He said every one of us would encounter someone we needed to forgive. So I'm taking his advice and forgiving you. I know I should have done it first."

"Well, thank you for letting me have that privilege."

"Did Lydia arrange this?"

"Yes. What a beautiful lady she is."

"Oh. I've never seen her."

"I think you have—better than I have."

"Don't tell me you're blind."

"No, but eyes are only distractions when it comes to that."

"Well, now I have to forgive her for taking this upon herself."

"Really?"

"I see what you mean. Okay, she has to forgive me for .... Felix said grudges are toxic. I subjected her to that."

"Are we all clean now? I counseled hundreds in the jail. It usually takes time to get it all out of them. But they couldn't be released until that happened. It's amazing how they hang onto the uttermost farthing. We can't let them out until they pay it because it's demonic for some of them. I don't sense that in you. Lydia did a good job."

"Do you mean—"

"Yes, she softened you up more than you know."

"Claudia was still behind bars when I left Salem. I sensed a bit of smoldering anger in that jail cell."

"Her case is different—a more difficult issue for her. She forgave me readily, and spiritually she had gotten quite clean. But she was working off a financial penalty that she owed to another artist. The root of envy is anger directed at God."

"She has to literally pay with the uttermost farthing."

"Sometimes it comes down to that. You know: the last shall be first and the first last. All the paupers were once billionaires. I see Lydia is standing patiently by. I will give you back to her. Just one more thing: go easy with Ms. Lolomi."

With that he left the lounge and Lydia resumed her place next to Samson.

"Samson, now since you and Alvin are getting along so well, I'm going to let him take over and deliver you to Ms. Lolomi when we get to Haifa. If you want him to, he will stay with you and make sure you get all your necessary accommodations."

"When will I see you again?"

"Silly man, you never have seen me."

"I have a clear picture of you, nevertheless."

"Did Alvin try to describe my face?"

"No. And I wouldn't ask him."

"Then you may keep your clear picture as long as you like."

"You haven't told me where you plan to go in the Land."

"Marching to Zion, of course."

"I have no business there. I'll be going back home with or without sight in my eyes."

"Oh, you do have business in Jerusalem. Everyone does, and you're no exception."

"Do you plan to stay there long?"

"As long as I'm able."

"How will I know you?"

"You would have to close your eyes because you will never know me with your eyes open. If you hear my voice and open your eyes I'll be gone."

"I would almost rather stay blind, then."

"You may learn to be blind to outward appearances in time. Then perhaps we will meet again. But I'm afraid your memories would lose something. So I think it is better the way it is. This way you will never stop seeing me as I am."

"I would like to have something to look forward to that's as pleasant as you've made this voyage for me. But I understand what you're saying."

"Isn't it always this way? You can never hold onto anything that's worth anything without losing it. And the converse is true too, so I predict that you will never lose Leila."

"Then you must believe that I'll never lose you."

The Mediterranean leg of their sea journey presented more vessel traffic and even some land sightings. Everyone on board was eager to have the voyage come to an end, and that eagerness drew more of their attention to the sights outside. The weather was fine and visibility good, providing stunning views of the land after so many days of empty horizons. The city of Tarifa could be clearly seen on the port side as they rounded Gibraltar and entered the inland sea—or the part of it called the Alboran Sea upon which they spent the entire day and the next. The following morning they passed Tunis, visible on the starboard side, and at noon they came close to the little island of Malta, also on the right, while Sicily lay in the hazy distance to port. Two days later they passed Crete at night but saw nothing, for apparently it had not many lights. After that they did not expect another view of land before reaching the eastern end of the sea, for the ship was on a middle course roughly equidistant from Turkey and Egypt.

After two days Cyprus was barely visible to the north and the mountains of Lebanon and the shore of Israel began to rise up out of the sea in the evening. Through Lydia's eyes Samson had not missed any of the land sightings, and he got detailed descriptions of the vessel traffic. He told me he could picture it all very well.

The next morning they were in port. As the ship was docking, Alvin approached Samson with some news:

"The captain asked me to arrange for an escort for you in Haifa. He got word that Ms. Lolomi will not be able to meet you here as she had hoped to."

"I will take care of that," Lydia said immediately.

"I was going to do it myself," Alvin objected.

"Then we'll both go with him," Lydia declared.

And so they did.

After finding a knowledgeable person who spoke English, they made some inquiries and ascertained the location of the Ministry of Health. A free trolley took them within a short walk of their destination. At the reception desk Lydia presented Samson's letter from the eye surgeon in Salem.

"I have no record of an appointment for Ichabod Samson. ... No, there is none for anyone with Samson for a first or last name."

"Can you make an appointment now based on that letter?" Lydia asked.

"Yes, but the soonest we can get him in is a year from now."

Chapter Twenty-Three

S amson now had to decide whether he was going to wait a year in a foreign land or travel back home. He was inclined to make arrangements for the return trip because there would be nothing for him to do in Haifa but wait, and his travel document limited his stay in Israel to three weeks. I'm sure various schemes for making the return trip were running through his mind, none of them depending on my assistance, I'm afraid.

But his companions had other ideas. Lydia wanted to take him to Jerusalem and plead for an audience with the King. Alvin invited him to go with him to Kibbutz Tzorah west of Jerusalem where he had a year-long employment arrangement to work in the winery. He thought they might find a way to allow Ichabod to stay for whatever duration was necessary.

In the end they decided to go together to Tzorah. Lydia would continue from there up to Jerusalem. Ichabod would have to decide whether to go with her or stay at the kibbutz should he be given an invitation to do so.

They found overnight lodging at a hostel in Haifa. The next day they boarded a train for Tel Aviv and arrived there about noon. The tourist ministry office at the train station informed them that their destination was beyond the reach of regular transportation. They were able to take a trolley north to the edge of the city and from there hire a cab (horse-drawn) to the town of Beit Shemesh.

For the last leg they found a wagon and driver willing to take them and their baggage to the kibbutz. On the way they had a nice view overlooking Sorek Valley, but of course Samson was unable to enjoy it.

It so happened that the kibbutz had two rooms in the main house that would be vacant for a week, and the management was willing to let the two unscheduled guests have them. Al said he would donate his wages toward Ichabod's room and board, which was gratefully accepted.

Among the residents of Tzorah was Rabbi Ahijah (not the same prophet Ahijah from Jeroboam's day) who took a particular interest in Ichabod when he learned he was an Exceptional, because Exceptionals did not fit into the Big Picture as Ahijah saw it.

The topic of the Big Picture came up again the next day when Huldah, a resurrected prophetess, and her former husband, Shallum, arrived for their scheduled vacation holiday. Earl and Ahijah were lingering at the dinner table when Earl asked him to explain what he meant by the Big Picture. At least he thought he was asking Ahijah. Huldah answered.

"If you want to explain evil, you have to look beyond the usual limits of theological inquiry. Is that what you mean by the Big Picture?"

"Ahijah mentioned the Big Picture yesterday," Samson answered, "but he didn't get around to explaining anything about it."

"How much time do you have?" Ahijah inquired of them. Quite obviously he was eager to share his thoughts. Samson said he was not going anywhere. Huldah pulled out a chair and sat down at the table across from Ahijah. Her companion, Shallum, acquiescing with less enthusiasm, took the chair next to her and facing the blind man.

Ahijah: "A place to start is with the beings the Bible calls 'sons of God.' By the way, we use the Christian Bible here, Huldah."

"Yes, of course. You're referring to Genesis six," she said. "They messed around trying to start a race of giants."

Ahijah: "'Sons of God' appears again in Job. In Job we get a glimpse of these divine creatures who contend with God about his designs and policies. And yet they continue to operate."

"Clearly," declared Huldah. "Because Paul's 'principalities and powers in heavenly places' refers to more than Satan."

"Absolutely," Shallum chimed in. "Satan is the prince of powers of the air, and being counted among the 'sons of God' in Job he's obviously the chief of a whole tribe of devils."

Huldah added, "The common Old-Testament word used for God is *elohim, and* it's *plural.* For example, God (*elohim*) said, 'Let us make man in our image.'"

Ahijah: "That's true, but I want to emphasize that the Big Picture is framed within one supreme, all-sufficient Creator of heaven and earth. We know nothing outside of that frame, nor can we. But within the frame we find these lesser divinities whom God made in his image."

"Perhaps you should define what 'in his image' means," Shallum suggested.

"At minimum it means having free will (or being a significantly free moral agent)," his former wife replied.

"Which includes moral discernment and freedom to independently choose a course of action," Shallum added.

Ahijah: "Now let me continue. Satan has his name mentioned over fifty times in the Bible. But 'gods' (not specifically Satan) are mentioned well over two hundred times. While most of the time those *elohim* refer superficially to physical idols, the Bible acknowledges that standing behind idols are seducing spirits and doctrines promoted by demons."

Shallum interrupted, "So if no other beings existed that could be called gods, Scripture would not need to make a big issue of the *name* of God. Why would he need a name if he's the only one?"

Samson: "I want to hear his name from a Jew."

Huldah: "In spite of some English Bible translations hiding his name in LORD, to us it is Y-H-V-H, meaning *the self-existing, timeless one,* or *I am that which I am,* as was explained to Moses, a name so revered that often he is distinguished in other ways, such as 'the God of Abraham, Isaac, and Jacob' or 'the Holy One of Israel' or 'the most high God.' We pronounce it Yah'-weh."

Ahijah: "All right. Now in order to make any use of what the Bible reveals concerning this issue we must set aside the simplistic notion that pagan mythology somehow covers it all. Old- and New-Testament Scripture presents these lower gods as real. Some of them are named, and most significantly they're associated with particular nations. While Yahweh became God of the nation Israel, other nations had acquired their own gods that influenced their cultures. Genesis tells us Yahweh fostered nations and languages when he broke up the early civilization in the land of Shinar. Roots of some seventy nations are traced in biblical genealogies. Did the gods then assign themselves to particular nations? Or did Satan oversee the assignments? Actually, Yahweh made the assignments—like a king allocating territories for his sons to rule. If he made the assignment of nations to gods (or gods to nations), he left one region to himself: this land where we live, where no intermediary deity could legally prevent him from reigning directly and supremely."

Shallum: "From that vantage point we can take Melchizedek, king of Salem and priest of God Most High, as evidence of Jerusalem, at least, being reserved for him."

Huldah: "Yahweh constantly reminded Israel that he is God Most High and the *only* God with whom they were to be concerned. And we prophets beat back the illegal intrusion of unscrupulous divinities by ridiculing their idols. 'Yahweh, your God,' Moses told them, 'is God of gods and Lord of lords.'"

Ahijah: "This land Yahweh God reserved for himself was first named after Noah's unfairly-cursed grandson. Would it not be an act of war and yet entirely within reason if Yahweh's adversary-in-chief urged everyone living in Canaan to serve other gods? That's what appears to have happened."

Huldah: "And as a counter measure, Michael, the great angelic prince, was appointed to stand for us in times of trouble."

At that point Lydia, who had been working in the kitchen, appeared in the doorway with notepad in hand saying, "May I join you?"

"Yes, please join us," Ahijah said.

Huldah: "It's not necessary to assume that pagan pantheons are as scandal-ridden as their poets describe them or as grotesque as their idols and ritual practices would suggest. Things happen in war that would not necessarily be predicted by the personalities overseeing the battles. While these 'sons of God' have become known as demons (from Greek *daimon,* meaning divine power), we need not think of them as being evil originally. But many of them certainly became sponsors of wickedness in their efforts to maintain their grip on their territories."

Samson asked, "Weren't people in those territories aware at all that there is a Supreme God?"

Huldah: "Yes, they were—as every thoughtful person is. The lesser gods managed to keep them from seeking God by feeding them lies such as, 'The Creator is too busy to care about you.'"

Ahijah: "My analysis of the origin of evil hangs on God's astonishing revelation that he created beings distinct from himself yet in his image. In other words, he made others significantly similar to himself with the ability to relate to him in a positive way like nothing else—but by that same freedom they might decide to oppose him."

Shallum: "Theoretically, it need not go entirely one way or the other. As with any society, there would be degrees and shades of obedient loyalty to one's superior *vs* loyalty to one's own self-interest."

Lydia: "We who bear the joy and burden of this divine gift of freedom understand very well that rudiment of psychology."

Ahijah: "If we're tempted to question the divine wisdom by which God voluntarily subjected the world to these demon rulers, the book of Job gives us pause. Job and his family were submitted to suffering and death in order to answer Satan's argument, which is that creatures of free will are not only inherently corruptible, they're sure to turn against their Maker when tested."

"If you ask me, the key to everything is right there," Samson volunteered.

Ahijah: "Yes, but the key is not shared with Job. In answer to Job's perplexity about why he was so severely tempted, God elaborates on a few things in creation that are astonishing as well—on a different level but as inexplicable in their own way. Job is never told that it was his outstanding *piety* that put him in a position where God—not Satan—could single him out to endure the trial. But the reader is aware of this, and the apparent injustice of Job's suffering is the foundation of the ironic narrative. The entire book of Job, including the introductory negotiation with Satan and Job's rewards at its conclusion, may be taken as a cameo of the Big Picture."

"That's exactly what I said when I preached my first sermon," the blind man said, letting them know he was no stranger to that line of reasoning and probably had a fair idea of the Big Picture.

There was a pause to let Ichabod go on, but lacking visual clues he was reluctant to say more about himself.

Ignoring Samson's remark, Huldah reverted back to fallen angels: "In Scripture we have good angels (Yahweh's heavenly army from the phrase 'LORD of hosts') and an opposition appearing as Satan's 'fallen' angels. How did they fall? Someone said it seems that Satan pioneered the 'know thyself' movement and gathered a following of a third part of innumerable angels celebrating their self-expression."

"How was their 'fall' necessarily an act of war?" Samson asked.

Huldah explained: "It became an act of rebellion because it usurped the right of Creator God to receive undivided honor and loyalty. Going their own way on the impulse of their own judgment in defiance of Yahweh's superior authority would inevitably begin an erosion of the structure and peace of heaven. Is it not reasonable that such a movement would have to be opposed at all cost?"

"Yes, of course," said Samson.

"But we empathize with Satan, do we not?" Lydia proposed. "We are a little lower than angels and even gods by nature.[1] We were born into and live within the same wilderness of self will that he discovered. What are we to do when we find ourselves with this godlike ability to think and act independently and to map out our own reality?"

---

1. "I said you are gods/And all of you sons of the most high." Psalm 82:6

Huldah: "Well, we do it, of course. We explore our gifts that enable us to develop the wilderness. But then what happens if someone waxes great by personalizing his gift of administration and discovers that he is greatly admired by his associates? How does he manage the accolades and worship laid at his feet? Does he automatically say, 'I reject this praise: all glory goes to my Creator who made the wilderness that I've explored and beautified?' Of course not."

"Because free-willed beings are by definition self-aware and not automatons," added her former husband.

"Right you are, Shallum," said Huldah. "So we understand how it would be easy for Satan, even in his original perfection, to develop an intoxicating taste for celebrity and stardom."

Lydia: "In fact, it would be unreasonable to fault him if he were to claim that his drive to build his own empire was merely an unfolding of something that was intrinsic to the design of his very being."

Shallum: "'Angel,' if you don't know already, appears to be a term that can include any agent involved with heaven's communications with earth. Though it's usually associated with a particular being and circumstance, it's a term of function more than a term of essential being. For example, an encounter with '*the* angel of the Lord' sometimes is interpreted to mean an epiphany of preincarnate Christ. So 'gods' and 'angels' are not mutually exclusive labels. Even human messengers are referred to as angels on occasion."

Samson: "I know this seems uncomfortably technical and complicated, but is there any reason to believe that heaven is no more complex than we imagine it to be when we know that on the physical side everything is overwhelmingly complex?"

Huldah: "There's no reason, of course. So now we need to ask, 'Why did some angels descend into Satan's regime and not others?' Were they 1) conquered in some arena from which the loyal angels were absent? Were they 2) created different from the staunchly righteous angels, say more liberal and free to invent their own avenues of 'obedience'? Or 3) were all angels created the same and the fallen-away individuals simply less successful at managing their free will? Think about those possibilities for a moment."

"I'm thinking," said Ahijah. "What do you think, Ichabod?"

Before he could answer, Huldah prompted him: "Why would the Creator imbue all of his servants with a potentially explosive element that might be ignited by a spark of pride and set his entire kingdom ablaze?"

"Okay," said Ichabod, "We have to conclude that the majority of angels were created with the needle of their moral compasses fixed on the worship of their Creator and unable to deviate from their original holiness for any reason. ... How's that?"

Huldah: "I agree. You're right. We have to conclude that."

Ahijah: "Indeed, it seems unreasonably generous that he allowed *any* of the angels *any* measure of moral freedom at all."

Samson: "Having more than a third of them able to rebel seems absurd unless he were not the supreme Creator."

Huldah: "So may we assume that two thirds were, shall we say, conservatively designed? They are intelligent and powerful beings who are 'hard-wired,' dedicated servants of Yahweh."

Ahijah: "Yes, by design with no mechanism by which they might experience an impulse to independent scheming or putting self-determination first. Therefore, lacking that significant freedom to indulge in self-inspired choice, they are not to be counted among the 'sons of God' made in his image."

Samson: "Then what about the others? Did the 'sons of God' *have* to fall?"

Ahijah: "No, but if the potential for pride and self-will exists, the dynamics of life guarantee that the potential to act independently of God will be activated as a temptation if nothing else."

Lydia: "This too we understand well."

Samson: "Does anyone think Yahweh was surprised when Satan swept all the 'sons of God' into his corner?"

Huldah: "Of course not."

Samson: "Though Satan's behavior is somewhat reasonable, it appears unreasonably tragic that his fall left his Creator with no trustworthy beings truly made in his image."

Huldah: "Yes, it *is* unreasonable. But within the Big Picture I think Ahijah is going to show us that ultimately that is not so."

Lydia: "Please go on."

Ahijah: "If there is a war, what is the evidence on earth and what does the action look like? When Yahweh got a people together and led them out of Egypt, away from the nations and their gods, and brought them into the land he had promised to them (and to himself), he first had to purge the area of demonic cultures that Satan and his cohorts had planted there. Yahweh was the farmer who had the harrowing task of recovering a field overgrown with weeds in order to raise his chosen crop. Since the field belongs to the farmer, no one will fault the owner if he gives it a new name and plows the weeds under—will they?"

Shallum: "Well, they certainly did. From earliest times they called unfair what Yahweh did to reclaim Canaan and rename it Israel even though the reclamation was never completed."

Huldah: "Jebusites, the original inhabitants of Jerusalem, were excepted and not expelled from the land, for example."

Shallum: "A large part of the Old Testament is about those battles. Thus, the land Yahweh reserved for himself is a well documented theater of the war—especially Jerusalem, the city of the great King."

Ahijah: "This is where we need to understand the reason why earth—and I believe the whole physical universe—was created. In war, both sides typically pay a terrible price; but if the conflict may be resolved within a limited theater, the damage is limited. When Yahweh made this earth and declared it very good, he was not unaware that it would become a battlefield. So did he mean by 'very good' that it was very good for that purpose? Yes, but the Bible said all along there would be peace on earth, so he meant that too. He knows the end from the beginning, and while the dark part of the end is victory over Satan, his fallen angels, and their followers, the bright outcome we are experiencing now features an incorruptible, eternal Bride for Christ, *re*made in his image."

Shallum: "It was at the risk (or perhaps the certainty) of an insurrection that God created beings in his image."

Ahijah: "It was a daring thing to do, and any philosopher, applying the most basic principles, would have warned him that chances of everything going perfectly well were slight."

Samson: "We wouldn't be here if God were a philosopher."

Ahijah: "But having taken that step, Yahweh could not let his willful sons establish for themselves permanent principalities in defiance of his authority."

Shallum: "Speaking of conflicts, it would be surprising if there were no wars among those rebel 'sons of God' themselves, with repercussions here on earth."

Ahijah: "Yes, indeed it would. We understand that God's essential nature is love and therefore that his purpose in creating beings in his image was to build a glorious edifice of familial fellowship grounded in love. But should systemic discord develop along the way, he would have unlovely rot in the foundation to deal with. Why did he not eradicate the agents of evil by immediately unmaking them?"

Samson: "Two reasons come to mind: 1) as far as we know, only things within material time can cease to exist; and 2) gaps or voids in the foundation of the building would be detrimental to the overall plan, perhaps much more than we can guess."

Ahijah: "But eventually the rot must be cleaned out, of course, and safely separated from heaven and earth."

Samson: "It follows logically that the Creator had to create a secure and isolated place for rebels and malcontents to be contained and kept from undoing his designs and polluting heaven's atmosphere of love, joy, and peace with the fallout of discord."

A pause followed this offering, putting blind Samson at unfair disadvantage because he could not measure his audience's reaction to his dispassionate description of hell.

Ahijah continued: "But a legal problem currently prohibits the use of the prison. We understand that God must uphold justice in order for him to command respect and obedience. He said he loves justice. So the question Satan would certainly have raised is whether it would not be an act of *in*justice for his Creator to condemn him for exercising the free will which his Creator had bestowed upon him. If his Creator did not expect him to explore his own potential as a moral pioneer, why was he given that ability? In other words, was it even possible for him and others like him to go on forever without developing his own realm in which self admiration and self determination would be proven an effective (and therefore legitimate) means of doing things—in his case managing a host of angels? We might call it a class-action lawsuit by Satan on behalf of all the 'sons of God.'

"How would God answer that argument? And how could he justify condemning Satan—and now all the rest of us—if he cannot answer it? If Satan argues that he rules his band of angels as competently as Yahweh did—or even better—where is the objective proof that his, or any free agent's, independent policy is criminally inferior?

"What do you think? Does this supposition about angelic psychology seem to have veered away from the biblical data?"

Lydia: "No, I wouldn't say that. I think that all beings created in God's image are similar and compatible to the extent that we communicate on the same issues."

Shallum: "This must be so, for if we take at face value the visitations of angels as recorded in Scripture, we find that they are sometimes indistinguishable from humans."

Lydia: "Zechariah even saw Satan in the form of a man."

Shallum: "Apparently, they are able to materialize at will, and it is not a phantom image because it is on record that they enter into conversation, eat food, and engage in battle."

(If this sort of biblical lore seems fantastic and optional, try removing everything that has to do with angels from the Bible: the Scriptures come unglued; nothing works without them.)

Ahijah: "So I think God set this world up to test Satan's claim to immunity from prosecution. He told Satan he would use a separate material universe designed to host a fresh, neutral being. 'Let us make man in our image,' he said; thus man would be free to rebel. And furthermore, this new world would be open to inspection by all the angels and gods; nothing would be hidden.

"To Satan it was an opportunity to prove his legitimacy—or at least he would have a good shot at corrupting the new creature, thus adding evidence to his argument. What did he have to lose?

"When our universe sprang into being (very quickly in heaven's timeless view), the sons of God shouted for joy. Yes, the physical marvel that unfolded held so many possibilities for development that it surpassed, in its own way, the beauty and potential of heaven. I imagine that Satan lectured the other 'sons of God' on not letting it become a playground and a distraction from their serious business. 'Watch this,' Satan said. 'I'm going to turn the human-creature to our advantage.' And he attached a puppet spirit to a dumb serpent-creature he found roaming the Garden of Eden and set himself up as its ventriloquist."

Shallum: "By the way, you often hear it said that because of the vast size and apparent age of the physical universe, its purpose must include more than what goes on here on this little earth. The error in such thinking is the assumption that size has some fundamental significance, which it does not. Even in human experience we know that by means of a suitable algorithm on a computer, vast constructions in virtual space and time require no additional effort and cost almost nothing. And physical matter is certainly a manifestation of information. The initial design of the infrastructure that yields the world is everything; to fling out any number of derivative versions is comparatively nothing. Or if the original design makes use of process in its execution, then any number of by-products of no independent significance may be generated (but in that primordial project intelligent beings made in God's image would not be included, for we will see that our genesis is distinctly different). So the stars, the mere debris of

Creation, may have no significance other than to remind us that we owe our Creator a profound sense of awe for what it took to make planet Earth.

"If you seek a more equitable reason for the galaxies, try the experimental genesis idea on for size: the vast universe was the essential outcome, and the planet that served his purposes best was chosen. But note that scientifically speaking our flesh and blood could not exist under any other conditions—even slight variations in a number of physical conditions would prohibit life—and I think Yahweh was very particular about the kind of flesh and blood *he* would take on."

Huldah: "Although the idea is ridiculous that billions of galaxies with no life in them is a shameful waste, the gods do play to that notion and make sport of the physical heavens. The planets, they say, are their manifestations and together with the sun and stars their plans are on display."

Shallum: "And to divert attention away from Yahweh they continually promote myths about visitors from far-away places when in fact the evidence they present consists of illusions they fabricate themselves."

Ahijah: "So God designed and established this physical world to be inhabited by novel creatures made in his image with this new feature of a physical extension. While the moral part of man remains essentially spiritual, his spirit's physical habitation is an energetic part of him. Just as the 'sons of God' could chose to disobey, so could the human being; therefore, it was a valid demonstration God set before Satan. Truly, it was skewed in Satan's favor because the physical side of man introduced a host of potential temptations for him to explore and exploit to help mankind assert independence."

Shallum: "If Satan's wisdom had not been compromised by his own failure to fear God, perhaps he would have wondered about that instead of rejoicing over it."

Ahijah: "Based on the male/female principle of mutual attraction, earth's residents were designed to never tire of multiplying.

Let us assume that for a being made in the image of God this was a novelty made possible by the physical side (contrary to pagan lore where the gods and goddesses manage to achieve their own procreation). I think the loyal angels were horrified when Eve emerged while Satan and his sexless gods were fascinated by her potential. Let me explain.

"Is it not surprising that the Creator would link to earthly time-bound flesh his unique ability to generate spirits? That he would embed this sacred genesis in temporal creature-stuff must have been seen as an extravagant and insecure sharing of his power. It seemed to put physical nature in control of creating spirits: God would have to respond to a physical circumstance and supply the spirit to inhabit the physical body. 'He sends forth his spirit and they are created.' In other words, he regulates conception; but in the case of mankind, our god-like free will is definitely in the picture as well because the spirit in his image which he puts on each human being is significantly like the spirit of God. The prognosis of the security of this design was not good: it opened another avenue for devilish interference, allowing the 'sons of God' to insert their own materializations.

"Satan was quick to see his opportunity, and he went right to it, taking it upon himself to test the stability of the pristine human pair by exploiting the division of the sexes. But it was too easy, and one wonders again if that did not make Satan wonder, especially after Yahweh slaughtered a pair of lambs in order to clothe the flesh of the sinners rather than making them skirts of plant material."

Shallum: "The shockingly crimson blood that spilled onto the ground must have startled the gods the first time they beheld it: they wondered what it meant."

Ahijah: "Having destroyed the possibility of a blessed and obedient race developing on earth and forcing Yahweh to put the brake on nature's cooperation and bedevil mankind's use of the planet lest things spiral out of control immediately, Satan proposed that he and his rebel gods be allowed to prove that they could govern humankind successfully. At any rate, they were given the opportunity to do so. Each of the gods (or perhaps an association of them) was promised a territory on earth to govern and thereby prove or disprove their competence while Yahweh would keep a portion for his own governance to which theirs were to be compared.

"But I have jumped ahead. I need to go back to Genesis six, and with all respect for the ancient text, take the liberty of adding a bit of color as we paint the Big Picture.

"Things were going well for Satan. He had shown right away that Yahweh's new creation was morally fragile and subject to the same isolating pressure caused by free will that he experienced himself. But some of the angelic sons of God pressed their freedom too far. They were fascinated by the power of the self-replicating genesis design, the genius of it at the human psychological level and particularly the beauty it bestowed on the human female, which surpassed anything in the angelic realm. There was more significance in Adam's rib than they could account for. They were intrigued by the variety it gave the faces of mankind—whatever the underlying mechanism was—and they desired it for themselves. They discovered the back door God had designed for his own use by which they could force him to create giant beings in *their* image. Or something like that. This biological intervention on the part of angels has far-ranging implications, of course.

"But that was a blatant violation of the ground rules, and it landed those angel mavericks in prison. It also necessitated a wash-down of the battleground theater. God had said that Creation was good in every way, and so it was, but if the satanic crowd would not abide by the rules, he would have to tell them that he was sorry but the contest could not proceed because the field of humanity had become infested with demon-possessed semi-human criminals out of which he had harvested but one Enoch. Rather than call the whole thing off, however, he saved a single family whose genes were free of satanic meddling and he flooded out the rest. This too must have made Satan wonder: the flood potential had been built into the planet and was there from the beginning!"

Shallum: "Jesus gave us a parable that can apply here. A field was sown with good seed, and then the enemy came along and sowed tares. Bible teachers may identify the good seed as those obedient to the Spirit of God and the tares as those seduced by lies of the devil. But that is not how Jesus interpreted it: he said the good seed are the sons of the kingdom of God and the tares are sons of the evil one. Apparently, Jesus' interpretation of his own parable—if taken literally—is too shocking to be repeated out loud. But it becomes more reasonable if we note that it agrees with the fact that devilish personages have appeared and influenced the world in every age, and they are only the tip of a sprawling criminal underworld."

Ahijah: "Even though he knew all this ahead of time, Yahweh set out once again to show Satan that his free-willed creatures would obey him if properly taught and governed. But there was no logic in it because Satan had forced his hand and gotten him to curse the earth and distance himself, making strict obedience virtually impossible. Yet Yahweh seemed to be willing to carry on with the compromised arrangement. He gave those 'sons of God' who were still free exactly what they wanted: an opportunity to show that their methods of educating and governing could achieve stability and therefore be worthy of perpetuation.

"But Satan and his demons had walked into a trap of their own making: their devilish administrations were doomed because they hated the newcomer made in the image of God. Yahweh, on the other hand, spoke and acted as though he loved humans, regardless of how badly they behaved. He was bound to keep providing fresh spirits for their offspring, and due to the confluence of two streams of flesh and one of divinely crafted spirits, every newborn was unpredictably unique. (The angels, I suppose, all look pretty much the same, at least within each type and rank.) This meant there was an ever-present danger that a child would grow to upset everything the devilish rulers had accomplished. They despised humans for being immersed in lowly matter yet capable of lofty achievement as they learned to exploit the material creation—and should the curse ever be lifted, the wretched creatures would have the means to enjoy heaven on earth.

"In spite of such dangers, the devils were compelled to press and entice men into the material realm in order to distance them from knowing and obeying their Creator. While this immersion in profane matters boosted science and industry, it plagued the whole of civilization with material addiction, making human society increasingly unresponsive to any outside influence either good or bad. Developments in travel efficiency made it increasingly difficult to keep people from regularly migrating across borders and thereby causing quarrels among their demonic overlords whose policy was to keep them locked down and dedicated to the gods of their native nations."

Huldah: "Yes, this earth was the theater of heaven's war. It was all about the governing principalities and powers trying to prove their worthiness by establishing permanent ownership of a realm and thereby becoming indispensable. Since our physical bodies were transient, the disposal of our eternal spirits is what mattered. To the overlords, the physical comfort of the masses was unimportant. If enough souls could be bent into images of a governing demon and persuaded to worship him, then that god would have collected a pool of witnesses to testify to his competence. But humanity develops in ways that cannot be predicted by intelligence less than possessed by Creator God himself."

Huldah: "Evil far beyond that was going on! As the governing gods were free to educate by any means they wished, it was not long before they discovered that the human frame is capable of harboring multiple spirits and that it is possible to plant demon agents within a person, attaching them as robot-like parasites to the God-given spirit and thus not only securing the following of that unfortunate soul but possibly creating a hybrid with extraordinary ability. This was their answer to the natural generation of genius and prodigy in the human being, and by means of these super-tares they compete with Yahweh for establishing stable cultures on earth. Trans-humanism is not a new thing."

Shallum: "Hence we had wars occurring among nations as demon surrogates worked to fulfill their lust for power by organizing campaigns using and abusing the common humanity they despise. Though emperors often reached beyond their legitimate borders, Yahweh did not allow his servants to indulge in wanton aggression. The purpose of this planet was not to host games wherein gods try to unseat brother gods; but it did come to that, which put a tool in Yahweh's hand that he used to discipline his own nation when he allowed us to be overrun and defeated by the forces of the foreign gods we defiantly worshiped—because thereafter he had the right to turn around and punish the nations for their illegal aggression."

Ahijah: "So the centerpiece of the Big Picture was this cosmic contest that could have defined, and may still define, what will be allowed as good and what, if anything, will be damned for being evil. Inescapably, we were not only surrounded by but immersed in that war since the habit of rebellion had become natural to our fleshly seed much earlier, and by then the imprint of rebel cultures profaned every brain."

Huldah: "Whoever despises hell welcomes perpetual evil. While nothing negates God's intrinsic love which he extends to all his creation, if evil is to be eliminated from heaven and earth, at least some of his creatures will have to be cut off and eventually isolated. If not that, then the rival hope of the 'sons of God' will be realized and heaven will forever tolerate legitimized evil throughout its domains."

Ahijah: "The purpose of earth was never to become an anthropocentric paradise—contrary to what many suppose. To believe that is to discredit God's wisdom. Fundamentally, earth's purpose was to be the theater in which the argument between God and Satan is played out, that the manifold wisdom of God might be made known to the rulers and authorities in heavenly places. Satan would have understood that the physical arena was designed to limit battle-damage in heaven, but he should have wondered why the advantage seemed to be all on his side. From our vantage point, we see that Satan's advantage was transient, but we marvel at the price heaven was willing to pay to allow it."

Huldah: "Yes, and bear in mind what we know about the character of our God. He is not a tyrant. He is patient, loving, and kind. He demands obedience because free will is highly explosive, and we need guidelines and training to avoid being hurt by it. Sin consists of disbelieving his warning; and willfully disregarding the warning is what potentially delivers one into the company of devils."

Lydia: "How can anyone avoid being a rebel when we are born with that tendency?"

Ahijah: "The day of final reckoning has not arrived yet, and there is still much more to the Big Picture. Scripture tells of a future time that must make Satan tremble as it draws near. But why hasn't Yahweh condemned him by now to rid heaven of the fallen angels and earth of their followers?—for they truly have failed to maintain peace on earth. Why has he locked them up temporarily instead? Does his patience indicate weakness? Impossible. Was the (what we suppose) early development of evil in his original plan a purposeful thing to help define or accentuate ultimate good? Certainly not! These questions must have made Satan wonder too.

"But from Satan's desperate point of view the urgent and practical thing was to forestall judgment until he and the rebel 'sons of God' had hit on a successful demonstration of Utopia. Yes, peace on earth by whatever means, even if achieved by severely degrading human freedom, responsibility, and even human nature would have served their purpose because in Satan's view this was never about the welfare of humanity—only the welfare of himself.

"To briefly recap: Yahweh's opposition had corrupted his good creation early on, but the Bible lets us in on the secret that this earth is still capable of producing a peaceful family in his image, free and sharing in his love. Satan has a contrary purpose, and it is not simply to mess things up. He is determined to demonstrate that he is capable of successfully managing mankind, which he hopes will validate his brand of godhood and prevent his permanent ejection from heaven. Everything Satan does is aimed at that end because he realizes it is his only hope to preserve his autonomy. If you enlist to help him achieve his victory, as many did for lack of knowledge, you become a member of his army, and that makes you his property. Where he goes you go.

"The good news is that Yahweh has provided a means of rescue from human nature's free fall into Satan's kingdom, and it explains how Christ will push Satan aside. He is demonstrating the second part of what he meant by "very good" when he created earth. In the aftermath of that day of wrath we are reappearing on earth as redeemed people who are beyond judgment because we have been remade in his image without sin, justice having been fulfilled by Christ taking our penalty upon himself. This is the bomb shelter from the wrath of God to which everyone was invited and which the demons tried to cover up.

"Thus is answered Satan's fundamental argument that free will cannot long stand without committing sin. He is right technically, but he never foresaw how God would apply divine love and step in to become a powerful sacrifice more than equal to the penalty that had (and will) accumulate on behalf of his beloved sinners. Satan never believed it could happen. Who would? The cost was unimaginable to Satan as it is unimaginable to everyone. Fortunately, we were so made that we needed not imagine it before we understood the simple gospel and let it apply to us.

"The final chapter is now being played out; the practical success of the redemption of humanity is being demonstrated. In Satan's view it was imperative that the world never get to this place. The prophets' prediction of an age of peace with freedom and prosperity was Satan's nightmare that he determined must not be allowed to come to pass. Satan's version of the age of peace saw mankind's free will disabled, cooperation coerced, and freedom severely curtailed.

"The shock and wonder of Creator God becoming man struck like lightening in Satan's kingdoms when the Spirit of Christ marched forth clad in ordinary humans inaccessible to demonic manipulation, lawfully challenging satanic institutions and establishing churches for Jesus Christ. This called for a direct counter by the 'sons of God.' Satan slapped the 'God' title on one of his fallen angels, a moon deity, and opened a channel to him in the name of his prophet, disseminating a bastardized religion that marginalizes Jesus. He waited for the organized church of Christ to get bogged down with bickering over relics and other petty concerns and then constructed an imposing shrine on Jerusalem's temple site and took the world by storm. Though having lost many wars over the centuries, the aggression was not over yet. By coercion and violence it continued to obscure and stamp out true knowledge of Jesus Christ; and the shrine on the temple mount long stood against the fulfillment of end-time prophecy.

"As Satan worked to break those prophetic Scriptures in which Christ sets him aside and brings about a nation of obedient sons and daughters on this earth, he had his useful theologians among us who insisted that the prophesied age of God's rule was not to take place quite as prescribed in Scripture. They sidelined our essential preparation for future offices of obedience by hiding the kingdom millennium from view, dangerously ignoring Jesus' stern words about the dreadful future awaiting those of his would-be servants who neglect to invest their talents in preparation for faithful service later in his coming kingdom.

"The turning point in the war that occurred when God entered the human race was not a surprise entirely. Ever since the events of Genesis six there had been speculations by seers and poets that this could happen. However, when the reality came it revealed more about the love of God for his Creation than anyone imagined, and even Satan didn't get it. Although hidden in the Scriptures was a prediction that Messiah would arrive in the womb of a virgin, the implication was not understood. If the Son of God had made appearances before that, those events were inconsequencial compared to this. If this had been explained to Satan beforehand, no doubt he would not have agreed to a theater of war where God would literally be born and die on the stage. The Incarnation tied God to Planet Earth and Planet Earth to God. There was no longer any possibility that Creation would not be shown to be good in the end.

"Satan knew the birth of Jesus was a bombshell, but since human life was not permanent, the potential for damage to his case by this transient influencer within captive Israel was not evident or not believable to him at first. Satan's initial counter-offer to Jesus demonstrates this lack of understanding. The devil's proposal was to hand over the rule of the nations that had been maintained by the "sons of God" if Jesus would forego his perfect dedication to Yahweh and not declare himself *the* "Son of God" but instead join the "sons of God" under Satan's leadership.

"Evidently Satan did not know (or believe) who Jesus of Nazareth was at that point, or if he did he did not foresee the full significance of the resurrection promised in Scripture. Yahweh had preserved the continuity of our nation, but it was still morally corrupt and not significantly better than any other nation with respect to the foundational markers of holiness. What Jesus was about to do was necessary in order to fulfill the promised resurrection of human bodies, but even more significantly it would make possible the moral purity of free-willed beings that so far had been unattainable. That was the game changer and essentially the end of the war. But few recognized it, and so the war raged on under a false pretense and satanic hope that the kingdom of Satan would coerce peace and produce a valid example of sustainability.

"Of all the nations, only Israel was offered this amazing opportunity for resurrected life. None of the 'sons of God' could promise this. Though reincarnation is set before them as a ruse to keep them in line, salvation from the dead end of sin could only be arranged by the Lawgiver himself and only if no law were violated in the process, including the law that death is the payment for moral imperfection."

"When we looked around at the religious cultures of the world, we were not be surprised to find rumors and even evidence of supernatural events everywhere. No doubt all of the 'sons of God' are able to bring about some of that. In the biblical records there are seers like Balaam and magicians like those in Egypt. The miraculous does not signify a way of salvation from sin. Only the substitutionary atonement of Jesus Christ has the power to do that; thus it is said salvation is of the Jews. By the light of this we see that shamanism was likely connected to the 'sons of God,' not to God Most High. Regardless of what truth and practical advantage there may be outside God's Anointed, the end is bound to be deadly. The resurrection through Christ is where the war has its consummation as we are called to partake of his death and be absorbed into his glorious body. Every other story was a counterfeit script devised by demons.

"It should be clear why Jesus prescribed that prayers be in his name. We had to be unambiguous when there are other gods on the loose, and even now they are only restrained. Tacking something like 'in your name' to the end of a prayer didn't necessarily qualify. Beginning the prayer with 'In the name of Jesus' was much better. 'In the name of Jesus Christ' made the message doubly secure. But either 'Jesus' or 'Christ' was sufficient. There were no other gods named Jesus, and only he had been anointed; that is why we find the apostles freely referring to him simply as 'Jesus' when the context makes it clear that ordinary humans are excluded; otherwise, 'Jesus of Nazareth' serves to narrow the field to a point. Throughout the Bible we find the 'name' being emphasized. His name is holy precisely because it separates him from other gods. And that applies today as much as it did in ancient times because those other gods are still around, and the default salutation might fit the god of the nation you happen to be in! While as Christians we belong in the holy meta-nation of Christ, it is still advisable to display your colors, which signifies that you are aware of the battle and have no interest in addressing one of the adversaries of Christ.

"If in some secret 'prayer language' we did not know exactly what we said and to whom it was addressed, we needed to beware! All the gods are capable of causing supernatural manifestations designed to deflect sincere prayers. And we should not assume that by using the name of some saint that a prayer is safe from being hijacked by the enemy. In fact, using any other name in prayer amounts to idolatry. How destructive and wasteful this particular lack of understanding was I suppose no one knows; hopefully the Spirit of Christ secured the door we left unguarded.

"Ironically, the leaders of the Jewish nation were prompted by Satan when the blessing promised in their Scriptures materialized, and we must assume that Satan failed to see that what he had led them to do was truly according to their Scriptures until it was too late to reverse the momentum. When Jesus resurrected, he demonstrated a miraculous body, the first of its kind but not the last. His small band of disciples were the first to receive the Holy Spirit whom he released, but not the last. The Spirit of Christ conferred to them was contagious and no respecter of nations. It spread throughout the Roman empire and everywhere, right under the noses of the 'sons of God' because every missionary effectively extended Yahweh's territory as he or she set a beautiful foot in foreign lands, revealing to all the manifold wisdom of God that Israel had carefully preserved in writing.

"This upset the whole economy of the gods. An individual person could walk into a thoroughly pagan territory, thus making an opening for the Spirit of Creator God, carving out a new segment for the body of Christ, and effectively extending the nation of Yahweh—but not without opposition from the demon masters, for this encroachment of what they consider their sovereign right was not expected."

Hildah: "Not that the territorial divisions were ever strictly sacrosanct, because the Spirit often found an opening through gifted prophets even before Christ's resurrection, but Satan could readily squelch the effects, as for example in Nineveh and Babylon."

Ahijah: "Basically, the land of Israel, and the temple in Jerusalem in particular, was the place Yahweh chose to be heaven's embassy, as intermittent as it turned out to be. But the missionary principle seemed to have been active all along. For example, how was Yahweh allowed to destroy Sodom if it belonged to another god? Answer: He placed one of his own there. Lot was not the missionary type, but he got involved with the politics of the place though he was not consciously sent there for that purpose. He was an anomaly, a righteous man in a corrupt culture. Yahweh sent him there as a legal foothold that gave him an opening to send in angels and manage the culture; and the change he made was drastic and permanent and a foreshadow of things that would come when he returned bodily to earth at the end of that age.

"We must not make the mistake of thinking that someone is worthy of more than their experience in life offers them. To be brought into existence at all, with the opportunity to try out on earth and perhaps leave progeny, is a gift that never imputes debt to the giver. If someone suffers a painful existence and shortened lifespan, the tragedy, if there is one, is due to uncured corruption of their spirit, for the never-dying spirit takes into eternity marks made in time. Human casualties of angelic wars must be seen in the context of Christ's strategy where evil was not immediately eradicated but allowed to grow along with good. There is little justice, no fairness, and never equity under conditions of war!

"The old world order seemed to be dissolving, but that was not so. We knew this because the prophets predicted violent destruction of the anti-Christ nations at the time of Messiah's return. The 'sons of God' would not be entirely out of business until then. Satan hung onto his hope that not enough faithful and able bond-servants of Christ would be brought into the resurrection age to successfully apply Christ's enforcement of righteousness throughout the world. When I looked around at what Satan was doing in those days, I found him opposing the development of sanctified saints who were being prepared, once released from unholy flesh, to prove that free will is not essentially corrupting.

"Christian teachers assisted Satan when they ignored the Big Picture. Christians were taught that the world was created for them and that to be blessed by God here and accepted into the eternal bliss of heaven was their goal. Sanctification and obedience were loosely tied to salvation and seemed scarcely necessary. They had it backwards. Satan was happy to have everyone tucked away safely in heaven. What he feared was many sanctified servants in resurrected and glorified bodies exercising their gifts as rulers in Christ's kingdom on this earth: a host of exhibits positioned to be Yahweh's evidence in the ultimate trial to prove that the 'sons of God' miscalculated about the inevitability of sin. At the conclusion of that trial, the guilty verdict having been unanimously approved by a jury of twenty-four angels, Yahweh will demand that the demons and every other rebel be delivered to a place separated from concourse with heaven, which translates to incapacitation by chains of pain in what is referred to as hell or the lake of fire, an outcome of shame and everlasting contempt.

"The takeaway from my rambling tonight is that if we haven't learned something in our former life that will be useful in this one, we need to get on with it. It is not enough to merely acknowledge Christ and look forward to happiness in heaven. We also have an obligation to risk applying our faith toward something of value as a return on the Master's investment in us. There is no safety in ignorance if you have heard me tell you this!

"Our only safety is in *successfully* investing the talents we were given. This is a cosmic battle in which we are the territory to be won by Christ or lost to Satan. Always remember what Jesus said in that frightful parable about the one who thought he was playing it safe.

"You might ask, 'Who are these obedient citizens? Do you know anyone who could qualify for being a perfectly and permanently reliable servant of God who will never, ever falter?' My answer, of course is, 'No, I don't.' Then how is it that God can have this confidence in people? Is the resurrection so transformative that we enter as world-loving saints and suddenly become trusted servants ready to brush off every worldly temptation? No, because he chose us in him before the foundation of the world that we would be holy and blameless.

"But this is also the point where we must take seriously some things Jesus said, such as the way being narrow and few finding it. Again, remember the servants in Jesus parables who were rewarded with posts of responsibility for making wise investments with the master's money. The surprising doom of the servant who played it safe and merely preserved what he was given is evidence that if we don't learn to be profitable now we'll be worse than useless to him then. So the exercise of investing our talents to benefit our Master and not ourselves is of far more practical importance than we had been led to believe. Being detached from worldly ways is preparing to joyfully use our resurrected bodies effectively and learning to laugh at any temptation to self indulgence.

"If you have doubts about this picture, recall that its mainspring is how it explains the persistence of Satan without making him equal to God and without seeing God as needing evil to achieve his purposes. The former heresy is a simplistic doctrine common in Eastern religions. The latter heresy is less obvious and by default slips without opposition into otherwise good Christian doctrine.

"As you read the Bible with this Big Picture in mind, you may be amazed, as I am, at how much additional material there is that easily fits and supports this perspective."

Samson excused himself at that point. Although the subject was not new to him, he had been unable to contribute very much. He was not feeling well either physically or mentally.

The next day Lydia announced that her search for arrangements had been successful and she was leaving for Jerusalem. Her intention was to return in a week to see if Samson needed to find other accommodations.

That evening another discussion took place. It began with Samson sharing his perplexity about not being informed of the reason for his call to the future after several years of homelessness and tenuous employment as an undocumented exceptional. There ensued speculation about his exceptional leap over time and the reason for it. Ahijah said that such a departure from regular procedure and indeed reality could only be explained as a miraculous act of God, and he asked Ichabod if he had any hard evidence. Samson claimed to be not as old as the calculation from his birth date would indicate and that he had verified that by comparing his skin with other naturals who had been his contemporaries. Other than that he had no hard evidence that it had actually happened. Though it was not brought up, he knew that his amnesia about the missing years and the journey halfway across the continent could be explained as a psychological aberration. Most tellingly his complete lack of knowledge about why he was called to the future made it seem unlikely that there ever was a reason, and if there was no reason then very likely it had not happened.

The discussion then turned to what seemed to be a favorite topic: What would the resurrection develop into ultimately?— say in a million years. It seemed they had already talked through the transition following the millennium, and various speculations about the city of gold and its setting had been discussed at length.

After breakfast the next morning Samson was left to himself. Without eyesight, his movements were limited, so he lay on the bed in his room, listening to the birds singing. He imagined people walking between buildings when sounds of footsteps and voices came through the open window, for he had received no orientation and knew only a small portion of the house he was in.

Suddenly, his imagination was challenged by sounds seeming to emanate from a horse-drawn carriage. He understood none of the words the driver spoke which undoubtedly were Hebrew, but the manner of speech betrayed an errand of importance. Then he heard footsteps within, then a knock on his door.

"You're leaving us, Samson. For better or worse, I don't know, but the carriage outside has gold markings of the crown on it, and the driver says you have been summoned by the King."

A hijah had developed his Big Picture over the course of several weeks during which time he shared it with members of his kibbutz. On the day after Samson left, a question-and-answer session was held which had been scheduled and announced earlier. In addition to nearly all of the kibbutz residents, people from outside had heard about it and had come with questions. For the most part they were naturals, but resurrected folk were interested as well. Notes were taken and copies were made. Lydia received an English copy which she gave to me when I expressed interest in it. I have included most of its questions and answers in this chapter. Does this mean that heaven endorses the Big Picture? Well, from heaven's perspective this is elementary material which would be expressed in far fewer words.

Q: How can we be sure this Big Picture is true since it draws from the Christian Bible exclusively and ignores or rejects perspectives from science and established dogmas of religion?

A: Either the Bible is God's perspective on man or it is one of man's perspectives on God. It can't be both because they are incompatible. You have to make a choice and go with one or the other. If you want to integrate science and history in such a way that it modifies or sidelines biblical data, you're in the latter camp.

I take it that God wants us to see things from a particular point of view because he is trying to adjust our values to align with his intention for mankind. As we accustom our hearts to agree with the Bible, its message grows wider and deeper for us. We find the Word is not only nourishing food, it is medicine to cure the disease of pride and ignorance. For those criticizing the Bible, the medicine has been ineffective: for some it works, for others it does not.

If you have determined which parts of Scripture are gifts from God and which parts are from man, keep it to yourself or else be honest and acknowledge it is a gift from you.

Q: You appear to be unaware that there is a rich literature on celestial hierarchies that goes far beyond what you have gleaned from the Bible. There is a lot of information about the past, present, and future of the universe and its purpose from a spiritual perspective.

A: It's easy to determine the worth of such systems. Simply ask two questions: 1) What is the source: upon what authority does it rest and how does that compare with the Bible? You will find that the Bible is considered to be authoritative by orders of magnitude beyond the systems you speak of. Yes, they attempt to incorporate Christ and Christian theology, but they take things out of context and their interpretation is wrong. 2) How is evil dealt with? You will find that evil is not really evil in these systems. The biblical Big Picture faces the origin of evil squarely and clearly presents the very exciting terms of its resolution.

Q: What does "investing talents" mean in practical terms?

A: To answer that we must look into the expression of our Ephesians 2:10 works and then figure out what investment would deliver increased value to our Master.

The Big Picture informs us that Planet Earth is a platform on which God has set out to prove to Satan that beings created with freedom to disobey can truly obey and adore him in spite of being free to assert independence—in other words that free will does not inevitably have to become marred by unlawful indulgences of self-will. Given that the blood of Christ has conferred legal innocence, and new or regenerated bodies have severed us from slavery to the First Adam and placed us in the royal line of the Second Adam, by what means will an individual deliver talents of increased value to the King in our theocracy? Some are literally participating in governing cities, applying skills learned in the former life. That sets a vocational pattern, but not everyone will be called on to continue an old vocation, so we can't rely on that. The common denominator for everyone is the value of our vastly increased reliability, which has its root in the disciplines of our past lives. In other words, regardless of vocation, our return on the Master's investment in us will be proven by applying what we have learned about being faithfully focused and trustworthy in times of testing. Because in the end it is the perfect record of uncorrupted loyal service that will qualify us for being exhibits in the trial which must turn out proving Satan's argument is false if he is to be removed from heaven and earth and condemned.

But if someone who received talents to invest comes through a thousand years being afraid to have those talents be tested in the crucible of real service, will that person be ushered out of the courtroom along with Satan and his demons? What do you think? What does the Bible say? I will leave that for you to ponder and answer for yourself.

Q: The so-called "parable of the talents," which this perspective is largely based on, ends with the cautious servant being absolutely condemned. This is hard to explain. Can the Big Picture explain it?

A: The version in Luke adds a verse which helps explain it: "But these my enemies, that would not that I should reign over them: bring them here and slay them before me." Now, realize that this is in the language of the parable and therefore not necessarily to be taken literally. The kernel of it is in "would not that I should reign over them." The Big Picture explains the origin and resolution of evil, and this attitude definitely is seen in the origin. In other words, this attitude is essentially a threat to the stability of heaven and must not be allowed to persist anywhere after the devils are eliminated.

Part of being saved by grace is walking in the good works which God has prepared for us. Discerning and pursuing that path is included in the gift of eternal life. You cannot avoid being his workmanship, so make the best of it that you possibly can.

Q: Micaiah (I Kings 22, II Chr. 18) had a "word from Yahweh" in which a "spirit" volunteered to put lying words in the mouths of Ahab's prophets. Was that spirit one of the fallen angels?

A: Note that just before he said that, Micaiah had spoken sarcastically to Ahab, telling him a lie which everyone present knew was merely an insult. The two kings who had summoned Micaiah on this occasion had put him in a difficult position, and this was his way of expressing his displeasure and contempt for Ahab. So can we be sure that what he said next was intended to be taken literally? He did not say the "spirit" (literally "breath") was an angel. Basically, Micaiah was saying that Ahab's prophets were false prophets, and the way he said it was well within the style of Yahweh's prophets. But is there some truth in the picture of Yahweh consulting his hosts of angels? This gets into the question of the purpose of the angels, which I never thought was to advise their Creator. Additionally, the matter at hand, which they were supposedly unable to answer after extended debate, is so trivial that we must take that whole scene with Yahweh and the angels as being Micaiah's transparent fabrication.

Q: It appears that Israel's division and civil war was caused by King Rehoboam's incompetence. Yet the Bible says it was brought about by Yahweh. Can the Big Picture explain this?

A: This was a strategic move, not a punishment. It looked like punishment due to the fact that Rehoboam's father, Solomon, had not made a strong stand against idolatry. But as long as demons had their surrogates living in the land (whether free or retained as forced labor) idolatry would be a problem. So the failure to stand against idolatry goes back to Joshua's day—and earlier, for idolatry was always present from the very beginning of Jacob's family.

Northern Israel became a sacrificial shield for Jerusalem against attack from pagan nations. Also it was a vivid demonstration to Judah of the fruits of unmitigated idolatry. The eventual dispersion and occupation of northern Israel was not a clear victory for Satan because knowledge of Yahweh was spread thereby. The same benefit of dispersion must be noticed for the two major defeats of Jerusalem: the tribes were safer in dispersion; they came back in time to birth the Messiah; and we have now come back to restore Jerusalem and all of the land promised to Jacob.

Q: Why was David denied the privilege of building the temple in Jerusalem? He designed it, gathered materials for it, and greatly desired to see it come into being. The answer he was given, that he had blood on his hands, is rather cryptic. What does that mean?

A: David was a warrior, and during his life he engaged in bloody battles that pushed back the enemies of Israel. Then, building on his father's kingdom, Solomon presided over a remarkably prosperous empire. The question might be asked: Did Solomon make the temple glorious, or was the temple the reason for Solomon's glorious reign?

The temple in Jerusalem was patterned after the tabernacle which had been designed in detail by God. The mercy seat within the tabernacle was recognized far and wide as a visible connection to Yahweh. And so the temple was destined to be not only a monument to the God of Israel but also a place where Yahweh would manifest himself like no other place. Thus it proclaimed Yahweh to the world of demon-god worshipers. If the temple had been built during David's reign, Yahweh would have been seen as a deity of war and military conquest. As it came to the attention of the world during Solomon's reign, Yahweh was seen rather in the context of prosperity and peace through strength.

This foreshadowed our time when the return of Christ necessitated a forceful subjugation of our enemies before the glorious reign of peace could begin during which the temple design that was revealed to the prophet Ezekiel was to be built.

Q: Does the Big Picture interpret the "pearl of great price" parable?

A: Yes. In fact, this is at the very heart of the Big Picture. The pearl is a treasure *to* Christ, not Christ himself directly. The kingdom of God must include gentile pearls if it is to win against Satan's argument that no such thing is possible. Every pearl came at a great price: it cost Christ everything as we count costs. The parable of the treasure hidden in a field says the same thing. Christ finds his pearls that have escaped the evils in the church (leaven and birds in the parallel parables). He treasures his pearls because he spent himself to form them, and they are one with him as his bride. His pearls validate his kingship. Satan has nothing to compare. Christ enjoys his pearls and his pearls love being worn by him. Significantly, the gates of New Jerusalem are styled as great pearls.

If you take these parables the other way around, Christ being the treasure to be found and bought, there is some truth there on the surface. But underneath it turns out to connect to the way of self gratification, the road that leads ultimately to destruction. Many go that way on the ill advice of some Bible teachers.

Q: If the "sons of God" are the evil influencers in the world, why was it said that "an evil spirit from *Yahweh* was upon Saul"?

A: The Hebrew word *ra'* translated "evil" in that quotation is not the kind of moral evil contemplated in your question. Rather, as a masculine intensive noun, it means distress or adversity. The spirit of Saul's kingship anointing, which was given by Yahweh, had been taken from him, and thereafter he became Yahweh's spirited adversary by violating his vow to never execute David.

Q: In Daniel chapters 4 and 5 it is written that the Most High rules in the kingdom of men and gives it to whomsoever he will. That seems to indicate that Yahweh rules the nations, not the "sons of God."

A: This passage is about a lesson that Nebuchadnezzar, king of Babylon, learned after his aggression in Israel. Yahweh had earned the right to overrule the gods of Babylon, and he did so very effectively through Daniel. So this was a penalty against Babylon's demons and not the general rule for all nations. It worked for the good of Babylon for some time as Nebuchadnezzar learned that his success was not due to his own excellence but rather the God of Israel. But originally it was Yahweh who made the assignments, and there is no indication that they are necessarily invariable.

Q: Who are the "watchers" in Daniel 4:17?

A: They are "holy ones," that is, they are angels who watch over the affairs of earth and, according to this passage, have authority to override natural causes by their own decrees.

Whether they did so on behalf of Yahweh or not is not clear. They are mentioned nowhere else in Scripture under "watcher" terminology, but that does not necessarily indicate a unique kind of creature or office because Yahweh's angels are often found intervening in the affairs of men.

Incidentally, it is mentioned here that the lowest or basest of men are given to rule over the kingdom of men—by decree of the watchers, the holy ones. The reason? That the "living" may know that the most high rules in the kingdom of men. Otherwise, full credit might be reasonably given to the man for his achievements —if they happened to last—and he might be confused with and worshiped as the Messiah. But more to the point in the Big Picture, this seems to indicate that Yahweh reserves some say about the administration of the nations outside of Israel, which may be taken back to the fact that he creates the spirits of all living beings.

Q: You mentioned Michael, the archangel who guards Israel. In the book of Daniel he appears to be joining in forceful opposition to the "prince of Persia" and not respecting the national boundary.

A: The "prince of the kingdom of Persia" is clearly one of the "sons of God" who has dominion over the king of Persia who would be Cyrus at that time. Cyrus happened to be Yahweh's anointed and so is being aided by Michael. There are complexities always.

Q: Why is the Bible virtually silent about literal details of heaven? There is so much speculation based on a few verses that probably are not literal and do not really make sense.

A: As the Bible is silent about the literal details of heaven, so is the Big Picture. The human mind is based in the material world. Heaven is outside the material world and outside the frame of the Big Picture. The frame is very important and stands as a barrier to nonsense. Certain Bible interpreters, having a dim view of the frame, continue to speak of heaven as being literally located within the material universe. Obviously this is nonsense because if heaven is God's "dwelling place" then it must be quite distinct from the universe he created. Time as we know it is a property of physical matter, so to speak of time in heaven as necessarily being in step with our time is nonsense as well.

But certainly heaven has much to do with earth, and by looking at the principles regarding heaven's involvement, we may arrive at something useful to our minds and in that sense true. This is not peering beyond the frame but rather looking at evidence of heaven's impact within the frame and using our imagination to pair the evidence with what we know about as humans made in God's image. The principle that allows us to do that is the principle that we must remain essentially human (not necessarily physical) or else being made in God's image means nothing and we become nothing because we become disconnected from everything we know.

There are some illustrations of this duality in the visions of Isaiah, Ezekiel, and John where we find images of men and animals mixed with otherworldly elements. These are breakthroughs from behind the frame, which is why they are difficult to interpret and of little use to us directly other than to testify that the Big Picture is not everything.

Now in our day we are hearing about New Heaven from people who live there. Nowhere is this found in the Bible explicitly—like the church is not found in the Old Testament explicitly.

Q: As recorded in II Chronicles and Ezra, Cyrus, king of Persia, said that Yahweh, the God of heaven, had given him all the kingdoms of the earth. How does that square with the nations being controlled by the "sons of God"?

A: First to note is that what Cyrus said is not what Yahweh or one of his prophets said. Isaiah named Cyrus long before he was born and predicted that Yahweh would anoint him to subdue nations—not that he would own all the kingdoms of the earth. The culture from which Cyrus arose was monotheistic, and Cyrus knew of Yahweh, which could mean that many in Persia had escaped the dominion of demons. Yahweh had told Isaiah that he would enable Cyrus to subdue nations and open the "gates of hell." Yahweh stirred up the spirit of Cyrus, a messianic figure who loosed the gates of tyrannical strongholds, ultimately to proclaim the release of the Jewish captives.

The arrangement that allows the "sons of God" to exercise dominion over nations does not prevent the knowledge of Yahweh from crossing borders and lodging in the minds and hearts of individuals who may influence their cultures. Another example is Solomon's influence in Ethiopia through the queen of Sheba which persists to this day. Paul the apostle began the movement that broke demon strongholds in western nations.

Q: How could theologians, Bible students, and preachers not see the Big Picture? Is the focus too narrow in the New Testament?

A: Consider Ephesians 3:8-12: "This grace was given to me, who am less than the least of all saints, to preach the unsearchable riches of Christ to the Gentiles and to make all men see what is the dispensation of the mystery which for ages has been hidden in God who created all things: to the intent that now it might be made known through the church to the principalities and the powers in the heavenlies the manifold wisdom of God, according to the eternal purpose which he purposed in Christ Jesus our Lord in whom we have boldness and access in confidence through our faith in him."

Who are these principalities and powers? Paul uses the same phrase in other places. An example is Ephesians 5:12: "Our wrestling is not against flesh and blood but against the principalities, against the powers, against the world-rulers of this darkness, against the spiritual hosts of wickedness in the heavenlies." Is this not a perfect description of what we have been calling the "sons of God"?

Paul is admitting that there is a larger purpose behind evangelism—larger than simply winning souls for heaven. The "eternal purpose" is to demonstrate the wisdom of God to the principalities and powers through the example of the church—the church being that mystery hidden in Christ comprised of Jew and Gentile raised in him to a new resurrected life of unqualified obedience.

In Colossians 1:16 Paul confirms that principalities and powers were created by Christ and for Christ. Then in the next chapter he says Christ triumphed over them. In other words, the stage was set for their defeat (for they were still quite active then).

In Titus 3:1 Paul uses "principalities and powers" to refer to human government with the implication that the wickedness in the heavenlies does not necessarily manifest as pure evil on earth. This is as we would expect, because the principalities and powers in the heavenlies, while in rebellion against Yahweh, are intent on governing nations to demonstrate their own competence.

The reason this is missed by most theologians goes back to ignorance of the war in heaven caused by their failure to pursue an answer to the continuing activity of Satan. I hate to say it, but could Satan have had his hand in promoting this ignorance?

Q: Why did Jesus, if he is God, spend so much time in prayer —far more than is recorded of anyone anywhere else in the Scriptures?

A: Being in the flesh meant he had temporarily "laid aside" some of his normal abilities. Or better said, he was necessarily handicapped by being in a human body. But still, Jesus was God: all things were made through him and for him and by him. So we might well imagine that he and the Father had discussions about "holding all things together." The plan to defeat evil was at its most critical stage, and the enemy was on high alert. The transition to the administration of the Holy Spirit, if not to the Kingdom, was at hand. Was that an open question? Another consideration is that the sanctification of Peter and the other apostles was central and critical. Were these prayers divine sovereignty at work shaping free will? There was much to discuss!

Q: Does the Big Picture explain how conspiracies can form? It's somewhat of a mystery because if you look closely you see a lot of stupidity and incompetence on the part of those who are supposedly conspiring.

A: That is virtually proof that strings are being pulled by principalities and powers beyond the human level. Also, the eventual failure and implosion of grand designs proves that those powers are not very competent themselves and are inevitably failing to demonstrate their right to keep their offices.

Q: Why didn't Satan foresee the possibility of Christ's incarnation and object to it at the outset of the experiment?

A: Yes, Satan might well have wondered why the Son of God invested so much care when he made this universe. Amazing handiwork would be expected, but far beyond that was the plethora of marvels and beauties hidden like treasures that would beg the question, "Who made this?"—in case anyone doubted or forgot. Also, I believe there was an uncanny resemblance to heaven, and if Satan had thought of the implication of that instead of shouting for joy as if it were his gift and playground, he might have seen that it had been fashioned such that God could actually walk on this planet. This was of a different order from the "back door" in the design of the human being that the devils discovered and exploited later. While the affinity of earth for the stuff of heaven made it possible for the two to coexist, the thing that Satan apparently did not notice when man appeared was that the human being was made little lower than the angels in such a way that not only could the Spirit of God inhabit him but also God could fully and independently participate in the time-bound human frame. Who would have thought that the Creator would ever want to do that?

Q: Doesn't the Big Picture contradict the Bible's speaking of God ruling the world with equity?

A: Several psalms include that language, but it is always about the future Kingdom. "Let the nations be glad," says the psalmist, "for you *will* judge the nations with equity and govern the nations upon the earth." But even if it was taken as a statement about that time, there was no contradiction because the "sons of God" who temporarily ruled the nations were not doing so in place of God. Yahweh is always the overarching Monarch whose purposes are never subverted, and the reason we can say that is because the frame around the Big Picture means that. If God is not timelessly sovereign, there is no Big Picture and we know nothing. It follows that, as a practical matter for all people everywhere, God is personally accessible regardless of the state of nations. There is nothing in the arrangement allowed to the "sons of God" that prevents you or anyone else from punching through the principalities and powers in high places and obtaining access to the saving grace of Jesus Christ and the God of all comfort.

Q: Suffering can be viewed in various ways, none of them being entirely satisfactory. How does the Big Picture reconcile suffering with the goodness of God?

A: Within the frame of the Big Picture we see God having placed himself in the way of suffering: loss of peace in heaven, rejection of his love, and subjecting himself to the weakness and mortality of human flesh. We cannot say that suffering is the direct result of sin unless we define risk-taking as sin, because the risk inherent in the highest order of creation looms behind the emergence of evil. So it is logical to say that suffering is the inevitable result of love, but also common experience tells us this is so. The universe is so constructed.

Q: Why were Jews generally unwelcome (except as slaves) in every nation but Israel?

A: Satan wanted to break the prophecy that has Jerusalem standing and waiting for Christ at his return. In particular, the temple which validates the prophecy could be built by no one but Jews. So the fewer descendants of Jacob the better in Satan's view. Many Jews were not Zionists, but they were still capable of producing offspring who may have participated in the building of the temple. This applies to Gentiles who support Israel as well. Secondarily, the rulers hated to have to make exceptions for Jews, for they did not obey and blend in well. Jews have customs that render them resistant to regimentation. Thirdly, Jewish blood produced exceptionally talented individuals whom the demons could not help but admire—and fear losing control to them.

Q: Hindus worship thousands of gods. Are they all "sons of God"?

A: The Bible reveals little of angelic ranking, but we are given enough to know that they are not all on the same level. So the answer could be that among the fallen angels the "sons of God" represent a natural level of leadership over any number of lesser demons. But whether or not Hindu mythology bears any relation to reality is uncertain.

Q: Gog and Magog are mentioned in Ezekiel and also in Revelation, the former placing them sometime before the Millennial temple comes to be and the latter at the far end of the Millennium period. Where does the Big Picture fit them in?

A: Magog refers to the area or the people, and Gog is the "prince" or "son of God" who has sway over the human leaders in that area—which is north of Israel and appears to be Russia. There are those two distinct invasions; each one is described differently in Ezekiel. Gog seems to think his imagination supersedes the Bible, for in about a thousand years he will attempt another invasion which will fail.

Q: For someone to like the Big Picture they would have to like the Bible. But is there any way to present the Big Picture to an atheist?

A: Yes. The atheist sits within the Big Picture just like everyone else does. Only he refuses to take seriously the fact that without God there is nothing: there is no atheistic explanation for a single particle, let alone the entire universe.

Every living soul experiences the battle between good and evil. Is your atheist scientifically inclined? Then let him test all the theories and see which one best fits the evidence. Is he negligent about the evil lurking in his soul? Then he is not up to dealing in philosophy and so is not really an atheist. In that case he may be open to entertaining the Big Picture.

Q: There's a proverb that says Yahweh has made everything for its own end, even the wicked for the day of evil. So how can you call it heresy to say that God created evil?

A: You might balance that with the proverb in the following chapter which says, *He that justifies the wicked is an abomination to Yahweh*. But note that your proverb is not a moral statement: it merely points to the moving parts of world history.

Q: Does this theater of war in the Big Picture rule out the "gap" theory of there being a period in earth's history between the beginning of creation and the earth as we know it?

A: The Big Picture has no view of a significant era in the cosmic battle that predates what we know from Genesis. It would be hard to fit that in, given that the purpose of the entire material universe is wrapped up in Christ preparing his answer to Satan.

Scripture presents the genesis of the universe as proceeding perfectly from the wisdom of God, which is contrary to the idea of chaos and reset. By wisdom and understanding Yahweh founded the heavens and earth. In other words, the physical universe unfolded from an exceedingly wise design that we can only observe one instant of and try to understand its mechanisms.

Q: Does the Big Picture explain the Tree of Life?

A: By Yahweh's own words we know that the Tree of Life in the Garden of Eden needed guarding in order to keep sinful man from eating fruit that would undo the penalty of death that came as a result of disobedience. This makes poetic sense, but it raises several more questions: 1) Why were cherubim assigned to guard the Tree of Life and not regular angels? 2) Why were the cherubim placed eastward or on the east side of the garden? 3) What does the flame of a sword that turned every way represent? 4) Does this tree still exist and if not, why not? 5) If the Tree of Life still exists in some form, then does the garden exist too? 6) Does it imply that there is a "fruit" other than the blood of Christ that would allow humans to live forever? 7) How does Yahweh's statement that the man has become "like one of us to know good and evil" relate to the need to guard the tree?

Obviously, the garden and the trees go together; otherwise we would have to ask why the trees were there. The whole scene is about the whole of mankind. In other words, the fact of man being created in the image of God requires the moral free will which itself is the soil in which the tree of the knowledge of good and evil grows; and the tree of life is the divine nature which can withstand evil without dying. But the surprising thing about this marvelous metaphor of the trees—which could stand alone and cause us no difficulty—is that it links not only to wisdom, obedience, human health, and longevity but also to the throne or seat of God, which is where we normally find cherubim acting as guardians. So the tree of life must be important.

We find "tree of life" occurring twelve times in the Bible and looking like bookends in Genesis and Revelation. In the middle, Proverbs applies "tree of life" as a metaphor representing an ongoing supply of some life-giving benefit. In Revelation the tree of life is presented as it is in Genesis (not a simple metaphor but perhaps a symbol), but in the end it is no longer guarded by cherubim or the flaming sword.

To answer the first question we need to know what cherubim are. The word appears nearly 90 times in the Bible, counting "cherub," the singular form (and not counting the man named Cherub). Images of cherubim decorated the tabernacle and temple in addition to the sculptures over the mercy seat where they are described as having wings and faces. They are first mentioned in Genesis without explanation as if their existence and purpose were common knowledge. Where did Moses get his information about them? The Hebrew word seems to be original, providing no clue as to their purpose or appearance. Psalm 18, echoing II Samuel 22:11, images Yahweh riding on the wings of a cherub, inspired no doubt from the concept of him being enthroned above the cherubim carvings over the mercy seat in the tabernacle. Ezekiel, in his vision of a future temple, informs us that each cherub had two faces, one of a man and the other of a young lion, and that the sound of their wings was as the voice of God, while another description counts four faces, adding the face of an eagle plus the cherub's own face and human-like hands under their wings. Apparently, the images used in decorative carvings showed two faces because more than two would be difficult to depict. The body in the artistic depictions may have been four-footed, perhaps like an ox because in Ezekiel chapter one an ox is listed instead of the "cherub" face. But when actually encountered in visions they are complexes of motions and symbols speaking of another world beyond three dimensions.

The famous passage in Ezekiel about the king of Tyre (that confuses many) is resolved in the Big Picture in which "sons of God" actually exert control through human kings and princes. It makes the most sense if we allow that the king of Tyre was possessed by Satan himself because of this key geographical location on the Mediterranean and its proximity to Yahweh's territory. The description in this passage looks through the king of Tyre and speaks to Satan: "You were the anointed cherub that covers; and I set you up upon the holy mountain of God." From this we might draw the conclusion that cherubim are an angelic class of the highest order, and if that includes Satan, it may also include the "sons of God." However, "cherub" could be a term of lesser specificity, covering more than one class of living beings in the angelic realm. The Big Picture supports this in that we have made a material distinction between fallen angels and loyal angels. The description of the king-of-Tyre cherub is vastly different from Ezekiel's description of cherubim. So if fallen angels may be called cherubim, while other cherubim are in a very different class, the term refers to their functions rather than their essential beings. Thus our question #1 might be answered by pointing this out and noting that the cherubim guarding the way to the tree were not necessarily like the ones around the throne of God.

Question #2 wonders why only the eastern approach to the tree of life was guarded. All kinds of answers to that may be imagined. It does say that the flaming sword was omnidirectional. The simplest answer is that it firmly grounds the tree of life by this geographic citation while other features of the garden disappeared beyond the edges of the Big Picture frame. So we can expect that the tree of life will be revisited.

Question #3 asks what the flame of the sword represents. Since swords do not have flames, it is a fair question. If the flame is a symbol, the sword must be a symbol too. Could the sword represent the Word of God? Several of the Proverbs use "tree of life" metaphorically to mean a continuing action like a tree replenishing its fruit. Psalm 1 promises that one who meditates on the Law of God will be like a tree yielding fruit for being planted near a stream of water. The flame symbolizes the vitality of the sword, or the Word of God on which it depends..

Question #4 asks whether the tree still exists. If the tree symbolizes the source of fruit that comes of meditating on the Word, then the tree equates to the Holy Spirit or perhaps one of his several facets as mentioned in Revelation.

Question #5 contemplates that the tree of life was an integral part of the garden. The Big Picture answers "not so" because the Garden of Eden was transitory with no future purpose.

Question #6 zeroes in on the eternal life-giving property of the fruit and sets it against the blood of the atonement. This question sounds simplistic, but it is not. It asks, "If the fruit could confer immediate immortality, then would it not have been an alternative to the redemption we know?" The Big Picture has the answer showing in plain sight: this would win the war for Satan; sin and sinners would become permanent.

Question #7 takes in the context which connects the two trees. The knowledge of good and evil is what forces the tree of life into the future where it appears again in the New Jerusalem with fruit for healing of the nations! If we may take this symbolically, the healing is relative to the scars of Satan's past dominion, and it will be effective and safe to administer because the truth about Satan is out in the open. As long as there was knowledge of good vs. evil, there was compromise or attempts to reconcile the two. Put the tree of life in that environment and you have the setup for perpetual compromise with Satan.

Q: How is Heaven made any more stable with human inhabitants replacing fallen angels?

A: There can be no guarantee that Heaven will never again experience a divergence unless free will is no longer free and humans are no longer in God's image. But one thing about humans that angels lack is gender, and that may dampen the energy of independence whenever it moves from potential to kinetic. Minus the procreation mechanism, there remains an underlying male/female dynamic that gives birth to a variety of humbling manifestations and connects with the basis for the relationship between Christ and his church, which is love and worship. If redeemed souls in this life love to worship their Redeemer, how much more when the old nature is a memory and only a memory?

Q: Why are the psalms and songs of the saints so focused on glorifying God, as if we can add to his glory?

A: The reason for this should be plain by now: our corrupted nature means that by default we glorify Satan. Not that we would ever contemplate worshiping the devil, but like him we are fallen from holiness, and so we need the pressure of the discipline of consciously glorifying our savior God, reveling in his love, and learning to obey his first and foremost commandment first and foremost. This extends far beyond devotional exercises. Obviously we must not align our energies with any organization or effort which disrespects Christian principles. Not so obvious is that in this war, neutrality is beyond our reach. We must intentionally glorify God or we risk glorifying the demons who rule the world and would have us glorify anything and anyone else. From this viewpoint we must say that nominally-Christian nations and communities and homes and individuals are as riddled with idolatry as was Israel under its worst king—because neutrality is an illusion.

Q: Explain the final verse in our Bibles where Jesus says that surely he is coming "soon" (or "quickly," depending on the translation).

A: This is an important data point because it sets a limit to our confidence in understanding heaven's relation to our physical existence. When trying to correlate times in heaven and earth we meet the magical mirror that views a thousand years as a day in one direction and a day as a thousand years in the other. In light of that, the best meaning, if not strictly a translation, of "soon" is "certainly." To put it another way, our apparently time-ordered universe is illusory from heaven's point of view. As the Great Lion said to Lucy, "I call all times soon." Fundamentalist expositors bring "soon" down to earth by insisting that it really means "quickly once it begins," which has the unfortunate side effect of lowering the barrier to dreams about heaven posing as reality.

Q: Does the Big Picture help explain why prayer seems necessary to move the hand of God even in cases where it is about something that is promised in Scripture and in his will?

A: The usual answers to this revolve around the concept that God wants us to develop in some way, such as increasing our faith, learning more about his will, becoming more dependent on him, etc. But another idea, which falls in line with the Big Picture, is that when we find ourselves within territory that has been allocated to the "sons of God," we are the only legal channel that Yahweh has available for doing things his way. In other words, we are the army of God in enemy territory: we are not at home here, but we bring the Spirit within us who because of the treaty with the demons does not have freedom to act apart from a prayer.

Q: What can the Big Picture tell us about heaven—that is, the experience of heaven we all look forward to?

A: One's first impression might be that since our world was made for war, we serve as parts of a military machine—cogs in a wheel that will become unnecessary when the battle is over and Earth has served its purpose. But if we step back and really look at the larger picture, it becomes clear that Jesus Christ has permanently connected us with himself and therefore the godhead. This view supersedes everything else. What Christ became and did and continues to do stands to certify a most glorious end for his bride and members of his body. We must realize he is the creator of all we know, including our time, and that compels us to see him the same at the beginning as at the end. So we are not a species invented for the sake of the war. Our being in God's image must be precious not only in this world but for eternity. We have infinite value to him. It's a love thing.

Now, we are shaped in body, mind, and soul by this physical earth. So in order for heaven to be comfortable for us it must be very much like earth with events taking place in the kind of time and space we are familiar with. Are there any residents of New Heaven in this room? Apparently not. If you get a chance to speak with one you may hear that it is a very pleasant place.

New Heaven was created for us by the eternal God. In other words, for us the frame around our biggest Big Picture will always be there—unless we somehow metamorphose into creatures that inhabit what we cannot presently imagine: but that sort of lore is completely foreign to our Scriptures which promise a new heaven and new earth. I think that means a heaven that is as much like this earth as it can be and also as much like the blessed company of God as it can be. That means "Jacob's ladders" connecting the new heaven with the old earth are possible, and of course we know they are being made use of during this resurrection age when God demonstrates to all the demons that his creation is very good.

Q: How does the Big Picture reconcile the sovereignty of God with the free will of man?

A: The Bible makes no apology for mixing election and responsibility to choose and act responsibly. Raising this question is ignoring the frame surrounding the Big Picture, which is the horizon beyond which dwell the infinities of God. It is futile to try to explore outside the frame because it represents the limits of the human mind. This much we can understand: while we are free moral agents, God creates our spirits and shapes our talents. But there remains a divine mystery.

Q: Many people believe there is an "atmosphere" of spiritual or metaphysical information and power that permeates physical reality. Is this compatible with the Big Picture?

A: No, because that is an atheistic idea which turns reality inside out. In reality our physical universe is merely a little picture within the Big Picture. It is the handiwork of Jesus Christ in which his Spirit is active through his Word and nothing else. Whatever distracts from that is of the devil, and that includes all the esoteric teachings which are merely demonic dreams.

Q: Are miracles exceptions, or are they built into Creation?

A: With this Big Picture in mind, small details like so-called miracles become less problematical. The primitive idea that the physical universe encompasses everything and the spiritual world exists as a sort of glow within it relegates miracles to the margins. The truth is that the entire physical universe is an artifice within the domain of God. Therefore, any anomaly within what we call the laws of physics is no less "natural" within the Big Picture than is our entire physical universe. Once you see it, this truth is obvious, and you escape the confines of materialistic science in which there is no reason for the existence of anything. The Architect of our universe may prefer to be constrained by certain "laws" or conventions of his design, but we have no grounds for supposing that he is absolutely bound by those particular constraints that we happen to be aware of—or that he must rigidly stick to the laws of his own making and never indulge in embellishments. Those physical laws that we know of are reflections of the main structure of Creation, but they are not everything.

Q: How can we rationally suspend disbelief of biblical miracles that seem to be mere embellishments?

A: Take an outrageous miracle like the "smart" earthquake that opened certain tombs in Jerusalem, out of which came sympathetic resurrections. Forget the unlikelihood of this occurring under the regime of physical laws. Look at it as a preview gifted to murderous Jerusalem confirming the Nazarene's claim that his death is the key to the future resurrection of the saints. Certainly it is not beyond human ingenuity to make up such a happy scene, but let us not give human imagination credit for what God has included in his story. If it is anyone's imagination, it is his.

Q: First Peter chapter 3 verse 22 says, speaking of Jesus, "who is on the right hand of God, having gone into heaven, angels and authorities and powers being made subject unto him." Yet the Big Picture seems to show the evil powers still ruling over nations. How is that reconciled?

A: Consider Colossians 2:15: "having despoiled the principalities and the powers, he made a show of them openly, triumphing over them in it." Both passages are about the resurrection of Christ. The Big Picture never diminishes the overarching authority of the triune God, so passages such as this must be seen in their context.

Q: With so many authors making contributions to it, how did the Bible escape being corrupted by Satan?

A: When Yahweh began conversing with Abraham Satan might have known the conversations would be remembered and recorded and inevitably the promises spoken by God to his nation would become its treasure and define its character. Perhaps the devil was smart enough to anticipate that one of Jacob's offspring might be educated in Egypt's famed university and learn the art of writing and preserving history. To lessen the likelihood of that happening, the Egyptian overlords put into Pharaoh's mind to stop further genesis of Hebrew males by having them murdered at birth or drowned shortly thereafter, neither of which were effective. One Hebrew baby floated into the heart of Pharaoh's daughter and became a prince named Moses. No doubt he received the best education Egypt could offer and learned to love writing and history. Who knows when he began the project that became our Pentateuch? The book of Genesis might have been his doctoral thesis. Being rather meek as a speaker, Moses favored writing. Once a writer always a writer, and the subsequent adventure in the exodus and beyond gave him plenty of material for a second volume. Having found himself becoming the father of a nation, he was thrust into the position of a legislator and legal adviser, and therein he put his writing skill to good use, laboring forty years on Leviticus and assembling information in Numbers.

Satan found that what Moses had begun could not be stopped from growing into the veritable counsel of Yahweh who declared it his right to protect and guide its development. The many counterfeit and substitute scriptures of devilish sponsorship never had the same appeal to so many as did the truth about the love of God.

Ultimately Israel's Bible grew to encapsulate not only her history, but also heaven's plans as they were subtly revealed within the writings of Hebrew prophets.

Without the Hebrew Scriptures there would be no charter for Israel and no literary womb of expectation living in the minds and hearts of Jews when it came time for Messiah to appear. Thus Jesus of Nazareth stepped into a story that had been outlined for him. It fit him well, and he brought it to life and fullness such that it inspired twenty-seven more books to be added to the library of sixty-six books that we call our Bible.

Satan continues to try by every means to hinder the dissemination of the Holy Scriptures, but the Bible carries its own guarantee of its preservation in the power it has to make unfailing disciples of Jesus Christ. And now with billions of copies in thousands of languages the overwhelming success of the Bible cannot be denied. Yet scholars who find it's popularity unwarranted write critically of certain elements that appear to them unhistorical or unscientific, as if their petty complaints could somehow undo the success the Word of God has achieved. It's like political critics of a great military leader pointing out that while the campaign he led was a resounding success and no soldiers were actually lost in battle, two or three of them were injured and so the victory is not really a victory.

Q: Where do "liberal" Christians fit in the Big Picture? For example, those who associate themselves with a religious organization that fails to uphold the divinity of Jesus Christ.

A: They would appear to be on the sidelines or not even aware of the great contest, whether it is by ignorance or blindness or worse. But regardless of the cause, by not being faithful servants of Christ they are not simply dwelling in neutral territory, because everyone is under the sway of some higher power. In wartime, unclaimed assets do not remain unclaimed for long! If they are not actually in Satan's reserve army they are very vulnerable to being pulled into his service. The chances are not even: as Jesus said, the way is wide that leads to destruction and few find the narrow way that leads to life. The reason, of course, is that they think they have as much life as anyone.

The question we need to ask is, would they be happy in heaven, assuming it were possible, being clothed in filthy rags while others wear the glorious righteousness of Christ; or would they be too ashamed to stay. The idea that everyone will somehow at some time become sufficiently enlightened and compliable to love God while serving him on his terms, not theirs, is a violation of the principle of enduring free will which continues to separate Satan from God.

Q: What can we say about the character of glorified saints who have not only been made righteous legally but also perfected morally?

A: It is easy to say "Christ like," but truly, Christ is unique. We will never be omniscient because that would destroy peer-to-peer fellowship. So what that leaves us with is fully ripened fruits of the Spirit. My enjoyment of Love will mean that there is no one I care less for than I care about myself. That lets me into an almost unimaginable freedom where I can enjoy spending unlimited time with anyone and everyone, which of course is not possible because we each respect the other's time. Or to put it simply, we want the best for everyone.

Imagine encountering your favorite author in heaven and finding that she would like to know all about your attempts at writing and would love to read them all if at all possible, and in fact that would truly make her happier than anything else at the moment! Of course you would much rather discuss certain of her writings, so if you could ever stop laughing together about it you would both have to get serious and work out a compromise. How many fruits of the Spirit are involved in that?

Q: How could Satan have miscalculated so badly?

A: The history of the world confirms that the material creation was never appreciated for what it is by the "sons of God," and of course neither is it understood by those influenced by demons, which includes almost everyone at certain times and places— though not to rival those whose birthright intelligence becomes subverted by a satanic insanity that propels them to inflict terrible damage on their countries. In general, the "sons of God" refuse to believe that the human heart is not enough: in truth, everyone needs the love of God like they need a physical heart. Demons believe they can prop people up by artificial means and put them to work in a system that sustains minimal prosperity without being threatened by individual ingenuity; but as long as what they ignore is primary and what they accentuate is secondary, it cannot succeed. Simply put, their empires fail because individual motivation cannot long be sustained without individual ownership and freedom of choice.

If societies are not in accordance with nature, economic and moral weakness leaves them vulnerable to a more energetic rival —if they do not simply collapse from their weak production. These ruling demons keep trying to subvert nature because if they are to prove the legitimacy of their rebellion they cannot simply imitate the way Creator God treats his subjects. Should a Cyrus achieve unusual success, it is because Yahweh planted within his spirit an enlightened desire to follow the demon-defying philosophy that imitates Yahweh's policy by recognizing and rewarding individual contributions to the prosperity of the country.

At the end of the former age, I imagine Almighty God called a meeting of the "sons of God" to inform them that in spite of all their efforts to corrupt the gospel, enough of us had been sanctified, and it was time to begin the resurrection during which government without demonic influence would prove that free-willed beings can be perfectly obedient. Though Satan will lose his appeal in the end, he must have known he had miscalculated when Jesus rose out of the grave to promise our resurrection.

Q: Since the Big Picture looks at the controversy between Satan and God, does it shed any light on the "temptation of Jesus" in the desert?

A: Yes. This is very significant. We need to explain how Matthew and Luke knew about this—or did they? It bears the marks of a theological statement in story form. The theology behind it was well understood by the time the Gospel records were written. The story may have been invented earlier by someone as a way to express the theology, which it does in a compact and unforgettable way. Possibly Jesus was the source of the story, but there is no indication of that other than the deduction that no one else could have known about it as a literal event. But of course it cannot be taken as essentially literal because there is no literal action, only a series of Satan's proposals in symbolic form and Christ's rejection of them.

Ultimately the origin of the story is the Holy Spirit who also brought it to Matthew's mind and for the good reason that it confirms the relative supremacy of Satan in the world, the super-supremacy of Christ as the confident Father's Son, and the desperation of Satan to prove his legitimacy by tempting the Son of God to join his side.

The three "temptations" tested Jesus' character in three particulars: 1) managing physical appetite; 2) respecting the plan of God; 3) rejecting religious heroism prized by demons. When we pray, "Lead us not into temptation," we are relying on him to deliver us from those evils.

Q: Where is there evidence that humans can ever become incorruptible and permanently dedicated to serving Christ and not prone to self-preservation?

A: The martyrs. The evidence of the Scriptures being true has always been people who stake their lives on it, especially those who choose to undergo unspeakable persecution and death. Many of the Old-Testament prophets were such, up to and including John the Baptist. Jesus Christ is the fountain-head of the blood shed by disciples who are pleased to suffer and die rather than be disloyal to him. Humans will sacrifice their lives in wars and for convictions that are contrary to the truth of Scripture, but their support is visible. The martyr passes the ultimate test by the invisible power of Christ.

Q: In Genesis, God said all green plants are for food. But some are poisonous. Did the "sons of God" have anything to do with that?

A: There are very significant implications from the revelation in Genesis chapter 6 where "sons of God" cohabiting with daughters of men sired monstrous anomalies. If demons could do that, what limit can we put on their ability to understand biology and manipulate it to their own ends? Given the fact that spiritual beings can bring about physical manifestations, what limits their ability to genetically re-engineer God's creation to the extent of producing novel variations? We have no idea how much of evolutionary science is invalid for ignoring this or how much of apparent evolution has been falsified by the efforts of demons. Are we prone to disease more so than the patriarchs were? If demonic invasion of human bodies is possible, as we know it is, what gives us the right to be simple-minded about this and assume they left no permanent marks on the flesh we inherit?

Q: The Law as given by God through Moses never was tried to its full potential; rather, it was partly obeyed, often forgotten, and ultimately corrupted. We learn from the apostle Paul that it functions as a schoolmaster who gives such poor grades that we must look to another Way to be right with God. In the Big Picture is there more to it than that?

A: True love never springs from a commandment. Isn't it curious that the First Commandment is a contradiction within itself? This is because it is a prophecy. When Jesus said the Law will be fulfilled in its smallest detail, who was he talking about? Certainly not the humankind he knew. Yes, he fulfilled the Law on our behalf in the sense that he shields us from its penalty and also in the sense that he imputes to us righteousness that the law demands. But that's distancing us from the Law itself as well as the effects of it; yet we are promised that the Law will not pass away until every detail be fulfilled. Of course it's easy to smooth this over theologically as is commonly done.

In the Big Picture, where the kingdom of God comes and his will is done, our greatest joy is in obeying the first and second so-called commandments. The Law is about now, not back then. Nevertheless, if we were to get here, we had to keep our eyes on it.

If we thought of the Law as an anachronism as far as Christians were concerned, we had it backwards. Wasn't there some comfort in looking forward to joining the psalmists in their passionate praise of the Law? Really, if we were to get right with the Bible we had to agree with it that the Law was good in its every detail. Israel's perfect response to those details now during this time when Satan is disabled will prove that God was right in the beginning when he said his Creation was very good and in the middle when he gave the Law. Our obedience that is being proven by the intricate demands of the Law will prove that Satan is wrong in maintaining that free will necessarily leads to disobedience.

Naturally, there were the animal advocates and myopic ministers who protested temple sacrifices, but these days there are not enough of them to justify Satan's argument.

Q: When Korah and his company opposed Moses, it seems that the ground opening up and consuming them is a punishment disproportionate to their trespass. Does the Big Picture answer critics who read it as a story manufactured by the priesthood?

A: The Big Picture provides the context. It informs us that establishing Israel as a nation in Canaan was central to Yahweh's plan in which he is raising up a family to disprove Satan's contention that free will inevitably leads to rebellion. It was inevitable that Satan would send demonic influences while Israel was in the desert no-man's land and infiltrate the ranks under Moses, which would have fractured Israel before it could stake its claim in the promised land. By the way, Korah and his company of princes who intended to fracture Moses' leadership is an analog of the rebellion of Satan that intends to fracture the domain of God.

Q: After the war is over at the end of this age and evil disposed of, what will become of this material universe? Will Earth have been so damaged that it will have to be abandoned? Will our earthly Jerusalem finally be abandoned forever? Or will there be mercy for archaeologists (among many others) who would shed tears if the city where God lived and died is no more?

A: That comes under the question about New Earth. Is it physical or spiritual—that is, temporal or eternal? An unending series of temporal planet-earths would be eternal. But is there any reason why New Earth could not be "spiritual" in nature? By "spiritual" we usually mean a realm where things do not decay or wear out. Actually, we know almost nothing of the spiritual realm because our senses are physical. But we can assume that it will not be something we perceive as shockingly different from what we see and hear and feel in this temporal life; otherwise, we would not be prepared for it, our minds would have to start over, and we would be like newborn babies. Worse than anything would be a bodiless spiritual existence with no senses. Can we imagine living without bodies? Only fools think so.

So we can reason our way into "seeing" what the eternal New Earth is like: superficially a lot like this temporal one. We have evidence that biological reproduction will be a thing of the past. A great number of internal simplifications can be imagined as a result of that change, which would not impair our ability to move and speak and recognize one another. If an image on a screen can look real to us, chemistry and biology of glorified bodies could be different and still leave the world seeming much the same.

Actually, the name "New Earth" tells it all: it will be a "planet" with most things outwardly like this earth. This material earth will have served its secondary purpose, which will be seen then as its primary purpose.

I say let Old Earth live on for a long, long time as a museum at least, and let the gardeners among us make it flourish like Eden. Not that what I say matters, but I feel it may be Yahweh's idea. After all, the incarnation of our Lord was not temporary. People living in New Earth will visit Old Earth like the glorified saints do now. Indeed, their "New Heaven" may be New Earth.

And what about New Jerusalem—that three-dimensional city seen coming to join Earth? It suggests a complexity in heaven that models the Millennial kingdom on earth lifted to a new degree. Does that mean there will be second-class citizens in heaven? Apparently so, and some higher than first-class too: "They that are wise will shine as the sun and they that turn many to right-eousness as the stars for ever and ever." Not everyone will have a place to live in New Jerusalem, for nations exist on New Earth outside of New Jerusalem's walls—places where healing is still required and is being administered—perhaps healing of minds.

Many will purify themselves and make themselves white and be refined, but the wicked will do wickedly; and none of the wicked will understand, but they that are wise will understand.

Q: Was Yahweh perfectly honest when he sold this theater of war, or did he trick Satan into accepting something which he couldn't win?

A: Satan has won throughout history. The demons have main-tained the control they desired and largely prevented develop-ments that would fit God's declaration of the good creation. God has lost beloved souls to demonic possession and ultimate food for demons. The perfection of saints which the trial will require in order to benefit God has an enormous price; the battle to win them is genuine, and Satan does not believe all is lost, for he still owns much. It is by *our* faith that we know he could not win.

Q: How does democratic government fit into this theory?

A: Democracy limits direct demonic influence, but it can only be sustained when enough people live according to principles of honesty, generosity, and self-sacrifice—in addition to hatred of dictatorial injustice. This puts the people, not God directly, in opposition to the demons, so it is perfectly legal under the terms of the war. The great danger to Satan was people learning what government requires and how to participate in it, which made them candidates for serving today as ministers of the crown.

Q: Is it possible for people to be happy under demon rule?

A: If that ever happened, it would tend to prove the opposite of what Satan needs to show in order to win his argument. This is why examples of governments that foster happy society are almost nonexistent.

Q: Why have the "sons of God" not learned to quell the turmoil on earth after at least six thousand years of trial and error?

A: The spirits Yahweh places in human souls are made in his image, not the image of demons. So as long as there remain humans unconverted to the image of Satan's obedient demons there will be active resistance to tyrannical government.

Q: Why was Israel not charged with spreading the knowledge of the true God by sending out missionaries and establishing worship centers in foreign lands?

A: Because it would violate the rules of the contest. Yahweh had reserved Israel for himself, and the "sons of God" were given dominion over every other nation. That rule still holds today. When the nation became well established under David and Solomon, the temple in Jerusalem became the center of learning and worship of Yahweh. It was open to other nations as Solomon declared in his prayer of dedication, but they had to go to Judea; Israel was not generally charged with going to them. Yahweh had the right to a temple. As long as it stood, that was his one material witness. The secondary level of this is that individuals who carried the knowledge of Yahweh with them could not be prevented from traveling and sharing the truth, yet the fact that there was but one true God was represented by the one temple on earth dedicated to him. But if Satan destroys the temple, Yahweh maintains his witness in his servants, and they are free to build worship centers anywhere, albeit under the opposition of the local overlords, which would vary.

When Jesus Christ arrived, he brought within himself an alternative to the temple in Jerusalem, and when they destroyed that temple he raised it up in three days in such a form that the Spirit of God was dispensed to every believer. They became his temples empowered to evangelize the world. This is how Yahweh maintains his right to a temple on earth as long as there is no temple in Jerusalem. Jonah's mission was not a violation of the rule because he was preaching repentance based on their knowledge of the true God which they had learned by their visits to Jerusalem.

Q: Did the prophet Jonah actually spend time in the belly of a fish, preach repentance to Nineveh, and convince everyone in Nineveh to repent?

A: Jonah revolted at the very thought that God would send him into enemy territory as a missionary because he adhered to the official doctrine that the nations were to come to Israel to meet God. For him to preach in a foreign land ruled by Yahweh's adversary was contrary to any protocol he had ever heard of. It turned his world view on its head. All his life he had known that God would someday send the Messiah to punish the nations and rule the world from Jerusalem.

Now consider the parallels between Jesus and Jonah: 1) Both were called on to execute a plan different from what had been revealed through the prophets; 2) Both were from the area in Israel known as Galilee; 3) Both were held in the belly of death three days; 4) Both were brought back to life; 5) Both went on to bring people to repentance who were and remained enemies of the Jews; 6) Both saw the enemy they had brought to repentance readopt pagan idolatry in the years following; 7) Both were disowned by the Jews in Jesus' day and thereafter (Search the scriptures, they said: did any prophet come out of Galilee?); 8) Both had to bear the sorrow of their people being persecuted by those they had saved. Jesus said Jonah, son of Amittai, was a sign relative to himself.

Clearly the book of Jonah was put in their Scriptures so we can look back and see that the plan Jesus executed was the plan all along. By the way, the name Jonah means *a dove*—not that that's significant or anything.

Also Peter was the disciple who had to be convinced that Gentiles were to be included in the great gift of salvation. Peter's father's name was Jonah—not that that's significant at all. Unfortunately, the Big Picture stops there—with the story of Jonah and the whale being a sign on the verge of being a parable for us to look back at—and whether or not it is also factual is a question that falls below the granular level of the Big Picture.

Q: In Jeremiah 25, starting with verse 15 to the end of the chapter, Yahweh names twenty nations that he will punish and then goes on to include all nations on earth. Doesn't this contradict the Big Picture where the "sons of God" rule the nations outside of Israel?

A: You can look at this the other way around: since the dispensation in that passage is different, it must refer to a future time, the time often spoken of when Christ will return to bind Satan's powers and subdue his principalities.

Q: Why did Satan have to ask permission to inflict Job but not Paul?

A: The story of Job is a miniature of the Big Picture. Job is analogous to Israel, the nation Yahweh reserved for himself. Paul stepped out of Israel into Satan's territory where he met demonic forces head on.

Q: What is the origin of God?

A: Within the Big Picture we know the reason for the physical universe, but we must stop there and not fantasize about the reason for God: the picture is mounted within a frame that represents the limit of biblical truth and indeed the limit of the rational human mind.

Q: How do we reconcile Isaiah's "day-star son of the morning" that is interpreted to refer to Satan, with Christ referring to himself as the "bright morning star" in Revelation.

A: Seeing that a couplet in Job establishes the equation of "sons of God" with "morning stars," the Isaiah passage that uses the phrase "day-star son of the morning" must refer to one of them and certainly it is Satan. When we get to the very end of the Bible we find Christ referring to himself as the "bright morning star" after Satan and his host are removed from the picture. So "morning stars," like "sons of God," is a broad descriptor of heavenly beings who bear the image of God. This clears up the apparent clash of terms when members of the church are promised the morning star. It also suggests that the new name given to each believer is a private name by which Christ will be known to the individual; so once the minor gods are out of the way, God has the freedom to be known by many names for his special significance to each human, without confusion.

Q: Who is the "prince" in Ezekiel 44-48?

A: We are given a glimpse of the perplexity of real life that we naturally assume is not there unless it is explicitly described. This prince does not coincide with Jesus Messiah, but yet he is prominent in Jerusalem as a priest and prince under the King. Jesus Christ may be physically present as King in Jerusalem, but the presence of the prince on earth makes it possible that he be reigning from the New Jerusalem in heaven. I would have said this prince would be David in resurrection, but now we know he is David's son Solomon, which really makes more sense when you think about it.

Q: If the Big Picture explains odd things found in the Bible, what about Balaam?

A: As prophets go, Balaam was not unusual. The prophets who wrote books in our Bible were unusual. Balaam typifies the conflicts under which prophets operate as they open themselves to direct influence of demons. He understands the supremacy of Yahweh and the privileged position of Israel, but he lacks the moral integrity of a true servant of Yahweh, so he stands apart, admiring Jacob from afar while making his living serving pagan clients.

The Balaam lore in the Bible is in the form of poems which celebrate a foreign prophet who feels constrained to speak truth about Israel. The stories perhaps have a loose connection with history, which is normal for that type of literature.

Q: Why are there walls and gates in New Jerusalem as it is pictured in Revelation?

A: The walls tell us something about ourselves. Walls surround the holy city to remind the residents that war could happen again. Free will cannot be made harmless because it is a characteristic of divinity, and the walls remind us of the awful responsibility we have being made in the image of God.

Q: The impulse to sacrifice appears in virtually every religion. How does the Big Picture explain this?

A: Free will tends to oppose authority. This is obvious to everyone. So there is a common, innate feeling that heaven is offended by what we do. The sacrifice is an acknowledgment of that debt and an attempt to pay it with something of real value. How valuable does the sacrifice need to be? Generally the troubling circumstances of life are interpreted to answer that question —be it lack of food, health, or security. Thus if a particular sacrifice doesn't bring an end to some trouble, more (and more costly) sacrifice is required.

What Yahweh did for his nation was define offenses in terms of comprehensive law and prescribe appropriate sacrifices; so there was no longer a need to interpret omens and quantify offenses. Since offenses between man and his neighbor were included, this was a tremendous advancement in religion and civilization in general. But it was no cure for conflicts caused by the fundamental appetite for self advancement.

The law reflects the nature of free will but does not sanctify it; it only serves to validate Satan's contention that it is an incurable liability. Sacrifice, if measured and carried out equitably, makes peace and prosperity possible in theory, and to some extent in practice, but the system depends on corruptible priests and judges.

The complete cure would require a holiness of spirit that would entail adding a divine structure to the human soul, something that was not included within the bounds of Creation and could only be done by the Maker participating in human flesh, becoming the ultimate Sacrifice himself, and thereby sanctifying the sacrifices he had prescribed.

Q: Jesus said to the sick man, "Thy sins are forgiven." How was he able to do this before he went to the cross and became the sacrifice for sins?

A: God specified shedding of innocent blood for forgiveness, but not the date of payment. When Jesus said he had authority to forgive sins as he spoke to his critics, he knew they would have a part in enabling him to pay the debt.

Q: How is Israel's theft of treasure from Egypt at the exodus justified?

A: 1) This is the winners booty from the war of the gods that had taken place. Far more damage than that was inflicted in that war. 2) The Egyptian people were not happy with their priests and politicians who were demon puppets; they sympathized with the Hebrews and willingly compensated them for their mistreatment. 3) Egypt eventually recovered its loss when Shishak king of Egypt came up against Jerusalem and took away the treasures of the house of Yahweh and the treasures of the king's house: he took it all away including the shields of gold that Solomon had made.

Q: What god ruled the Vatican?

A: All the kingdoms of the earth were under demonic over-lords. The Holy Roman Empire inherited the demons who dominated Rome, but there is no reason to believe the arrangements were static. A particular "transgender" demon who called himself the "Queen of Heaven" seems to have wielded influence there.

Q: Does the Big Picture re-frame our outlook on fellow humanity?

A: Yes. By emphasizing that we are spirits assigned to inhabit bodies and minds and environments that are strange to us initially and always perplexing, we recognize that we all face essentially the same struggle. None of us asked to be here. But we are so designed that we instinctively take courage and make the best of whatever we are presented with—unless we encounter love, which changes everything, more or less. But if we feel unloved we irrationally conclude we are uniquely unfortunate and therefore entitled to optimize our own ends at the expense of others.

Q: What can we say about the animal sacrifices now that they have been resumed during the kingdom age?

A: In other words, what is their purpose and effect? Assuming that the purpose is the same as held forth in Leviticus and that the effect matches what is anticipated there, but with less corruption, a simple thought experiment will point to a remedy for the nominal faith of believers who eschew works.

Imagine someone being in the habit of ignoring his neighbor's need. He has excuses, but he knows that disobeying a command is a sin, so he prays for them but never takes further action. If this is not quite what he is commanded to do, he knows that forgiveness is guaranteed, so he needs not worry much about it.

Now introduce the new element: having committed a sin he is expected to acknowledge it by killing a perfectly good animal in order to be reminded that the lamb of God died for that sin. Which is more difficult: helping his neighbor or buying an expensive animal and watching it go to waste?

These rituals were spoken by God directly to Moses. Their detail is amazing and bears evidence of careful design for some purpose that is not apparent. If there is beauty in simplicity, there was no beauty in this.

The fact that no room is left for human invention or augmentation makes a statement that man can do nothing to overcome the destructiveness of sin; if there is a remedy, it depends entirely on God. The fact that blood is central to the rituals makes a statement that sin is a debt payable by the currency of death. The fact that the sinner does not suffer other than by the loss of property makes a statement that physical pain has no efficacy in removing the blot of one's sin. All of these statements stood against pagan rituals and insulated Israel from pagan religion.

But the outstanding thing to notice is that these God-given rituals point to Christ without taking the place of Christ. For those who took the Bible literally and accepted that the practice would be resumed during the millennial kingdom, they stood against sentimental idealism about the millennium.

Q: Does the Big Picture add anything to help understand the mystery of the humanity of Christ?

A: It certainly does. Satan's whole argument is basically that the design of beings in the image of God makes the peaceful monarchy of heaven impossible. By living a perfectly obedient and sinless life in truly human flesh, Jesus of Nazareth demonstrated that the design is good. Though a special case, his humanity was genuine, and it has perfectly human "offspring" on this side of our resurrection. The satanic attacks on the doctrine of the hypostatic union reveal that acknowledgment of this is essential. The body of Jesus began as the natural egg of a woman which bore the imprint of the turmoil of her ancestors yet it produced the second Adam able to undo the curse of the first, another proof that the original design was good. The record shows a perfectly balanced personality in spite of the spoiled social and religious environment.

Q: Did the removal of the faithful church prior to the return of Christ have a place in the Big Picture?

A: If Scripture did not mention the Rapture, reason would have us hypothesize that living saints must be spared the outpouring of wrath that immediately preceded the return of Christ. Here is one way to reason it out:

1. This millennial age with Christ ruling on this earth is central in the Big Picture because of the trial of Satan. Fully sanctified, talented, and reliable saints are the exhibits God will use to disprove Satan's contention. This is no time for equal opportunity.

2. In keeping with divine interventions in history, the miracle of Christ's second coming did not instantly remake everything. While his appearing as told in Zechariah changed some of the local terrain, there was no drastic alteration of the earth mentioned. The population such as it was after the Tribulation remained in place and had to be managed as well as judged.

3. The "saints of all time" were not all resurrected to serve at that point because it would be a massive invasion requiring a massive miracle to manage the logistical requirements.

4. Those arriving with Christ were in positions to rule the nations and so had to be familiar with contemporary cultures, methods, and technologies. There is no reason to believe that resurrection should confer knowledge and skills that transcend whatever interests and abilities we developed originally. The souls and spirits of the Christ followers who became qualified for these tasks were taken in the Rapture for final training and sanctification and then were the first to appear with him at his coming to Jerusalem. Angels cleared the way by carrying out the judgment of nations, but the government is on Christ's shoulders while saints rule under his command as promised.

5. The purpose of the Rapture, therefore, can be seen as a harvest before the devastating storm, the produce from which was essential to standing up the kingdom of God on earth.

6. This, by the way, did not necessarily exclude from the Rapture Christians who were not qualified for one reason or another to be among the first to be placed in positions of service. Some, along with older saints, were glad to stay in New Heaven and never be given assignments on earth.

7. I rest my case. Only this I would add: if the passage of time, as we count time, is involved in completing the sanctification and training of saints in heaven before their qualification to rule on earth, then it seems that the process of conferring such graduate degrees would fit better into seven years than into no time at all. But I've heard that the passage of time for them was different.

Q: Can the Big Picture help us interpret Revelation, the last book in the Bible—especially its views of events from heaven?

A: Chapters four and beyond take John on an amazing tour in heaven, or what we say is outside or behind the frame of the Big Picture. Therefore, many of the scenes are ambiguous and puzzling when we try to link them to events in history. On the other hand there are things in John's Revelation that the Big Picture clarifies, because certain of its revelations are anchor points for the Big Picture.

Here are several of those points:

1. The war in heaven is brought to the forefront, and more clearly than anywhere else in Scripture we see Satan's desperation to maintain his legitimacy by destroying the womb of Messiah whose prophesied kingdom will challenge his theory of sin.

2. The thousand-year duration of the kingdom age spans the lifetimes of the first humans when God declared his creation was very good. A test of 70 or even 150 years would not be convincing to Satan.

3. Satan's being bound for the duration reveals that a scientific test of innate human loyalty apart from preexisting conditions is being conducted.

4. The climax is the culmination of the purpose of the earth, which is the conclusive disposition of Satan and his fallen angels.

5. There comes an end of grace and mercy when seeds of future rebellion are blown away: souls harboring illicit spiritual alliances; halfhearted lovers of Almighty God; minds unable to discern truth; perverted images of God; souls unable to believe; and timid souls unable to stand reward. The line is drawn: every scrap of Satan's legacy is barred forever from heaven.

6. Satan has lost his bid for legitimacy when he recklessly leads a rebellion at the end of the millennium.

7. The swift disposition of the devil and his demons rebuffs both dualism and benign permissiveness.

· · ·

When Ahijah gave me permission to publish this he added seven questions which the reader should be able to answer:

Q: Why was Satan not disposed of at the time he rebelled?

Q: What is the purpose of the millennial reign of Christ?

Q: Why was Yahweh not made known to every nation as he was to Israel?

Q: Why are governments always enslavers?

Q: Why do dictators seek to be worshiped?

Q: Why did Jesus ask the identity of the demon?

Q: Might Satan win his argument, breaking Scripture and allowing evil to go on forever? If so, who would be at fault?

Earl Meets the King

Chapter Twenty-Five

The carriage driver was a man of few words, and when he did speak, Earl had to ask him to say it again more slowly.

It was not long before the relative silence of the dusty carriage lane gradually gave way to noises: clattering animal hooves, rattling wagon wheels, and many voices. Earl tried to imagine scenes fitting the sounds he was hearing. By listening for echoes he judged the nearness of buildings, and he knew they were entering the city well before the driver announced it. Less than an hour had elapsed, but they were still far from the palace complex, for greater Jerusalem, including the prince's extensions, had grown quickly and was far larger than it had ever been. Ezekiel was right.

After an additional two hours, as nearly as Earl could estimate, the driver told him this was as far as he could go. When he asked for directions to the palace entrance he was told that someone would be there to guide him, and indeed someone was there.

"I'm here, Ichabod!" came a voice from outside the carriage.

Earl produced two coins from his pocket as the driver got down and opened the door to let him out.

There was no mistaking Lydia's voice. "I was told to come to this spot and wait for your arrival. We're not far from the palace gate. Just a short walk and there's a visitor's waiting area inside."

She led him to what appeared by its echoes to be a great hall, for it was rather noisy. Bits of overheard conversation told him people were constantly coming in to see the King, which seemed odd if they were all expecting an audience with the world's monarch who must be attending to a thousand other things as well.

"Do I need to register somewhere?" Samson asked Lydia.

"I was told to have you wait here. That's all."

After walking nearly the length of the hall they found two vacant adjacent seats. They sat and waited, questioning how this many people could visit the King in one day even for five minutes —or if they would have to wait days for Ichabod's turn.

It was not long, however, before Earl found himself being led by someone's hand away from the noisy waiting area, down a long corridor, around a corner to another corridor, and finally into another large gallery where a young woman's voice greeted him. He knew instantly to whom the voice belonged by the way she addressed him:

"Mr. Samson, do you remember when you cleared the drain in my sink? This is Laura. I'm here because of you! I'm sorry about your eyes, but we will make this work. My job is to show you through the royal baths. Before anyone can visit the King they go through these baths. I'm leading you now to the door of the first one."

She directed his right hand to a nearby door handle.

"When you enter through this door you will be in a room with a pool of warm water. Stay close to the wall on your right, and you will come to a bench where you can leave your clothes. Then carefully feel your way to the edge of the bath. It's deep enough to dive in, but I recommend you sit down on the edge and slip into the pool from there. You will know when it's time to get out. Then you'll find a robe hanging next to where you left your clothes. Put on the robe because you won't need the clothes you came in with ever again.

"The exit door is right there too, and it lets you into another room where there's another pool. But the water is cold in that one and not very deep. You must immerse yourself in it, robe and all. It will not be pleasant, but stay in as long as you can. When you get out, get out on the opposite side and search the wall on that side for another door, which goes to another pool.

"That one is very warm and only about knee deep. Lie down in it and enjoy the warm water, but not for too long because you will find that the pool seems to grow larger and get deeper, and if you stay in for too long the sides will become so high you will not be able to get out. When you do get out you will find that your robe dries very quickly and feels clean and smooth. Then you will be fit to see the King.

"Call for me when you're ready, and I'll come in and lead you to the hall of the judgment seat," she said finally.

Earl was glad to be relieved of his concern about proper attire for an audience with the King, and if it took three baths before being dressed properly, so be it. But he did not like the sound of "judgment seat."

He was sure the first pool contained something besides water, for it felt slightly sticky. His body sank easily into the warm liquid, and it seemed to have a cleansing effect without any effort on his part. He imagined it actually loosening the outer layer of his skin, which in his mind's eye floated away like a shed reptile skin.

The next pool was cold, just as Laura had warned, and it was not pleasant at all. It felt gritty, and it made his skin itch all over, compelling him to scratch, and as he did so he realized more of his skin flaking off. "At this rate I'll have no skin at all," he said. Since he was told to stay in as long as he could, he busied himself pursuing the itch, which scratching alleviated, fortunately. He waited for some time after that and finally decided there was nothing to be gained by succumbing to hypothermia.

The outrush of heated air was very welcome when he opened the door to the third pool. The warm water seemed to burn his feet when he tested it, but soon he adjusted to the sensation and crouched down, pulling his robe tight about him and letting the hot water rise to his neck. It startled him when he noticed that the water was getting deeper. He reached up to the edge of the pool, and just as Laura had warned him it seemed that he was growing smaller, not that the pool was becoming larger!

He did indeed feel smaller, even small like a child, standing with water dripping from the robe onto his feet. Uncharacteristically, his only thought was gratitude that the material became dry very quickly. He felt his way along the wall, searching for a door other than the one he had come in by. Then he remembered that Laura had instructed him to hail her when he was ready.

She appeared immediately with the dark glasses he had left in the first room. And she led him out.

Earl understood that his immediate destination was the judgment hall where he assumed he would face the famed judgment seat of Christ. But he pushed that aside and thought of Laura; no one else in all the world would he rather have leading him.

Yet he was apprehensive because he had in his mind the customs as described in the Bible which would require that he kneel and prostrate himself before the King on his throne. He told himself he would do that if Laura would orient him, but he did not know what the proper thing to say would be. He was about to ask her when she announced,

"Mr. Samson, you are now in the presence of the King. This is the royal judgment room. ... Now feel this right here."

She put his hand on what felt like a piece of furniture.

"Move your hand along the edge and tell me what it is," she said joyfully. Sooner than he could respond she told him eagerly, "It's a grand piano! I requested it be brought in here for you to play for the King. I know he will love your playing."

Thus Earl's apprehensions vanished. Apparently the King had agreed to Laura's plan as if she were his young daughter whose every desire he was happy to accommodate. It did seem very odd that there were no words of formal introduction.

"What would the King like me to play?" Earl whispered.

Since he had not been oriented to the layout of the judgment hall, to him the entirety of the place was Laura and the piano. He was not sure that she was not deliberately withholding information from him as he had once done to her.

"Play anything," was Laura's answer.

Then came the shock. The King spoke, and his voice was strangely familiar. "Play your favorite Beethoven, if you please."

Earl was astonished and relieved. His normal reaction would be to laugh, but instead he nearly cried. He felt the keyboard and settled himself on the bench. How unbelievable it was to be performing in a bathrobe before the King of the world—even the Creator of everything. Yet he had to believe, as a child would believe. Finding the keys, Earl began playing "Moonlight Sonata."

As the last chord died away, Laura, in her childlike enthusiasm, exclaimed, "He liked it: he's smiling!"

"What would you like me to do for you, Kenneth?" came that familiar voice. Earl was sure it was not the voice of any person he had ever known, but it instilled confidence into him, for love and peace were in the tone, which somehow prompted him to say, "If it please your majesty, your servant would like to see the moonlight tonight."

"Stand up and remove your glasses," came the King's command. "Just lay them on the piano. ... Hold still now, and don't flinch when I touch your eye. ... How is that?"

"I see light."

"Now let me do the other one."

"Yes! That's good. Both are good."

Earl blinked and beheld a man of his own height and build dressed in a simple oriental style. But at first he only saw the King Jesus' face, for his face almost glowed, and he smiled.

"Would you like to go for a walk with me in the garden?"

"Yes, please, I would love to."

King Jesus led the way through an arched opening to a long corridor out of which were many doors. He stopped at one, and Earl thought he saw his name on it. The door opened onto a country road well lit by the moonlight.

"That field beyond the fence reminds me of a field near my home when I was a boy," Earl said.

"I think so too. Let's go see what it was like."

"That barn I remember well. Even at night."

"I'm sure you do. I thought what you did with those dogs and the sparklers was a jolly good scene until they went into the barn and caught the hay on fire."

"I'm sorry. It was my revengeful nature, and I'm afraid I never got over it."

"Of course it was. It's the nature I gave you, and actually you handled it well. I enjoyed every minute of it. We had a lot of laughs—secretly, of course. Outwardly we had to be repentant."

"It wasn't so funny when I had to pay for it."

"Oh, you mean the barn. But you did splendidly: you followed every cue and we got it paid off more quickly than anyone expected."

"I thought it was my own cleverness. I'm sorry."

"Well, that's true too. Partly it was. But there's no need to be sorry because you needed plenty of inborn talent for the tight spots we would have to deal with."

"Like when the police were looking for me and I passed for a jazz pianist in Peter's restaurant?"

"Well, yes. And like tonight."

"If that was all in your plan for me, I don't know what to say."

"You can thank the young woman who calls you Mr. Samson."

"Are you referring to Laura?"

"Indeed. Laura prayed for you as much as she did for her parents during that week. And this week she began praying for you again."

"She must have a lot of sway here."

"Truly she does."

"I'm not sure I understand. Does she know all I've been through?"

"No. But she knew you were blinded. No one told her. It just came to her."

"So if she had not known of my condition, I would not be here tonight?"

"But she did know. Now back to your stunt at Peter's Japanese restaurant. When you apologize to Officer Headworthy for what you did with his gun—that wasn't necessary, you know—you will be surprised at his gracious reaction. So have no fear. He enjoyed your rendition of 'I don't know enough about you,' and he will tell you that."

"I have already encountered him. Did he recognize me?"

"No, but that was your chance. There will be another."

"Must I go looking for him?"

"It will be arranged. Why were you there, by the way?"

"Do you mean why did I skip town?"

"Yes. You don't have to answer because you don't know. Ask Carmen next time you see her. She will tell you."

"I haven't revealed myself to her yet. I wasn't sure she would be happy to see me."

"She knows. I think you know that she knows too."

"I was thinking it was likely. By the way, thank you for that felicity with the piano that came naturally with little effort."

"And what about thanking your father who provided the instrument and insisted that you take lessons?"

"Where is he now, may I ask?"

"You will meet him, so have in mind what you would like to say."

"I never tried to go far with the piano. But in other things why did I always push beyond my limits?"

"What did you know about limits?"

"I see what you mean. I knew nothing. No one told me. Except in aviation and baseball where rules are everything. Otherwise, as long as no one stopped me I felt I could set out to do anything."

"Yes, and sometimes even when they tried to stop you."

"But I never succeeded, really. I started and rushed to get something done then ran out of time, and in the end it wasn't worth anything. Well, there were the boats that turned out okay— after the first one."

"You were fun to watch because you had this naïve hubris such that it never occurred to you that you might fail the next time too."

"It would have been too much if I had understood myself."

"That's right, and you wouldn't have done anything. So I gave you a brain that always thought of interesting things to do and forgot to look back."

"I never counted the cost; I worked up a vision and went ahead."

"But the flip side of your foolishness was genius. Actually, it was your faith in me though you didn't know it—or confidence that what I had made was good. But you needed to add persever-ance to it, which time allowed you to do with the boats."

"I'm surprised you don't count my flaws as serious matters."

"Your heart is the serious matter, and that's what we need to talk about."

"I know I kept it safely out of sight."

"You did from an early age. After that you were always lonely."

"How did my father figure into this? Did he influence me more than I was aware of?"

"Of course he did. You never knew him, really, because he never recognized your genius, only the foolish things that went with it, so you were not easy for him to befriend."

"So I had to fill a void."

"Yes, he influenced everything you did in that way. But you only knew it as your independence and self-reliance which you thought was normal and better than having friends who were obsessed about trivial things, and of course that doubled the lone-liness that comes of caring nothing about small matters. And that made you vulnerable to imagining fulfillment where there would be none. I knew that would happen, which is why your mother was able to successfully make you halfway a Nazarite and some-what in the mold of Samson."

"You knew I would have trouble with women, then."

"Yes, of course. Every man does. But you never thought you would."

"I know that's true, but then why was I shy and walked away whenever I was approached by one?"

"That was for their protection. It gave them a chance to avoid getting hurt."

"If one gave me a second opportunity I was ready but knew nothing about how to proceed."

"Yes, by then you were all wound up and the poor girl was con-fused unless she had a real need, and then you became her shelter for awhile until she realized you were a piece of work like none other and she sought refuge in a normal person."

"I wouldn't say my wife's second husband was normal."

"Well, compared to you he was easy to understand."

"I never understood why women liked me and men just thought I was nuts."

"You were mysterious to them, that's why. But they soon grew to distrust your wild boldness."

"Shouldn't my mother have taught me how women think?"

"Your mother had her own ideas. But she was a true enough mother and she was your first friend."

"She never taught me about respecting boundaries. She let me grow up thinking all formalism was useless."

"The reason you minimized rules and boundaries is you lacked the ability to assemble them and make sense of them in your mind. Anything that seemed arbitrary might just as well not exist as far as you were concerned. But you did apply yourself to convention when it was the name of the game."

"I actually enjoyed it as part of flying. That was a marvelous game."

"And you studied baseball well enough to please a small town."

"But I failed the NSA and never took the paper or the gym very seriously. They were only means to make a living."

"What you had to give you gave and it was priceless, Earl. You were a leader in an unconventional way, fostering community spirit by your benevolence."

"I saw needs that I could easily meet if I could do it my own way, that's all."

"That's why you're exceptional. It's not that you have some unusual merit in heaven. It's that you don't know how to evaluate your failures, and so with a few notable exceptions you never correct them. You think whatever seems good to you is acceptable to me and others. You have no use for authority and rules, and you usually get by without respecting them. I had to make an exception in order to get you into this age without further damaging your already-damaged body. Look: here's what I saved you from."

They had come to what appeared to be an exhibit on the grounds of the palace, perhaps of some ancient ruins below ground level, for a red glow from down below could be seen reflected on the railing that surrounded an opening in the ground. Earl wasn't prepared for what he saw when he peered over the edge and down into the pit, for even though he had read the last verse in the book of Isaiah he had not taken it to be so literal.

> And they shall go forth and look upon the dead bodies of the men that have transgressed against me, for their worm shall not die, neither shall their fire be quenched; and they shall be abhorrent to all flesh.

Earl was aghast and speechless.

"Is it hell?" he asked the Jesus.

"In a way it is, but hell is not within this universe. What you see is a model of hell intended to awaken your heart if not your understanding, to the horror of it. I want no one to go there. This is an unforgettable warning that I hope you will remember whenever you encounter someone who is transgressing the laws I have established. Tell them about seeing this."

From there—they did not spend much time on that spot—the King led Earl along a path that reminded him of other times in his life. He didn't share these with me. I knew there would be no benefit to my knowing all that was brought out. I went through a similar interview with my Savior, and I came away with nothing but gratitude and appreciation for what the word "salvation" means.

Finally, it came to making an arrangement for Earl's next step.

"But now I have a problem," said the King. "There is an issue regarding you that I have to settle. I think you know what it is."

"You haven't mentioned Leila."

"What am I going to do with her? What does that secluded heart of yours say? You love her, do you not?"

"Well, yes I did. Or I thought I did."

"Be honest with your God."

"She stole my heart, and I don't know what she's done with it."

"She's stuck on you, Earl. Do you want to be like her or not?"

"You mean I could visit her in heaven?"

"I mean would you like to become a glorified man?"

"How is that possible?"

"Remember Enoch."

"I will be what you will have me be."

"I am asking you to make the decision. You see, that rule of choice holds for everyone made in the image of God."

"I'm not sure I would like having the travel restrictions."

"I'm not sure you're ready for heaven, Earl."

"Would a resurrection body be possible?"

"You would have to die first, and those bodies are all taken."

"Well, I should get along pretty well in this one since you've restored my eyesight."

"It was Leila's desire that we get you here to be healed. She assumed you would choose to become glorified. You have just made it more difficult for me because now we have to get you back home. Lydia is choosing to go back to Alaska, so you two can travel together as far as Salem where you left your airplane. Fly her up to Sitka if you will. You will find fuel there. They will tell you their tanks are empty right now, and they are.

"Since neither of you have enough money, stop by the travel minister's office—someone will direct you to it—on your way out. Take the train to Haifa. They will have arranged for you to return by the way you came. Take care not to complain this time; you're Ichabod no longer. Let no harm come to Lydia. You will be surprised when you see her face, but don't let that concern you.

"Is there anything else you would like me to do for you?"

"Is there any reason I need this lame leg and weak arm?"

"You tell me. There's no reason that I know of."

"I love your humor, your majesty. Please, then, I ask you to heal my limbs."

"Lydia is praying that your limbs be healed. Give her my greetings, and both of you come see me again as soon as you can."

Back in the waiting room he saw that Lydia had her head bowed. Presently she looked up.

"I've been praying for you, Ichabod, did you feel anything? Look, your leg is straight, isn't it? I think it is—and your arm! Oh! And you're looking at me. Can you see?"

"I can see. I've met King Jesus. He healed my eyes."

"Now you can forget that eye clinic. Are you going back home right away, do you think?"

"I think so. Have you had any success in your search for Bible characters?"

"I met Samson and Delilah!"

"You did?"

"Leila introduced me to them."

"She was here? ... Leila was here?"

"She came to Jerusalem while you were at the kibbutz. She almost went down there to see you, but transportation is always a problem for glorifieds. I don't think I would want to be one even if I was given the chance."

"I feel the same way."

"Is there any reason we need to stay here now that you've gotten healed? Do you still have something to say to the King?"

"We had a very good meeting. It started when he asked me to play some Beethoven. ... No it started before that in the first bath; I know now he was there. There were three of them and it was all a preparation. An amazing young woman I somehow introduced to Jesus, essentially by accident, was there as my guide while I was still blind, you see. So I played the only Beethoven I know, and Laura said he liked it. That's when he asked me what he could do for me. It was the Moonlight Sonata I had played, by the way, and I said I would like to see the moonlight. Then he touched my eyes one at a time and made them work like new."

"That's a lot of dream for so short a nap."

"I wasn't napping. It wasn't a dream."

"But you've been sitting here all the time. You dozed off just for maybe five minutes at most. Let me see your eyes. ... Where are your dark glasses?"

"I must have left them on the piano."

Back Home
Chapter Twenty-Six

Everything went well for Samson after that. The journey from Jerusalem to Sitka by ship, train, and plane was enjoyable for him and his companion. There were no breakdowns or delays, and having gained decisive confirmations of their callings they both felt great relief and new freedom,

Lydia filled the hours on the ship and train composing a historical supplement to Judges thirteen through sixteen based on her interview with the real Samson, a quiet and humble man in his resurrection, and his petite and reticent Delilah, both of whom had graciously shared their recollections. Her book will present stories and details from their past lives and also offer an interpretation of the biblical text. Lydia learned that what she had written previously was accurate in making a continuity of Samson's adversaries in Timnah and Sorek to explain Delilah's treacherous teasing and Samson's perplexingly playful dismissal of it.

Earl had finally received the reason for his summons, and he turned it over and over in his mind, trying to find an angle from which to understand it. The only way it made sense was without the piano episode, yet that was the stated purpose of his calling and the only thing that was required. The rest was the result of his own wishes. It made sense as a dream except for the fact that he had been blind and now he could see. The healing miracle could have happened if he was slumbering and dreaming, but his eye patches had disappeared and the dark glasses were missing. Even his cane was gone. What would cause the disappearance of those material objects if it had been merely a dream?

But clearly the reason for his summons had not been for physical healing; that was merely the vehicle that got him there. The brief piano recital the King required of him was of no value to Earl, yet he would have paid any price for what he received in return. Was there a lesson in that?

"I think so," he said, "unless it was pure and simple irony like everything else seems to be in this world."

Speaking of dreams, I had not forgotten my daydream of spending a leisurely afternoon on the lake with Earl and his sailboat; and it came to pass on a beautiful autumn afternoon not many years later.

Never lose sight of your dreams! Someday they will be fulfilled.

Our conversation touched on certain broken and oddly shaped pieces of our lives which, as we looked upon them, appeared to have been fitted into a frame by some masterful workmanship. There was no trace of the fractures and sharp edges so prominent when we viewed the pieces separately. Our histories had been melted together and recast in a mold that made all things very much worth remembering.

But mostly we were enjoying the grace of our Lord who made all things work together for us to be there on that happy day, a crowning reward which left nothing to be desired. At least that's how I thought of it until Earl asked me about my future plans.

"Would you say things are going well in your management position?" he asked me.

"Yes, you know they are. Why do you ask?"

"I know they are because you're not at work. You're here on vacation with me, and we've spent time together prior to this. That means someone is filling in for you when you're out of your office."

"Yes. I could leave everything to Everett permanently, and he would carry on very well. But it's my assignment and still my primary responsibility."

"Yet you could turn it over to Everett."

"The powers above might do that, I suppose. But what else I'm fit for I don't know."

"Are there no opportunities in heaven you might look into if you were given the freedom?"

"Yes, there are many."

"What, for example?"

"Play writing. You already knew that."

"I did, of course. I think we all need an opportunity to be creative."

"Do you really think so? I don't feel a need. Or I wouldn't call it a need. My feeble attempt to create that drama you're remembering was based on a story from Scripture. So it wasn't really a creation. I'm not sure any of us are capable of creating things. That's the exclusive domain of our Creator God."

"Yet you had that urge to write a play, and you finished it, and we rehearsed it, and if ever I were to get my lines down well it might have blessed a small audience."

"Are you suggesting that I might go in that direction someday?"

"Would you enjoy writing plays in heaven? I understand that the arts are a big part of heaven's culture, yet they're merely magnifying the divine creativity from which they're derived. If you set yourself to the discipline of play writing, might you perhaps please your maker as much as you're doing now?"

"I see a possibility in that, but I don't know where it would lead. Maybe my efforts would amount to nothing in heaven's artistic marketplace."

"When Salim was young, did his artistic efforts ever fail to please you?"

"No. I see what you mean. Every child has the urge to be creative because they're made in the image of their parents who are made in the image of the Creator. So there's a little bit of the Creator in each of us. But there's a limit, isn't there? You like to build sailboats, but would you be happy building boats forever?"

"That's what I'm getting at. I could experiment with different designs to forestall monotony, but to build a different boat just to be different wouldn't satisfy me. Let me put it this way: There are certain nooks and crannies in Yahweh's good creation that he left undeveloped and ready for *creatures* in his image to delight in being *creators* in his image. When we find a place which matches our creative gift and we work to glorify him, everyone is happy. But there must be a balance and a respect for the overall design that we're building on. There will come a time to be finished with the adornment and move on. Pressed beyond a certain point, creative inspiration goes in the other direction and you have ungodly elements creeping in to maintain novelty. But if we're within the zone of sub-creators after his image, our work will add to the beauty of his creation for others to enjoy for a long time. And I think that means it adds to his enjoyment as well."

"What would you like to move on to?"

Earl pointed to the east. "Have you gone exploring those mountains? I don't think you have. You told me how the woods terrified you one time. But what if we could join with others in teams to tame the inaccessible wilds and make accessible gardens of them and places for people, as well as wildlife, to enjoy?"

"If that's God's plan, then there will be enough to keep every would-be gardener happy for a long, long time," I said.

"How long is eternity?" he asked.

I had no answer for that argument. Nevertheless, I said, "We could keep changing them, trying new arrangements."

"For what purpose? Just to keep busy?"

I knew what he was getting at, and I saw no way not to have things end. "The earth is large, but eternity is infinite," I said.

"What about other planets?"

"Well, now that you bring that up, I understand heaven may connect everywhere the same as it does here on this earth. But I don't expect there would be a Jacob's ladder where there is no Jacob."

"Perhaps suitable worlds exist elsewhere in the universe for organic life as we know it."

"And suitable for creatures in the image of God?"

"Not yet, perhaps. But once evil has been sealed off from everything, there could be races of beautiful creatures created in the image of God who might be taught by us to worship their Creator and avoid the dangers of their moral freedom."

"Do you mean that such creatures would be fruitful and multiply while enjoying unbroken fellowship in the Trinity?"

"Yes. Wouldn't you like to meet them?"

"Would they be immortal?"

"I think not. Long-lived, perhaps. The lifespans equivalent of a thousand years, I suppose."

"Then their immortal spirits would add to the population of heaven?"

"Aren't there other heavens?"

"Yes, I see. A heaven for each planet. Then if we could visit other heavens, the possibilities would be enormous."

"Yes, but not infinite, strictly speaking. But since this universe was created, there could be another. That's how eternity works without stagnation and without cycles of swelling and shrinking or learning and forgetting. As long as evil is kept from corrupting there need be no cycles."

"Then do we eventually become infinite in a sense?"

"No, there's no 'becoming' infinite because there is no infinity outside of mathematics. To us, infinity has no end. Infinity means there's always more."

"If, as you say, there's no forgetting, wouldn't one's memories become an overwhelming burden?"

"That's the problem which is solved by the cycle theories. But they create a bigger problem in that the closed cycle is indistinguishable from nothing. If the end is the same as the beginning, it has no beginning. If it has no beginning, is it anything? They don't know. We might say the theory of cycles is a clever magician who vanishes the Creator and vanishes creation."

"Then what is the answer to the problem? Do we add another memory storage bank to hold the next thousand years of memories?"

"Memories aren't stored, they're recreated, which sounds like a cycle. But time is not the master of anything. You remember by going back and replaying some form of the program. That gives you access to your memories without being burdened by them."

"It sounds like the same thing to me. How would I know to go back and relive something if I don't remember it?"

"Think of a library of books, all of which you've written. You need not keep the contents of every volume in mind in order to have access to every word in the library. You only need to be familiar with the titles and what they stand for. Then you can go straight to the thing you wrote and reread it. The cycle theorist thinks in terms of starting over again, which makes the books you wrote and the library an illusion that has no absolute existence."

"Does everyone get to read your books?"

"No, but you can read them to anyone you like."

"I didn't know you were an amateur theologian."

"I'm not. This is what I learned at Sorek Valley, when I was blind."

"From what authority?"

"From the rabbis."

"Not the resident rabbis at that kibbutz, I hope."

"Well, yes. They sat and argued about those things all day."

"I thought so."

We had been running before the wind, wing-on-wing, and had traveled southward many miles, for the breeze was keeping the promise it seemed to have made to the sunny day. I knew we would be much longer sailing back against the wind, but I wished the day to never end, even though I was already low on energy.

"Am I going to be returning late?" I asked Samson.

"We should have turned back before now," he admitted. "If you will manage the tiller and swing our course ninety degrees to starboard, I will bring the jib around."

My job was easy. I pulled the tiller to port, which swung the bow to starboard, and though he did not mention it, I knew I would be taking in main-sheet slack as well. As soon as the jib lost its wind he released the starboard jib sheet and quickly pulled in the jib sheet on the port side and took a turn around the cleat before the sail had time to billow out on the opposite side. In just a few seconds our little ship had settled down on a broad reach, soon becoming more like a close reach, as *Wind Chaser* gained speed through the water.

"I know you and *Wind Chaser* prefer this point of sailing above all others, but we're not shortening the distance we have to travel to get you back to heaven before you faint on us."

"Aye, aye, Captain. Say when."

"Bring her up into the wind a bit at a time. Can you manage the main?"

"Here we go."

It always surprises me how much stronger the wind is when we head close to it. I had a little trouble holding the tiller while adjusting the main sheet, and I rounded up too much in order to accomplish it. It's also surprising how quickly headway is lost and how much noise the sails make when they're not full. An experienced sailor would laugh at my surprise, but Samson told me I had done a good job.

We got her settled down as close to the wind as her sails would allow. This would be our configuration (is that the right term?) as we worked our way back north, only switching to the opposite tack each time we approached the east or west shore of the lake.

The wind was straight out of the north and had been building all afternoon—and building the waves which had not seemed formidable at all on the down-lake run. Now with *Wind Chaser* tossing and plunging as she encountered ever steeper waves, Samson relieved me at the tiller.

Samson knew the lake. It was deep, but shoals were not uncommon on the west side. Sometimes I could see where waves broke, suggesting shallow water farther out. Samson always called the moment to come about and change to the opposite tack as we zig-zagged up the lake. It was a decision balancing the slight variations in the wind strength and direction with the headway lost during the tack as we approached each shore. When it was time to come about I took the tiller and called "helm's a'lee," as he had taught me to do so many years ago, while he brought the jib around.

Was I afraid? No. If Samson was not afraid, and I was sure he wasn't, I had no reason to be afraid.

I never felt invincible, though perhaps I was. What I felt was a pleasureful excitement being in Samson's presence. I might have worried about something going wrong on the boat that would prevent me from getting back before I had lost all my vitality for the day. As far as I was concerned the boat was perfect because Samson had made it. It never occurred to me that Larry Link, the one who had been maintaining *Wind Chaser*, might have neglected to replace or repair some part of the rig that had corroded over the years. If the stress on the forestay had caused it to part, the mast would rotate straight back and come crashing down over the cockpit. But fortunately I never worried about such things.

If I had any apprehension it was about Samson. He was getting up in years, as they say. I knew there would come a day when he would need me and I would come down every day to take care of him. But that was far from my mind. He seemed to be looking a little pale, and he was not saying much. I doubted that he would have gotten seasick, but that is what came to mind.

As evening approached, the wind became less and we still had a long way to go. We had enjoyed the downwind sail without considering that sailing against the wind would be much slower. At least I had not considered it. I began to wonder if Samson had not been feeling well and had not calculated well for that reason.

"I need to go lie down in the cabin for a little while," he said to me. "I think you can manage both sails when it's time to come about."

"You're not seasick?"

"No. I have a bad headache."

I knew he got headaches, and lying down with his eyes closed tended to ease the severity.

"The wind is much less now, so I think I can do it."

"I know you can."

I let her get close to shore before coming about because the wind was less there so the sounds would be less likely to wake Samson if he had gone to sleep. It went well, but it took longer to regain momentum than it ever had before.

I was more concerned about minimizing noise and motion than about making progress toward home, and on each crossing I became more successful at doing so. I was enjoying the elements and pleased with my ability to allow Samson the sleep he needed. On each tack to the west the sun had declined noticeably, which did not alarm me, for the sky was clear, and I knew as long as there would be starlight I would see well enough to keep making progress toward home. But when the sun set and daylight faded away quickly so did the wind.

It got to the point where *Wind Chaser* was ghosting along, finding slight currents in the night air while stars dazzled my eyes. Once before I had stayed on earth beyond sundown, so I knew what to expect, but in the midst of the lake, far from trees and hills, the dome above was very much broader, and reflections of the heavens shone on the surface of the water as well. The sharpness of glorified vision brings out stunning details and distinguishable shades of color in planets and stars and galaxies, like a good telescope with an immense field of view.

"How are we doing?" Samson said as he crawled up out of the cabin. I think he knew exactly how we were doing.

"How is your headache?"

"Gone with the sun," he said. "Now we need to get you back before you fade away too."

He got out the oars and began rowing. I held the tiller and kept a straight course toward the entrance to our harbor which I could see well enough, but with Samson blocking my view ahead, I had to stand up to get the bearing and pick out a star to steer by.

He rowed steadily and, it seemed, easily. I believe we were making better speed toward home than when we were sailing best, but still it was slow progress. Neither of us spoke. This day of my dreams had used up my energy. I was worn out. I imagined angels looking down, wondering how much longer I would last.

By the time we got to the dock I had faded alarmingly. Samson carried me to the house and up to the second floor then on up the narrow stairway to the attic where my ladder to heaven waited.